PRAISE FOR
RARE METTLE

"... a gripping fictional account of a serious real-world problem. Touching on contemporary issues of big-data mining, drones, and human rights, Bridges builds a plausible and frightening story about America's absolute dependence on Chinese rare earth metals and the head-in-the-sand behavior of Silicon Valley elites and DOD bureaucrats when all the warning signals were flashing red. *Rare Mettle* should serve as both an entertaining read and a cautionary tale about the lengths to which regimes will go to insure their survival."

–Robert H. Latiff

Ph.D., Major General (retired), USAF

"*Rare Mettle* offers a chilling tale of a scenario that has the potential to become reality. Written like a rare earths industry insider, Ann Bridges offers ... a suspenseful backdrop of characters caught in a web of political intrigue ... keeps the reader guessing as to the eventual resolution to a problem that threatens the essence of American technology."

–Anthony Marchese

Chairman, Texas Mineral Resources Corp.

"*Rare Mettle* is fast-paced and exciting ... Ann Bridges delivers a believable characterization of Chinese politics, and mimics the behind-the scenes maneuvering of business dealings ..."

–William DeVincenzi

Executive in Residence, Director of Gary J. Sbona Honors Program and
Thompson Global Internship
Lucas College of Business, San Jose State University

"Ann Bridges' exciting, reality-based *Rare Mettle* is packed full of corporate and government agents engaged in an economic and geopolitical battle across cultures and vast geography ... her story foretells America's weaknesses and possible consequences of decades-long, compromising policies chasing China's cheap manufacturing promises and stable global alliances ... the underlying technical facts are true; therefore, her depiction of the current commercial and National Security situation is accurate, valid and deeply relevant to U.S. economic standing in the world . . ."

–James C. Kennedy
President, ThREEConsulting.com

"Ann Bridges captures the dragon spirit of both Silicon Valley and China—bold, ambitious, and intelligent. With attention to authentic detail, she moves the story through the perspectives of powerful, complex characters, all grappling with universal issues—power and control, love and sex, fear of failure and drive for success. Best yet, she understands how to communicate the delicate balance of two fast-paced cultures, each vying for supremacy in a high-tech, high-pressure world in an entertaining, captivating thriller . . . "

–Margaret Zhao
Former Enemy of the State in Mao's China and Award-winning author

"I was motivated to read *Rare Mettle* after having read *Private Offerings* . . . Bridges' stories . . . tend to be fast-paced, full of twists and turns, and feature good guys who are not always good, and bad guys who are not always bad . . . In the context of a venture capital playbook, behind the scenes of public diplomacy between the U.S. and China, and the very sensitive and real issues like control of rare earth elements, Bridges writes like she has 'walked the walk.' . . . In the end . . . you are left wondering if a complete resolution will be found in the next book or in tomorrow's newspaper."

–Stephen Tritto
Award-winning author, Retired Silicon Valley executive

RARE METTLE
A Silicon Valley Novel

Hardcover ISBN 978-1-939454-64-5
Softcover ISBN 978-1-939454-69-0
Epub ISBN 978-1-939454-76-8
Kindle ISBN 978-1-939454-77-5
Library of Congress Control Number: 2016932754
Cataloging in Publication data pending.

Published in the United States by
Balcony 7 Media and Publishing
530 South Lake Avenue #434
Pasadena, CA 91101
www.balcony7.com

Edited by JZ Bingham www.balcony7.com
Cover Art by Anthony Grimaldi
Cover & Interior Design by 3 Dog Design *www.3dogdesign.net*

Printed in the United States of America

Distributed to the trade by
Ingram Publisher Services
Mackin
Overdrive
Baker & Taylor (through IPS)

RARE METTLE

A SILICON VALLEY NOVEL

Ann Bridges

media & publishing

Prologue

BARCELONA, SPAIN

Early Evening, November 1

"Where the hell are you?" Paul Freeman's voice reverberated through Kay Chiang's brand new cell phone, purchased just that morning. She had left behind all traces of her former life two weeks ago.

She'd even put off checking in with Paul, her boss at the Defense Intelligence Agency. Since he'd recruited her directly from college, Paul grudgingly granted her a lot of freedom in her undercover roles. But she'd really pushed the limit this time.

"Barcelona today. Tomorrow—who knows?" She kept her eye on Charlie Wilkin's back as he bickered with a street vendor for tonight's dinner. He'd surprised her. He reveled in the back and forth exchange with fishmongers in each tiny port they visited, proud as a schoolboy when he bested them for their prize catches. He even tried his hand at cooking the local dishes for their dinner. Like Kay, he preferred a low profile for now, and tooling around the Mediterranean on a leased yacht was no hardship.

"Uncle Sam has been very worried about you," Paul scolded. "Du lost a great deal of face with the Taiwanese Maoists when he didn't acquire the technology you promised him."

"All because he assumed a woman was easily controlled." Kay sniffed. "Serves him right." She wiped the sheen of perspiration from her brow with her free hand. Even in her skimpiest sundress, the setting sun's rays set her aflame.

Out of the corner of her eye, she watched Charlie wave as the fisherman wrapped up his catch in paper. Only a few moments of privacy left.

"Listen, Paul, I'm sticking close to Charlie Wilkins for a while. He has a whole network of contacts in China's black market. He's really low on funds, so I bet he'll try blackmail again soon."

Kay waved back at Charlie and lifted one finger to give her another minute alone. "With those kinds of military contacts, he could be tied into the biggest technology theft rings we're tracking."

"Doesn't he need U.S. security clearance for leverage with those contacts?"

"I'm not sure. Let's reactivate it so we can use him while I'm his shadow. Give him free rein just to see where he leads us."

"Agreed."

"I'll be tracking technologists now, not the financiers. I may run across more of their precious engineers with high clearances who aren't trustworthy. They'll have to deal with these leaks somehow."

"They'd probably rather not know the truth." Paul sighed.

"Tough! They're not the only ones concerned about national security," Kay retorted. "I'll activate my secure email account so you'll know where we are, and keep you updated via phone when I can."

"I'll pass that on to the senior division head. He's been desperate to get someone inside those technology circles ever since we signed that trade agreement with China. It kills him to see our intellectual property pirated."

"The Communist Party still doesn't get it. Intellectual freedom has to be part of the equation." Kay fought to lower her voice, passion rising from her very core. "If people are afraid to think for themselves in day-to-day activities, how will anyone feel free enough to innovate? Until free ideas flourish, the country will flounder. After all, isn't that what my great-great uncle fought for?"

Glancing over her shoulder, she saw Charlie approaching rapidly. "Gotta go!"

She swung toward Charlie and opened her arms wide, forcing a welcoming smile. He wrapped her up in a bear hug and she relaxed into her other persona, the one that would keep her alive until she accomplished her current mission. Whenever that was.

Deep in her heart, she knew it would probably take her whole life to bring full freedom to her Chinese compatriots—to those who hadn't had a chance to flee the tyranny. She intended to help them in any—and every—way she could.

Chapter 1

MOSCONE CONVENTION CENTER

*San Francisco, California
Morning, November 1, 1 Year Later*

"I give you our latest breakthrough phone!" Victor Turtino held his arms up in a triumphant stance and stepped to the side of the enormous stage.

Thousands of his throng roared their approval, holding up cell phones and snapping photos. The huge screen behind him flashed stunning pictures of Snazzed Up!'s newest product. Vivid color options and unimaginably thin add-on components danced in a glitzy video trailer, simultaneously fed to the Internet. Accolades poured in from around the world. The comments appeared in bold type behind him, in real-time glory.

Victor grinned at his largest investor, sitting in the front row, applauding with the rest of the audience. The New York banker had railed against Victor's decision to move all his manufacturing plants to China. But Victor had just proven him wrong.

Snazzed Up!'s quarterly profits shattered all its previous records. China's cheap labor proved a boon for shareholder returns. And given the crowd's enthusiasm, Victor could spend his guaranteed year-end bonus on a custom-colored Tesla to match his company's showcase phone.

He jogged down the stairs leading from the stage and waded into the swarm of admiring fans, shaking hands. This is what he'd worked for all those years: the tributes, the fame, the sheer jubilation from betting it all and making it big. The ballooning bank account didn't hurt, either.

Business journalists gathered around his chief financial officer, probably prodding her for specific numbers to justify the huge uptick in their stock price. It had been on a hockey-stick trajectory for months leading up to this newest product launch. Victor hesitated. Should he join her and divert them from asking the hard questions? The truth might not go over well with the American consumers who bought his products.

All his newest technology relied on rare earths processed exclusively in China, so why not move the manufacturing line close to the supply chain? He'd made that decision with eyes wide open—it made sense. Besides, auto manufacturers and defense contractors made the same shift years earlier. Everyone applauded their savvy and how it padded their bottom lines.

Other Silicon Valley CEOs warned him he'd pay a price—China's inevitable, identical replication of the manufacturing facility and his product line. Intellectual property rights held no meaning to the Chinese. Knock-offs were a way of doing business. Had Victor made it easy for them to mimic his success and capture the bulk of the growing middle-class market? So far, relying on China was a one-way street, heading in his direction. He doubted it would change. Not with his new phone the darling of both the holiday season and Wall Street.

Victor shrugged off any worries and greeted the next wave of admirers with high-fives. His innovations always carried the day. No one would dare hold his technology hostage. He was the poster child of Silicon Valley success.

He'll be on top for decades more to come.

Chapter 2

DEFENSE INTELLIGENCE AGENCY

Washington, D.C.
Late Morning, December 18, 47 Days Later

"How the hell did you lose Kay Chiang, Freeman?" Hank Shaughnessy's rebuke bounced off the conference room's soundproofed windows, and the distant, snow-capped Washington Monument appeared to shiver in fear. Paul Freeman could relate—his boss' fiery Irish temper was a thing to behold. And one he'd become adept at avoiding over the past two years. Apparently, this was not his lucky day.

Paul glanced around the polished mahogany table at his co-workers and met only blank stares. The wall-mounted TV's black screen magnified their unsympathetic expressions. In this town, one kept close to the person in power and avoided any loser like a steaming cow pile. Right now, Paul was undoubtedly the piece of shit in this elite unit.

"I didn't lose her," Paul corrected, keeping his voice confident and almost as loud as Hank's, doubling down on his bet that he could keep this botched situation from coming under scrutiny. He remembered his high school football coach's lecture—a good offense was always the best defense. "She emailed me a month ago warning me she was going deep undercover and in sporadic contact."

"She violated regulations!" Hank banged his fist on the table. A dozen encrypted smart phones jumped from the impact. A banana slid from the tempting tower of fruit centered in front of the meeting participants and landed in the cream-cheese tub next to a poppy seed bagel. "Weekly check-ins, no exceptions—especially our civilian operatives. She may be dead—or worse."

"Really?" Paul pushed down the anxious bile rising from his gut. "What's worse than death?" He couldn't stop the sarcastic taunt. Nor fail to notice Hank's forehead turn an even deeper shade of purple.

"Treason, torture, switching to a double agent—and that's just off the top of my head." Justin Collins just had to chime in with his usual two cents.

Paul raised his eyebrows at Collins' token comb-over. Collins twisted his jaw, adjusted his ever-present red bow tie, and rearranged the wave over his gleaming bald patch.

"Good to know one of those three actually had Chiang's safety in mind," Paul seethed. Goddamned selfish career bureaucrats. He was the only field liaison with actual military field experience. They thought running a global intelligence network entailed pushing buttons on a computer. The incoming data usually overflowed their capacity—both analytical and technological.

Paul knew better. Highly trained agents and patriotic civilians sacrificed their lives every day outside the protected walls of this insular town, beyond the country's cozy borders. However, Hank's ire was warranted. Kay Chiang was definitely a rogue operative. Always had been, always would be—if she survived. Using an alternate email address for her last communiqué meant she was in even more danger than either had anticipated when she started this unusual assignment.

"We'll talk about this later, Freeman," Hank growled. "We have other agenda items to discuss. Everyone look at the file I sent out this morning."

Pulling up the spreadsheet on his computer tablet, Paul squinted at blurry numbers. Damn it . . . he wasn't forty years old yet, too young for reading glasses. Hank droned on about budget cutbacks, staff reductions, and all the inevitable nonsense accompanying a new administration promising fiscal discipline. Never once did they cut their own plush, private limousines, or pare their ample staff. Instead, fighting men put their lives on the line, ill equipped.

Eyelids drooping, Paul lifted his coffee mug and drained the caffeinated sludge, amazed at the hint of warmth after five long hours. The rest of his image-conscious team patronized the corner gourmet coffee shop multiple times daily, like sailors on a short shore leave visiting a brothel. Paul preferred carrying coffee from home in the thermal mug Tina decorated for him three summers ago. Superimposed on the side was a picture of the two of them clowning it up on the beach in Savannah, their blond curls mingling as they wrestled in the sand. Using it brought a wisp of happiness instead of regret about what couldn't be. That kind of jolt got him moving these dark mornings.

Hank checked his watch and grabbed the TV's remote, powering the unit on.

"Breaking news, guys. Pay attention to the top story," Hank said. All heads pivoted to watch.

The TV was already pre-set to CNN, which kept its relevance by leaking upcoming stories to the right people in D.C., including the exact time they would first air. Apparently, Hank achieved a coveted spot on its distribution list. Hurrah for ass kissing.

"New threats from China put the State Department on high alert this morning," reported the bland, brunette anchor. "China pledged to block all future shipments of rare earth elements to the United States if we sell our newest military technology to Taiwan."

Paul leaned forward. His brain raced from the familiar kick of adrenalin.

"These refined metals are used in the manufacture of laser-guided missiles and our newest weapons," the reporter continued, "among other high-technology products contributing to the booming sales of mobile devices. China's Northern Province of Inner Mongolia mines and processes over 93% of the earth's supply of these minerals. We'll keep you posted as the story develops."

Hank flicked off the TV. "Our leaders learned about the possible embargo two hours ago, and are discussing an appropriate response," he stated in official monotone, but the telltale twitch of his nostrils clued Paul into how seriously Hank took this threat. "We need to touch base with all our field personnel for insights into potential solutions or risks."

That explained Hank's focus on Kay. Her last email disclosed advanced military technology using those obscure minerals, hiding under a cloak of tiny Chinese game companies. Kay's cover as an interpreter for an American venture capitalist in Beijing worked wonders getting her behind closed doors.

Her most recent missive was surprisingly cryptic. But in the last two weeks . . . nothing. Had whatever she stumbled onto provoked this diplomatic muscle-flex from the Chinese Communist Party? And put her in greater danger, too?

"Which elements are so rare? I mean, were these recently added to the Periodic Table of Elements, or did I space out during high school chemistry?" Tamara Mostiacelli's dry comment drew chuckles. The newest and youngest team member, she was the brainiac of the bunch. No one ever stumped her. Tamara tossed her purple-streaked hair over one shoulder, her fingers tapping the screen.

"Basically, we're talking about Elements 21, 39, and numbers 57 through 71," Paul said, striving to simplify his research over the past year. "Key elements for defense, for example, are Yttrium, used in laser-based weapon systems; Terbium for advanced radar and sonar; and Holmium, for the latest in directed energy weapons like rail guns. These purified rare metals are the new building blocks for our high-tech military gear."

Paul swallowed hard, stomaching painful memories. "However, the broader economic implications could be devastating if China carries through on this threatened blockade. They could potentially shut down every automobile, computer, and cell phone assembly line outside of China. Those firms all rely on some number of purified rare earth components."

"Our mission is national security, not to protect the private sector," Collins said. "Only defense applications are priority."

"And how do you think all this national security is paid for?" Paul waved a hand at the state-of-the-art video-conference setup. "Taxes collected from successful companies supplying those high-tech products, and from their well-paid employees, that's how."

"The American consumer can get along without a new smart phone every year, and the auto makers should have stockpiled what they need. Besides, they can engineer their way out of it with the older technology." Collins pursed his lips like a disapproving old maid.

"But our soldiers won't survive without the best equipment," Paul muttered.

"Gentlemen—enough." Hank ran his hand over his head. "Touch base with all field personnel. Let me know if you find anything of use to either the Defense or State Department. Deadline is three o'clock tomorrow afternoon. Meeting adjourned."

Paul jumped to his feet and checked his watch. Could he squeeze in a quick phone call? Nope. He'd have to call from the cab.

"Freeman, hang on." Hank gripped his arm, pulling him from the milling bodies. "We need to talk."

"Sorry, it'll have to wait until after lunch." Damn it, he was a professional, with more important commitments than an ass chewing, no matter how hot Hank was to deliver it.

"Freeman, don't fuck with me today." Hank tightened his fingers. "I won't accept made-up excuses for family emergencies, either."

Jerking his arm free and throttling his snide response, Paul headed toward the door. "I'll return at one o'clock, and be in my office all afternoon. Catch me then."

Chapter 3

Opting for the stairwell to avoid the elevator's piped-in Christmas carols, Paul chanted the reasons he chose this job in time to the rhythm of his thundering footsteps. In return for precious time with his family, he was just a cog in a big wheel, supposedly with no stress. Unfortunately, the Yin of mind-numbing frustration undermined the Yang of teamwork.

Paul tapped his phone directory on the second floor landing, searching for Colonel George DuMont's home number. Although recently retired, DuMont would probably have a few choice words to say about China's embargo. Paul relied on his previous team leader's sage guidance more often than he'd care to admit.

He placed the call, impatient for the sputtering rings within the unreliable stairwell tower to clear up as he made his way to the lobby.

"DuMont." The colonel's gravelly voice had lost some of its power over the years but none of its authority.

"Hello, Colonel. Paul Freeman here." Exiting the building, Paul flagged an idling taxi and pulled open the door. "Did you catch the news story about rare earths?"

"Shit yes." DuMont huffed. "I warned the procurement officers for almost ten years about China using rare earths for blackmail. Apparently, the higher-ups decided to ignore all my advice."

"Good thing you gave me the heads-up." He covered his mouthpiece and pointed in the direction of the Potomac River. "Arlington Cemetery— and hustle." The cabbie nodded and accelerated away from the curb.

Paul removed his hand and spoke into the phone. "I finally managed to assign a civilian operative in China to monitor this. She's following developments on any new uses of rare metals in high-tech military applications. I've already passed her findings onto my boss for inclusion in his intelligence briefings."

"Gonna take more than a civvy's word to blow open the cover-up going on at the Pentagon, son."

"Cover-up?" Paul pitched his voice lower. "What are you talking about?"

"Warfare 101, Lieutenant." DuMont took on the sonorous tones of a classroom lecturer. "Have you forgotten the basics of your military training? Modern warfare is based on logistics and procurement. How the fuck can we make sure we have the weapons we need if we rely on a foreign power to provide them to us?" His heavy sigh echoed in Paul's ear. "At least that's the argument I made to my CO. Then he handed me my walking papers and wished me a happy retirement."

"Are you telling me they pushed you out because you brought to their attention a potential issue of national security?" Paul's brain raced at the implications.

"I'm telling you that the fate of this nation hangs on whether our military can actually get its hands on critical high-tech gear when we need it, not when China decides to process metals for our defense contractors," DuMont barked.

The cabbie revved his engine at a stoplight with matching urgency.

"But the rare earth mines that operate outside of China are our back-up!" Paul's protest sounded lame even to his own ears.

DuMont snorted. "None of those operations have the metallurgical capabilities the defense industry needs. Only China does."

"Which means?"

"Figure it out, Lieutenant. Your goddamn intelligence services have reported on increases in non-Chinese rare earth production, sure. But they failed to point out that all those producers still send their raw materials to China to be upgraded and refined for our newest weaponry."

"So any non-Chinese rare earths production is basically worthless to our defense and technology companies . . . until China gets its hands on it . . . Whoa . . ."

Paul's stark statement hung in the air for long seconds. The light turned green and the cabbie darted left onto the main boulevard, filled with the usual lunchtime rush-hour traffic.

"Lieutenant, let me be perfectly clear. America and its allies don't have a single company in this space anymore. We sold all the intellectual property and purification expertise to China years ago."

"That doesn't make sense, Colonel. Why we would do that?"

"Because a Chinese company offered the highest bid, and the idiots in charge at the time didn't stop to consider the consequences of transferring this key technology." DuMont paused, as if waiting for his comment to sink in. "And by the way, the owner of said, same Chinese company was none other than the son-in-law of the Chinese premiere. How's that for coincidence?"

Politics. It always comes down to who you know, Paul thought with cynicism.

"But surely the Pentagon stockpiled enough refined material or necessary components to cover supply-line logistics in case of war." Paul scratched his head. "Isn't there something like the Strategic Petroleum Reserve for this stuff? I mean, with a budget of almost $800 billion, some of that money had to go to procure the rare earth metals we would need, right?"

"Doubtful. And nothing guarantees we won't go to war with China or one of its allies in the future. Then we're up shit creek without a paddle beyond the first foray. China has two mining cities with a combined population of seventeen million people working in and around their refining industry, no doubt with a goal of advancing its global dominance in rare earths. We wouldn't stand a chance in any war without China's cooperation."

Paul winced, staring out the window at snow-dusted trees silhouetted against government buildings. He tuned out the raucous automobile horns, considering the full repercussion of DuMont's conclusions. And realized he, too, had ignored the elder warrior's wise anticipations of the worst-case scenario.

"What you're talking about is economic warfare, aren't you, sir?" Paul mused.

"That's nothing new," DuMont answered. "War has always been a violent tilt toward a new economic equilibrium. What we're experiencing today is a radical evolution instead, and the Pentagon's career bureaucrats are unwilling to accept this new reality. It's just like boiling frogs—raise the heat slowly, and they never realize the danger they're in until they're too lethargic to jump free."

"So what option is left if China has already leveled most of our industrial capabilities? Seriously, how do we gear up for war if our defense contractors are reliant on China's continued willingness to supply these key materials at a price we can afford?"

"That's the question I asked, son . . . and it cost me my career," Dumont said without emotion.

"They just ignored you, sir?" Paul's empty stomach clenched. The taxi sped through an open intersection and onto a narrow side street, weaving around double-parked delivery vans. Paul fought back nausea.

Silence.

Paul could picture DuMont wiping his ebony skin of perspiration in his usual fashion, weighing an appropriate, measured response. He hadn't made it far up the military ranks by flapping his jaws.

"Son, what I'm about to tell you is confidential. Do you understand?"

"Yes, sir." Paul threw an ironic glance up at the Watergate Complex towering above, recalling its tainted history of Washington secrets and political ambitions. For a brief moment, he considered ending the call abruptly and avoiding the truth altogether.

No, DuMont deserved a full hearing after his years of dedicated service.

"Last month, I met with the Assistant Secretary of Defense, along with a top metallurgist and one of his own Asia policy experts," DuMont said. "Do you know what that asshole said to my face?"

"I'm assuming you mean the Assistant Secretary," Paul said with a wry twist of his lips.

"Actually, they all meet that description." DuMont chuckled. "But yeah, the Assistant Secretary had the balls to look me in the eye and tell me that all our weapons still work without rare earths. That's the official policy of the Pentagon."

"In other words, 'Shut the fuck up.'"

"Yep. While it's true that some of our older weapon systems will work in a degraded form without rare earths, none of our laser-based systems will work at all. All those new, precision-guided weapons relying on surgical targeting won't perform worth a damn. I should know. I spent half of my career searching out the technology to give America's military a leading edge."

Paul swallowed hard. "Sir, I hope you won't take offense at this, but how the hell can you just retire knowing he flat out lied to you?"

"Oh, I still have a few friends in Congress who keep a close eye on the goings-on at the Executive Branch. They tracked down whether your agency's documentation in the Congressional Armed Services Committee reports had ever seen the light of day."

"And?"

"Nope. Edited out. Plus, a staffer told me that asshole Assistant Secretary met with the ranking members of the committee just last week and reaffirmed the Pentagon's official position on rare earths. So he lied to Congress, too." DuMont tutted.

Holy shit.

DuMont was right. Most of today's military hardware increasingly relied on rare earth metals. And the Pentagon was engaged in a cover-up that included lying to Congress about their significance and its impact on national security.

The Pentagon, the most respected bureaucratic organization in the world, had lost control of its own procurement process—and to China, no less. Acknowledging that failure could embolden our enemies. The single most important building block of a successful military is logistics, starting with identifying and securing uninterruptable supply lines. No beans, no bullets—no army.

No one's Beltway career could survive a failure of this magnitude. They had to cover it up.

The taxicab scooted onto the Arlington Memorial Bridge, built decades ago as an honorable passageway for the country's fallen soldiers. Its graceful, powerful arches supporting the road mocked the reality of today's military's weakness.

"I just scanned the DOD's updated Inspector General's report this morning, sir," Paul said. "Based on what you're telling me, that's just another whitewash. And, with U.S. and NATO weapon systems one-hundred-percent reliant on China's good will, the defense industry can't afford to piss China off. They'd lose their key supplier."

"In today's world of shrinking defense budgets, our defense contractors can't stay in business based solely on Pentagon procurement orders. They rely on selling a whole range of products worldwide in order to be profitable. It makes sense the defense industry is in on the cover-up, too."

Paul shook his head. "How did this happen?"

"Son, I pushed this issue to the wall and no one listened," DuMont sighed. "I'm a modern-day Cassandra at the Pentagon, and an old man at that. It's time you youngsters take the lead before we lose our future."

Paul opened his mouth and snapped it shut again. For the last decade, DuMont worked a desk job in Washington while Silicon Valley percolated at warp speed with new inventions. Maybe today's high-tech companies had more options for America's defense than DuMont knew. Paul remembered that when DuMont first recommended Paul's transfer to the DIA, he'd insisted Paul resurrect their old engineering connections. Maybe it was time to give them another call.

"Are you volunteering me to rock the boat, sir?"

"Only if you have the backbone to make it happen, son. No telling what the new military industrial alliances might do to stop you—in both this country and in China."

Good point. Was China now exploiting the nation's ultimate weakness—arrogant economic confidence in a borderless world? Paul rubbed his jaw. It seemed painfully obvious that balance sheets and bottom lines had created blurred allegiances. Who was the defense industry defending these days? American citizens, their shareholders, or the new biggest customer in the world: China?

"I'll do my best, sir, and keep you posted when I can. Goodbye." Paul pocketed his phone, his conscience already warring with old, embedded fears. How many more soldiers had to die defending freedom? Too many lives would be in jeopardy if he stepped away from this duty.

The cabbie swung between the gates of Arlington Cemetery and wove past acres of rigid marble saluting heavenward. Paul swallowed back the guilt, bubbling like a science experiment in his belly. What made one man the target and left the other unharmed? Poor leadership, or did God have a special role determining life or death, happiness or heartache for the soldiers' families?

Paying and dismissing the driver, Paul climbed the final hilltop in the frigid cold and spied Guillermo's figure towering over Ernie's gravestone. Paul waved and loped the remaining distance, unwinding his scarf from his neck.

"Paul! Hey there!" Guillermo's enthusiastic hug calmed Paul's inner turmoil. Never recrimination for his brother's death, only quiet understanding of Paul's heavy burden of responsibility—and willingness to offer support each year over his grave.

He clenched Guillermo's broad back, breaking away and scanning the surrounding grounds. "Only you and Oscar this year?"

Oscar scuttled around the nearby tree with all the impetuousness of his ten years. Guillermo stuffed a knit cap into a pocket of his familiar, worn army jacket and pulled his nephew to his side.

"Mom's getting re-married, Uncle Paul." Oscar's face scrunched with bewilderment, a mirror image of his father. The same unruly cowlick decorated the crown of his black hair. "Mom says I should respect Dad's memory, but says it's better if we don't visit every year. But Uncle Gui wanted to come and tell you what's up."

A volunteer stepped forward bearing a Christmas wreath, placing it with reverence onto Ernie's grave with a salute. Guillermo tugged Paul away from Oscar, who sniffed the evergreens and peppered the volunteer with questions.

"Time heals." Guillermo squeezed his shoulder. "Oscar never knew Ernie beyond the framed pictures on the mantle—and these cold visits." He shrugged. "It's time we let him go, and rest in peace the same way he is."

Paul hunted for the right words, elegant platitudes to echo Guillermo's simple homily.

"I can't," he blurted. "Not yet."

"Problems at work?" Guillermo crossed his massive arms.

"Yes...no...maybe." Could he tell Guillermo? Meeting sympathetic brown eyes, Paul gripped the back of his neck and cleared his constricted throat. "I still have nightmares," he confessed. "Of the screams, the chaos..."

"Is someone in danger?" Guillermo pinned him with his gaze. "What are you doing about it this time?"

Guilt slammed into Paul. He grabbed Ernie's rigid headstone for support.

"Not enough," he admitted in a gruff voice. Straightening, he took a deep breath. The frigid air braced his soul. "But that's gonna change."

"Helping the living is a higher priority than mourning the dead—and your mistakes." Guillermo thrust out thick fingers and shook Paul's hand. "Let it go, man. Just let it go." He waited a heartbeat, his eyes drilling Paul's. "I forgive you. We all do."

Paul crossed to Oscar and enveloped the boy in a bear hug. "Merry Christmas, kiddo. Don't break my gift for at least a day, you hear?"

"What'd you get me, Uncle Paul?" Paul's coat muffled Oscar's curiosity. "A new game player? Huh? I sure hope so!"

"You'll get it in the mail soon, but you have to wait until Christmas morning to open it." Paul winked at Guillermo, ruffling Oscar's hair. "Didn't you hear? Time waits for no one, including Santa Claus."

Chapter 4

Paul sidestepped a forlorn bulldog puppy dressed in red velvet and reindeer horns. He shook his head, giving the mutt a sympathetic glance, and stepped inside his office building. Its stolid gray facade showed no hint of roiling turmoil hidden from view like a burgeoning tsunami.

He felt strangely detached from its intrigues. His responsibilities had narrowed to only one: manage Kay Chiang's mission to successful completion. Only how could he? She wouldn't give him the tiniest bit of information so he could keep track of her. DuMont's dire warning reminded him—get creative. They'd flat run out of time.

He tapped the elevator button and rubbed his frozen ear. The cold metal of his wedding band nipped his lobe. The highlight of this year's sex life—and last year's, too. With a muttered curse, he yanked and the ring popped off his finger with all the finale of flat champagne. Stuffing it in his pants pocket, he walked down the empty corridor with bowed shoulders, toying with it in a final, silent eulogy.

Unlocking his door, he shoved it open and tossed his phone over the ribbon-topped game box perched on the metal corner. It looked as out of place in his utilitarian office as a berried sprig of holly in a war zone.

"We still have to talk, Freeman." Hank's rumbling baritone came from the far corner.

Paul started, casting a wary glance to his right. Sighing, he hung his coat and sank into the chair. He braced his feet on the desk and faced Hank head-on.

"So what burr's under your skin, Hank? My Army recruiting officer wasn't this eager to talk to me."

"This fiasco with Chiang isn't good, especially with the current China situation." Hank leaned forward, his hands locked between his knees. "I've gotten a lot of complaints, although I cut your load virtually in half. The team is tired of picking up the slack."

Paul acknowledged the stark facts with an abrupt nod. Hank gave him breathing room to shake off his bouts of panic after Daisy arrived at his office, divorce papers in hand and moving van packed. A few months ago, he pulled his head out of the fog and faced reality again. Kay's troubles topped his short priority list, sucking up all his work time and then some. Apparently, he was not back on his game.

Time to kiss ass—big time—and re-join the team.

"You're right, Hank. Assign me a full load and let others enjoy more family time. Lord knows I found out the hard way this job can be death to a normal life." He forced a smile to his face.

"Remember those budget cuts?" Hank shook his head.

Paul tensed, sensing the axe hovering over his neck.

"Of course, and if I can help scrounge for savings in our department—"

"You're missing the point." Hank lifted a hand, palm outward. "I have to eliminate one liaison from our payroll immediately. Your only responsibility has been to track Chiang, gather her current intelligence and, especially, ensure her safety. You failed. No amount of arguing erases that black mark with this rare metals hoopla taking center stage." He paused. "You're fired."

Fired? What else could go wrong today?

"However . . ." Hank rippled his fingers against his jaw, tossing Paul a stern look. ". . . I'm willing to cut you a deal to keep your medical benefits intact—for you and your family—longer than customary."

His office shrank into a vague blur. Paul could hear Daisy's screams now if he lost medical coverage. The federal government's plush benefit package trounced what he could command in the private sector. Maybe Daisy would get a job so he wouldn't have to cover alimony payments in addition to all of Tina's support.

Dream on.

His chest tightened. Or maybe Daisy would remarry—soon. He shoved the depressing thought aside. He needed a job—fast. Who would hire a guy with more black marks than a goddamn zebra? He couldn't count on Hank's glowing referral. And he'd just promised his best to Colonel DuMont.

Wait. Hank hinted at a deal. Paul heaved a deep breath. The room drifted back into focus. Hank's toe rat-a-tatted on the linoleum in impatient rhythm.

"What do you have in mind?" Dropping his feet onto the floor, Paul rested his forearms on the desk.

Hank grabbed a folder tucked into the chair and scooted forward, plopping it under the desk lamp. He nudged Oscar's present. "Secret Santa gift? I would hope our agents are too old for video games."

"It's for the son of Private Ernesto Nieves, my fallen squadron teammate." Paul set the box on the floor and snapped one farewell salute to Ernie.

"You care too damn much, Freeman." With a derisive snort, Hank flipped to a paper-clipped page. He ran one finger over the tiny, typed entries and stopped, tapping the sheet repeatedly. "Your personnel record indicates you have contacts in Silicon Valley. Correct?"

"Yeah. At DARPA—the Defense Advanced Research Projects Agency, in case you don't know what the acronym stands for . . ." Paul loved having a chance to use the sarcastic dig, "my job was to recruit the best technology minds from American universities for defense contractors and hush-hush military projects in Silicon Valley."

"Students? Those are your wonderful contacts?" Hank mocked.

"Students, all grown up," Paul corrected. "My recruits earned the top jobs and I kept in touch, including with the tight engineering circles at local universities–Stanford, Berkeley, San Jose and San Francisco State."

Paul paused. "I personally recruited Kay Chiang from Berkeley," he admitted, clearing his throat and opting for full disclosure. "She didn't study technology but we needed her to infiltrate companies selling into China to learn how our secrets were leaked."

"Is that why you requested to be her liaison?" Hank shot him a shrewd glance.

"Partly," Paul said. "I felt responsible for bringing her in, and she never received extensive field work training because her specialty was corporate espionage. Since her assignments often overlapped my contacts, it seemed a natural fit."

"Hmm." Sitting back, Hank placed his ankle atop his other knee. "With this rare earths situation threatening, I've been asked to shake up Silicon Valley. Find companies working on substitute processes or metals, or frankly anything to give our defense contractors options besides being beholden to the Chinese."

DuMont had been right on the mark. Too bad it took this crisis to wake up the Defense Department. But at least he had an official direction now.

"Where do you want to begin?" Paul's chair squeaked as he tilted back, rubbing his forehead.

"First, we want to entice the venture capital community to bring to market whatever technology looks promising ASAP, even if it takes a couple extra years to reach profitability. We're willing to forego our usual claim to intellectual property rights to make this happen."

"That should grab their attention." Paul cocked his head. Was there a viable rare metal solution in the high-tech pipeline already? DuMont would be happy, but conceivably Paul would work himself out of a job way too fast.

"The defense industry hopes Silicon Valley will ratchet into high gear again, like it did during the Cold War," Hank continued, scrubbing his auburn crew cut. "They'll make it worth their while."

"They'd better." Paul wondered how much it was worth to those same defense contractors to avoid going toe-to-toe with the Chinese—or the Pentagon.

"Second, we must convince one or more venture capitalists to consider investing in old mining sites to kick-start our own production again. The last one declared bankruptcy last year and its investors won't put another dime into it until we can guarantee them customers." Hank slapped his thigh. "Damn it! The country needs alternatives. Including, as you so graciously pointed out in the meeting, the private sector. Otherwise, our economy may tank. Silicon Valley is the engine driving us all forward."

"So . . . what? I'm to work for the government, but undercover?" Paul's tension eased. He could handle reassignment again.

"Not quite. We hope you'll act on the government's behalf, keeping national security in mind. But we cannot keep you on the payroll."

"You said—"

"No, Paul. My decision is final. I can put you on unpaid leave of absence and extend your medical coverage for one full year—that's quadruple standard termination benefits. Plus, if you do a good job on this . . ." Hank twisted his mouth to the side, ". . . we may consider reinstating you at the agency."

Paul took a long, deep breath. On one hand, he'd have benefits. On the other, he would need to land a good job in Silicon Valley, putting him in the right circle of people—without the overt sanction of the government. Tricky. Maybe Eric Coleman could lend him a hand, especially if DuMont prodded him first. But Hank hadn't mentioned the huge—and definitely pink—elephant in the room.

"What about Kay Chiang? Who follows up with her in the middle of this rare earths cluster fuck?"

Hank slapped the file closed, the finality of the gesture irking Paul. He wouldn't decide anything with Kay's welfare a big question mark.

"She'll be reassigned to another liaison—who may even find her."

Hank's sarcasm wasn't lost on Paul, but he wasn't ready to stop fighting for Kay's welfare. Not yet.

"Why not assign Tamara?" Paul hesitated. Hell, what else could Hank do but fire him again? "Please don't ask Collins to watch her back. He couldn't hold a candle to her methods of communication. If she's in trouble, only creativity will pull her out."

"She's possibly gone rogue," Hank said, scowling. "She requires an experienced handler to gather whatever information her venture capitalist cover managed to find about China's military use of rare earths—and fast."

Paul opened his mouth, and Hank held up his hand

"I didn't offer you my job, Freeman. I fired your ass. Chiang's not your concern any more. What don't you understand?"

"Fine. OK." Paul clamped his lips together. "You do your job and I'll do mine. Frankly, I trust the geeks in Silicon Valley to pull our butt out of this rare metals wringer more than I do all the diplomats in China and D.C., combined."

"Actually, so do I." Hank rose, a slight smile curving his lips for the first time. "Maybe your lone-wolf style will work better in Silicon Valley than here in the Beltway. You used to have it in you, according to your records. Don't let us down." He waved his hand over the desk. "Clear out your personal belongings. I'll call Personnel to deal with the paperwork and escort you out." He tapped his phone and lifted the device to his ear.

Personal stuff? That comprised one special coffee mug and the coat hanging on the door. And years of effort he wasn't ready to give up on.

Focus—what else can I do before I leave?

Priority one—keep Kay safe.

Priority two—there was no other priority. When had his job become just one woman's welfare? Months ago? Years?

They'll yank his security clearance as soon as he signs the paperwork, and they certainly won't let him carry out information relating to company business. Thank God he kept his original recruitment files on Kay at his apartment. Buried in a box, no doubt, but at least not in Georgia with Daisy.

Paul opened his top drawer. He palmed a memory stick and placed it next to his computer, hidden by his oversize coffee mug. Whistling his favorite country tune, he banged the drawer shut hoping Hank would turn slightly so he could—

Yes! Hank frowned, plugging his free ear with one finger and turning his back on Paul.

Jamming the tiny device into the matching receptacle, he saved his email folder. He rummaged under his desk for a jumbo-sized shipping carton and set it between his feet, managing to tape one end shut. He stuffed papers relevant to Kay's mission inside—scribbled notes from his months' long research, memos with emergency field contacts, plus the agency's internal directory with cell numbers and email addresses.

"A rep from Personnel is on his way," Hank said. Muttering under his breath, he scrolled his phone's display. Praying Hank would stay distracted checking new messages, Paul grabbed a mailing label and gnawed on a pen.

He couldn't send a box to himself. That would create a record. They could hold his medical benefits over his head, as potent a threat as kidnapping to ensure his full cooperation. Ditto for sending it to any family member. His personnel file contained all their contact numbers and addresses.

The red bow on the video game caught his eye. Of course! Oscar's Christmas present. Chuckling to himself, he pasted an innocent expression on his face.

"Hank, would you mind if I mailed this kid's gift on the way out?" He lifted the game box and waggled it, retrieving the computer memory stick in one smooth motion with his other hand. "His family's address is in my files." He poised his fingers above his keyboard, pretending he wouldn't dare access any information without Hank's express permission.

"What?" Hank blinked. "Oh, sure. The Agency will pick up the tab instead of throwing you a farewell party."

Containing competing glee and ire, Paul scribbled the Nieves' Baltimore address on the label, surreptitiously scrawling a short note to Guillermo asking him to hold all the contents for him. Affixing the label to the package, he made a show of stuffing the video game inside the box, patting the bow on top, and slipping the note and tiny drive in alongside the other papers. He sealed the box with care.

"Hank?" He cradled his empty mug between his hands and stacked it on top of the box, protecting its precious contents with his forearms and wrists.

"Now what?"

"May I send a short note to Chiang's last known email addresses, telling her of her reassignment to another liaison?"

"Go ahead—but I'll review it before it's sent." Suspicion crossed Hank's face.

"Of course." Paul widened his eyes. "I'm no longer officially an employee. But I appreciate your professionalism . . . in this case."

Hank flushed red, his eyes narrowing, and waved at the keyboard.

Paul pulled up Kay's multiple email addresses and started typing.

Kay. What's up—long time no hear! I've taken another job in the States and will be busy for a while, but I have a friend who asked to talk to you about your insights into Beijing's cultural treasures. He's taking his family on vacation there next summer. Is it OK if I have him contact you?

Re-reading it, he cringed. His words seemed so uncaring, eager to shove her off with one last missive. He gnawed on his cheek. The elevator dinged its arrival on his floor—probably the pit bull from Personnel. Only seconds remained to reassure Kay she could contact him no matter what, especially if the intelligence community failed her.

He continued.

FYI, visited our old haunt in Berkeley the other day, and couldn't help remembering the laughter and fun last time we were there. Hope we get a chance to visit again as soon as you break free from your demanding schedule. Miss you. Take care. P

Satisfied he struck the right tone in the cryptic email, he motioned Hank over to review it. After a brief scan, Hank nodded his approval. Paul hit enter and crossed his fingers. Hopefully one email address would work. Even with China's top-notch surveillance monitoring her, and this ratcheted-up military rhetoric, he wouldn't stop looking for her until she arrived safely home with whatever intelligence she'd gathered.

Guillermo is right—I can't let it happen again.

Chapter 5

GOLDEN SEASONS HOTEL

Beijing, China
Evening, January 2, 15 Days Later

The wide halls of Beijing's luxurious hotel reverberated with the raucous cadence of Chinese entrepreneurs hawking their best ideas in a race to capture easy wealth. Compared to their grandparents sweating in southern rice fields, it was a step up for these young men.

Kay Chiang checked her delicate gold watch and frowned.

It wasn't like Charlie to be so late. Especially after prevailing on her to attend this geek fest. Pulling her phone from her tiny leather purse, she checked the display. Nope, no messages, voice or text. No missed calls, either.

She ignored the jostles of the crowd drifting toward the exit. With the technology conference officially closed, hard-core players would sniff out the most desperate engineers and negotiate better ownership positions or favorable contract terms. Or wheedle inside information from tired exhibitors.

Should she join them? Oh, why the hell not? What else to do until Charlie deigned to appear?

Damn it. Her feet hurt from spending two hours in three-inch spikes on this barely covered concrete floor. She craved a cup of hot tea and a bath, not mission creep.

I'm going to kill him when I get home.

Charlie would get a piece of her mind instead of a piece of her ass tonight. Unless he'd gotten into trouble . . .

Shoving aside her little warning voice, she chose the next target, tucking her black, heavy hair behind her ear. She never once broke eye contact with the engineer, whose tongue barely stayed in his mouth. Sauntering up and smiling, she pointed to the prototype propped open on the conference display table. Wiry guts and etched board lungs spilled out of its plastic casing like a mechanical autopsy.

"*Ni hao,*" she greeted, switching to Chinese. "Does this use the latest in 3-D vision goggles?" She bent from the waist for a closer look. "The ones requiring those expensive, special minerals?" Her assignment included identifying Chinese start-up companies who might be shills for their government's intensive research into laser-guided missile systems. Some even had sub-contracts from American defense contractors, in clear violation of Defense Department rules on procurement and technology transfer. It was amazingly easy—and excruciatingly tedious—to extract tidbits of information from these young men.

Hoping the entrepreneur wouldn't notice, she memorized the serial number etched beside the layers of chips and storage modules. Charlie would track down the rest of the manufacturer's customers using those rare earth metals. They'd apparently become quite valuable with Charlie's black market dealers.

"I . . . I . . . think so . . . yes," he stammered, raising his eyes and flushing a deep red. She straightened, deepening the vee in her blouse with her index finger. "But I'm the software engineer. My partner is the hardware expert."

"Hmm. Is he here?" Kay angled away so he could have a better view of her legs anchoring her snug mini skirt. She scanned the thinning crowd. "You must be a genius to come up with a new way to develop games. Everyone else here in China just copies Silicon Valley's technology." She turned and shot him a naughty wink. "I just love geniuses."

"Uh, we, uh, we just landed new government funding last month." His voice cracked. Sweat appeared on his forehead. His wide-eyed gaze darted to her chest and lingered, hope and disbelief warring across his expression. "We're better than anything developed in America." Shaking his head, he cleared his throat. "Are you directly interested in investing in our technology? I have time for an office demo now."

Kay bit her cheek, throttling the grin. He must be even younger than she thought. Did he actually think she'd go with him at this time of night? The kid had balls. Or was incredibly horny. Or both.

Of course, Chinese embraced the 24/7 mantra to conduct business across all time zones. Restaurants catered to the night crowd with full menus. Bike- and man-pulled cabs trolled the business districts as thickly as prostitutes did, and office lights shimmered an eerie brown in the moonlit smog.

Sighing with false regret, she tucked her hand around the engineer's elbow and pulled it into the side of her breast.

"Sorry, I can't come tonight," she crooned for the umpteenth time this evening. "If you give me your phone number, maybe early tomorrow morning . . ."

Her implied promise lingered in the smoky air. Kay hoped he would pack up his display and leave. The fewer who knew, the better, at least until Charlie checked it out. He was much savvier than she on the engineering mumbo-jumbo, except she unerringly got the men to spill their secrets. They made a formidable team.

Her idealistic entrepreneur offered a sweat-dampened business card, pressing it into her fingers with the air of a secret rendezvous. Kay shrugged mentally. She chose early on to blend the traditional path of corporate life with the challenge of leveraging her brains and beauty together to support her country. She never imagined she'd choose to act the part of a dumb bimbo. But that was half the fun—not knowing what she might be involved in next.

"Don't tell anyone besides your partner I'm coming," she whispered, brushing his ear with her lips. He tensed immediately and nodded. Mission accomplished, and with time enough to brief Charlie and lay out an action plan.

She turned away, scanning the hall again for Charlie.

"Hey! What's your name?" the young man called.

"Kay." She waggled her fingers in farewell and stepped to the wall. She checked her cell again—nothing.

What meeting would keep Charlie three hours? His caller insisted on privacy and spoke enough English so Kay's interpretive services weren't required. Charlie hinted at secret information related to the Chinese government's military investments, so she planned to finesse the information from Charlie later.

Leaning against the wall, she slid one foot out of her high-heeled pump and wiggled. *Ouch!* She would kick his perfect ass—as soon as her toes recovered.

Well, Charlie could take care of himself. He'd learned months ago to navigate the neighborhoods south of Peking University and Tiananmen Square to the Zhongguancun district—Beijing's own Silicon Valley. The spanking new buildings epitomized the ongoing chaos of invention, genius, and ambition.

Propping her hands on her hips, she regarded the beckoning exit. If she were lucky, Charlie had outlived his usefulness to the DIA and she could return home with her sparse intelligence and a long break.

God, wouldn't that be wonderful! Or just wishful thinking?

She had no home.

Not that a home was the be-all and end-all. In her scarce moments of elusive peace, she basked in poignant memories pulled out like holiday decorations. Old favorites resurrected once a year, dusty and dingy from their last exposure to light. A time when she could be who she really was, not the person everyone else imagined.

She'd meshed her emotions with work once before. Never again. Losing her edge in this business could cost her career. But if she lost her soul in the meantime, what was the purpose of living? Her heart skipped a beat.

Taking a deep breath, she shook off her negativity, concentrating on the problem at hand. After all, that's what she signed up for and committed to. And damn if she wouldn't succeed!

Chapter 6

"This is amazing! The Party will be so pleased with your discovery, Minister." The hushed female tone broke through the rumblings of male voices echoing in the emptying hall. A small crowd gathered around an outsized monitor. Images flashed from a tiny, hovering drone with dizzying speed and astonishing clarity, provoking gasps of astonishment.

"Possibly—too often a meal's aroma outshines its taste, heh?" The rich, masculine voice resonated with assurance and joviality, in stark contrast to the serious expressions of his companions.

Kay's lips twitched in amusement at the Chinese idiom. What enticed a Communist Party official to this obscure technology gathering? She sidled up to the group's periphery, her eyes focused on the elegant gentleman wearing a perfectly tailored pin-striped suit, his posture proud and erect, his head well above the bystanders. A network of fine lines cut across his temples, but not a single gray hair appeared in his precision cut.

To his right stood a squat, fifty-something woman, her stiff, respectful bearing and black boxy pantsuit slotting her as his subordinate. The squared-off, bobbed haircut didn't flatter her round face, adorned with glasses. Too bad she couldn't take as much pride in her feminine features as she probably did her job.

Kay nodded to her, sliding into the group and moving directly in front of the official. Keeping her eyes lowered in deference, she bowed slightly. She raised her chin, met his gaze, and blasted him with the full wattage of her practiced smile.

"I think any meal with you would smell—and taste fantastic," Kay murmured, lowering her voice so the surprisingly handsome official would lean forward and breathe in her body's natural perfume.

His eyes gleamed in appreciation. "I noticed you earlier, talking with one of our young innovators." A confident smile brightened his face and he raked an approving gaze along her body. Kay smiled in return, charmed.

The older woman glared at Kay, bringing a cigarette to her mouth, taking a quick drag, and exhaling noisily into Kay's face.

Kay ignored the acrid plume.

"I'm surprised a person of your stature would attend such a lowly conference," Kay breathed, arching her brow and flicking her gaze over him in return. Close-up, he was truly a fine male specimen, fit and healthy. She'd bet good money he tucked away a first wife, who bore his one allowed legitimate child, and enjoyed mistresses to provide the traditional variety.

"Likewise, I am surprised a woman of your exquisite beauty would bother with boring business and technology gatherings." He inched his way close, angling his shoulders and creating a private cocoon.

"You are so kind." She winked with a naughty smile. "I confess most of this is beyond my understanding."

"Ah, we must remedy that." He withdrew a card and offered it with a small flourish and sly smile. "Feel free to call me—anytime—and I will advance your education in whatever you desire." His low tones throbbed with sexual intensity.

Tilting his card toward the light, Kay coughed back a gasp and dropped her head, grateful her long veil of black hair would hide her expression. *Wei Jintao, Minister of Industry and Information Technology, Beijing District*, the card proclaimed in bold type. One of the most powerful men in Beijing, if not the whole country. He could order Internet cafés shut, email dissidents jailed, and blogs reporting government corruption squelched in a heartbeat.

If he had any inkling she authored Charlie's email to Paul about his findings on rare earths, she could be in a world of hurt. Is that why he flirted with her? The idea crossed her mind and sent her heart into a solo riff. What if the Chinese government snagged it in a random perusal of outgoing emails last month? Would this guy know? Be forewarned? Should she turn tail and run while she still had a chance?

With a quick prayer she was only a small player in the world of rare earth shenanigans, she swallowed hard. The opportunity to get close to such a high-up government official was leaping out and biting her in the ass. If she accepted Wei's blatant invitation for a liaison, she could ascertain if she and Charlie had already blown their cover. And possibly uncover more state secrets between the sheets than any man could ever worm from his mouth. She ignored the warning bell clanging in her head of more hypocrisy and games, not the fewer she craved.

Kay extended her hand. She brushed Wei's chest with her glossy fingernails, the less-than professional gesture a subtle acceptance of his offer.

"Minister Wei," she acknowledged, squeezing his hand and taking a deep breath, anticipating espionage's familiar razor blade. A surge of adrenaline filled her veins and heightened her senses. "I am Chiang Kay, a distant American relative of Chiang Kai-shek." She prayed choosing immediate truthfulness would deflect any suspicion of her honesty.

His brows narrowed, just as she expected. His female associate stiffened and stepped forward.

"I apologize for my rudeness," Wei said, turning to include the other woman in their conversation. "My subordinate, Han Mai, studies new technologies and their importance to our nation. Han Mai, this is—may I call you Kay?"

Kay nodded, lifting her brows and meeting Han's eyes with all the composure she could muster. This woman had disliked—or suspected—Kay on sight. Was she looking for a catfight in front of her boss? Did Kay dare respond in kind? With a wistful sigh, she let that fun fantasy float away.

"Chiang?" Han echoed, darting her eyes back to Wei Jintao. "The family of the traitorous rebel who destroyed our countryside, stole our treasures, and led his cowardly followers to hole up on Taiwan like shivering dogs?"

Gritting her teeth, Kay held onto her temper instead of slugging the old bitch. Defending her family's honor wouldn't win her any points.

"I work daily to overcome the shame of my great-great-uncle Chiang Kai-shek." Kay wasn't used to groveling but she could act with the best of them. She squared her shoulders. "In fact, the reason I am visiting Beijing is to see for myself its great splendors and learn of China's modern accomplishments, instead of simply believing the many untruths my relatives in America tell me."

"Ah, good!" Wei nodded, tossing a dismissive hand. "I will share with you what has made China great since your uncle and Chairman Mao's famous altercation."

Han pulled her head back, her homely face tinged red. What could she say, really? Giving homage to this high-ranking Communist Party official was part of her job. Wei could have fired Han for her rude comment.

Better only a few people learn Kay's family name. She could manage the impact of immediate hostility but not ever-increasing gossip and speculation. Whispered rumors would only get her into deeper trouble. Well, at least she could lessen this woman's antagonism some.

"I doubt I would ever be as learned as Han Mai," Kay demurred, bowing to the older woman. "But I may call you, Minister Wei, if you think it is worth your while to spend any of your precious minutes with me."

"It will be my pleasure," he assured her, angling to the side. Out of sight, his hand skimmed down her back to her waist, rested, and skated across her bottom with the barest brush of fingertips. His eyes slid to hers, gleaming with laughter and aplomb. Should she take offense at his audacity? Nah. This shrewd old dog simply confirmed her potential power over him.

Snapping his fingers, he drew his entourage on to the next table. The entrepreneurs scrambled to unpack and re-display their wares. Wei's opinion, time, and connections mattered. Not so different from the venture capitalist community in America, Kay mused. Except he wielded the power of the state—including its punishments—not the marketplace.

Chapter 7

Kay walked the hotel corridor one last, futile time. Still no message from Charlie. Putting her phone away, she fingered the worthless assortment of business cards in her purse. She would have been better off soaking in a hot bath and relaxing away her chronic tension than putting on a show. Would she ever be more than a hypocrite again? She sighed.

Her nail scraped the embossed state seal on Wei's fancy card. She obviously snagged his interest, plus an invitation to the next step. Did she dare? Would it put her in more danger—or less?

She didn't relish handling another of Charlie's jealous tirades because she flirted with a powerful government official. So far, she'd placated Charlie—mostly because there wasn't any information worth pursuing for more than a few minutes' investment. Kay suspected Wei would demand far more.

God, why couldn't she decide what to do?

She needed a break. Her aching toes seconded the idea enthusiastically, pointing her toward the renowned little tearoom off the main lobby. Decorated in the style of a traditional courtyard palace, with dark wood walls topped by red tiles swooping in a wave from a high peak, it served the highest quality green tea—at exorbitant prices. Kay was too tired to care. She put herself in the hovering waiter's hands, who escorted her to a small window table. Taking her order, he bowed and backed away.

Kay stared at fat snowflakes drifting down and disappearing into tiny puddles. So like her pretty life, buffeted by larger forces, yet only moments away from becoming an inconsequential smear on the street.

The waiter presented her with tea decorated with tiny little flowers. As she sniffed the fragrant aroma, she wondered how Paul would advise her. She trusted his professional judgment—usually more than her own. He never let her down, despite his disapproval of her flirtatious methods. Oh, he never came right out and said so. Simply reminded her that Mata Hari was so last-century. Sexual blackmail didn't work as well these days, so why do it?

Her cell phone tinkled a high, muffled note. It's about damn time!

Draining the last drops of warm tea, she pulled the phone out of her purse and rose, dropping bills on the table. She peered at Charlie's text. *On my way home.*

That infuriating man. No apology or acknowledgement he missed the conference entirely and he was hours late. Nope, just a "see ya later."

A smug smile twisted her lips. She imagined appropriate sexual payback for such rude behavior. Maybe locking him to the sink in her velvet-lined handcuffs and doing a very, very slow striptease. Make him squirm and ache while he waited for once. Yeah, that might do it.

Retrieving her long, woolen coat and matching black beret from the front desk, she tipped the sleepy young man with coins and a large smile. Out on the street, she hailed a cab to give her still-protesting feet a break.

The waning moon glowed through the window, mesmerizing her, reminding her of mothers' stories about the moon's power. Well, she felt as pathetic as tonight's fading moon, searching for her essence against a black backdrop of slowly dissipating time. Where was the girl heroine with strong convictions, an unerring sense of right and wrong, and the courage and fortitude to face tough decisions? Buried so deep under this promiscuous persona she could never reclaim her?

Tapping the driver's shoulder, she pointed to the narrow alleyway leading to their modest flat, impossible for a car to traverse. He pulled to a hard stop. She tossed him the fare, pushed open the door, and stepped right into icy, wet slush topping the low sides of her high-heel shoe.

"Shit!" She shook her foot free and crossed to the walkway's relatively drier side, concentrating on avoiding another misstep in the meager light. Rats scurried and scattered in their nightly foraging, interrupted by her measured paces. Teeth clenched, she fought back a shudder.

This was one hell of a way to end a lousy day.

A loud roar of motorcycles reverberated in the distance. Throbbing motors echoed in ever-increasing rumbles. The wide boulevards built for the Olympic Games changed from paved roads to bumpy cobblestones, testing the riders' abilities to prevent skidding out on the deadly turns.

Glancing over her shoulder, Kay spied twin headlights turning down the alley. She hurried the final fifty yards toward her doorway, hoping to avoid their zooming splash.

The cycles slowed, throttling back and pacing themselves to her speed. Her familiar door beckoned. Still too far away for refuge. Turning her head, she noted three figures—two on the front bike, one on the second. She carried little money in her purse. Her body was her only prize. And she wasn't offering it to brutes.

She slipped off her shoes, ignoring the bite of cold stones against her feet. Tucking her long hair into the neck of her coat, she scooted her tight skirt up her thighs. She'll kick and claw her way free if necessary.

The passenger on the front bike angled against its plane, poised to jump. Kay readied herself for attack.

The cycles skidded to a stop, blocking the entrance to her flat. Motors revved to a deafening roar in the narrow passage. The riders wore dark jackets and leather leggings, with caps pulled low over their faces. She absorbed each detail with a professional glance. Unfortunately, the gang chose a perfect locale. No witnesses, no light, and they outnumbered their target three to one.

Too bad. Kay tensed and balanced on her toes, fists raised, legs spread wide, eyes fixed on the passenger, anticipating an air-borne pounce.

Instead, he slid to the pavement. His body hit the stones in a boneless heap. The driver of the front cycle flipped him carelessly with a booted foot, kicking his face into the sliver of light trickling between the buildings.

"Charlie!" Kay gasped. Her heart pounded double-time. She surveyed the extreme bruising on his left side, his blood-soaked clothes, and his utter stillness. Adrenaline surged. Ignoring her lover, she shrank back, keeping to the shadows.

"You're next, you traitorous whore!" The biker waved his fist. He spun in a whirl of wet spray, and accelerated away. The second biker followed. She caught a glimpse of a familiar crest decorating the cycle's back—the official image of the Great Wall, reserved for police insignias and China's currency.

What had Charlie gotten them into?

Chapter 8

CHINATOWN

*San Francisco, California
Afternoon, January 23, 21 Days Later*

A horn blared in Paul's ear. A bright red Porsche cut in front of him and zoomed up the steep hill, swerving and leaving a wake of chaos and brake lights. Startled back to the present, Paul barely avoided rear-ending a double-parked delivery truck. His Jeep engine stalled out.

"Way to go, Freeman," he muttered. These San Francisco hills almost required three feet to operate the damned manual transmission, and certainly commanded more attention than Paul gave it.

The audiobook "Learn Mandarin Chinese in 10 Easy Lessons" coughed as he cranked his motor and continued its placid tones over his flooring the accelerator.

"Today is Wednesday," it crooned. "*Jin tian xing qi san*" rang out a nasal twang.

Paul shook his head in frustration. He tried for weeks to get the hang of Chinese but it escaped him. The language used emphasis and slight variations in tone and cadence. He still fumbled with beginner words. So much for impressing Kay's family.

He couldn't wait any longer to approach them. Hank blocked his efforts to pry new information from his old teammates six weeks ago. The obvious conclusion—no one was even trying to find Kay.

Her troubling vanishing act led to late nights searching the Internet for information about China's newest arrest procedures, just in case she'd gotten into real trouble. What he discovered scared the bejesus out of him. Instead of the promised transparency, a tangled web of military bureaucratic nonsense about anything related to rare earths blocked him. The sudden disappearance of a number of key scientists and researchers was also jarring.

Political refugees told U.S. Congressional Sub-Committees of years-long imprisonment without charge in unidentified holding cells, unable to receive visitors. In fact, many said their families weren't told anything—the accused traitors simply vanished.

And for what? For challenging the official Party line. These were loyal Chinese citizens, but with no political connections—just like Kay. Paul could only imagine what a Taiwanese-American undercover, civilian operative caught for spying on military secrets might face, especially those using these goddamn rare metals.

But he was damned if he would fail a teammate again. He brought her into this line of work, so he'd get her out. Even if it wasn't officially his responsibility anymore.

Spying a car exiting a prime parking spot, Paul zipped across a lane and maneuvered into place, barely keeping his Jeep's rear-end out of the traffic lane.

Locking the car with its annoying beep, he climbed the steep hill, its top already shrouded in misty fog. Street signs covered with both English and Chinese characters guided him to the right address, a grocery store with an apartment above. He stopped and caught his breath.

Bright oranges in neat clusters were piled high near the doorway. The tangy odor of fresh fish mixed with the damp air. Customers chattering a mix of English and Chinese poked and prodded strange-looking leafy vegetables and pale roots. They bargained with loud enthusiasm with the courteous young man behind the counter.

One of Kay's three brothers, Paul recalled. He grabbed the recessed door leading to a staircase. A gust of wind tore the door out of his hand. He fought it closed and tackled the stairs two at a time. Reaching the top in the half-light, he knocked twice, glancing at his watch. Right on time.

The door opened a crack. A squinting brown eye topped by gray hair appeared. Kay's father, Paul guessed, frantically trying to remember the appropriate Chinese greeting of hello. The door opened wide. A row of shoes and slippers lined up like a military parade along the beige wall.

"*N-Ni hao*," Paul stuttered, praying for correct pronunciation. He bowed his head and extended his hand. "My name is Paul Freeman, Kay's friend. Thank you for agreeing to see me."

"Hmph." The elderly man stepped back and motioned him inside the flat. Wearing a sweater vest over a dress shirt and polyester slacks, white cotton socks covering his feet, he would blend in with any retirement community in the country. "This is usually our time of rest," he informed Paul in slightly accented English. "We work hard every day, and we are not getting younger. We rely on our children to help us, especially as our community prepares for our Spring Festival."

Remembering what his guidebook told him about manners and protocol, Paul toed off his loafers. The entrance led into a combined living and dining area, where a battered wood-carved loveseat faced an aging television. Two matching armchairs covered in faded red and gold stylized dragons flanked the windows, their drapes pulled aside to let in the fog-dimmed light. Black and white portraits, and color snapshots of children speckled the wall in formal groupings.

"Your business looks very prosperous," Paul said. "And the young man working there handles the many customers well."

"That's our youngest son, Howard," a female voice announced with pride. An older woman entered the room carrying a tray with a steaming pot of tea and porcelain dishware. Setting it on the endtable, she straightened and gave him an assessing stare. "And I am Kay's mother. It is nice to meet you, Mr. Freeman." Jet-black hair coiled at her neck in a thick bun. She wore a loose fitting floral top, black pants, and bright yellow cotton slippers on her feet.

"*Xie xie ni.*" Paul thanked her with all the graciousness he could muster.

A small smile flitted across her face. She nodded and settled in the chair next to the tea tray.

"I meant to say 'thank you,'" Paul hastened, positive he'd mangled the pronunciation and politeness stopped her from correcting him.

"I understood you quite well, Mr. Freeman," she reassured him, smiling wider. "We rarely hear anything but Cantonese. Most of Chinatown's immigrants come from the southern regions of China, not Taiwan like ourselves. We have adapted accordingly." She began pouring the tea in a choreographed dance of fingers and wrists. "Please sit, Mr. Freeman. Tea?" Using both hands, she offered him the steaming beverage.

Paul accepted the delicate cup and settled into the opposite chair. Chiang shuffled toward the loveseat, next to his wife. She placed a saucer in his hands with the identical gesture. Pouring her own, she sat back and took a dainty sip.

"Mr. Freeman, perhaps now you will answer me about our missing daughter," Chiang said. "How do you know she is in China? And what is your relationship with Kay?" Chiang's tone demanded a full accounting. Paul promised he would disclose the details face to face, not over the phone. With less than five hours to concoct a believable cover story, he prayed it would match whatever the Chiangs knew of their daughter's job.

"Kay and I met at Berkeley." Paul forced an easy smile to his lips, sticking as close to the truth as he could. "I expected an email months ago about joining her in Beijing while she was there interpreting for an American businessman. I tried reaching her by email and phone but got no reply. I'm concerned she may be ill, possibly on her own in a hospital, and only wish to help her. Who might she contact in Beijing if she were in trouble?"

"Our family has ties to Taiwan, Mr. Freeman, not to Communist China." Chiang stiffened, his spine as straight as a parade marshal's, his eyes narrowed and suspicious. "If you know Kay, you understand this."

Paul scrambled to recover from his obvious gaffe. "Yes, I understand you are descendants of the brave leader, Chiang Kai-shek, and therefore have no friends on the mainland." He gulped his tea in one swallow, ignoring the liquid fire burning his throat.

Mrs. Chiang rose gracefully and walked to the largest portrait on the wall. A wide grin beneath a thick mustache split the face of a Chinese man relaxing in his garden, hat in his hand. His well-defined cheekbones and jovial eyes repeated in Mr. Chiang's features, and reminded Paul of Kay's identical beaming smile.

Reverently touching the glass, Mrs. Chiang spoke. "Chiang Kai-shek is our country's hero, Mr. Freeman, and the role model for our family." Paul strained to hear her low tones. "We encouraged all our children to have the same courage and loyalty to family, the same vision to protect our country's heritage and greatness. Anyone we knew living those ideals is no longer living in Communist China."

"Of course not," Paul agreed, confused by Chiang's grim and unforgiving face. "Perhaps you are aware of her friends working or visiting there now."

"We do not recognize our daughter anymore." He sipped the last of his tea and set the cup in its saucer with a rattle. "She turned her back on our wishes. If she is in trouble, it is because she must pay for her choices."

"That's a little harsh, isn't it, Mr. Chiang?" Paul's hackles rose. "She's still your daughter, no matter what she has done."

"Kay refused to respect our family's lustrous heritage." Chiang sprang to his feet, pacing to the window. "She dishonored our family with a career we disapproved of strongly."

"She was always a willful child," Mrs. Chiang said, returning to her seat and quietly placing the empty cups and saucers on the tray. "We tried to guide her in the ways of our cultural heritage, but she grew up loving America, not China." A sad expression wreathed her face.

"Our eldest, Bob, manages the store for us, very profitably, while still retaining our traditions." Chiang pointed with pride to a photograph of a young man in cap and gown. "Our next son, Steve, studied at Harvard and is now earning his UCLA law degree. And you saw Howard, our youngest son—he works every day so we can rest our feet." He strolled past the row of pictures, all boys, nodding.

"Where's a childhood picture of Kay?" Paul couldn't resist the prod.

"She disobeyed us one too many times." Chiang kept his back to Paul and shrugged. "We removed it."

"What did she do that was so terrible?" Paul aimed his question at Kay's mother, hoping she wasn't as hard-hearted.

"We asked her to marry a wealthy older man who would have been an asset for our business and desired a family of his own." A wistful smile flitted over her features. "Kay refused her father, claiming she had better things to do than raise children." Her eyes lifted to his, compassion and worry in their brown depths. "She said she wanted to change the world."

"You mean imitate her ancestor?" Paul gestured to the portrait. "Or does courage and loyalty only belong to the men in your family?"

Mrs. Chiang covered her mouth, too late to block the escape of a tiny gasp. Chiang whirled, stalking three paces and stopping directly in front of Paul, his eyes glittering.

"A woman's role is as a mother, first and foremost. This modern view of family is destructive. Consider what they require of women in China—forcing them to have so few children!" He shook his head and dropped down on the loveseat.

"Who will take care of elderly parents?" he continued. "A woman goes with her husband and supports his parents in their waning years. A family should have many children so family traditions can carry on, so young children can learn the wisdom of all their grandparents, aunts and uncles, and older cousins, and . . ." His voice trailed off.

Mrs. Chiang cradled her husband's hand and met Paul's eyes.

"Kay is a member of our family, yes, Mr. Freeman," she said. "However, family and traditions are greater than any individual. Our Chinese customs fill our daily life and give us purpose. Is it wrong to honor our forebears by passing their values onto our children?"

Paul stayed silent. He studied Chinese culture voraciously this last month to understand both Kay's and America's options against Chinese threats. The Chiangs fervently defended their way of life, one never questioned because their honored parents admonished them to continue the traditions. And so they did, for generations. Even the way the family name came first reflected the individual subsuming to the family. Conformity, rather than the vivid individualism sparkling throughout American culture.

The image of Kay standing among a group of proud recruits, hand raised as her high-pitched notes solemnly swore allegiance to America, not China, popped into his mind. Kay considered herself an American, not Chinese-American, and certainly not Chinese. Perhaps the Chiangs either couldn't see or couldn't accept her identity.

"*Duibuqi.*" Paul apologized. "I'm sorry if I offended you in any way. Clearly Kay made different choices with her life, and—"

"Bah!" Chiang exclaimed, throwing away his wife's hand and jumping to his feet. "She spends her life with one man after another. She is no longer fit for a man's first wife. I would not arrange a marriage for her with any respectable man if she came home begging me to do so!" He stomped from the room.

Paul's eyes widened. Did Chiang think his daughter a whore? He shot Kay's mother a quick glance. She raised an embarrassed gaze to his.

"Mr. Freeman, we have relatives in Taiwan who may be able to help you find Kay," she whispered, glancing down the hallway after her husband. "I will send you a list if you leave me your email address."

"Thank you, Mrs. Chiang." He handed her a card. "I'd appreciate any names you give me. I promise to be discreet," he added. She might provide more leads if she felt she could trust him.

"You are still here?" Chiang stalked back to his wife's side.

Mrs. Chiang elbowed him. "My husband will take you to our warehouse. Kay's landlord delivered her belongings when she left the country. Perhaps you will find what you seek in those boxes."

"If they are still there." Chiang threw his wife a dirty look and shuffled toward the line of assorted shoes near the door. "I told Bob to create room for next week's shipment of holiday decorations and firecrackers."

A slow burn began in Paul's belly. Loyalty to the family only worked one way, it appeared, at least for the women. It must have been impossible for a girl with Kay's zest for life and freedom to live up to their views of a dutiful daughter. He bit back caustic words.

"Thank you, Mrs. Chiang, for the tea, and your hospitality," Paul said. "I will tell you if I find out anything."

She offered her hand with an imperceptible nod, picked up the tray, and disappeared into the kitchen.

"This way." Chiang opened the door to the stairs and slid his feet inside plastic sandals. He clattered down two flights of stairs, leaving Paul yanking on his loafers and running after him.

"Over here." Chiang led him to a carton-crowded corner. He pointed to a short stack of boxes on the bottom of a shelving unit.

"The freight elevator lifts to street level at the store entrance." Chiang started towards the far corner. "Are you parked nearby?"

Paul nodded, fumbling for his keys. "I'll pull in front and I can load my Jeep. Thanks for storing these for Kay. I'll make sure she gets them when she returns home."

"Good riddance," Chiang muttered, slapping the freight elevator button.

Paul grabbed the smallest box and headed up the steps to load his car with the remnants of Kay's life.

Chapter 9

SILICON VALLEY, CALIFORNIA

Late Afternoon, January 23, Same Day

Cruising south along Skyline Boulevard with the setting sun on his right and the flat-topped office buildings of Silicon Valley offering peek-a-boo views on his left, Paul was intent on making good on his promise to check in with Eric Coleman today, despite the late hour. Pulling off next to towering redwoods, he found Eric's programmed number in his phone, hit the call button, and zoomed back onto the paved surface again with a rattle of gravel. He raised the volume to his car speakers.

One of his most successful DARPA recruits, Eric and his wife Lynn were now legends in the Silicon Valley venture capital community. With Colonel DuMont's blessing, Paul contacted Eric after packing up his D.C. apartment and gave Eric a heads-up on his unofficial interest in the rare metals industry. Paul sought a job referral to a company relying on China's supply. Instead, Eric asked Paul to consider joining his namesake firm as a consultant, so he and Lynn could enjoy their three-month old daughter. Apparently, Paul's experienced eye for innovative defense technologies was a godsend to the pair.

Paul hadn't yet disclosed Kay's dilemma to Eric, and hoped he wouldn't have to, given their run-ins at Eric's first technology company. Paul wouldn't blame Eric one bit for doubting Kay's integrity.

The rings stopped. Paul yanked his mind back to the present.

"Coleman." Eric sounded more harried than last time.

"Eric, it's Paul Freeman. Sorry I'm so late in calling, but—"

"Don't worry about it. Are you free tomorrow morning at nine?"

"Sure. You wanna grab a cup of coffee? I found a great place in Los Gatos—"

"No time. Meet me at DOD Tech and you can have coffee during the board meeting. I'll email you the address."

"Meaning I'm acting as your consultant?"

"Meaning another board member just quit at DOD Tech so there are two vacancies. I nominated you for one since it's right up your alley. They design rare earth-based components and research alternative solutions using less of China's purified metals. I'll send you our standard contract with compensation fees and stock options for a board seat, plus what I have in mind for your other work with Coleman Partners." Eric paused. "Sorry. I'm handling this with all the finesse of a freight train. Are you ready for the Silicon Valley pace?"

"As ready as I'll ever be." Paul couldn't help but laugh. "You can count on me to give it my all."

"Good enough. Review the material I send you and if you have any questions don't hesitate to ask. I'll see you in the morning."

He terminated the call, and Paul scratched his jaw in wonderment. Eric still hadn't asked him one question about why he'd left his job at DIA.

Of course. Eric probably got an earful from DuMont. Shrewd business people respected their earliest contacts, and DARPA's team leader, DuMont, had kick-started Eric's career decades ago.

DuMont had a knack for honing analytic and people skills, offering Paul a break from command right when he craved it. It seemed a safe and sane choice. People didn't die working for DARPA.

Later, DuMont pushed Paul into putting his field experience to use helping covert operatives; thought it would help Paul deal with his persistent demons. Paul agreed, partly because Kay was out there on crazy missions. And then both he and DuMont pointed her to the craziest one of all, chasing rare earth leads in the heart of China.

Two months later, and still no word from her.

Driving down the long driveway of his remote rental home, Paul wrestled slippery tires. Mud splashed his windshield, reminding him of his fun and crazy teenage years driving in the red clay of Georgia hills. Before chasing girls became his whole life. When life was free and easy and oh, so simple. Could it ever be again?

He parked in the carport, appraising the threatening clouds. More frigid rain, ready to deluge soon. Snow in January he could handle, but he loathed icy rain pellets against his face.

Welcome to Northern California.

Grabbing the smallest box, he juggled his keys and let himself into the cold, dark living room. He flipped the hall switch on with his elbow, dropped the box on the wood-planked floor, and cranked up the thermostat. He lit the kindling, thankful that this time the wood was dry and he wouldn't have to stumble around the acre of property searching for the damp woodpile. *Be prepared*, the motto of his Boy Scouts reminded him after that fiasco.

Paul lugged in the rest of the boxes, avoiding the first drops of rain splattering on the roof. He clapped his hands once and the lone torchiere lamp in the corner instantly blazed. Inky shadows receded through floor-to-ceiling windows.

Nudging Kay's boxes close to the fire, Paul settled on the huge sheepskin rug. He'd already excavated every nook and cranny in his old files, searching like a man obsessed—and maybe he was. No way did he want to add to his nightmares, which he would if he lost her the way he lost Ernie. Not this time. Not because he delayed.

Even if he blamed her for dropping out of contact, he hadn't pre-arranged a signal if the situation turned dicey. Or yanked her little butt out at the first sign of trouble. Her job was civilian reconnaissance, damn it, not full-blown confrontation. What was she trying to prove?

Or were there greater forces at work in D.C., protecting career bureaucrats' jobs over her life, like so much collateral damage?

Fumbling for his pocketknife to break the seals, he hesitated before invading her privacy. Of course, she had abandoned her apartment and belongings to take off with Charlie Wilkins in the middle of the night. Perhaps she didn't have anything to hide.

He sifted through a box of skimpy lingerie, discovering a couple of sex toys he couldn't figure out how to use. Shaking his head, he left the rest of the contents untouched. Too many intimate secrets. She'll probably tear him a new asshole for pawing through it.

The next box held a near-complete collection of Nancy Drew mystery books, numbered and in well-used condition. He imagined her as a skinny pre-teen, snuggled into the chair he'd just vacated in her San Francisco apartment, reading in the dim light. Wedged in next to the books were several dolls he recognized as part of a Barbie collection, complete with sets of outfits and tiny high heels stored in zippered plastic bags. Nothing here except a clue as to how Kay developed her unshakable desire to become a modern-day heroine.

Pushing that box away, he grabbed the last one. Small, heavy and filled to the brim with papers clipped in small stacks. Hopeful, he shuffled payment stubs, bank statements and expense account reports. No address book, no journal. He neared the bottom and his heart sank. Still no inkling on her whereabouts.

Digging further, he touched soft, flexible paper. Curious, he lifted it from the box and tilted it to the light.

Coffee after this? His own handwriting leapt off the paper napkin in bold black strokes, the emblem of Berkeley's Claremont Hotel embossed on the corner.

"What the–?" He'd slipped it into Kay's hand after his recruiting speech. He never played favorites, but her astute questions, aura of commitment, and direct approach resonated deeply in his gut. His marriage was on the rocks—in spirit, if not in fact—so he broke his rule and invited Kay out.

Why keep such a personal note? Better yet, why stash it among dull, financial records?

His cell phone rang. He pulled it out of his pocket, flopping down on his back against the hard floor.

"Yeah?" He stared at the ceiling.

"This is how you answer your phone? How rude!" Paul almost expected Daisy to give him a wet Bronx cheer in the best Jar Jar Binks imitation.

"Uh, sorry. My mind was elsewhere. What's up?"

"I wanted to remind you Justina's school lets out in mid-May and she's flying directly to California. Could you have chosen a more inconvenient location?"

"Jeez, Daisy, I'm sorry I don't let you run my life anymore. Maybe you should have thought about that before you divorced me."

"I thought plenty," she said in a raised voice. "Including the fact that you were and still are a lousy father. How can you be involved with Justina if you're three thousand miles away?"

"Phones still work, don't they?" he retorted. "AT&T doesn't care if they're connecting us from one block or one country away. Besides, we email weekly."

"Well. Warren is much more in tune with us. You should prepare Justina for accepting him with more grace than she's shown."

Paul couldn't help his grin. "Tina isn't as taken with him as you are, huh?"

"No, and it's all your fault. Tell her to be nicer to him—"

"Stop right there. I won't tell Tina who to like or not like."

"Well, you better, soon. All she does these days is bury her face in her computer and text her supposed friends. She's becoming a nerd," Daisy wailed. "At this rate she'll develop no social graces."

"She's only fourteen."

"I dated at her age," Daisy snapped. "And you were eying girls, too. Don't bother denying it."

"Uh, yeah—but she's still just our baby girl." Paul dreaded Tina dating horny teenage boys with no Dad on hand to kick their touchy-feely asses. "She'll mature in her own time."

"Not if she keeps spending her days at Naomi Quinn's house. She dates constantly, according to Justina."

"Who's Naomi again?" Paul's mind raced, trying to remember details of his last conversations with Tina. Damn, Kay distracted him for way too long. Daisy was right. His fathering skills needed a lot of work.

"She's Justina's best friend. Remember?" Daisy's sigh dragged on. "Her parents divorced, and she and her mother live with her grandmother, clear on the other side of town. Speaking of which . . ."

Paul grimaced. The other side of town was Daisy-speak for their African-American neighbors. So what if Naomi was black, yellow, red, white or blue? Daisy's racism annoyed Paul more times than he could count. And embarrassed him in front of DuMont at one Christmas party.

"C'mon, Daisy. Let Tina make friends with whoever she wants. You don't have to socialize with them."

"That's not the issue," Daisy shot back. "Your mother is."

"My mother?" Paul's mind raced in another direction. He hadn't talked to Mom for six months, trusting Tina would keep him posted. She adored his mother, for which Paul was eternally grateful. At least Mom defended his side of the divorce argument to Tina. "Is something wrong?"

"She contradicts everything I say to Justina," Daisy huffed.

He flashed a thumbs-up. Way to go, Mom!

"Look, Daisy, next time I talk to Tina I'll ask her to show you and what's-his-name a little more respect. Gotta go. Talk to you soon." He punched off, shaking his head at the scattered papers littering the floor. The napkin faced up, reminding him of his supposed top priority. He smacked his forehead, remembering Eric's promised email, too. He'll be awake all night cramming for tomorrow's meeting.

Leaning forward, he grabbed a loose paper in the bottom of the last box. Blurry numbers wavered in imprecise columns on the page. With a sigh, he raised it to the stark light and squinted. Nope. With a muttered curse, he shoved the new glasses onto his face.

He was too damned attached to these things.

Strings of numbers shot into focus. Bank accounts? Credit cards? Who cared? He needed a list of the financial institutions and passwords to access them. Maybe she stuck those in a safe deposit box. But where?

Damn it Kay. Why didn't you stay in touch?

Frustrated, he kicked the box, sending it spinning crazily, corner over corner. A flash of white caught his attention. Tackling the carton against the wall, he reached inside. His finger touched a single square of slick paper jammed into the bottom. Bingo! A forgotten photo. He yanked it out and flipped it right side up. Air rushed from his lungs.

Kay's graduation day at Berkeley. Kay begged to see him before her first assignment. They met at Oakland's Jack London Square, wandering the foggy waterfront, talking about her future and shivering. Wrapping his Georgia Tech sweatshirt around her shoulders, he ignored her teasing nickname, Georgie Porgie.

They innocently mugged for the street vendor's camera, her long hair tangled in his shoulder-length curls. Or so he remembered. Now he discerned lust tinging his usual cherubic air, matched by obvious adoration on hers. She had been so young—and he left to recruit more idealistic students for DARPA. He recalled casually mentioning Daisy and their baby girl, pretending purely professional interest.

He may have fooled himself then. What was his reason now? Obsession? Guilt? Sure, Kay jumped at the chance to serve her country. But perhaps she was simply trying to please him.

Jesus, he prayed that wasn't the case. Despite his protests, Kay never changed her modus operandi, trusting her 4.0-grade-average brains would serve her well while leveraging the one-two punch of her knockout body. Maybe she convinced herself her tactics were worth it—but never him. He worried some asshole would treat her no different from a well-paid prostitute snitching for the police, and put her in a world of hurt someday.

Collapsing into the recliner, he rested his forearms on his knees and dropped his head in his hands. His only significant find comprised a list of account numbers, a candid photo, and an unsigned, years-old note. Only he would recognize that handwriting.

What are you trying to tell me, Kay?

He grabbed the three items and headed toward the small bedroom fashioned as an office. Powering on his PC, he tapped the desktop, considering how Kay's brain usually worked. The cursor blinked invitingly, and he flew his fingers across the keyboard, testing possible combinations. Forty-five minutes later, he fell back, astonished. Transposing numbers to letters, he found a Yahoo! email account, User ID *Claremont*, password *GeorgiePorgie*. And blinking in the desk lamp's eerie fluorescent light, an icon cheerfully informed him of incoming mail—sent almost three weeks ago.

He took a deep breath and clicked it open.

Paul, Help me get out of here. Charlie's been killed following up on rare metal lead. Possibly tried to blackmail the wrong person, not sure. They assume I was involved and are threatening me. I don't know much about his last contact except they spoke English. Afraid to use regular channels. Have moved to a different safe house. If I don't hear from you in 2 weeks, I'll try new contacts.

Paul glanced at his desk calendar. Too late again!

Chapter 10

TIANANMEN SQUARE

Beijing, China
Late Afternoon, February 5, 13 Days Later

Kay propped her heavy bicycle against the brick wall and tightened the coarse black shawl across her face. A blast of Siberian winter settling southward whipped across the vast expanse of Tiananmen Square to its outskirts. She huddled, shivering, behind a square pillar and watched the sparse crowd disperse under a threatening sky. Chins tucked into scarves, brows covered with hats, and eyes unanimously downturned directed numerous booted feet on the treacherous, icy pavement. Soon, only an elderly couple joined a camera-toting tourist to stare at the gigantic portrait of Mao Zedong on the adjacent wall.

Who else sensed the deep-rooted danger floating in the dusky light? Or cast furtive glances in all directions, lingering too long in the emptying square and glancing at a watch? Who else dressed in disguise, looking for a stranger for the briefest of meetings?

No one. Kay's heart sank. The storm warnings kept the usual throngs away. Did she really think this last-ditch effort to contact a rebel journalist for help would yield results?

Nightmares of the menacing growl telling her she was next still woke her in a cold sweat. She had grabbed her stash of cash and a change of clothes from her old flat and rushed back out, ignoring the rats skittering over poor Charlie's body. She opted for life, convinced his murder sent a message to other spies—and their sponsors. *Don't mess with China.*

Or was Charlie specifically targeted because he'd pursued that rare metals lead? In the past six weeks, official Chinese announcements headlined every newspaper, denouncing Japan's belligerent tactics and proclaiming China's right to retaliate by withholding exports of those highly refined metals.

Fortunately, her pre-arranged safe house, a flat in the flashy section of Beijing, allowed her to blend in with tourists visiting the neighboring Buddhist shrine and locals haunting the cafes day and night. For weeks, she assaulted the red tape protecting China's political secrets, battling a bureaucracy that ever so politely insisted she couldn't leave the country because her papers weren't in order. No more detail, just a civil dismissal toward an inevitable fate of limbo.

Establishing a new screen name at a nearby Internet café, she perused stories of official corruption and inhumane policies that brought her to tears. One journalist's name popped up repeatedly. Also a Berkeley graduate, Tan Yannan's stories unabashedly took the Chinese people's side, crying out for justice, equality and opportunity. Her recent exposé decried the plight of the indigenous population, displaced from their northern ancestral lands by the huge industrial mining enterprises.

Kay emailed Tan and asked her to meet and discuss an American's view of Inner Mongolia, gambling that a public email might be temporarily safe. Tan pushed to find out more but Kay stayed silent, not wanting to end up as dead as Charlie. Finally, Kay volunteered her last name and link to Chiang Kai-shek in a desperate, last move. Tan capitulated and agreed to this morning's meet, but insisted it take place at Tiananmen Square, the biggest public gathering place in Beijing.

What other choice did Kay have? So she agreed, hoping to keep a low profile. How crazy was that?

Kay tugged her ragged clothes close, stamping her feet in the felt boots. She changed her appearance daily—sometimes an office worker in colorful skirts, other times an industrial worker in plain pants and jacket. Today, mismatched scraps haphazardly hung on her frame. Underneath she wore long silk underwear, yet the frigid wind penetrated the gaps with unerring precision.

A flash of pink and blurry yellow captured her attention. Peering left in the diminishing light, she glimpsed a young girl running in circles and capturing fat, heavy snowflakes on her tongue. Carefree giggles mingled with suddenly hushed silences, her enthusiastic claps of joy muffled by yellow mittens. A matching beret topped shoulder-length black hair. Bundled in a bright pink jacket with a huge familiar Barbie face emblazoned on the back and on each front patch pocket, she appeared a schoolgirl playing hooky. The required red tie peeked out from her coat's neckline and the black pants of her school uniform were tucked into sturdy boots.

Kay smiled at the girl's infectious laughter. Had she ever been so young? No, she always had a damned heritage to live up to.

A camera flashed a respectful distance from the girl's antics. Probably the tourist who would go home with a mistaken impression of China's youth. The rigid conformity required of schoolchildren clashed with her obvious love for the American icon, Barbie.

Kay stiffened. Healthy children didn't skip classes. Where were her parents?

Was she spying on Kay?

BOOM!

Kay dropped to a crouch, searching for danger. She spotted a pink blob on white pavement. Grabbing her skirts, she straightened and rushed toward the little girl. What reckless instinct drove her to protect this child rather than herself? An affinity for Barbie in a foreign country? Idiot!

The low throb of a racing engine filled the air. Terrified, she spun around. She spotted a young couple straddling a motorcycle, the man fiddling with its controls. Of course. A backfire. The little girl jumped to her feet, inspecting her snow angel in the fresh powder.

Kay slumped forward, flooded with relief.

I'm certifiably nuts if I fall to pieces over this tiny shit!

One thing was certain—Tan's tardiness risked putting Kay under unusual scrutiny from the numerous security cameras dotting the high walls. Tucking her shawl close to her face, she grabbed her bike's handlebars and strolled toward the main exit.

"*A yi! A yi!* Wait up—please!"

The high-pitched Chinese words barely penetrated the thick wool covering Kay's ears. Relieved the little girl's aunt had arrived to escort her safely home, Kay pressed on, maneuvering her bike in the deepening snow the few miles to her flat.

"Auntie! Auntie!" The girl's voice sounded closer. There was no one in front of her, no one to either side. Shrugging, Kay plodded on.

A sharp tug on her sleeve forced her bike's front wheel into a crazy angle. Kay spun around, releasing the handlebars. The bike skidded sideways. The pedal's teeth scraped across her shin, snagging the silk and banging the bone hard enough to bruise before it fell with a dull thud.

Fists raised, legs wide apart, Kay's rushing blood warmed her in a second. A soft bundle of pink catapulted into her arms, hugging her waist hard and hanging on.

"Auntie!" the girl cried again, more quietly this time, her gaze not as innocent as Kay imagined. Her black eyes sparkled with intelligence, not mischief; her smile forced, not carefree. "I've missed you!"

Kay couldn't force a reply past her constricted throat. Was this a trap? Simply a case of mistaken identity?

The girl furrowed her brow and licked her lips.

"Do . . . you . . . speak . . . Chinese?" she said in halting English, dismay a poor replacement for her earlier joy.

"*Wo hui shuo guo yu,*" Kay reassured her. "Who are you?" she continued in Chinese, glancing at the small number of people left in the plaza. The tourist with the camera, a solitary guard, and an older couple carefully plodding their way to the exit were all outside of earshot.

The little girl stood erect. "My name is Li Fangqing." She threw Kay a mischievous grin. "My father respects my wishes to use the American version of my name. You can call me Fran."

"How do you do, Fran." Kay bowed a few inches. Now what? She didn't dare give a stranger her name, not even a precious child.

Fran grabbed Kay's glove with her mittened hand, spinning her to face the photographer.

"That is my other Auntie, Auntie Tan Yannan," she said, flicking her eyes in the woman's direction. "She asked me to meet you here today."

"You! You can't be more than ten years old!" Kay blinked. "You should be in school, not risking—" Maybe this precocious child didn't realize her part in this meeting. "Please introduce me to your Auntie Yannan."

Fran shook her head, turning Kay toward the exit with the stragglers. "I'm twelve years old, and I love to go shopping." She darted a glance upwards and held Kay's gaze. "We can walk your bike there—please? Maybe you would also enjoy a cup of tea."

Kay allowed Fran to drag her forward, not daring a peek in Tan's direction. She'd done low-down things in her career, but this was the worst—accepting a child's help to bail her ass out of the fire. What should she do? No doubt she could ditch Fran, although clearly the girl understood the game. Why would Tan put her niece in danger? Was she even a real aunt? The Chinese language used precise names for each family relationship. *Auntie* was a catchall used for family friends and distant relatives. Exactly who was this little girl?

"I often help Auntie Yannan." Fran scanned the wide expanse of the emptying plaza. "No one pays any attention to me because I look so young." She shrugged, lowering her head a tiny bit. "My father's name is Li Ying. Have you heard of him?"

"No. Should I have?" Kay kept a close eye on the soldier guarding the gate.

"He says he is famous among Americans." Fran kicked a clump of snow off the toe of her boot. "Auntie Yannan said to tell you Charlie was a friend."

Warning bells clanged in Kay's head. If Tan figured out her connection to Charlie, this little girl could be dangerous.

"Did you meet Charlie, too, honey? Did he visit your father?"

"No, I never met him. Daddy said he was interested in the games he made for his company."

"What kind of games does your Daddy make?" Puzzle pieces clicked in Kay's brain.

"Games boys enjoy, with guns and airplanes blowing stuff up." Fran flicked her wrist. "You know. Not girl games with Barbies." She sighed. "I think Daddy is doing something he's not supposed to, and that's why he talked to your friend Charlie. He was asking for help from America." She lifted her face, her mouth quivering. Tears filled her eyes.

"I'm scared, Auntie. I love my Daddy, and don't want him to leave me." She sniffed. "Mama died when I was born, so it's . . . it's my fault."

"Oh, honey." Kay tugged the little girl to a halt, dropping to her knees and hugging her right in front of the soldier. "It'll be all right. Your Aunties will figure out a way to help your Daddy."

"Promise?" Fran wiped her nose with her mitten and searched Kay's eyes. "Because he and Auntie Yannan are the only family I have."

Kay hesitated. Hardly anyone in China was bereft of family. At the death of one of their own, grandparents, cousins, distant aunts and uncles hovered and stepped forward to care for orphans. How could this little girl only have her father and one supposed aunt?

She opened her mouth to ask. The soldier's glare stopped her.

"We'll talk later. Let's get you back to school." She made sure her voice carried to the soldier. He eyed her and Fran, shrugged, and turned his gaze to Tan and the elderly couple. Rising to her feet and pulling Fran up, she pushed her bicycle along the path.

With a little skip, Fran chattered about her school and favorite subjects. Kay scrutinized the passersby, the little girl's enthusiastic prattle a balm to her frazzled nerves. After walking two blocks, she checked over her shoulder. Only Tan Yannan followed them into the nearby shopping district. With a deep sigh, she relaxed.

"Daddy promised to take me to America." Fran skipped ahead and clasped her hands in front of her chest. "We'll go to Disneyland, and Hollywood to meet an American movie star. I love Jackie Chan, of course, and practice Kung Fu every day with Auntie Yannan. She says if I get good enough I can be in an action movie, too. I love those spy stories, the ones where they have to escape prison, and fight the bad guys, and—" She giggled into her mitten, tossing Kay an impish glance. "—kick butt!"

Kay laughed. Fran changed topics so fast it made her head spin. Her energy catapulted upwards in tandem with Fran's continuous chatter of naïve dreams and childish fantasies, almost daring Kay to reclaim her youth. What a contrast to her missions' usual companions of liars, con men and grifters.

She would take her life back. Finally. And all because she was inspired by this little girl's enthusiasm.

Go figure.

Chapter 11

"In here, Auntie." Fran pulled her into a dim teashop on Anlin Road. A heavenly aroma drifted through the heavy curtains. Three tables were empty. The fourth held two elderly women with their heads together, sipping from chipped cups.

A man's crinkled face appeared in a gap of the room divider. He stepped forward and clapped his hands, telling the old ladies they must stop gossiping and leave now. They grabbed their small parcels and left with noses in the air. The proprietor turned his window sign to *CLOSED*, hovered near the door and peered out. Beckoning Tan Yannan inside, he disappeared into the back, emerging moments later with a steaming pot of tea, cups, and a little plate of crescent-shaped cookies.

Kay sat with her back against the wall. Tan Yannan unwrapped a long plaid scarf from her neck. Stylish short hair framed her wind-chapped face in attractive wisps and spiky bangs. She wore a thick turtleneck sweater topped with a fine-grained leather jacket, black jeans, black leather boots and gloves. Finely arched brows capped a small nose, and her tiny rosebud shaped mouth twisted in matching assessment.

If she were in America, I'd mark her as a tough biker chick.

Fran reached for the teapot and poured three cups with a playful expression on her face.

"Auntie Yannan, this is my new friend, Auntie Kay . . . right?" She seemed amused by the clandestine antics. A sense of protectiveness stirred in Kay. How could she keep this innocent little girl ignorant of life and death games?

"Kay, I'm glad to meet you." Tan extended her hand. "Please call me Yannan."

Kay shook it and settled back, crossing her arms. She peered around the quiet little room. "Is it safe to talk?"

Yannan nodded. "The owner's a friend of our network."

Kay took a deep breath, uncertain where to begin. Yannan quirked an eyebrow and waited.

"How and what do you know about Charlie?" Kay threw a warning glance in the little girl's direction, hoping Yannan would leave out the details.

"Fran's father, Ying, married my sister," Yannan said. "Ying came to me last month, a week after he shared information with Charlie. He was . . . concerned . . . he hadn't heard back from Charlie. We later found the official news of his death." Yannan's face expressed sympathy, not censure.

"What else aren't you telling me?"

"Quite a bit." Yannan met her challenging stare with one of her own. Five seconds passed. She broke her gaze and took a sip of tea, tracing her finger along the tabletop. "And you aren't telling me everything, yes?" Yannan's mouth curved into a half-smile. "Okay, I'll go first."

Drawing her chair close, Yannan leaned toward Kay.

"You contacted me because of my investigation of the forced relocation of Inner Mongolians, right?" Yannan pitched her voice low. "Well, the impetus for my investigation was Ying's work with the rare earth elements they mine and process there. You are familiar with the significance of China's rare metals initiative?"

Kay nodded, bringing the cup to her lips and drinking in long, slow sips.

"The Chinese military directs the industrial effort for these precious metals," Yannan continued. "This justifies keeping China's total output secret. Our diplomats proclaim the world can trust us as supplier for all modern technology. No worries—China believes in free markets. Bah!" Yannan slammed her closed fist on the table. "Rumor is they'll soon distribute the highly refined metals only to friendly governments."

"How did Ying learn all this?" Paul had speculated about such a possibility as a tenet of her mission. With her American schooling, Yannan's insights would carry a lot of credibility in the DIA—if Kay could only get this confirmation back to Paul somehow.

"Ying was hired right out of Peking University to work at a secret research facility in Beijing. He engineered a better way to purify rare earths for commercial products, and eventually the government required him to work on military applications. He overheard his superiors boast of their true goal—worldwide dominance by manipulating the price and controlling the supply of rare earths. So he rebelled."

"Courageous man. Did he get in trouble?"

"Not yet. But we think he will soon."

"Please help Daddy," Fran whispered, grasping Kay's hand between both of hers and staring up with troubled eyes.

Kay suppressed an ironic laugh. Here she thought Yannan would rescue her. How the hell could she aid them? She feared for her own life every day.

Suck it up, girl! This intelligence is worth a lot to America. Kay switched to professional mode.

"What's the current situation with Ying?"

"Ying told only a handful of people of his knowledge outside the Chinese mining industry . . . and all of them have . . . disappeared . . . like Charlie," Yannan said. "He contacted me to publish his information— but I can't and still take care of Fran." She winced. "Do you understand? We don't have American-style freedom of the press."

"What a contrast to attend Berkeley, yet choose a life in China." Reaching across the table, Kay squeezed Yannan's hand. "You have courage, too."

"Not so much." Yannan blushed, shaking her head. "We can push the envelope on some stories, but ones concerning the military and the Communist Party's ambitions—those are too dangerous. Journalists disappear too." She sipped her tea. "An underground network of pacifist forces is slowly rallying support. But now, surveillance cameras and tiny drones watch our every move. Our emails are read and blocked, our computers confiscated, and web sites shut down daily."

Kay nibbled on a cookie. Would this new network of pacifists facilitate her safe passage home, even if they could? Maybe video cameras already captured her and Yannan together in Tiananmen Square, compromising them both more than her email ever would.

"I tried tying into the Taiwanese battling the Communists." Kay gambled that her pursuit of family connections wouldn't surprise Yannan. "They weren't able to help me. Have you contacted them?"

"Yes, though frankly, they can't quite grasp the new threat China presents to the world. They care only about protecting their little island enclave, and the memories of Chiang Kai-shek in his glory days." She gasped, eyes widening. "Oh, I am so sorry. I didn't mean to insult your ancestor. I'm sure he was a great man."

"Don't worry," Kay said. "I'm not so sure of his greatness. Remember, he aspired to keep China's political structure the same after they defeated Japan, not move it forward. Who knows what would have happened if he stayed in power instead of Mao?"

"I know about Chairman Mao," Fran chirped. "My teacher told us what a great man he was."

"Did they tell you what great policies he dictated?" Yannan's voice dripped with sarcasm. She turned to Kay. "They don't teach the current generation any historical facts. They just declare certain people twentieth-century heroes. It's ludicrous."

"Isn't that Chairman Mao's picture hanging in Tiananmen Square?" Fran's forehead wrinkled. "Isn't he a hero?"

"Your Daddy's a hero, honey." Kay hugged Fran's tiny shoulders. "I'm sure your Auntie Yannan will share many stories about Mao when you're older." She slanted a wry grin at Yannan.

"If I live that long," Yannan muttered.

"Amen." Kay gulped. Her turn. "My visa was mysteriously revoked or lost, or whatever bureaucratic nonsense they came up with to keep me in China. I've tried every avenue I dare, and still nothing. I suspect I'm being watched, but no overt confrontations . . . yet. My communications to the U.S. may or may not have gotten through. I hoped you could help me, frankly."

"I figured." Yannan crossed her arms. "Do you work for your government?"

Kay kept her expression blank.

"Got it." Yannan tossed money on the table. "Let's trade favors. I'll see if I can expedite your departure, you think of anything to help Ying. When you get back home, I expect you can do much more." She leveled her gaze on Kay.

Fran jumped from her seat and hugged Kay with thin, trembling arms. "Promise me you'll help Daddy," she whispered. "Promise!"

"I promise," she whispered back. Fran's simple demand tugged on Kay's heart. "I'll visit Disneyland with you and your Daddy." She released Fran, meeting Yannan's wary eyes. "I promise to disclose the facts, and try to keep Ying safe—and you, too," she added. This meeting with Kay undoubtedly put Yannan in more danger

"Have another cup of tea before you leave," Yannan said. She rose, tugging on her jacket and helping Fran with hers. "If you must get in touch with me, call the paper from a public phone and leave only your first name. I'll come to Tiananmen Square at the same time the next day."

"I have no safe way for you to reach me," she confessed.

"That's why you'll help us," Yannan said with a grin. "You have no other options." She opened the door and led Fran out into the driving snow. Fran's farewell wave became a yellow beacon of hope.

Kay watched thick flakes convert her bicycle into a lumpy white snowdrift. Glum, she thrummed her fingers on the empty teacup, considering her two problems—getting out of this country safely and protecting Li Ying and his vital information.

The U.S. surely anticipated the potential threat of a rising Chinese military power as an adjunct to their growing economic influence. Didn't the strategists grasp the difference between playing outlandish scenarios in the bowels of the Pentagon and having sworn testimony with hard facts? From what she had gleaned from Paul's initial mission parameters and Charlie's mutterings, China could dominate the next generation of military hardware simply by controlling rare earth metallurgical processing, eliminating any competitors through its monopoly pricing.

Kay grimaced. Only one option left, like it or not.

Wei Jintao. The answer to every woman's prayers. She would contact the government official and hope he remembered her from the convention. Could she enthrall him without compromising her safety? His influence could keep her in China forever—alive or dead.

At least he was attractive and physically fit. Sex shouldn't be too awful. He would expect her allegiance to America. However, in his position he could track down her ties with Charlie . . . and now Li Ying. He'll demand significant proof of loyalty to him in return.

She squirmed in her chair. Her reluctance to pick up the burden of subterfuge again surprised her. Living as a double agent, even for a short time, hadn't occurred to her when she joined freedom's fight with stars in her eyes.

Fran's woebegone features danced in front of her eyes. Kay could relate to the little girl's search for heroes in a world gone sideways, where family support was sparse, and fictional characters rushed to the rescue. She wanted to help Fran, and her father too, honor-bound to expose the terrible outcome of his research. Plus her aunt, who risked her life exposing state secrets.

Kay could do no less. She just needed to get Wei Jintao into her sphere of power—and get out of this country.

And now for the sixty-four thousand dollar question: How?

First step, get word to Paul. He'll climb out on this cursed limb she clung to and rescue her, no matter what. He wouldn't give a rat's ass about protocol or following the DIA's rulebook.

Only Kay didn't dare risk any former channels. Too many people knew of her ties to the Taiwanese, and to Charlie's circle of contacts. New help from Yannan's rebel group was too iffy. She needed a new network with its own agenda to subvert the Chinese government. Who in Beijing fit that profile?

A flash of orange color caught her attention. Sounds of a muffled crash filled the air. She jumped up and yanked open the door. Her bicycle lay on its side, trapping a slight figure beneath. Muttering in an incomprehensible dialect, a bald man tugged furiously at his thin robe, tangled in the chain. His ankle twisted at an odd angle.

Kay dropped to her knees and jammed her fingers inside the chain guard. She spun the wheel one link at a time. Glancing up, her apology died in her throat.

Not an old man's face, but a clear, unlined one stared back. A Tibetan monk, of course. Kay took in the sandaled feet, distinctive saffron-colored robe, and shaved head. Averting her eyes with respect, she pointed to her progress and turned the wheel, hiding her glee.

Around the next corner sat the Yonghe Temple, appreciated the world over for its historical and spiritual significance. She'd often wondered why the Communists kept this religious relic a thriving part of Beijing's center. Undoubtedly a popular tourist destination, it compelled pilgrimages from Tibetan monks too, in an ironic contradiction to the Communists' ongoing battles with the exiled Dalai Lama and his separatist movement.

If anyone else fought for life against the Chinese government, it was a Tibetan. And one now lay at her feet. Kay jumped at the unexpected opportunity.

"You are going to the temple, yes?" Kay enunciated her words with care, uncertain as to the nuanced accents of the far West regional dialect. The youth nodded. She helped him place weight on his ankle and noticed his wince. "You can ride there on my bicycle and I'll push you." She shooed away the gathering crowd. "My greatest apologies it caused you to fall."

The monk nodded again, mounting the bike in an awkward motion. Kay counterbalanced his weight with hers, hoping the bicycle could maintain traction on the slippery streets. They inched their way to the Buddhist Temple while she mentally composed the communique she might be able to send via the Tibetan network. How long would it take to reach Paul?

Chapter 12

LONGEVITY CLUB

Beijing, China
Late Evening, February 7, 2 Days Later

"*Guo Nian!*" The subdued cries of arriving guests wishing him a Happy New Year grated on Wei Jintao's nerves. His annual Spring Festival celebration carried only one bright spot: a special guest who interested him far more than stilted, predictable discourse with his political peers and business leaders.

He settled against the wall, keeping a close eye on the door. Let them think he simply wished to welcome tardy guests as a responsible host. Instead, he saluted the heady rush of anticipation firing his blood. Why did Chiang Kay titillate him so?

With age, the thrill of being desired replaced the thrill of the hunt, enough to fill an old man's dreams for many nights. So he waited, tracing her communications using his showcase design, dubbed China's

Great Firewall. For years, his ingeniously engineered controls blocked pornography and other offensive material on the Internet. Now, friends in the right places and back doors he installed to satisfy his cravings, gave him the desired result—watching potential traitors very, very closely. He loved beating the Americans in their supposed expertise of technology. And Chiang Kay would be quite a prize.

He wasn't yet convinced Kay represented a menace. Certainly, that Wilkins fellow put his nose where it didn't belong. His threats to disclose military secrets compromised the Party's parallel diplomacy with ambitious countries eager to knock America off its perch. So he had to go.

But was Kay smart enough to understand her translations' significance? Was she using family ties to ask the Taiwanese for help? Did she only reminisce with that journalist about their alma mater because she felt isolated and alone? It could be coincidence.

Admit it—this American girl bewitched you!

Yesterday, her sultry tones and distinctive accent reached through the phone and squeezed his testicles as she asked to see him. His policy meeting was forgotten in a heartbeat as he reveled in fantasies of youthful skin and tantalizingly firm buttocks. He hastened with an invitation to tonight's gathering and his private suite afterwards, whooping aloud at her husky promise and ignoring the disapproval on his elderly colleagues' faces.

Snagging a shot of whiskey from a passing waiter, Jintao indulged in one tiny sip. Otherwise, this evening's enjoyment could turn into a fiasco. He delved into his trouser pocket, fingering the months-old, bubble-wrapped purple pill. *Wei Ge*, the Great Brother, helped him more often than not. He desired fireworks in bed to match the exuberance and power of those soon to explode in the skies above Beijing's skyline.

A man's sexuality was still his own, the one stamp of individuality the Communist Party hadn't targeted for extinction. And Jintao reveled in every private second of his hedonistic fantasies. Kay desired him after all, and pursued a liaison with him. No one else. She was his now.

The crowd drifted toward the sumptuous buffet. Whole salmon and cracked lobsters artfully depicted the *Year of the Monkey*. Herb-infused steam rose from the perfectly carved chickens and duck, their crisp brown skin invited sampling. Bite-sized dumplings flanked fresh vegetables carved as intricate flowers. Nestled among gold-flecked plates and bowls, tiny bejeweled monkeys adorned the tops of ivory chopsticks. Bottles from France's exclusive Pétrus winery graced the table's ends, and expensive tea leaves beckoned the most discriminating teetotaler.

Commanding the large armchairs, high-ranking men barked orders. Jintao's hired young women fetched food at their every whim, kneeling by their sides and offering portions in the time-honored tradition of subservience. The other guests lined the walls, deftly juggling plates, glasses, and chopsticks.

Snippets of conversation drifted in the smoky air, overwhelmed by Han Mai's unmistakable, strident tones. Jintao winced, tired of her incessant nitpicking and tattling. Her new assignment in Inner Mongolia restricting the news of its native population put her far enough north of Beijing to keep her away for long weeks, yet close enough to prevent her aristocratic feelings from being offended. She still believed her father's sterling reputation during the Cultural Revolution gave her leeway to step on others.

"It is our duty to advance China's greatness." Han Mai paused, lighting a cigarette. Surrounded by a sea of tuxedos, her garish purple pants and gold tunic made her look like a street clown, undermining her esteemed image. "If precious metals lie deep in our mountain's bowels or hide beneath our vast plains, should we not use them to leap ahead of our Western competitors? Even if it means relocating a few hundred thousand people to our cities to do so?"

A tense silence met her bold statement. Politicians and bureaucrats rarely spoke of those forced from their homes. They simply became the new urban poor, an unfortunate consequence of great progress.

Jintao straightened and strolled over, steering clear of the smoke spewing from Han Mai's mouth. "China has been and always will be great," he interjected with a polite bow in her direction. "We are blessed with many resources, including our Chinese compatriots who strive to maximize their usefulness, wherever they can. However, we must honor our ancestors. Everything our government can do for those asked to sacrifice their homelands, we should."

Dipping his head, Weng Yu moved a scarce half step away from his outspoken wife. A meek descendent from expert miners, he competently managed the industrial output of the northern regions. Jintao wondered how often Han Mai stepped on her husband to further her political career. They probably married for connections and convenience, not any kind of affection. Jintao shuddered at the thought of sharing a bed with a woman of such calculating harshness.

"Of course, Minister Wei, we must always protect our citizens." Han Mai returned Jintao's bow. "However, do you not agree it is also our responsibility to safeguard our resources, as well?"

Jintao chuckled, tilting his glass in mock salute. "I fail to see how anyone could steal minerals out of the ground without your husband noticing." He shot a conspiratorial wink at Weng Yu, who smiled companionably.

From the corner of his eye, Jintao noticed the suite's door crack open. He held his breath. Two elderly men entered. He exhaled in a disappointed rush.

"Husband Yu, what's the name of that brilliant engineer working for you? The one who works with rare earth elements."

"Li Ying," Weng Yu murmured, wringing his hands.

"Yes, Li Ying." Han Mai nodded, preening like a hen in front of disinterested roosters. "My husband keeps the boy busy seeking out new applications for his ideas. His excellent education at Peking University should further our cause, not create Western toys or silly television displays." Her cheeks disappeared to suck in fresh nicotine. "Our Great Wall halted Mongol invaders years ago. Wei Jintao's Great Firewall protects our children from Western filth. Now we must take our turn protecting those who will catapult us to our rightful leadership among the world powers!"

Jintao jerked his head toward the next room, throttling his irritation. The obedient circle of men followed his silent directive and headed for the bar. How rude of Han Mai to introduce politics during a New Year's party! He never should have invited her, despite the long-standing protocol. Next year he'd know better.

"Weng Yu, perhaps you would ask one of my pretty assistants to arrange a plate for you and your wife while I discuss a matter of great importance with her," Jintao murmured, pointing Han Mai in the opposite direction. Once out of immediate hearing distance, he let loose his anger. "What is the meaning of this inappropriate tirade?"

Han Mai sniffed, extricating a cigarette pack from her handbag. Jintao shook his head, even more appalled. She was well aware he hated smoking.

"It is prudent for the most connected politicians to understand the implications of my husband's and my success increasing our mining output." She tossed her head. "We face discontent in the Tibet and Inner Mongolia regions. What does it hurt to stockpile our resources instead of selling them to the foreigners? The Party officials should have all available tools at their disposal."

"What concerns you? The Party—or your career?" Jintao placed his hands on his hips.

"They are one and the same. The individual always is second to the State, of course."

"And the State must handle its power responsibly. Otherwise we will have a repeat of the violence emanating from sheer, military might. Do you wish for this?" he hissed.

"What is the proverb? '*You can't wrap paper around a fire.*' Yes, this is exactly what I mean. China is exploding fast and our technological discoveries significant. The West can no longer stop us!"

"Those fires are the burning ambitions of our people experiencing the headiness of prosperity for the first time in generations." Jintao frowned. "If we wrap them too tightly, their passionate flames will indeed destroy the paper. Only if we keep our control loose and accommodating can we steer the right course for our economy."

"Bah! Only a person afraid of power's responsibilities would say such drivel."

Fury drummed in his forehead. Inching closer, he thrust a finger in her face.

"Are you calling me a coward? Or simply powerless?"

Han Mai blanched. "I apologize," she said with haste. "I spoke foolishly . . . with patriotic fervor. I did not stop to consider all the wisdom you offered." She bowed, backing away in tiny steps. "I—I will see what keeps my husband. Thank you for your kind advice. Enjoy the fireworks." She turned and hurried away, a red flush creeping up her neck.

He marveled at her career trajectory despite such a poor grasp of human nature. The West had a unique term for it . . . The Peter Principle. Promoted beyond her capabilities. Unfortunately, her ambitious quest for power could get her . . . and him . . . in a great deal of trouble.

Chapter 13

An imperious knock carried to Jintao's attuned ears. He hastened to the vestibule, glancing at his watch. Five minutes to midnight. His heartbeat resembled the pounding of a *taiko* drum, drowning out his guests' murmurs of anticipation. Waving away the club's surprised waiter, he took a deep breath and opened the door. Another colleague or his personal fantasy?

He locked his waivering knees in place and bowed deeply. Straightening, he flung his arms wide and stared at the image facing him.

She wore a dress of sheer red lace. A delicate, dense pattern covered every inch from neck to wrist to ankle, taunting him. He peered close, hunting beyond the material to the flesh it masked. A skin-tight, flesh-toned fabric blocked his view of patterned glory.

Chiang Kay stepped forward. Her long leg split the side of her dress to the top of her thigh, fulfilling his most fervent hope for bare skin. The briefest of stilted sandals adorned her feet. Red toenails caught his gaze, enticing it up her slender calf, delicate knee, and lean-muscled thigh. Her next step repeated the torture, the lacy dress catching for the tiniest of seconds between her legs, outlining the distinctive contour of her femininity.

Swallowing a satisfied growl, Jintao captured her extended hand. He stroked his middle finger across her wrist once, and released it.

"Welcome, my dear Kay," he murmured, meeting her eyes at last. Her hair was pulled back in a simple fashion with two diamond clips. Their sparkles matched her expression. She'd perfected her makeup's enhancements, outlining her eyes in smoky black. Her lashes curled long and beguiling. Rosy red lips matched her nails, sending his mind immediately to other female body parts with the same vivid hue.

Smiling, she stepped closer than convention allowed. Her perfume wafted into his nostrils, teasing him with its familiar mix of sweetness and musk. She leaned forward and exhaled warm breath directly in his ear.

"Thank you for inviting me," she whispered. She eased back, holding his stare and giving him a slow wink. Running her gaze down the length of his body, she paused below his waist for the briefest of seconds. She licked her lips. "I hope I haven't missed the fireworks. All those explosions make me shiver."

He glanced over his shoulder at the whispering crowd and adjusted his trousers over his heavy arousal, twisting his lips into a rueful smile. What a time for his body to respond with such immediacy! Kay's eyes twinkled with mischief. She handed her coat to the hovering waiter and snuggled to his side, grinning.

"So much gossip tells me you're a fascinating man."

"As you are a fascinating woman." He tucked her hand into the bend of his elbow. "Let me introduce you to my guests."

Satisfied beyond measure by his prize, Jintao suspected Kay would never agree to the label of casual mistress. No, she certainly sought testing the full extent of her sexual power over a high-ranking official.

He'd give her all the chances she desired to turn him on. And watch her every second.

Chuckling, he spied Han Mai closing in on them like a furious ox, dragging her husband after her. Then again, perhaps he stayed a step behind to hide his expression. The way Weng Yu's eyes bugged out of his head, he would sacrifice a testicle for a few private moments with Kay.

"Minister Wei, I did not realize you invited Chiang Kay to our exclusive gathering," Han Mai said with forced politeness. She threw Kay a hostile glare and nudged her husband's foot. "Husband Yu, this woman is a descendant of the infamous Chiang Kai-shek."

Her voice resonated off the walls—purposefully, Jintao was certain. No matter. The Party would never question his loyalty, certainly not because of the direction his cock pointed. Han Mai couldn't compete with Kay's sexual power, so she reverted to raw politics instead. How did men manage to balance both?

Kay . . . his Kay, he marveled . . . jumped into battle. Tossing her hair back, which thrust her luscious-looking breasts forward, she gazed down her nose at Han Mai. Her high heels gave her extra height for pure domination.

"Han Mai, I am so glad to see you again. And this wonderful gentleman is your husband?" Kay blessed Weng Yu with a brilliant smile. His jaw dropped. Jintao smothered a chuckle.

Han Mai elbowed her husband in the ribs, her expression wary.

"He is built like a man who could easily give you wonderful children, and with much pleasure in the process." Kay's mocking whisper was loud enough to carry to those nearby. "How many are you blessed with?"

Han Mai turned beet red. "None of your business, you harlot!" she hissed. With the speed of a rattlesnake, she rose to her full height, her eyes venomous with hatred. "We adhere to the wise policy of our great Party to limit ourselves to two special children."

"Hmm." Kay tapped the side of her nose. Weng Yu's expression stayed stony. "Perhaps Yu has indeed fathered many more than two children in a joyful bed—just not with Mai?" Kay arched her brow, a mocking smile dancing on her lips.

Weng Yu's gasp confirmed Kay nailed the truth with one blow.

"Watch your step, you damn whore." Han Mai pointed her husband to the balcony. "You don't appreciate who you're dealing with." She stomped off.

"Don't I?" Kay taunted after her, peeping at Jintao with a questioning air.

"Yes, I'm sure you do," Jintao sighed, tucking her hand back into the crook of his arm and leading her to the foyer. "You enjoy playing with fire, don't you, little one?"

Kay threw her head back and laughed a victorious, full-throated enjoyment. "Occasionally, I simply relish discovering the boundaries of true power."

Jintao halted, enthralled. She sounded so sincere, lowering her guard in the flush of success and sharing innermost thoughts with a trusted lover. Is this how she perceived him? If so, he would soon have all the dominance he ever craved over one so lovely. He shuddered.

The first explosion of Beijing's massive fireworks display rattled the windows. Its echo called all the guests to the open balcony. Jintao grabbed a passing waiter and demanded he retrieve Kay's coat.

Smoothing the wool across her shoulders, he pressed his crotch against her back.

"You deserve better than this for your exquisite form," he murmured, undulating his hips. "Perhaps a black sable or a silver fox. I'll give it more consideration."

"Now what?" Kay turned and winked, drawing her coat close.

He opened the door, settled his hand on her back, and nudged her down the empty corridor.

"Fireworks!" he whispered in her ear, reveling in the tremble coursing the length of her spine. Time to play with fire, and explore who held the real power.

Chapter 14

SNAZZED UP!

San Jose, California
Early Evening, February 16, 9 Days Later

"Hey, boss." His chief financial officer's gray-topped head popped through his doorway. "Do you have a minute before you take off?"

Victor Turtino closed the daunting list of incoming emails and dropped his tablet onto the sleek birch desktop. "Sure, Veronica. I'm here for a couple hours more."

Veronica Harris stepped in with his seasoned VP of manufacturing on her heels, both grim-faced.

"Nothing bad, I hope?" Victor waved them into matching wood-framed leather chairs facing the purple-tinged western hills. The sun had set hours ago, taking with it that extra bit of warmth and coziness. There were times when Victor craved his crummy, old office couch—and crashing into its comfort after working long hours. His new digs felt cold and sterile, especially during the winter months when sunshine rarely warmed his bare skin. But the interior design firm he'd hired had the best bona fides in Silicon Valley. He wasn't about to argue with their taste.

Serafín Perez cleared his throat. "Depends how much you believe in unicorns and Santa Claus."

"Not." Dreams of modern-day gold and Silicon Valley-sized ambitions to move mountains, yes. But dreams didn't put an anxious expression on Serafín's face. Victor ran his finger around the neck of his black sweater, releasing his body warmth's sudden build-up.

"Nor I." Serafín puffed out his already-rounded cheeks. "This afternoon I spoke with the supplier of flux amplifiers for all our communication interfaces. They ran out of the highly purified Holmium metal powders necessary to alloy the concentrators."

"Did you get our standard quarterly allotment?" Victor scrubbed his palms over his beard. He'd better re-think the major media push at next week's convention. The date of their new product launch might slip if they couldn't guarantee their already-public forecasts for first-quarter sales.

"Yes, plus everything I could get my hands on, with Veronica's help expediting immediate payment. DOD Tech's running low on cash, so they didn't hesitate."

Victor turned to Veronica. "Thanks for jumping on this."

"It's my job to control risks and manage assets." Uncrossing legs encased in her predictable beige pants, she edged forward, a worried frown adding another wrinkle to her forehead. "Victor, this has huge implications going forward. After we use up this inventory, our per-unit costs may skyrocket if there's a real shortage. We've got to identify an alternative solution for this component."

"Serafín, have you spoken with the engineering team regarding other options?"

"I prodded them two months ago, the day China first threatened to halt rare earth shipments." He jutted out his jaw. "I checked again—they haven't come up with a high-enough quality substitute."

Veronica rapped the desk. "If these essential components compromise our ability to manufacture Snazzed Up!'s flagship products, we have to go public with it. At least to our board."

Damn! Victor hoped to avoid that. "Thank you for bringing this to our attention so promptly, Serafín. I'm counting on your discretion. Let's keep waste to an absolute minimum on the manufacturing lines. Would you prepare a rank-order priority of products affected?"

"No problem." Scribbling on his pad, Serafín nodded. "I'll have it to you within twenty-four hours."

"If you will excuse us, I need to talk to Veronica in private."

"Of course." Serafín hastened out the door, closing it with a loud click.

Veronica leaned back and crossed her arms, her gaze steady . . . and uncompromising.

Victor rubbed his chin. A financial officer's fiduciary responsibility popped up at inopportune times—and this was one heck of a moment. "We can discuss it at the scheduled Board of Director's meeting. Don't fuss. It might blow over before then."

"Blow over? I'm sorry, sir, this interruption of our supply chain might risk our entire financial footing. We can't just float new shares or issue bonds when we choose." She threw up her palms. "Who knows what might happen to our market valuation if this news gets out. The S&P Index requires a minimum capitalization to stay on it, you know."

"Exactly. We can't afford a leak. Do you trust Serafín to keep his mouth shut?"

"To a point, but—"

He raised his hand. "I will talk to one board member in private immediately. Nikolai Herzog sits on Morrison-Meyer's board, too. As a defense contractor, they have similar technology and probably have excess components they could sell us in a pinch. We'll be fine, Veronica."

Rising, she wagged her finger. "I'm not sure I agree with you on this but it's your call." She hesitated at the door. "If you don't identify a better strategy within a month, I'll speak directly to the board's Finance

Committee. We may have to change our earnings guidance for next quarter and beyond." She slammed the door behind her.

Irked, Victor pulled up Nikolai's number. Their leading-edge solutions decimated competitors' models. His entire company depended on the performance of tiny gadgets built into each device. He wasn't about to compromise years of work because a start-up supplier couldn't negotiate with the Chinese for an adequate allocation. Besides, the public didn't need to know how he pulled off his technology marvels.

Once he got his new chief operating officer hired, his only assignment would be to find a second-source solution—preferably outside of China. Victor would buy him a one-way ticket until he got the job done.

In the meantime, Veronica had better adapt and bend her ethics to suit the situation, or he would find a new CFO who would. And fast.

Chapter 15

DOD TECH, INC.

Sunnyvale, California
Late Afternoon, February 17, Next Day

"We recommended to our largest customer that they stockpile ninety-days' worth of our rare earth-based components. Snazzed Up! just bought our entire supply. We're going to beat our quarterly numbers!" CEO Adam McQuirk's gleeful tone and smug smile grated on Paul's nerves. For a thirty-something kid, he sure sounded cocky. "At this rate, we can go public in six months."

Paul drummed his fingers on the clear lucite table with enough force to capture everyone's attention. The sharp rat-a-tat sounded like a drumbeat of war, even to his ears. He reminded himself that, as one of two attending board members, he was here to provide counsel, not to command. He glanced at Eric Coleman sitting to his right in this windowless conference room, double-checking the appropriateness of so much toughness with novice entrepreneurs.

Based on Eric's mild expression, he was comfortable letting Paul take the lead on this issue. Adam and Gideon Weinberg—the start-up's chief technologist—turned their heads in his direction, Adam's too-long ponytail following a second behind.

"By any chance, did you set aside finished product for your defense customer's equipment, too?" Paul studied his jotted notes. "Morrison-Meyer, right?"

Adam fidgeted in his faux-leather chair, his eyes downcast. "Um, they said they needed to process a bunch of Department of Defense paperwork first, so it would delay payment for at least two months." He shrugged. "I figured they could wait their turn."

Throttling back a flash of temper, Paul eased the tie around his neck and loosened his collar button. He felt like yelling with the ferocity of Hank Shaughnessy to wake these kids up. Only this was not meant to be a public whipping. Eric expected him to guide and advise, not to chastise. He strove for calm, motioning Eric to respond instead.

"Gideon, it's been a couple of months since China first threatened to halt all exports of refined rare earths. What else have you done to address alternate suppliers and keep the manufacturing line moving?" Eric tapped the papers piled in front of him. "We earmarked extra funding for R&D specifically for military equipment requirements. What results have you gotten with the money?"

Gideon cleared his throat. "I contracted with a Southern California firm specializing in purifying rare earth metals. Their cutting-edge solutions keep running up against the Nuclear Regulatory Commission's rules from the 1980s. I guess they need a type of heavy rare earth we used to mine but can't provide any longer due to some nonsensical rule regarding environmental impact. Not a problem for China."

Paul had read this about this conundrum too many times to count. Broad-brush solutions coming out of Washington rarely met the requirements of fast-growing tech companies.

"China scooped up our metallurgical technology for next to nothing when the NRC killed our domestic supply chain," Gideon continued. "Plus, any new solution we come up with still needs a guaranteed source of heavy rare earth oxides from China, otherwise commercial-scale production is impossible. This firm thinks it can solve the refinement problem, but not access to the core commodity. So that's that."

Paul sat on his clenched fists. God, this kid had balls. Yeah, he was some kind of brilliant engineer. An MIT scholar dedicated to his studies since condemned to a wheelchair due to spina bifida. And yeah, he impressed Paul with his sheer mastery of the ins and outs of metallurgy at the ripe old age of twenty-nine. Full of future ideas for alternative technologies to keep the U.S. competitive, the kid couldn't identify one measly, viable short-term option with an extra ten million dollars!

"A simple case of make versus buy," Adam said. "China supplies us with what we need at such a low price it's illogical to do it ourselves. After all, they'd been working on it since 1963. We've got enough on our plate growing our business. Why worry about finding a second-source supplier because of political hubbub? China's our trading partner, not our enemy." He leaned close to Gideon and held a whispered conference.

Paul grumbled. Eric raised a pacifying hand.

"Welcome to Silicon Valley," Eric said under his breath. "Produce technology for the best price, and don't get involved in global politics. Let the D.C. experts negotiate tariffs or whatever to fix the problem."

"Since when did the DOD rely on a single supplier for such key components?" Paul scratched his head.

"Since just-in-time supply chain management consultants recommended streamlined shipping and manufacturing processes. Pinpoint efficiencies can't handle too many choices." Eric shoved back from the table. "For little companies like this one, it's a gold mine. Once they land a contract, they can rely on a hundred percent of that business rather than worrying a bigger player will take a chunk of the orders away."

"You mean hurricanes and earthquakes haven't interrupted the supply chain at any time?" Paul lifted his eyebrow at the young men sitting across the table.

"Of course, that's why we recommend stockpiling key components," Adam said. "A good company always identifies their long-term requirements and plans accordingly."

"Long-term now equals ninety days? Wow." Paul didn't bother to hide his sarcasm. "You know, men, just because the virtual world can transmit data in seconds doesn't mean tangible goods move as fast. How quickly do you think Morrison-Meyer can produce and ship something as simple as night vision goggles to our guys and gals fighting half a world away? Last I looked it took at least six months—assuming you can still get your hands on enough refined rare metals to supply the components."

"You're right, Paul." Adam sat forward, frowning, his own hand raised to stave off Gideon's retort. His sapphire blue eyes glittered in the fluorescent light. "I take responsibility for my decision. Please don't take it out on Gideon."

Paul took a deep breath, struggling for control. Would DuMont be a giant jerk to these kids? No. DuMont understood what it meant to fail a mission. Even one as important as this one.

Of course, they didn't have a clue about his main worry—Kay and whatever intelligence she gathered. Talk about a failure. No matter that he worked every spare moment searching for her, contacting retired agents and leveraging their contacts, he couldn't discover her current whereabouts. Or if she still lived.

The door to the conference room opened several inches. Adam's assistant extended a piece of paper. "Adam, I think you should see this."

Adam stretched one long arm and grabbed the note. The door closed with a snap. Adam's eyes darted left to right and opened wide. He clenched the paper in his fist.

"China announced it's stopping all exports of refined rare metals to Japan immediately," Adam said.

"Goddamnit!" Paul dropped his head in his hands.

"What's their stated reason?" Eric ignored his buzzing phone.

"Apparently in retaliation for sinking a Chinese ship in the Sea of Japan last month." Adam glanced up, confusion warring with concern on his face. "What are the implications of this embargo?"

"Japan's electronic industry is trashed," Gideon concluded.

"Ours is next." Paul lifted his head. "As is our defense industry. We get sub-components from Japan, right? Japan will posture for a while and object to the WTO, but China probably has a competing set of components stockpiled and ready to sell to Japan's customers at bargain basement prices. Eventually, what can Japan do except back down politically?"

"You know, a lot more global technology firms will consider relocating inside China just to keep their production lines moving," Adam said. "Their investors will demand it to keep costs down."

"We'll be held hostage soon." Paul shook his head. "Didn't anyone anticipate such a scenario when we outsourced all our manufacturing to China?" DuMont's warning zipped through his brain.

"Any free market trade carries a certain amount of risk, despite the upsides," Eric said. "Regardless of politics, business flows to the least expensive option, drawing the world closer in standards of living and cooperative efforts to maintain peace. Everyone involved in the supply chain benefits, from having jobs to affording more and better goods at increasingly lower prices. And, with government contracts, those lower prices mean lower taxes on its citizens to fund the military."

"And the downside?" Gideon raked his fingers through his hair.

"War interrupts, if not destroys, the business chain." Eric shifted in his seat and tapped his pen in staccato rhythm. "Even with our own rare earth mines in California, Texas, Alaska, and Missouri, we can't upgrade these resources domestically."

"Unless . . ." Paul jumped to his feet.

"Unless what?" Gideon leaned forward on the arms of his wheelchair.

"Unless we outsmart them." Paul pinned Gideon with his stare. "The clock's ticking now. Are you ready to go head to head with these guys? Your ideas, not some other expert's. Something breakthrough, innovative. Something no one else has ever thought of. Can you do it?"

"Yes, sir. Competition is my middle name," Adam interjected. "Gideon, if we strip our engineering staff to the bone and concentrate on alternative elements and methodologies, let everyone else go, and slash our leased space, can't we make rapid progress within sixty days? Our current funding should last."

Gideon hesitated, glancing at the three men. "I have a couple of radical ideas I didn't make the time to explore. Now I will. So, yes sir, we can."

"Good." Adam's glance flickered between Eric and Paul. "I suggest we adjourn this meeting. We have our work cut out for us, and the sooner we get to it, the better." He rose to his feet.

"That's the spirit." Eric stood and pumped Adam and Gideon's hands. "Call me with a progress report in a week."

"Will do." Turning to Paul, Adam thrust out his hand. "Paul, thank you. We may have lost sight of our mission for a while, but we're back on track now."

Paul grasped the younger man's palm. He couldn't speak past the lump forming in his throat at the memory of his last mission and Arlington's haunting tombstones.

God, if only I could fix that error with an apology and sixty days grace period.

Like Adam, he'd lost sight of his unit's operational needs after requesting to lead the squadron. It was a fool's quest. And Ernie followed Paul's last, fatal order.

"I . . . I . . . want to say I think you have what it takes to head this company," Paul said. Which is more than he could say for himself. He lost his temper and fell to pieces too easily.

Adam squeezed Paul's fingers with a knowing nod, gathered his papers, and exited.

Gideon rolled over and shook his hand. "I'll do better this time." Whistling, he wheeled away.

Eric slapped him on the back, searching his face. Paul looked in the mirror enough times to know how haggard his features, how haunted his eyes. Too often he turned away, screaming inside, trapped in memories of failing Ernie.

"Why don't you come over for dinner? We'll discuss more options and get Lynn's perspective." Eric pocketed his phone. "Don Salazar and his wife are joining us, too. It's time you met my new baby girl, and get home cooking in the bargain."

"Sounds great." Paul grabbed his sports jacket, wondering if he should break the news to Lynn that her ex-husband Charlie was dead. After the fiasco Charlie and Kay had created with Eric's old company, SDS Technologies, perhaps it would be better to let sleeping dogs lie.

Chapter 16

Eric pulled onto Central Expressway with a satisfying roar, his classic Mustang rumbling beneath them. "Ready for a job performance evaluation?" He headed south in the dedicated carpool lane and flipped on the windshield wipers in the steady rain.

"Not really." Paul stared out his side window at the dreary one-story buildings nestled against the berm. The rush-hour traffic progressed in fits and starts. Tiny electric vehicles intermixed with old junkers splashing through pothole puddles and sending spray heavenward. "But I bet you're going to give it to me anyway."

"Why are you so sure I'll say anything negative?" Eric sounded confused.

"What else could you say?" Paul twisted in his seat, facing Eric. "I was way out of line today."

"You're right, you were—and you not only recognized it, you immediately addressed any hard feelings you caused." His fingers thrummed the steering wheel.

"Gideon's just a kid," Paul muttered, scrubbing the cherry red seat with his fist. "And Adam's not much older."

"True. You know, Adam founded a start-up before. That's why Lynn and I asked him to be CEO."

"Well of course. You require a track record of success."

"Actually, Adam's last company declared bankruptcy." The rain stopped with an abruptness matching Eric's comment. He flicked off the wipers and arched a knowing brow at Paul.

Paul sat straight, squinting at Eric in disbelief. Eric was one sharp dude. There had to be a reason he'd hire a failure.

"So . . . what was it? Adam went to school with a key investor? His daddy is a Wall Street banker who can smooth the path for an IPO?" Paul's voice wobbled. "Why the hell would you give a failure a second chance?" In his case, he was certain DuMont himself had gone to bat for him, playing off old loyalties and returning favors.

"Just because a person erred once doesn't mean he'll err again." Eric's confidence radiated within the car as powerfully as the setting sun's rays breaking through the silvery clouds. "If he learns from the experience and corrects faulty analysis, he actually becomes a better candidate than one who hasn't faced self-assessment yet."

"Tell that to all the hiring managers," Paul muttered.

"Lynn and I both do. I actually prefer a School of Hard Knocks graduate at my side. He or she grasps how to handle tough decisions. No whining, no regrets. Simply a clear-eyed assessment of what's required. And then executing."

"And you think Adam fits the bill."

"Adam knows exactly what he'll face in the morning." Eric flicked on his turn signal and glanced over his right shoulder, meeting Paul's eyes for a brief moment. "He'll lay off loyal employees who've done a great job. He'll slave every moment he's not sleeping, and I guarantee he cuts back on his shut-eye for the next two months. He's got to prove he can succeed this time."

Eric exited the freeway, heading the long nose of his car toward the sparsely treed, eastern foothills.

"Paul, no one is perfect," he continued. "In Silicon Valley, we seek motivated and talented people, sure. More important, however, is a leader who recognizes his own limitations and hires better people to get the job done. Yet Adam still lacks one key skill—the one you brought to the table this afternoon."

"To be an asshole?"

Eric chuckled, turning up a steep country road. "No, Adam already has that skill." He braked at a stop sign, pausing a long moment.

"You challenged them," Eric said quietly.

Paul met his eyes.

"You made them see their efforts have an impact that's bigger than their individual egos or their ambitious dreams," Eric said. "You reminded them of the reason they chose this particular line of work, this particular company—a fierce pride in America. You shared your unique background and insight, exactly what a great board member does."

Shock, gratitude and flushing embarrassment swept through Paul.

"I only said what I believe, Eric." He gripped his knees. "The Pentagon is really stuck behind the eight-ball this time. This rare metals brinkmanship is China toying with us."

"Perhaps. And perhaps it's a matter of an adolescent learning how to use its new body mass in an already mature world. China's still new to the game of world politics."

"No!" Paul pounded his fist on his thigh. "China's sophisticated political machine has been controlling its population for centuries, and they're still doing it today, but with an added finesse of modernity. Hell, they revere their ancestors' secrets in everything else. Why would Washington politicians believe they'd capitulate their precious heritage to a Western-defined one?"

"Politicians are human, too. Yes, China dominates their region now, both economically and militarily. Globally? Not quite yet. Our elected officials will avoid facing their own demise until they must."

"Yeah, I get it. But do they realize their policies encourage China's ascendancy over America? Have our ambassadors and trade representatives capitulated just because they have a larger population and cheap labor? So our politicians can crow about our economy's success when, in reality, they're just pushing numbers around to make it look good?"

Eric parked in front of a rambling house and turned off the engine. "I don't have the answers. I wish I did. America still has the edge in innovation. You're in the best place now to have an impact. We can recapture our lead in only a few years if we get it right." He stepped from the car and stretched.

Paul followed, his gaze encompassing the surrounding acres of green hillside.

"Nice spread," Paul said. "I can barely see the sky for all the redwoods around my rental, and any hard rain creates mud to my ankles."

"Yeah, it's our little secret." Eric laughed, heading for his porch. "We get less rain, more sun, and beautiful sunsets on the east side of Silicon Valley. Of course, drought years can be tough with higher fire danger, but I'll take it. Come on in and meet my special ladies."

Chapter 17

Paul covered his lips with a napkin, muffling a satisfied burp. He couldn't remember the last time he'd eaten a casual, home-cooked dinner like a civilized person, sitting at a table sharing events of the day with women. Three years? He shook his head. Way too long.

"So the best years of my life meant nothing." Don Salazar wiped his black-and-gray-peppered mustache and grabbed another beer from the six-pack carton in the center of the oak-veneered table. "DARPA used to make a difference. Now the whims of Chinese politicians control our military technology. God, who could have seen this coming?"

Paul studied the man he knew only slightly, hesitating to disclose all of DuMont's revelations. As previous Navy liaison for DARPA recruits, Don did a damned fine job mentoring young engineers to demanding, military-style requirements and the slow roll of DOD funding. Eric praised his buddy's gut instincts about the high-tech community, honed through a short stint at the FBI and his thriving private investigation business.

"What gets me is we worked so hard to keep the U.S. ahead of the curve." Paul tore the label off his bottle. "Remember DuMont's lectures? What happened to DARPA?"

"DuMont retired," Don grumped, lifting his bottle high. "Here's to DuMont and his vision of what government funded research delivered."

"Here, here," Eric cheered, and gulped down a slug.

Paul joined them, yet couldn't set aside the gnawing questions he'd lived with for months. "Do we have any politicians representing this region who take their job seriously? Ones worth pulling aside and discussing the real implications of China's Japan embargo on Silicon Valley?"

"Maybe DuMont still has contacts in Washington circles," Don said.

"He has contacts all right—starting with his daughter." Eric chuckled. "She was just sworn in last month to the U.S. House of Representatives for the northern Silicon Valley district. Not our rep, Don, but one whose ear we can bend."

"I'll say!" Paul thumped the table instead of his forehead. He should have checked in with DuMont since their December conversation. By now, he would have nagged his daughter's ear off on America's rare earths dilemma. "Let's convince her it's time America goes on offense and win this game."

A feminine laugh filled the room, followed by soft cooing. "There you go with those football analogies again, Paul." Lynn stepped to his side, rocking her infant daughter. Inez followed with a tray loaded with brownies and a pot of coffee. "Will you ever forget you're not a high school running back anymore?"

"Probably not." Paul held out his arms. "May I hold her? It seems forever since my Tina was this tiny." He settled back with the baby kicking her small feet. Turquoise eyes stared up at him, so serious-looking. His heart twisted with thoughts of Daisy's first baby, lost in her second trimester. He squeezed a little tighter.

Lynn tossed snow-white hair over her shoulder. "Eric, I talked with Alex this afternoon. He was so excited he couldn't wait for the next board meeting to tell us his findings."

"Yeah? What's new? Oops—sorry." Eric turned to Paul. "Alex Tran is a local college student who founded a company enhancing digital imagery with new algorithms. He swears he will blow our socks off when it's perfected."

"Well, apparently he's done it." Lynn broke a small brownie in two and popped half in her mouth. "He claims he can identify people via unique 3-D biometrics from source video captured via satellites, drones and security cameras. If that's true, he'll land a DOD contract for sure. Except . . ." She swallowed and gazed at her husband, her expression hopeful.

"Let me have it." Eric sighed. "What's the kid hankering after now?"

"He's limited to only a small database of identified people where he can crosslink their name and physical position for corroboration that his software works." She leaned against the doorjamb, her expression intent. "He needs a larger database of pictures and video images."

"Hands off my surveillance videos," Don warned with a wry smile.

Lynn walked over to Eric and placed her hand on his arm. "Don't you have archived digital images from SDS Technologies we can lend him? Lobby security video, that sort of thing. No one's using them—SDS doesn't even exist anymore."

Paul's mind raced. Kay's image should be stored in those files. She worked at SDS for months. Could this kid's technology help in his search?

"What do you say, Don?" Eric squeezed Lynn's hand, quirking an eyebrow at Don. "Any laws we'll be breaking?"

"They're yours to use as you see fit. However . . ." Don held up one finger, ". . . please confirm young Alex distinguishes between YouTube and his private test. I'd hate to go up against any privacy laws with leading-edge technology at stake, especially with the explosion of government and drone-based surveillance video. Best keep his capabilities under wraps."

"Yes!" Lynn cheered and lifted the baby from Paul's lap. "I'll text Alex the good news. Inez, do you want to stay with these grumpy old men adding to their waistlines or give me a hand?"

"Hey!" Don patted his trim waist. "I'll sweat these extra calories off in the morning."

"Sad to say, I prefer dirty diapers over exercise." Inez hefted to her feet. The two women strolled toward the hallway, heads bent together above the baby.

"Come on, let's get comfortable and join Fred." Eric shoved back his chair, grabbed the plate of brownies and his coffee cup, and gestured toward the living room entry.

Paul strolled into the snug front room. A combination of Japanese lanterns and rustic Mission-style table lamps flooded the area with light. A mixed-breed dog lay on the hearthrug, snoring. Their footsteps rang out on the wooden floors and Fred yawned, cocking his large head.

Motioning Paul to the coveted recliner, Eric and Don plopped on the twin sofas. Fred clambered to his feet, padded close to Don and dropped slobbering jowls onto his shoe, panting. The two old friends regaled Paul with stories of Fred's obvious favoritism.

"I got news today regarding our mutual friends from SDS Technologies, Eric." Don fingered the dog's long ears. "It still chaps my hide we were ordered to stop the FBI investigation." Leaning back, he scowled and stretched his arm along the sofa cushions.

Paul held his breath. Did they know of his involvement? Regret met with worry. He would no longer be welcome in their cozy friendship circle once they learned his secrets.

"National security required that," Eric said, smoothing his hair.

"So what's the news?" Lynn entered with Inez at her heels. They settled next to their husbands.

"Lynn, I . . . uh . . . I have bad news about your ex." Don stroked his moustache.

Paul kept his expression deadpan.

Don caught Eric's quizzical gaze and waited two seconds. "My FBI contacts informed me Charles Wilkins is dead."

Lynn gasped, one hand flying to her lips. The other grabbed Eric's. Her eyes filled with tears.

Paul clutched the leather arms and bit his tongue. That same official channel wouldn't share their intel with him. Who the fuck did Don know? Blood pounded against his temple.

"I'm sorry, honey." Eric hugged Lynn. "I realize you have good memories of him. But he did turn out to be a lying piece of shit."

"Eric." Inez wagged her finger. "Don't speak ill of the dead."

"There's more." All eyes in the room turned to Don. Even Fred raised his head.

"Kay Chiang lived with him in Beijing, posing as his interpreter," Don continued. "My sources tried to contact her. No luck. No one can find her. She's officially presumed dead, as well."

"No!" Months of built-up fury at Washington's politics and concocted alliances exploded inside Paul. He bounded from the chair. "They're not certain she's dead, they just don't care enough to find her!" He stalked the wooden floor to the entrance and back, ignoring their shocked expressions.

"Uh, Paul? What haven't you told us?" Eric approached him with the apprehension of a bomb squad leader facing an imminent countdown.

Paul whirled on Don, fisting his hands so tight his knuckles popped.

"Who's your contact? What's his name?" Paul's questions peppered Don. "What agency does he work for? How do you know he's telling the truth?"

Don tilted his head. His tongue poked his swarthy cheek outward. "Why don't you sit back down and tell me why I should answer those questions?" His quiet, controlled tones commanded obedience.

Eric laid a hand on Paul's shoulder, exerting subtle pressure until he got the message—calm down or else. All too late, he remembered Eric's tiny babe slept in the next room, and his wife's heartbreaking news. Forcing breath in and out of constricted lungs, Paul dropped into the recliner with all the dignity of a beached whale. He pulled at strands of hair. The pain brought him back to his senses.

Only Fred's regular pants filled the silence.

"I can't tell you much." Paul raised his eyes, flitting between Eric's questioning stare and Don's suspicious gaze. "It's a matter of national security."

"There they go again, Lynn, touting security clearance shit," Inez said. "Why do they think they're the only ones with big, bad secrets?"

Lynn blinked away tears, a wan smile crossing her pale face. She faced Paul, her expression somber. "Our husbands have the highest level of clearance, and they've entrusted us. Can't you see fit to do the same with friends if this matter causes you such pain?"

Paul opened his mouth in protest, and closed it again with a snap. Four compassionate faces looked at him. Was he so transparent—or were these four truly that special, offering help on a silver platter? He prayed for the latter because he had to trust them with the whole truth. Screw rules and regulations. The threats to Japan surely caused all hell to break loose within diplomatic channels. The only way Kay could leave China—if she lived—was with the most unorthodox assistance.

Running a trembling hand over his face, he took a deep breath.

"Kay Chiang was—is, goddammit—a civilian undercover operative for the Defense Intelligence Agency. I am—was, goddammit—her liaison, and I'm trying to find her."

"Well, that explains a whole shitload of confusion," Don muttered, throwing Eric a meaningful glance. "No wonder the FBI dropped all charges." He pivoted his large bulk toward Paul, his brow furrowed. "Did Wilkins work for the feds, too?"

"No, he was simply a convenient contact Kay exploited to fulfill her last two missions."

"Missions?" Eric threw his arms high in the air. "Damn it, SDS was my whole life! She tried to tank it with her interference."

"Convenient contact? What a horrible way to describe anyone who's dead!" Lynn cried, her eyes filling with tears again.

"Exploited, my ass. From what I heard, she's a prick teaser to the nth degree." Inez crossed her arms, an angry gleam in her eye.

Paul raised his hand. "I'll tell you more, but first I need answers to my questions." He pinned Don with his gaze, struggling to keep his voice neutral, not hostile. "Who gave you the information on Wilkins?"

"Do I have your word you'll treat him as a confidential informant?" Don stared back with equal intensity. "His name, his position, and his sources go no further than this room."

"Of course. I understand." Paul hesitated. "In the spirit of full disclosure, I've been working with confidential Agency files I...uh...I pilfered when I was fired. Eric, I apologize for not telling you the circumstances of my departure. They booted my ass out here on special assignment."

Eric's eyes widened with surprise. He took Lynn's hand and squeezed it. "That's not important to us."

"FBI Special Agent Emilio Chaboya is my contact." Don's matter-of-fact voice filled the silence. "He tracked Wilkins and Chiang into China. Like you, he was blocked a number of times, but seems to maneuver his way around the bureaucracy's secrets. I trust this information is truthful, not necessarily complete."

"Thank you, Don," Paul said. "I've never run across Chaboya's trail, so he must be good. Unfortunately, he's unaware of the most significant piece."

"Kay's mission." Lynn scrubbed her cheeks with her hands and took a deep breath.

Paul rose. He stood behind the recliner, clenching its back for support and gazing at their friendly faces. Would they cheer him on from the sidelines, or jump into the fray and give him the help he—and Kay—needed?

Only one way to find out, buddy. You've got to tell them the truth and then ask.

"This rare earths shortage has been on our radar for a while, and was behind Kay's clandestine sleuthing with Wilkins. Did you all hear the news today about China's curtailment of shipments to Japan?" Paul shot a quick glance at Don, Inez, and Lynn, receiving confirming nods. "Okay, I'll stick to high points. Wilkins uncovered Chinese government efforts to disguise advanced military technology in video game companies. My guess is Wilkins intended to sell the information to the highest bidder, and ended up dead instead."

"So you believe the Chinese government murdered Wilkins?" Don linked his fingers and rested his jaw on top.

"Oh, not so you could prove it," Paul said. "However, Kay thinks so, since she used his email account to alert me to his findings, just in case they were already onto her. Wilkins showed up dead, not Kay. Plus, this refined metals situation ratcheted up big time after she wrote that, so whatever Wilkins stumbled on must have been huge."

"Is it possible Kay double-crossed you so she could collect his money?" Lynn wore a skeptical expression.

Paul sympathized with Lynn's negative opinion of Kay since she usually played the part of what Inez called her—a prick teaser—to perfection. Too bad only he had ever seen her brains in action, mixed with real courage.

"Despite what you observed, Kay usually got results, albeit through unorthodox methods not always approved of in advance," Paul said with a wry twist of his mouth. "She admitted she crossed the line at SDS by putting Eric's life in danger, which was clearly outside her mission's parameters. That's one reason she's so hard to find. She's trying to atone by bringing home a stellar piece of intelligence." He ran his hands through his hair. "She delivered on some of the intelligence, all right. But she just hasn't made it home . . . yet."

"Why are you so convinced she's still alive?" Don's assessing eyes probed Paul's.

He twitched, dreading the question's implication.

"Because she has to be." Paul dug his fingers into the leather padding. "Because I want her to be," he admitted, dropping his head to his chest. "Because I need her to be!" He pounded his fist on the headrest. "I can't lose another person under my command. Until I know otherwise, I won't stop trying to get her out of China!"

Lynn rushed to his side and squeezed his waist.

"Oh, Paul, it's so obvious you care for her . . ." Paul drew back, looking askance. ". . . safety," she added hastily. "What can we do to help?"

Eric joined them and slapped his back. "Seriously, we'll help any way we can if it's in our power."

Paul gazed at Don and Inez on the sofa. Inez seemed proud yet resigned to Don's non-existent free time. Bulldog Don appeared ready to charge into the fray, teeth bared.

I didn't even have to ask.

"Thanks, all of you." He brushed a shaky hand in front of his eyes and stumbled back to the recliner. "Let me fill you in on the details. Maybe you'll catch something I missed."

Chapter 18

VILLA TOWERS

Beijing, China
Late Afternoon, March 21, 32 Days Later

Jintao studied their luxurious love nest with a critical eye. In the apartment's foyer, Birds of Paradise flowered in purple, yellow and tangerine hues in a perfect *Aloha* greeting. Fresh orchids spilled their mottled hues out of vases dotting glass tables. Peeking inside the bedroom, he admired the creamy magnolias intermixed with scarlet roses on the black sheets, beckoning him to seduce her once again.

Not quite the exotic vacation outside China's borders Kay begged for so prettily, riding him hard. But not bad with only nine hours planning.

His clamoring desires surprised him these days. Even though Kay couldn't escape China, he wanted her happy. That's one reason he'd settled her in this opulent high-rise. Would she forgive him for ignoring her veiled hints about clearing the bureaucratic tangles? The Party wasn't through with her yet—and neither was he.

Would he ever get enough of his precious Kay?

So different from his other women, she challenged him no matter the subject. He shared his opinions, eager for the intellectual clash and subsequent sexual tension. Then the little games could begin, provocative and titillating, until he overwhelmed her senses with pleasure. Proving he held the ultimate power as she begged for mercy.

And promised to keep her pretty mouth shut.

Any man seeing her tantalizing body would never believe she would tolerate a less-than-virile lover. She could have her pick of men. She chose him.

Mine.

Using the gilded mirror on the wall, Jintao patted each dyed strand of hair back into position. He sucked in his stomach and pivoted, eying the fit of his knit shirt. His extra gym time worked. Each year he re-doubled his efforts. Otherwise, the image he so carefully fashioned would wither away like an old man's pathetic erection.

Click.

Kay stepped through the entrance door panting, dressed in a pink sweat suit and running shoes. Her magnificent hair swept high in a bun, secured with pink chopsticks stuck through in a haphazard manner. He frowned. This ragtag vision did not match the florists' exorbitant prices or his other surprise.

"Jintao! What are you doing here so early?" Kay darted a quick glance over her shoulder. Fright flashed across her face.

"Why are you late?" He waved his arm. "And why would you wear clothes so . . . so . . . hideous? I filled the closets with outfits to display your beauty!"

She dropped her eyelids. A provocative smile flitted on her lips. She grabbed his hand, moving his fingers to the zipper tab of her jacket. Placing her warm palm on top of his, she slid their digits downward inch by unhurried inch. The slick cloth opened and revealed her flushed, moist skin. Her breasts heaved in rapid succession. Unable to resist, he slipped his hand under the snug cup of her running bra, squeezing her hard nipple.

"Didn't you realize a woman is wettest after exercise?" she whispered. "I love being all hot and ready for you." Pushing the jacket off her shoulders, she slanted her hips forward and slid her hands into the elastic waistband. "Wanna help me out of these, too?" She licked her lips, appraising his crotch. "Then it's your turn."

Jintao moaned and chuckled in the same breath, sliding his hand out with a final little pinch.

"You little minx," he said. "After all I've done to arrange a romantic evening. I think you should take a shower first and model the little outfit I placed on your bed." He swept his arm wide, hoping she'd notice his supreme efforts. How did this woman make him happy to beg for praise like a lap dog? No matter. She was his. "Welcome to paradise—Beijing style."

Her eyebrow tilted upward. She surveyed the wild tumult decorating his staid apartment, caressing the flower petals and releasing the orchids' heady perfume. With a delicate sniff, she slid her gaze to the bedroom and smiled.

"Join me in the shower?"

"Not this time, my little fox spirit," he murmured. "I desire watching you exit your bedroom wearing only a little bikini and your new sable coat. Remember how much you enjoyed fur caressing your bare skin?"

Kay shivered. Her body remembers, he exulted. He always strove for the ultimate sensual experience, perfectly matched to each of his women. He couldn't resist seeking out unique responses to a particular touch, private cries freeing them from China's mass mania, a world where they conformed to a certain set of behaviors, matching the other millions. In his world, he demanded each be herself, and only herself.

Only for him. He pointed to the bedroom.

"When you come back, I'll decorate your bikini straps with flowers. We'll sit at the fire and I'll feed you, satisfying one hunger while the other grows. Your skin will taste of crushed petals when I feast on my favorite delicacy—your moist inner flesh." Her breath quickened; her little gasp of arousal awakened even his ears. "Then, and only then, will it be your turn to pleasure me." With an exaggerated bow, he threw her a wicked grin. "I await your best effort."

"You won't be disappointed." She bowed back. Spinning, she shucked her pants and shoes, displaying her creamy skin. She shimmied out of the tiny thong and bra, tossing them in the air with a throaty laugh. As a last fillip, she yanked the sticks from her hair and shot them like darts, her thick hair cascading to her waist, tempting him to twist the tresses about his naked body and never let her go.

Mine!

· · · · · ·

A wonderful, cool breeze separated Kay's open lapels. The sable jacket was a little too warm for this mild weather, but it covered the daring mini skirt she wore in case Jintao surprised her again. Her bare legs ate up miles of trendy shops on Wangfujing Street. With every stroke of the soft fur, she imagined another life where a man loved her, kept her safe, and spent countless hours adoring her.

Jintao watched her too often with a calculating expression. No doubt, he knew every detail about her life with Charlie. Had he also sicced a watchdog after her now? A niggling sense of uncertainty hounded her every time she exited her lavish cocoon. Had she covered her recent tracks well enough on her clandestine visits?

Rounding a corner onto a rustic street of herbalists and acupuncturists, Kay rubbed her arm. The morning's hormone injection still stung. Finding a doctor to provide her with birth control shots was easy in a country dedicated to minimum population growth. However, Jintao's essentials weren't as simple to fill.

She pushed open the rickety door and entered the small store. In addition to powdered rhinoceros tusk and ginseng, apparently this shopkeeper carried authentic American virility pharmaceuticals too, all favored by the political class. Kay shook her head and closed the door. What would the Communist Party do for a pecking order when women made headway?

"Good afternoon." She nodded to the wizened man perched on a stool behind the counter. A cap topped long white locks and red gloves with no fingertips covered tiny hands. "I am to pick up a gift for an important man." She dropped Jintao's money onto the counter, praying he'd alerted the storekeeper as promised. Tiptoeing through a conversational maze of half-truths and innuendos required a facility with colloquial Chinese she didn't have, and could cause Jintao real harm if she misspoke.

"Heh," the elder muttered. Sharp black eyes framed by thick glasses studied her for silent moments. He undoubtedly tagged her as Jintao's current whore. Well, wasn't she?

Would Paul agree?

Kay blinked, surprised the direction her thoughts wandered. Her last communiqué may not have been received—or even sent. God only knew how long it took that Tibetan monk to journey home, figure out how to get the message out of the country, and finally send it to Paul. Weeks, at a minimum—months, a real possibility. Paul probably figured she was dead.

What she wouldn't give to hear him rip-roaring mad over her latest tactics, pounding the phone in frustration on his desk. However, thousands of miles and too many lost years made his censure moot. She faced the consequences of her choices all alone this time.

The storekeeper shoved a paper bag at her. Peeking inside, she spied the bubble-wrapped purple pills proudly popping up, plus an assortment of tiny envelopes scribbled with cryptic characters. She dipped her head and exited, concealing her face in the lifted collar, following Jintao's precise instructions. Talk about paranoid! Compared to her, his worries seemed trivial.

Turning onto appropriately named Heavenly Peace Avenue, she held the cell to her ear and blended in with the rich women shopping at exclusive boutiques. She chattered aloud in an empty conversation and checked her surroundings every thirty seconds. No one followed. Relieved, she turned in the direction of the café she visited yesterday on her jog, under the pretext of trolling the Internet for designer high heels and Hollywood gossip.

"Get back!" A string of oaths followed the harsh yell. A musical cacophony of shattered glass followed.

Filled with dread, Kay turned the corner and froze. Youths streamed from the Internet cafe's doorway. They shoved and tripped over each other in their haste to flee uniformed police.

Their hated insignia brought back vivid memories of Charlie's death. She ducked into the vestibule of a neighboring store, fisting her hand in her pocket and stifling a whimper.

Wielding heavy batons, the police whacked the heads of the few customers standing their ground and waving futile arms. Screams of anger and pain splintered the air.

A parade of six officers, each carrying computers, dashed through the melee to their waiting vehicles. They tossed their loads inside trunks, slammed them shut, and drove off in a merciless wail of sirens. Blood dripped in slow motion down the faces of the café's customers and staff.

Trembling, Kay shrank against a wall, her forgotten phone imbedded into her cheekbone. Five times already, raids closed a cafe she used the previous day. This was more than coincidence. Someone monitored her communications and hunted her. She felt like a scared rabbit caught in a rifle's crosshairs.

She must get out of China—now!

Did Jintao orchestrate this? She chewed her lip, considering. He hadn't assigned a bodyguard, nor forbidden her contact with anyone. She only used her phone for safe, innocuous conversations with hairdressers and the like, in case he monitored those, too. Conveniently close to his luxurious club, he often returned to her apartment after an evening out. He took calls in her presence, shared his schedule with her, and acted as a true lover.

If not Jintao, who dogged her?

His pissed-off subordinate? Han Mai carried a chip on her shoulder bigger than the original dragon lady's. Would Jintao call off Han Mai's investigation if Kay begged? Nicely, of course, with all sorts of pretty pleases and sexually nuanced promises, but begging nonetheless.

She swallowed the bile in her throat. It always came back to sexual power.

Chapter 19

High heels clicking a rapid tattoo, Kay crossed her fingers and whirled toward Tiananmen Square. She tugged her sable collar close and kept her head bent against the steady springtime wind whipping across the open plaza. Passing through the tower gates with a wary eye on the alert guard, she scanned the far corner where Fran and Yannan usually huddled.

Empty.

A large crowd massed under Mao's gargantuan portrait. Raised fists and placards celebrated the anniversary of the historic protests that rocked the world. Thank goodness Yannan and Fran weren't here today. China's large dragon jaws may finally be snapping shut around her.

Palming her phone, Kay hesitated. Finally time for a text message to Paul? Maybe she should buy a disposable cell first. Of course, they might track it, too. What would be the point? She'd run out of time.

Kay sank onto a bench and began typing. *CW death linked to me, blocked from leaving. Can't Uncle help?* Gnawing on her lip, she considered saying more. No, Paul would grasp this overt message meant she faced big trouble.

Bang! Whump. Bang! Whump. Bang! Whump.

Her eyes instinctively followed the commotion, at the square's center, finger halted in mid-air. Tear gas floated above the youthful crowd. Hands with cell phones held high twisted in every direction, pleas for help from the outside world. A tiny drone lifted above the crowd. It hovered and zipped in erratic patterns. Capturing incriminating video for the underground network of political dissidents, or sent by troops to capture the protestors' identities for later prosecution?

"Shit!" Kay had no excuse to be anywhere near this political demonstration. Certainly, no one would rescue her if she became part of a massive arrest. Time to go. She tapped her phone, sending the text message.

No Network Detected

"Shit, shit, double shit," she muttered. Holding her breath, she hopped on the bench and spun her phone high in the air for a viable signal. No such luck. All outgoing calls blocked. Seconds too late. Defeated, she sat back down.

Storing the text to send later, she grabbed her purse and paper bag, shivering underneath the warm fur jacket. Right now, she craved even the false sense of security within Jintao's apartment.

"Auntie Kay! Auntie Kay!" The child's voice rose above the crowd's clamors and roars. "Wait!"

Kay shook her head. Today was definitely not her day.

A pink whirlwind catapulted onto her lap, knocking her purse beneath the bench. Small arms squeezed her neck so hard she twisted her head to breathe.

"Frannie? Are you okay, sweetie?" Kay rocked the little girl, crooning comforting sounds and searching for Yannan.

"No!" Fran exploded out of her arms; her tiny hands slammed onto her hips. "Daddy's gone to jail and Auntie Yannan said you have to help him." Her face contorted and a torrent of tears spilled out of her wide eyes. "Please help Daddy. I need him home . . ." Her voice broke. She threw herself back into Kay's arms. Heartbreaking sobs shattered against her shoulder.

Kay was torn. How could she tell this innocent child she was the last person to confront Chinese bureaucracy?

She recalled Jintao disclosing an incident at the northern mines that Mai took great delight in quelling, to the detriment of her husband's career. Why hadn't she connected the dots to Li Ying? Li probably got into big trouble for flouting one of Mai's directives, just like Yannan predicted.

"Frannie, stop crying so I can understand you." Kay tugged the girl upright and handed her a tissue. "What does your Auntie Yannan say?"

"She said she couldn't be seen with you, otherwise she might be arrested, too. She has to stay inside, and I have to come home straight after school." She sniffed and blew her nose.

"Did you tell her you were coming to see me?"

"N-N-No." Guilt wreathed Fran's face. "But the last time we came, she forgot to give you this." She dug into her jacket pocket and retrieved a small photo disk.

"Do you know what this is?" Kay spun the disk in her fingers. Yannan wasn't a photojournalist–her power came from words. The guard glanced their way. Gulping, she stuffed it inside the paper bag.

"She's always taking pictures of me. Maybe she wanted you to have one . . . to remember me." She ended with a loud wail. Each sobbing, shuddering breath touched Kay's heart . . . and kicked her conscience.

How can I leave this precious child to face a world without either parent?

"Shhh . . . Stop crying and listen." She jiggled the little girl.

"Will Daddy come home?" Fran hiccupped and wiped her nose with the sleeve of her jacket.

"I'll get him home to you. Do you trust me?"

Two lone tears slid down Fran's round cheeks. She nodded. Hope replaced the woebegone expression.

"Then let me get to work." Kay gave her a squeeze. "We can't meet anymore. I'll send a friend, instead." Inspired, she leaned close. "We'll have a secret code, like in the movies," she whispered in Fran's tiny ear.

"A code?" Fran's eyes widened, delight vying with misery. "What will it be?"

"California Barbie," Kay murmured with a smile. "I'm Californian, and you're my little Chinese Barbie doll. If anyone brings you a message from California Barbie, it will be from me. Okay?"

"I'll remember." She patted the emblem on her outthrust jacket front. "I won't tell Auntie Yannan, either. It's our secret code."

"Fine, sweetie." Kay lifted her to her feet. "We've got to go." Clouds of tear gas drifted in their direction, creating a break between the crowds and police heading the opposite way. She squatted and reached for her purse.

"Goodbye, Frannie." She swatted her little rear end and pushed her toward the exit, juggling her purse and paper bag. Fran gave an optimistic wave. She prayed Fran would make it home safe this afternoon, and every night for decades.

If God really listened, she would love that, too.

· · · · · ·

Settling inside a taxi, Kay slid her shoes off and rubbed her aching toes, trying to recall the last time she walked so many hours in high heels.

The night Charlie died.

Prickles crawled up her neck like tiny spiders hatching within the lush folds of her fur collar. Shuddering, Kay jerked her head forward, shooing away imaginary pests with her nails and scratching under the heavy tresses.

The taxi halted in front of her apartment complex. She tossed a large bill over the seat, ignoring the driver's chatter of gratitude. Stuffing the paper bag with Jintao's pills inside the jacket pocket, she grabbed her purse and nodded to the bowing doorman opening the car door.

Entering the vestibule, she hesitated. Her nape crawled again. In warning? She dropped her purse and squatted, spinning and darting her eyes in a full circle.

No one paid any attention. And she considered Jintao paranoid?

Twisting her lips in a rueful smile, she thanked the hovering doorman and whisked inside, pressing the elevator button with relief. She would run a hot bath and wash away all these silly fears. Nothing changed in the last couple of hours. Jintao paid for the best in discretion and security Beijing could provide. Why should she worry so? She was safe now.

Riding the spacious elevator to the top floor, she imagined tonight's scenario. With the miracles of modern medicine, Jintao would demand intense, vigorous sex. Perhaps if she fulfills his every fantasy he'll grant her a favor. He wasn't a bad man, just one caught in his country's heavy-handed politics and his own pleasures. Surely, she could leverage one against the other for her own gain.

She stepped off the elevator and into the hall. Fumbling inside her purse for her keys, one of her nails broke. Damn! Now she'll need a manicure this afternoon, too. Examining the damage, she unlocked the door and shoved inward with her hip.

A blast of light greeted her.

"What the—"

A pistol dug into her temple.

Kay broke out in a cold sweat.

Uniformed police officers swarmed her beautiful apartment. The rare Ming vase from Jintao's prized collection lay shattered on the tile entryway, the lovely flowers a pungent smear of color. Framed calligraphy parchment hung askew; sharp edges of broken glass gouged the fragile antique. Ripped cushions displayed their innards in a shocking dissection of the sanctioned search. Loud crashes in the kitchen mixed with matter-of-fact male tones.

Kay swatted the pistol aside, tossing away her purse. She whirled and faced her attacker. A young man with that special insignia on his breast pocket met her look with a blank expression.

"Why are you here? This is my apartment!"

"Are you Chiang Kay?"

"Yes, but this is Wei Jintao's apartment. Do you appreciate who he is?"

"You said this was your apartment. Which is it?"

"Both." Kay held onto her temper. "He pays the rent. I am one of his mistresses. Understand now?" He nodded. "You confirmed your identity. You are under arrest." He reached for her wrist, his pistol held at the ready.

Kay flung her arm away. "Wei Jintao is a senior Minister of Information Technology in Beijing. He is an influential man with much power. He will not be happy you destroyed his apartment."

"My superiors demand I follow their orders."

Digging into her pocket, she shook the paper bag in his face, akin to a voodoo amulet.

"He sent me on an errand to pick up his private medicine. He will be angry if he does not get it tonight." Highly frustrated, more like it. "Do you wish his wrath upon your head?"

"I have no proof he is acquainted with you." The officer shrugged. "The apartment manager has your name on file."

Kay's shoulders shot full of tension. Suspicion and a sickening panic battled for dominance. Why would Jintao hide paying for all this opulence, yet not conceal her companionship? Was this his perverse way of using power, to yank all security away as soon as she felt safe again?

"Let me call him." She bent for her purse, dropping the bag on the floor. "I'm sure he'll clear matters up."

"No phone calls." He shook his head, snatching the purse away. A fellow officer joined them, aiming his pistol straight at her head.

Grabbing the phone, the first officer scanned the display, flinging her purse aside. Her cosmetics clattered onto the tile.

"Ah! Proof of her treasonous activities," he crowed. "We have done our job. Time to leave."

The trampling of their boots . . . the beating of her heart . . . both in sync . . . fast, furious.

She couldn't think. She couldn't breathe.

She couldn't escape.

Chapter 20

OFFICE OF MINISTRY OF INFORMATION AND TECHNOLOGY

Beijing, China
Late Morning, March 31, 9 Days Later

Han Mai pushed back the cuff of her crisp shirt and pointed her watch at Wei Jintao's young secretary. "What is keeping him? He is ten minutes late."

"I am sorry." A polite smile graced her pretty face. Surrounded by a lush array of plants and valuable paintings, she acted as pampered as Wei's mistresses. "He has someone with him."

Biting back a sharp retort, Mai shoved her glasses up her nose and settled back in the armchair, considering the vast political power housed in the cavernous basements below. China's robust communications networks came together there under Wei's complete command, all because of his long-ago idea for a Chinese firewall to monitor and block

Internet traffic. Brilliant, yes, because China's government officials demanded such complete control. Wei had since ascended the Party ranks with his smooth talk and political savvy, not due to any new contributions to their cause.

She should have known he'd dodge this confrontation. For over a week, he avoided pressing charges of treason against his American consort. Well, not any longer.

Grabbing her leather briefcase, she rose, smoothing the folds of her pantsuit.

"This will not wait," she said to the secretary with a toss of her head. Striding to Wei's office, she shoved the cherry wood door open and barreled in.

Wei stood near the windows, his face flushed. His trademark Italian silk tie hung to one side, an odd contrast to his symmetrical, handsome features.

"I will not tolerate pornography depicting children, do you understand?" Wei waved a sheaf of papers at his young guest. "There are enough resources to block these loathsome perverts as well as unharmonious and treasonous sites. Find them!"

Wei threw the papers into the air, ignoring their fluttery descent. He glared at Mai. His obsidian eyes blazed in a face twisted with fury.

"How dare you enter my office uninvited!" Wei roared.

"We have an appointment," she snapped. "You're late."

The unfortunate target of his last outburst fell to his knees, grabbing the loose papers.

"I decide what is important, Assistant Minister Han." Wei thrust back his shoulders.

Mai, emboldened, cast an eye on the remnants of his last discussion. "I think the Party leaders would want to know you spend time and money on sexual perversions, rather than matters undermining the nation's security."

"Get out of here!" Wei besieged the young man, frantically stuffing the last pages in a file. "And shut the door!" With a deferential bow, the man exited with a click.

Mai dropped into a guest chair angled in front of Wei's expansive desk. The Yanshan mountaintops glistened through floor-to-ceiling windows, the view bordered by two flags—China's and the United Nations'. Framed photos of Wei with every recent premiere decorated the adjacent wall, flanked by diplomas and national award certificates.

Exhaling noisily, Wei walked to his desk, sat, and adjusted his tie.

"It is inexcusable to interrupt my meeting," he said.

"Any more inexcusable than holding a private meeting in government offices?" Mai smiled. Wei dared not dispute stated Party policy. "Interruptions are so enlightening."

Leaning back in his chair, he picked up a palm-sized jade carving of a ripe peach, caressing it with smooth, delicate strokes as it rolled through his fingers.

She squirmed at the sensuous image, ignoring the warning bell in her brain. She would not allow his charismatic allure to distract her from her goal like a silly teenager. Smoothing her features into blandness, she hoped her attraction wasn't obvious.

"Minister Wei, we await your formal statement regarding your relationship with Chiang Kay."

"I have been busy." He rubbed the carving's rosy curves, licked his thumb, and probed one smooth crevice.

"That is no excuse." She crossed her legs, imagining such a caress, and luxuriating in a brief flash of heat. "The evidence she sent Chinese secrets to America is indisputable. That is why she sits in jail. Now, we must hold a trial, and send a message to other corporate spies of the consequences of such actions."

Wei's gaze snapped to hers. "What exactly is your sudden interest?"

"I . . . I don't want our department's reputation tarnished because you are treating her with favoritism." Mai couldn't look away from his mesmerizing eyes. Deep-set, dark brown, framed by thick lashes and elegant brows.

"This is not your concern." He replaced the carving on the desk with deliberate precision.

"My direct responsibility is the protection of secrets about Inner Mongolia's mining and distribution of our purified rare metals. Do you agree?" Mai straightened, attuned to his voice's nuanced scolding.

"Of course." He swiveled his head and glanced out the window. "I requested your assignment there because of your husband's expertise. A husband and wife working in concert make a formidable team." His gaze shot back to hers. "Do you enjoy having him by your side both day and night?"

Mai fought the blush working its way past the high collar of her jacket. Was he sarcastic or sincere? His expression revealed nothing.

"We work well together." She refused to disclose more. Her husband's fascination with his mistress' second son was no business of Wei's.

Jutting her chin up, she tapped her briefcase. "We must protect our military secrets. Hiding them inside game companies is not secure enough. Whoever determined it was smart to take capitalist's money clearly did not consider the future consequences."

"You dare question our premiere's policy on engagement with the West?" he challenged.

Mai cleared her throat and silently cursed her wayward tongue.

"Not the policy . . . of course not . . ." She scrambled for the right words. "Perhaps we did not fully consider how desperate the U.S. would be to steal our technological advances once they realized how dependent their businesses are on us. Perhaps their politicians fed our elderly statesmen lies." Her temple throbbed. "Perhaps . . . they have seduced us with their money and capitalistic promises of success, while they exploited our dedicated and hard-working citizens."

Scratching his jaw, Wei stared at her for long moments. His fingers moved to the desk, tapping a slow cadence. One finger, another, playing an invisible piano.

"Do you think doing anything more than detaining Chiang Kay won't provoke a full-scale diplomatic crisis?" He held up one finger. "Take a minute to consider this, Assistant Han. We cannot keep her forever. Jailing her would create an international outcry."

Mai slumped her shoulders, struggling for words. If appealing to his patriotic duty wouldn't sway him, daring a political gamble was her only option. Did she want to bring this one fascinating man down? A flash of sympathy for Chiang Kay ran through her. Perhaps the young woman fell under Wei Jintao's magnetic spell, too. She shrugged. China's billions took precedence over one man.

He rose. "Do you understand why I keep the UN flag displayed so prominently?" He pointed to the blue and white silk.

"It's rather unusual." She admitted.

"Yes, it is." He traced its folds. "However, when foreign dignitaries arrive puffing dragon fire over our censorship policies, their accusations of nefarious intentions fall away like flower petals since I so obviously pledge support to the goals of world peace and harmony."

"A ruse." She snorted. "I assumed as much."

"Not a ruse—a tool to keep relations between China and the world productive, not destructive." Wei sighed, rubbing his neck. "The tactics you propose for Chiang Kay would destroy much of the goodwill we've built."

"So what?'

"So—that is not your place!" He whirled, taking menacing steps toward her. "Leave Chiang Kay in detention. We will determine the best way to deal with her actions. She is not one of our dangerous revolutionaries."

"How can you be sure?" Mai jumped to her feet, arching her neck back to meet his gaze. "With her heritage of leadership, she could initiate a revolution that might break us apart—creating a separate

Taiwan, Hong Kong, and Tibet. To stay strong we must remain whole. We cannot risk failure!"

"We? Or you?" Wei's hot breath fanned her face.

"It is my responsibility to protect our state secrets from all harm—even if it exposes your dirty little whore!" Mai screamed, disregarding the spittle escaping her lips.

He reared away, his face twisting with revulsion. Pulling a handkerchief free, he wiped his cheeks and glowered.

"If you do this, all your father's connections won't save you," he said in a threatening tone. "This is not your decision."

"Bah!" She grabbed her briefcase, slapping it on the desk. "You old men running our country better step aside for a new wave of men—and yes, women—who see the world differently." She cast a final, derisive sneer at his crotch. "Mostly because we don't think with our penises!"

Mai slammed Wei's office door behind her, shaking with rage and fiery energy. She pushed open the door to the stairwell with the force of an embattled warrior.

Her mind whirled with how to handle Wei's recalcitrance. His involvement with this woman blinded him to the dangers. She pounded down two steps and rounded a corner, the echoes in the stairwell besieging her. She must escalate the situation. If it compromised her reputation and abandoned her in Inner Mongolia longer than she planned, too bad. She reached the ground floor and hustled through the lobby. To protect China, she would do anything and everything, including entrapment. Her father's honor demanded it.

Flagging a taxi, she jumped in, her breath catching at the audacity of her plan. "Take me to the Party Headquarters."

Moments later, while standing in front of Deputy Minister of Justice Cai Bo, the reality of her decision hit home. A stack of printed documents, probably awaiting his official seal, tested her resolve. Hurried footsteps rang in the modern corridor outside, accompanied by low tones of desperate pleas and adamant refusals. Other petitioners caught in the bureaucratic net necessary to secure China's future. She locked her shaky knees and tilted her chin high.

"Minister Wei Jintao refuses to cooperate. I believe we have enough evidence to pursue a trial of Chiang Kay on charges of espionage," she said. "Since the exposed secrets directly affect my region, I officially request the charges announced and a trial date set."

Cai Bo tapped fat fingers on his keyboard. His protruding stomach enveloped the edge of his desk, lank strands of hair hung in perfect symmetry over each rounded cheek.

"How unfortunate about Minister Wei." A smug smile flitted on his lips. "I must report his recalcitrance to the Party right away."

"I understand," Mai said. Too bad a handsome man like Wei would face potentially devastating punishment for his disloyalty. Well, she could never invite Wei to her bed, so what did she care?

"Very curious happenings, though." Cai motioned her closer, peering at the ajar door. "Wei Jintao arrived the day after Chiang's arrest and a paper bag with evidence mysteriously disappeared. I'm not sure we inventoried its contents, either. If it belonged to him, how did this traitor possess it?"

What did that bag contain? Since Mai couldn't get Wei to cooperate, maybe she could force Chiang to spill her secrets.

Cai hit one key with a flourish and leaned back in his chair, his hands folded on his middle. "Charges are now formally filed."

"There may be others involved." Mai tilted closer, casting a glance in all directions. She dropped her voice. "May I have the list of Chiang's contacts in case more exist in my region to oust?'

"Of course, of course." Cai tapped a series of commands. The printer whirred on the credenza. "I commend your loyalty and dedication."

Mai held her breath. The precious sheet of paper slid into her ready hands. Studying the long list of Chinese names, she recognized the troublesome journalist Tan Yannan, in addition to Li Ying's distant family members. But the one arresting her attention was American—

Paul Freeman. Someone new to investigate and bring under her circle of influence.

"Thank you for your assistance." Bowing scant inches, she offered her hand to Cai.

"Not at all, not at all." He shook her hand with too much enthusiasm. "Always willing to help a descendent of such revered ancestors." He pursed his lips. "Although it is a little early, perhaps you would join me at the club for a cocktail—or tea, if you prefer."

Mai bit back her retort. Did he really think women couldn't drink socially?

"A cocktail sounds perfect to commemorate the path of true justice." Tucking the valuable paper inside her briefcase, she waited as he locked his office. "Others may wish to join the celebration of our findings."

"No doubt, no doubt." Cai laughed, leading the way to the exit. "Perhaps Wei Jintao will retire early. They deserve a heads-up to the potential change in such an important Party position."

Mai shot her unexpected ally a sharp glance. How much should she share of her inner thoughts? "He is much older than he appears."

"And perhaps not quite as sharp, heh?" Cai gestured for a taxi. He held the door open for long seconds. She tossed her head, swallowed her pride, and entered first.

"Perhaps one of our colleagues noticed similar behavior." Mai plopped onto the seat and slid across, avoiding his crowding bulk. "I will brief my staff on the situation immediately and ask their help so we can identify all our potential enemies before they strike." She hesitated. "Even if more Americans are involved."

"Good, good." Cai nudged her knee. She jerked it away. "I will snag the premiere's personal assistant's ear at the club. He should be informed there is trouble brewing—and prepare for more trials." He stroked his jaw. "It wouldn't hurt involving our public relations department, too."

Smiling, Mai reached for her pack of cigarettes, offering one to her companion and flicking her lighter. The tip caught fire, working its way up the cylinder as she inhaled. That old saying was wrong. A fire could be wrapped in paper—if controlled by her every breath.

Chapter 21

UNITED STATES HOUSE OF REPRESENTATIVES COMMITTEE ROOM

Washington, D.C.
Late Morning, April 1, Next Day

"In conclusion, we believe the Chinese government systematically obstructs free speech by blocking key content on the Internet. It is the moral responsibility of the United States to call for unfettered access for all Chinese people." The Silicon Valley executive, David Rodrigues, dropped back in his chair with a quiet sigh, drained the last of his bottled water, and loosened his tie with the air of a young man unaccustomed to attire beyond a favorite polo shirt.

Congresswoman Janelle DuMont slipped reading glasses down her nose and considered the witness' testimony. After all, his firm's global headquarters were in her district. He deserved whatever support she could provide, even with this hearing's tiny audience. Unfortunately, the young man's cries for justice stretched credulity.

"Mr. Rodrigues, isn't it true your firm will benefit financially if you deliver unrestricted content to millions of new Internet users?"

"Yes, of course we would appreciate opening the Chinese market to our service." Rodrigues leaned forward across the wooden tabletop. "But more importantly, we seek freedom for our fellow man."

"Bullshit." Her administrative assistant's whisper echoed Janelle's thinking. Shoving a note into Janelle's hand, Sara Tanaka squatted next to Janelle, her petite body fitting between the chairs. "His firm agreed to censorship in the Muslim world without a squawk in return for access. We don't hold hearings on those countries, only China," she murmured.

Janelle smothered a smile and glanced at the paper reminding her of a fundraiser in less than an hour. "Unfortunately, Mr. Rodrigues, unless we wish to have our own constitution overrun by other countries demanding we follow their customs and laws, I doubt we should demand it from them. Don't you agree?"

Rodrigues scowled but stayed silent.

"Mr. Chairman," Janelle said, "perhaps we should adjourn and delay our recommendations to the Administration until we have solid proof it is in our national interest, not solely the interest of select technology firms, to insist on a censorship-free zone within China's sovereign borders. We have bigger fish to fry regarding China's human rights abuses in this afternoon's hearing."

Chairman Ed Freiberg picked up her cue. "Mr. Rodrigues, we all hope our precious First Amendment right of free speech will spread worldwide. Until then, however, the focus of this committee must stay on China's possible abuse of negotiated treaties with the U.S. or blatant human rights violations. We thank you for your time and testimony." He slapped his gavel. "This hearing is adjourned."

"Thank goodness that's over." Sara's knees popped as she rose, gripping the back of Janelle's chair so hard it dipped down. "You're already late."

"Since when do you care?" Janelle stuffed papers into her satchel. Her San Francisco assistant had jumped at Janelle's offer to join her in Washington. Sara's no-nonsense approach provided a refreshing contrast to long hours groping through her fellow politicians' vague conversations and doublespeak.

"Since our revered House Majority Leader demanded your attendance. Apparently, whatever you said to her last night didn't go over well." Sara handed Janelle her suit jacket.

Janelle sighed. She followed Sara out the door and into the crowded hallway. No, Barbara Cox was not happy with her refusal to join other members of her political party at a lavish weekend getaway to Bermuda under the guise of touring a new research center. The CEO of a multi-national company, hoping to grease the skids of current legislation working its way out of committee, sought ten more votes to beat fierce opposition. He apparently assumed enough money could buy the bill's passage.

"I reminded her my vote is not for sale, and never will be." Janelle shoved an unruly curl away from her cheek. "I can still face myself in the mirror. Speaking of which . . ." She rummaged in her bag for a wide comb as she shouldered through the restroom's swinging door. Sara followed.

The mirror crowning the pedestal sink reflected her weariness all too well. More gray hairs appeared daily but Janelle refused to dye them. Forty-three wasn't old, she reminded herself for the umpteenth time, leaning forward to paint lipstick on her full lips.

Dad turned completely gray at my age. But with Mom's Cambodian genes, I'll ripen into a fine old woman.

"Better have your guard up." Sara's warning floated out from the nearest stall. "Barbara Cox called in backup."

"You think they would have learned their lessons from the scandals of the nineties." Janelle leaned against the sink. "When the President sells Chinese access to breakfast at the White House, it's time to change the status quo."

"There's a new rumor floating around today." Sara popped out and glanced around the deserted room. "Our database of detained and jailed human rights protesters in China has been tampered with...in this country. Apparently a hacker halved the total number China claims they've investigated or convicted—and scrubbed pertinent details of specific charges and punishment."

"It's bad enough we rely on political refugees to piece details together." Janelle smacked her fist. "How could a vital, sensitive database be hacked with all our new security measures in place?"

"I think the question is who and why, not how." Sara washed her hands and reached for a paper towel. "Who in this country benefits by keeping your committee in the dark about the actual details of China's detention program? And why muzzle the dissidents' testimonies?"

"I have no idea." Janelle tucked another wayward strand behind her ear.

"You are so naïve. Didn't your Dad show you the ropes?" Sara rolled her eyes. "Perhaps your fearless leader knows."

"Barbara?" Janelle scrunched her forehead. "She was the loudest proponent of establishing hearings to monitor China's abuses."

"Consider what the famous bard once wrote, *'The lady doth protest too much, methinks.'*" Sara planted her hands on her hips. "Her motivations may have been pure twenty-plus years ago. Is she still impartial?"

"How many millions of dollars have flowed into her re-election campaigns?" Janelle wondered aloud.

"More than you alone can tackle head-on."

You were right, Dad. D.C. is a snake pit for the unethical and power-hungry.

Janelle massaged the tension gripping her neck. "I promised Dad I'd never take gifts. I mean to keep my promise."

"Then I better start looking for another job." Sara grinned, elbowing her in the side and opening the door. "You'll never raise enough cash to finance your re-election race at this rate."

· · · · · ·

Entering the lush Bay View Hotel in the outskirts of Washington's Beltway, Janelle rode the elevator to the tower suite. She agreed with Sara's glum assessment. Campaigning became her full-time job rather than representing her constituents' interests. She'd been so idealistic, convinced of the appropriateness of government to create a great society. Now she wasn't so sure. Power became a heady drug, addictive and alluring. A siren song with no conscience.

"Congresswoman DuMont, I'm glad you could join us today." The lobbyist's smooth-skinned palm grasped hers in the suite's foyer.

"I came to speak with Barbara Cox." Janelle tugged her hand free. "Have you seen her?" She peered over his shoulder, scanning the room.

Snagging two flutes of champagne from a table, he offered her one.

"In the far corner, I believe, meeting with visitors to the Chinese embassy." He tipped his head at the small gathering. "You wouldn't interrupt such an important discussion, would you?"

"Actually, yes." She pushed the glass away and turned aside, maneuvering through the crowd.

"Janelle—there you are!" Barbara Cox's polished tones grated on Janelle's nerves. As House Majority Leader for the last ten of her twenty-eight years in Congress, she epitomized the appearance of a gracious, unassuming do-gooder. Only those who spent time with her behind closed doors saw her as a fierce negotiator and unstoppable fund-raiser. Dyed blonde hair kept in perfect trim by the Congressional salon complemented nails polished to a high gloss. Her pastel designer suit screamed success.

Standing next to her, Janelle felt like a country bumpkin. She bought her clothes at the local warehouse outlet and wore her hair *au natural*. She towered above most women populating Washington. Unfortunately, without her mother's petite stature softening her father's drive, she couldn't play the feminine wiles card Barbara used so well.

"Barbara." She greeted the woman with the perfunctory, hypocritical air kiss, fighting revulsion. "You asked to see me?"

"My dear, these gentlemen wish to learn how they can help you keep your seat." Barbara's hands fluttered at the three men hovering around her.

"Ms. DuMont, my name is Zuo De." The eldest stepped forward, business card extended. "It is our honor to meet you finally." The others followed suit with quiet murmurs, offering their cards and stepping to their leader's side. All dressed in crisp suits with perfectly knotted ties and not a hair out of place.

Tapping the cards against her fingers, Janelle pursed her lips and angled her head in Barbara's direction.

"What did you tell them they could do?" she whispered out of the side of her mouth. "It's illegal for a foreign national to contribute to an election campaign."

"Of course it is, dear." Barbara's insincere smile flashed like a beauty contestant's. "That's not the issue. These gentlemen propose bringing jobs to your district. What a feather in your cap in your first congressional term!"

"All right, Mr. Zuo." Janelle smothered her skepticism. She'll give these strangers the benefit of the doubt. "What do you have in mind?"

A satisfied smile crossed his face, raising her hackles high. Well, she only agreed to hear them out.

"We intend to construct a new technology liaison office on federal land just south of the San Francisco Airport, with the intent of accelerating shared research and intellectual property transfers. Your Environmental Protection Agency requires a detailed analysis even of a non-manufacturing facility. Since this land falls within your district, we ask your help in expediting their review so we can advance with our plans."

"I don't inject myself into ongoing proceedings." Janelle raised a hand. "There is a reason the EPA exists. If they require more time, I support them."

Zuo stepped closer. "I can add to our land purchase an amount equivalent to one appropriate for a residence," he said in a low voice. "My real estate agent informs me it is a simple matter to swap ownership of one piece of land for another." He straightened his shoulders, chin notched high. "We would be happy to offer you a more suitable home than your current townhouse, matching your esteemed stature in the community."

Her jaw dropped. She darted a glance at Barbara, and met only sparkling eyes and quiet determination.

"This can't possibly be legal," Janelle said.

"Oh, my dear, you do have a lot to learn." Barbara laughed, placing her hand on Janelle's arm and squeezing a bit too hard. "Trust me, the Ethics Committee signs off on deals such as these all the time." She turned to Zuo. "Please budget street improvements for her new neighbors, too."

"No new house, no favors, and no deal." Temper firing, Janelle freed her arm from Janelle's lingering grip. "I do not accept gifts at all. From anyone. For anything. Got it?" She glared at Barbara.

"We'll talk more later, gentlemen. I'm sure we can find another suitable location for your business." Barbara's color rose, but she still managed her trademark smile. "Would you please excuse us?" She hustled Jannelle to a quiet corner.

"Are you a complete fool?" Barbara's blue eyes blazened into hers. "The economy needs those jobs, and you need to bring the bacon home to your district! Got it?"

Janelle drew herself up to her full, intimidating height.

"Barbara, no matter how many times you throw temptations at me, I'll refuse. So don't waste your time or mine again. Got it?"

So what if her voice carried? Let the whole world hear she kept an ethical standard. Politicians didn't have to become corrupt the minute they swore their oath of office.

"You just kissed your plum committee positions goodbye," Barbara hissed.

The threat gave Janelle pause. How would she uncover the truth about China's detention programs relegated to a back seat? Let alone help people struggling daily for their freedom.

"Only if you dare disclose the reason. I can detail this little bribe-fest to eager reporters." Janelle shrugged with feigned nonchalance and turned to leave. Meeting her colleagues' disapproving stares, she felt only sadness for her chosen profession.

Janelle hailed a taxi and crawled inside, her mind in turmoil. How could she have been so naïve? Trading favors was Washington's favorite past time. She couldn't escape unscathed. Barbara would make good on her threat in a matter of weeks—or days.

Not before she dealt with this alteration of public records, she vowed. That went beyond the pale of a simple hack attack. Someone was shielding the American public from the truth of Chinese dissidence.

She glimpsed the Pentagon's walls in the distance, reminding her to read the briefings for tomorrow's top-secret committee meeting on military technology. Last month, they discussed readiness in the face of a possible rare metals shortage. Did the top brass realize the legislators holding their purse strings bought and sold favors with the Chinese? Would the military just roll over to procure the supplies they need, or take a principled stand so China couldn't control America's future?

China's military spending increased dramatically this past year, consistent with their quest to become a great power. The U.S. risked falling further behind every day. What would happen if China played hardball? With U.S. defense contractors now relying on China's processing of the key metals needed for new, sophisticated hardware, would America have any choices left?

Last week's conversation with Dad ran through her mind again. His voice had been gruffer than usual. It pained him so to see the country he loved in such a quandary, but she didn't see how a freshman congresswoman could make much difference.

Even with his help getting her on key committees, she still sat at the end of the rows and received vital briefings last. What else could she do within the ethical standards she set?

Chapter 22

PANVISION TECHNOLOGIES

Cupertino, California
Early Morning, April 2, Next Day

"I gotta tell you, Eric, I'm kinda uncomfortable letting these military guys get their hands on my software." Alex Tran squirmed in his favorite rickety chair, tucking his phone under his jaw and studying the huge monitor framed against the closed window blinds. "Are you sure I should pursue this direction?"

"Your software is so far advanced, the military will pay top dollar for two years of exclusivity." Eric Coleman's reassuring tones mixed with his baby's soft cooing over the phone line. "That will buy you time to ramp up staff for a broad commercial launch without having the other VCs sniffing around and pushing you for a premature IPO. Isn't this what you intended?"

"Well, yeah, eventually, I'd like . . ." Alex trailed off, unwilling to admit his fear to such a top-notch advisor and initial investor. With Eric and Lynn's guidance, he stayed happily obscure, focusing all his attention on developing his software and buying the tech tools he needed. His business flew under the radar of other high-flying Silicon Valley tech start-ups who vied for media attention through designer offices and on-site playgrounds.

"I imagined private security companies would buy my software," Alex continued. "The federal government will take forever to decide. Jeez, it took them weeks to execute the NDA." He didn't have enough fingers and toes to count the number of horror stories about start-ups dying a slow death after chasing a big government contract.

"The military can procure advanced technology quickly if it fills a demand. DARPA funded my software after one meeting." A loud burp erupted. Eric cursed. "Honey, try not to spit up on Daddy's tie, okay?"

"Will I be expected to sign any contracts at today's meeting?" Alex inquired. Eric went to great lengths inviting these Department of Defense experts to Silicon Valley for the sole purpose of examining Alex's technology, including negotiating his use of top-secret surveillance images for this demonstration. Alex didn't dare jeopardize Eric's reputation within that tight-knit community. Eric had gone to bat already three times when discrimination against Alex's Vietnamese heritage blocked security clearances, despite his being born in California and raised a patriotic American citizen.

"Of course not. Besides, I'll keep those attack dogs at bay." Eric chuckled. "What's made you so uptight? Usually you can't wait to show off."

"I'm nervous about this next step." Alex toed the old desk's vanity panel with his sneaker, knocking away more of the aging veneer strips. "My parents and teachers warned me the military only uses advanced technology to kill people. I'm uncomfortable enabling weapons . . . I don't want anyone hurt."

Years of his parents' fears about the military pressed down on Alex. They'd fled Saigon's fall, pledging their loyalty and hard work to America. The terror of Viet Cong ransacking their village still gave them nightmares. Having spent their youth embroiled in war, they sought only peace and quiet for their growing American family—and a healthy distance from government authority. Alex still didn't dare tell them a VC funded him—a Venture Capitalist, not a Viet Cong.

"Hang on a sec." A rustling noise filled Alex's ear. "Take her, Lynn," Eric murmured.

Alex heard the soft click of a door latch, then Eric's rhythmic footsteps ringing in his usual pacing cadence.

"You know, Alex, we protect more civilians with technology than ever get killed, including providing tons of aid after natural disasters. These days we can target specific bad guys instead of using indiscriminate weapons from the last century. DARPA needs to visit. You can help them accurately identify terrorists. Trust me, they don't seek power to launch a third World War."

Perhaps Eric was right. Perhaps better technology could create a brighter, more peaceful future. Maybe he could even prevent wars with his breakthroughs.

It wouldn't hurt to tie into the hacking community a little more, though, and see what it was up to. Between the hobbyist hackers tackling firewalls in a game of one-upmanship and the professional hackers who invaded privacy to sell their findings to the highest bidder, the virtual cloud's promise created more opportunities than they could exploit.

"I promise to be open-minded, Eric. You've never given me bad advice."

"That's the spirit. Have you run a beta test yet?" Eric's tones carried a touch of atypical anxiety. Alex could picture him scratching his jaw in worry. "I specifically requested you get all recent surveillance files covering the mining regions in Inner Mongolia and the greater Beijing region."

Alex stared at the folder name with the downloaded images. *As soon as I open this confidential file, my NDA kicks in and I commit to considering military uses for my software.*

Taking a deep breath, Alex pressed the key. His screen flickered to life.

"Starting it now." Alex leaned back in his chair and nervously gulped cold coffee. "I'll run my program to compare all the SDS security and personnel facial images with the DOD's, right?" He wondered how routine Chinese surveillance files landed in U.S. hands. Eric's friends sure must be high up the national security chain of command.

"Yeah. It's a long shot, but if you can track down Kay Chiang in Beijing through your high-powered extrapolation algorithm, our visitors will kiss your feet," Eric said. "This rare metals issue really has our military in a quandary. They can't push China to release what we need, which has huge implications for our future weapons systems. They want to talk to Kay ASAP."

"I'm confused." Alex scratched his forehead. "Why can't they just call Kay and ask her?"

No answer.

Higher security clearance than his—of course.

"Sorry, I wasn't thinking," Alex muttered. "Don't tell me. I'll call you if I find anything, okay?"

"I'll keep my fingers crossed. Talk to you later." Dead silence filled his ear.

Alex scooted close to his monitor, scrubbing the thick bristles standing straight up from his head. If finding Kay Chiang was his assignment, he would pass with top marks.

He remembered Kay from the moment he met her at SDS—what male wouldn't? She filled his teenage dreams with vivid sexual fantasy. SDS engineers teased him about his infatuation, yet admitted they sported hard-ons for her, too. It would be so easy to scan for her unique facial features and body image—they were burned onto the back of his eyelids. His software went orders of magnitude beyond any other used today in deciphering discriminating details.

Pulling up his proprietary program, he integrated the SDS database with the government-provided imagery, pushed a button and let his invention do its magic, beginning with drone shots from barren Inner Mongolia. Maybe later he'll catch Kay in the middle of doing the dirty dance with a lover on the streets of Beijing. He imagined her ivory skin exposed to the sunshine, long, slender legs spread wide, and arms reaching in invitation.

Lost in erotic dreams, he almost missed the incessant BEEP alert. Alex stopped the program, frowning at the glitch. Beijing's matching images shouldn't occur until more than halfway through the file.

He squinted at the digital imagery. Green figures with dots indicating potential matches didn't tell him much. His fingers flew, enhancing the conversion file, impatient for a close-up of his fantasy woman.

The first image appeared. He gasped, unable to tear his eyes from the screen. He slowed the speed to slow motion, grasping its horrible implications. Jaw dropping, his fingers reached toward Kay's image of their own volition. Could he help her? This file was days old. What dangers did she still face?

Grabbing his phone, he punched re-dial.

"Come quick," he barked at Eric. "I found Kay. And she's not in Beijing anymore."

Chapter 23

BAOTOU JAIL

Inner Mongolia, China
Late Afternoon, April 5, 3 Days Later

The key grated in the lock, its harsh scrape better than a watchdog. Kay bolted upright and hugged her coarse tunic against her torso. She couldn't stop shivering.

This time it wasn't from the frigid cold.

The guard motioned impatiently to exit her tiny cell which, in comparison to what awaited her outside, seemed safe and secure. She rose with as much grace as she could muster and met her guard's gaze with contempt. His grinning leer resembled a two-toothed beaver.

Grabbing her arm, he propelled her into the late afternoon glare. Her bare feet stubbed the uneven stones. She said a silent farewell to the last of her pedicure. As they rounded the corner, he shoved her so hard she stumbled to her knees.

Hoots and jeers in various Chinese accents greeted her ignominious entrance, the usual beginning of the garden's grim gauntlet.

"Perfect position for a whore!" yelled an off-duty guard.

"I will treat her like the dirtiest dog she is."

Kay whipped up her head and speared the youngest with a glare. She tucked into a squat. Her blood pounded in her throat, faster and harder with each heartbeat. She eyed the far door and planned her circuitous path.

"No, no, I intend this whore to suck my cock." A hulking brute, the senior guard stepped into her vision and widened his stance.

"In your dreams," she mumbled, wiping the sweat beading her upper lip.

With a deep breath, she darted forward and swiveled hard to her right, ducking under the wooden table and diving out the other side. She ran past a line of grabby hands copping a feel of breast or ass. Yanking her worn garment free, she confronted her final obstacle. His fly was open, his hand aimed his erection at her like a weapon.

Pretending to cower, Kay let her legs buckle and wobble.

"Hey, boys, she's kowtowing to her boss!" A satisfied chuckle belched from his mouth. "Who claims her after I'm done?"

A clamor erupted. She sensed the crowd of twenty-plus men pressing closer, waiting for a peep show and their turn. Now or never.

She dove forward and slid between his spread legs. Pivoting, she placed a hard kick exactly where it would do the most harm. He howled and clamped his knees together. Scrabbling backward, she cleared the space beneath him. With a whimper, he dropped. His forehead hit the stones with a thud. The men roared with laughter.

Jumping to her feet, she slapped her hands in satisfaction. Who cared that today's gauntlet was more difficult than yesterday's? She'd won again. If she kept outsmarting them, she would be safe.

Knocking on the closed door with false briskness, she threw her shoulders back and wrapped cold fingers around the knob.

"Enter!" The brisk order penetrated the metal door.

Kay twisted her wrist and slid inside, shutting the door behind her. A thin beam of sunlight spilled through the high, narrow window and onto a lop-sided stack of papers piled on the steel desk. The feeble rays couldn't dispel all the shadows flickering over the features of the office's occupant.

Harsh lines bracketed his mouth. Determined eyes reflected that last stage of bitterness when the soul's only purpose was to rot—when the thin veneer of order-taking and -giving filled daylight hours, and screaming nightmares filled the inky darkness.

Warden Deng, jailer from hell.

For the last week, he hauled Kay in whenever he wished, day or night. Each time he interrogated her endlessly about what she knew, who she knew, why she was here.

If she only knew.

Accused of treason and espionage, yet no formal charges were filed. She lived in a convenient, indeterminate state of detention, with no legal recourse to dispute her custody.

"Do you have an answer for me?" He rounded the desk and bellied next to her. She gagged at his garlic breath. Pressing her lips tight, she forced the bile down and notched her chin up.

Kay met his gaze not two inches from her own. One of these days he wouldn't let her open the door, and she would be gang raped while he listened. But not today. Today, intimidation still fascinated him.

"Bah!" He grabbed a piece of paper off his desk and jammed it under her nose. "This says you are Wei Jintao's whore and suggests I treat you well. Do you think I care about his stupid order?"

Hope flickered in her chest.

"Warden Deng," she began, dropping her eyes and painting on a demure expression. "Perhaps your reputation would be greatly enhanced if you claimed Wei Jintao's whore for yourself. Your men would understand why you granted me special treatment, yes?"

"Hmph." He studied the paper again. "There are rumors Wei Jintao is infected with the AIDS disease. Why would I risk fucking a sick whore?"

AIDS! God, what else could go wrong? She considered and tossed aside possible strategies like a woman shopping for the perfect shoes.

"You don't have to touch me." Was she reassuring him—or herself? "We could pretend you do. I could corroborate your story in return for, let's say, two hours a day outside? It is so beautiful in the springtime. I only wish to see a little bit of blue sky, and smell the fresh air."

"And then you would come willingly?"

Kay laughed inside at the irony of that word's English translation. Orgasms were ancient news. She only craved survival. And this little taste of freedom outdoors might have to last for many years—if she lived.

"Yes, Warden. I will let all the others know I am your woman now, and you are a better lover than Wei Jintao."

Warden Deng grabbed her hair and jerked her head to the side, hard. Neck aching, eyes stinging, Kay met his gaze . . . and winked.

"Bah!" He threw her aside. She banged her hip on the desk, struggling to stay upright. "You will not speak to others. I will tell them what they require. Behave. Otherwise, no tie to Wei Jintao will help you. A sick old man's reach does not extend to Mongolia."

He pulled open the door and thrust her through, glaring at the lingering guards wearing hopeful expressions. Warden Deng scowled and crossed his arms across his chest. They scattered like cockroaches. Kay glanced back, wondering what he expected of her.

"Go. Dig in the dirt as a diseased, washed-up whore should." He shoved her in the opposite direction, to the courtyard's far edge where the inmates tried to grow any kind of food to supplement their scarce provisions.

The warden's words stung with the truth. What good did all her looks and flirtatiousness do her, jailed in Mongolia? She couldn't even parlay her sexuality for favors. Wei Jintao's ostensible protection came with a damning price to her health.

If sex was power, she just lost the war. Completely.

Staring at the early twilight sky, she faced facts. She was a washed-up whore. And if she didn't want to die here, she'd better change. Now. No more using sexuality as a tool. She'd better use her brains and figure a way out—fast.

I'll be lucky to escape with the skin on my back.

· · · · · ·

Warden Deng must have believed her ruse would work to enhance his stature, Kay mused the next morning. Otherwise, why would he let her come outside again so soon? She shrugged, intending to enjoy whatever moments of peace she—and Wei Jintao—had negotiated.

Sunshine warming her shoulders, Kay studied a particularly tenacious plant pushing upward between two stones. Twisted and deformed, it epitomized a unique defiance and triumph, growing and re-growing from a thick, callous root toward life-giving sunshine.

Was she rooted deep enough to get back what she valued most? She had become a random risk-taker. Sheer chutzpah, not mettle. Wasn't real courage acting on one's convictions, like Yannan? When had lies become her currency, rather than truth?

When she lost the courage to face life's consequences.

She was a coward.

No more! Damn it, if a lowly weed could survive Inner Mongolia, so could she.

So she screwed up her health and life—and mission. She couldn't turn back the clock. She'd have to deal with it. And stop counting on men. Even Paul.

"Is your name Kay?"

The low whisper came over her shoulder. Bare feet shuffled to the right. A dropped hand beckoned. The sole guard assigned to watch the privileged prisoners pissed against the far wall, his back turned. She sprang to her feet, keeping low, and ducked behind a thick rosemary bush leading to the cellblocks. The wonderfully aromatic smell contrasted with her horrible surroundings.

"Yes, I am Kay. Who asks?" Suspicious, she studied her fellow prisoner. His swollen cheek dominated otherwise average Chinese features. A purplish tinge on top of a fading yellow bruise ran from his jaw to his brow. Disheveled black hair swept his filthy neck and spilled over a ragged tunic identical to hers. The young man's eyes reflected intelligence and curiosity.

And wariness.

"Li Ying," he whispered, peering through the bush.

"You're Li?" Frannie's bright face flashed in front of Kay like a beacon, the distant echo of their joyful laughter seeming to float in the breeze.

"Charlie Wilkins told me about you, and I heard your name when you arrived. Do you know if my daughter is safe?"

"Well, yes. Fran still attends school."

"Thank God she's not in a jail." Li's shoulders sagged. "The government will probably only force her and Yannan to publicly denounce me."

Kay hesitated delivering the bad news. But wouldn't she crave the truth in his position?

"Actually, Yannan is under house arrest because of an article she wrote denouncing the forced relocation of Inner Mongolian natives," she said.

"She never could keep her opinions to herself." Li grimaced, watching the distant guard.

"Apparently, you share the trait." Kay couldn't keep the tart tone from her voice. This man had put his precious daughter at risk. "What are you charged with?"

"Betraying my country." Antagonism wreathed his face. "I love my strong, loyal Chinese people. I don't love corrupt leadership, nor the lies they perpetuate to keep us in lockstep." He pointed at the surrounding walls. "They promised us freedom, yet still cage us with their politics. Their economic jail might be larger, the food better, the clothes finer. But still, we cannot think for ourselves or believe what we wish."

He pounded his thigh. "Our current leaders are bent on destroying the lands and people of Inner Mongolia for a pointless dream of world domination through monopoly pricing of the world's rare metals. Didn't they learn the lessons from the 20th century? Those seeking ultimate power will soon lose it through war."

"Perhaps." Kay cocked her head, considering. "They also learned economic power can supersede military power. And they rely on ancient methods of negotiation—distract, deny, and defend by accusing your foe. If rare metals become the new currency, and China controls the output, they will win economically and, eventually, militarily."

"I can stop that!"

"How?" Kay tilted her head forward, eyes locked on the guard who scanned the yard. Charlie was dead because he discovered Li's secret. Did she want Li to answer? She couldn't do much with the intelligence in here anyway.

"Tomorrow," he breathed and crept away, motioning her in the opposite direction. Kay wriggled back to the garden bed on her butt. Maybe the guard wouldn't notice the imperceptible inches she covered with each pivot.

Almost there. Her struggling weed danced in the stiff breeze. Exhaling in relief, she wiped away excess dirt weighing down its stem. If she gave it a chance to grow straight, it—

Thunk.

A cruel boot crushed the weed . . . and her fingers. Pain shot the length of her arm to her brain.

"The Warden's whore only talks to him." The menacing growl accompanied a twisting motion by the guard's heel, pushing her fingers deeper into the loose earth. The weed broke in two, its root trapped in the soil again, its length decimated.

Grabbing her hair, he yanked her upwards, stretching her into an impossible angle. She muffled a yelp of pain and tangled her legs with his so he staggered, freeing her fingers. Scrambling to get her feet underneath, she rose, fighting back the urge to slug him. He wielded the power now, not her. Different time, different place.

"You have broken the rules. Warden Deng says you must be punished." He wrapped her hair around his wrist and forced her to her knees. He slapped her face. Hard. Again.

Her lip split open. Bitter blood coated her tongue. Whimpering, she grabbed his wrists with her hands.

"No more, please. I'll be good." She twisted her face and forced out tears. "Please don't hurt me."

Surprise crossed the guard's features, replaced by weary cynicism. "I have my orders."

Motioning another guard into his position, he hauled her to her feet and shoved her, bent double, through the concrete building's menacing doorway.

Twenty-three paces to reach her cell. Kay's brain worked in time to their hurrying footsteps. What could she offer for her safety? How could she bargain? Had reassuring Li used all Wei Jintao's protection?

They took an unexpected left turn, to an unfamiliar, large courtyard. Deng's dark silhouette lurked across the open space, elongated and threatening. She shivered, aware of her fragile humanity. Blood dripped on her chin. She licked it, relishing its warm saltiness. Proof her heart still pumped. For now.

She twisted in an acrobatic motion and managed to free enough of her hair to stand upright, ignoring agonizing pain shooting from her scalp. She met the warden's angry eyes, and squared her shoulders. Daring him to mete out his worst punishment.

Wielding a heavy knife, he waved the guard toward the sturdy square table in the middle of the courtyard. Metal manacles fastened with heavy chains graced each leg. Stains mottled the gravel in ominous patterns of pain and grief.

With an abrupt move, the warden grabbed her calves and snapped locks about her ankles. Shoving her to sit on the tabletop, the guard pushed her shoulders down and handily took care of her wrists in the same manner.

"Leave us." Warden Deng's raspy voice carried heavy overtones of anticipation. Kay closed her eyes for a long moment. A loud buzz caught her attention, and she opened them, searching for one last, brief glimpse of a bee roaming free. Or did she seek guidance from heaven? Yeah, right.

"Look at me!" His thundered command made her flinch. She twisted her head to the right. He tossed the weapon between his hands, his gaze raking the length of her body. He stepped between her legs and ran the knife up the outer pants seam to her waist. The threadbare fabric fell away, exposing her to the cold air. She shivered and locked her eyes with his.

Reaching forward, he slashed more fabric from her waist to her neck, nicking her throat's soft flesh. She prayed for a quick end. Wasn't that better than dying of AIDS in this forsaken prison?

No! She'll do whatever he goddamn demanded. As long as she lived.

"Warden Deng," she gasped, twisting her neck high. "You don't need to get infected with my disease. Let me pleasure you a safe way instead."

"Wei Jintao is a sly fox, notorious for spreading false stories to get his way." He yanked open her tunic and ogled her nakedness. "You must offer paradise between your legs for such a powerful man to lose face. I will find out for myself."

Payback is such a bitch.

She stared over his shoulder and spied the guards crowding the doorway . . . gawking, fascinated, eager. She cringed and tugged against her restraints.

Deng circled the table, resting the knife on her throat, a cold, wide pressure on her collarbone. A graze along her shoulder. A thin narrow blade beside her jawbone. He pivoted it with expert skill, drawing it up her cheeks with a lover's caress. It rubbed her hairline.

With a quick twist of his wrist, he flicked it beneath the heavy mane, shaving her nape. Tiny hairs released from her skin. Kay squeezed her eyes shut, imagining the coming, fatal slice.

He parted her hair with the knife like a comb. He stroked above her ear. A soft slither of loose tendrils slipped over her shoulder.

"You disobeyed my orders." He crooned in her ear. Repeating the gesture on the other side, she shivered. The unexpected, sensuous *tête-à-tête* warmed her.

Grasping her hair at the crown, he pulled her head back . . . back. Her hips lifted from the table, shoulders jammed against the wood. As her throat convulsed, she grasped for air. Desperate, she clutched the ends of her locks, reveling in their silky smoothness one last time.

He raised his hand high, eyes flickering across the distance, squinting and measuring. With a slicing motion, his hand dropped.

Chapter 24

PANVISION TECHNOLOGIES

Cupertino, California
Noon, April 6, Next Day

Paul blew on piping hot coffee as he made his way toward borrowed space, not even large enough to earn the label of an office. As soon as young Alex Tran had received the next batch of surveillance video, he and Eric raced to join him here in case these new files contained more images of Kay.

He prayed no more gauntlets. He couldn't sleep with that nightmarish vision pounding in his mind. And even though it was already noon, his brain refused to boot up until he had a few gulps down his throat.

Stepping through the open doorway, he set his favorite mug down on the listing tabletop crowded with reference books. He dropped into the plastic chair and opened his laptop. Punching its power button, he tapped his foot. Too bad he couldn't pour high-octane caffeine into its guts to get it moving faster, too.

Finally . . . an email from Carmen Mostiacelli's personal account. For the last three days, he begged her for any official news on Kay. Clicking it open, he scanned the brief words.

KC listed as MIA, no longer on current roster. Sorry.

Sorry. An inadequate word to a person who cared. The government fell short protecting those serving in foreign lands.

Don't go there.

Paul focused on the next set of emails, searching for another clue, another tool he could use to rescue Kay. Another way to pilfer images from official Chinese surveillance cameras populating the cloud. Anything to move the clock back four days.

His mind rewound the haunting images from Alex's huge monitor, her prison's idea of fun and games. Inner Mongolia appeared as forbidding and remote as the joke said—nowhere anyone in his right mind would choose to go.

Searching recent satellite imagery, he tried to pinpoint her exact position. Deep mines gouged the earth. Trucks barreled through barren terrain and onto the main highway. Refugees clustered too near lakes filled with toxic side-products of refining processes. According to his research, the poisons damaged the land for generations.

Clicking open another email, he prayed the VC community found alternative sources of refined metals, so at least he could eliminate part of his stress. Nothing. And DOD Tech had no breakthroughs, either. So much for their boasts.

Paul's chest tightened. China's embargo of purified rare metals to Japan remained in place. Despite scrambling to stockpile critical components, in only days the U.S. military might be forced to capitulate from a position of weakness—for the entire world to see—by negotiating high-end technology from China on their terms, not ours. Whatever they might be.

Assuming they negotiated, of course. If that happened, China would be poised with better military might . . . and no form of bargaining might appeal to them. Not when they commandeered the catbird's seat.

Shit.

Jumping up, he hurried to the break room and refilled his coffee mug. Tina's laughing features couldn't relax him this morning. She'll be his full responsibility soon. He remembered his meeting with the Chiangs and his heart sank. What did he know about teenagers? Would placing boundaries on Tina's independent streak create a next-generation Kay?

He stared at the vending machine. It took him ten minutes to choose between regular or nut-filled chocolate candy. How could he help anyone else?

Colonel DuMont's scowling face appeared in his mind's eye, questioning whether he still had the backbone for battle. Well? Did he?

He'll stick by Alex's side for answers. Alex poked around daily for new video on TOR, the informal website for dissidents and conspiracy theorists. He decrypted and enhanced both official and unofficial images, including those hidden within family pictures attached to innocuous emails. Their best lead came from surveillance video smuggled out of China in those encrypted files.

"Paul! Get in here—quick!" The intercom amplified the urgency coloring Eric's voice.

Paul dashed down the hall to Alex's office. A series of monitors displayed today's image haul.

"Is that Kay?" he croaked. Stepping close to the largest screen, he placed his hands on his knees and squinted. "Dammit!" He dug out his glasses and slammed them onto his nose.

"I think so." Alex circled the mouse pointer around the central image. "I put out a request to the underground hacker groups in Inner Mongolia to send drones with tiny cameras over this prison. They sent files from yesterday's foray. It . . . It looks like her . . . doesn't it?"

"Unfortunately, yes." Eric said, his hand anchored onto Paul's shoulder.

Garish figures with a greenish tinge moved across the screen, their actions clearer than their visages. A woman, clothes hanging in tatters off her slender frame, shackled to a small table. Long hair held tight by a large man brandishing a knife to her throat. She didn't seem to resist. Had she fainted? Been knocked unconscious?

Dead?

The jailer raised his knife high and plunged.

"No!" Paul jerked his head back.

Alex's body twitched. Eric's hand on Paul's shoulder tightened into a vice grip.

A cascade of green hair swirled to the ground. The knife hacked the sides and top. An uneven crown appeared.

"She's okay!" Alex exhaled.

Dropping the knife, the jailer circled the table, inspecting his handiwork. Waving his hand at something off the screen, he moved between her legs, lowering his pants to his knees.

The image wavered, shimmered, and became a rhythmic blur.

"Get her back!" Paul grabbed Alex's shoulders and shook them.

Eric restrained Paul with a tight bear hug and held on. "Calm down. Alex can only enhance whatever image we can get our hands on. That's all the video footage we've got."

"We can't wait! Can't you see the danger she's in?"

"Of course I can." Eric's calm demeanor was driving Paul nuts. "Do you see he didn't take the chance to kill her? There must be a reason," Eric pointed out.

"What? He thinks she's cute?" Paul threw off Eric's grip and spun around. "Gonna be the mother of his next child? Who are you kidding?"

"Maybe I can find out." Alex's subdued voice drifted between them.

Paul whirled on him. "How?"

"More smuggled surveillance footage from Beijing." Alex's fingers slapped the keyboard. "I identified Kay with a young girl and another woman in Tiananmen Square and tracked them to their various addresses. Kay lived in a swanky apartment high-rise, and the other two live in a flat near the river. I already sent search bots out over the Internet to find the addresses and their names. Let's see if they found anything."

"Give Alex time to work his magic." Eric nudged him into an empty chair.

Paul sucked in a deep breath, trying to shove back the images now seared onto his brain.

"I never should have let Hank force me out." Despair whipped through him. "DIA dropped her like a hot potato."

"Seriously?" Eric's voice hardened. "An American citizen is being harmed in a remote Mongolian prison and you're telling me our government isn't demanding her release?"

"Nope . . ." Paul's voice cracked as he cradled his head in his hands. "Not through official channels. Not with all this political posturing going on."

"Then it's time to work unofficial ones, isn't it? We can't wait forever for China's purified metals." Eric grabbed his cell phone and punched a number. "Don? Eric here. Who do you know who can move mountains in China?" He recounted what they'd seen, nodded twice, and scribbled notes on an empty pizza box. "Thanks. I'll be in touch."

Eric faced Paul. "Don will try to shake information loose from the FBI and get in touch with Janelle DuMont. She sits on the Congressional Executive Commission on China and may have pull with the State Department if Kay's been charged as a spy—or worse."

Paul remembered the last time he heard those words. How much worse could it get for Kay? He clenched his fists, helplessness battering his heart.

"In the meantime," Eric continued, "Lynn and I will network in Silicon Valley for non-governmental ways we can get her out. A few CEOs may step up and force this issue to a head, despite a potential hit to their stock price. Our manufacturing contracts are the backbone to China's economic success—the face of their pride in front of the whole world. If we threaten to shift the next generation of high-tech innovation to India or Brazil because of how China treats a U.S. citizen, we might just free her."

Eric's prosaic argument fell far short of comforting. He couldn't forget about the horrors Kay might be experiencing right this second. Screw this professional façade. He cared for her. Why, oh why, had she chosen this path?

Because he hid his feelings from her for years.

Guilt wrenched him tight. He leapt to his feet, pressured to move, to progress forward—not sit, watch and wait.

Not again.

The phone in his pocket jingled a notification. Paul glanced at the call log and moved the display back and forth.

"Does anyone know a monk in Tibet?" he frowned, studying the cryptic address on the email.

Eric and Alex turned, puzzlement lining their faces.

"It's from Kay." Paul skimmed the text and whistled. "She found out the name of Wilkins' last contact, an engineer named Li Ying. He has some rare metals secret worth killing for."

"Li . . . that's the same family name of the little girl Kay met with in Tiananmen!" Alex pounded keys and scrolled through his search results. "According to official notices, he was arrested as a traitor."

"He's gotta be at the center of all this," Paul declared. "Let's try muscling China back. The media loves to support Tibet. And maybe someone in Washington is already one step ahead of us."

Smart thinking, Kay. When outnumbered, pull in new allies.

Chapter 25

CHESAPEAKE CORNERS CONDOMINIUMS

Washington, D.C.
Midnight, April 14, 8 Days Later

Janelle slouched into her favorite armchair with a heavy sigh and powered on her laptop. Maybe she could get a head start on her emails instead of having to respond in the morning. Scanning the log of addresses, one jumped out at her.

Chinese characters filled the address box, but the subject line couldn't be clearer: Rare Earths Opportunity.

Wary of the usual scam, she clicked it open anyway.

Congresswoman DuMont: I am a neutral go-between representing a high-level Chinese government official. I request your help to grant political asylum to this person, caught in an untenable situation regarding China's official policies.

As proof of my client's position and influence, we disclose our Chinese hackers broke through the Congressional firewall and changed records in your database of our official prisoners. As a member of the appropriate committee, I trust you are aware of this recent security breach.

In return for political asylum, my client will carry to the U.S. a disk which contains breakthrough proprietary information on how other countries can purify rare earth elements to highly refined rare metals at the required level for industrial and military use.

Perhaps you now understand your opportunity.

If you are interested in such a trade, please reply to the same email server, account name Charlie Chan. You must keep all correspondence completely confidential. Otherwise, no deal.

Stunned, Janelle re-read the email—twice. Digging through her pile of papers, she found the recent brief on rare earths. Wind energy magnets, high-tech mobile devices, and precision imaging hardware for the military, all relied on one or more rare earth elements, purified to better than 99%. Only China could purify to that level. Dad had bent her ear about his take on China's intentions to monopolize this particular market, but she'd been skeptical.

If Dad was right, what Chinese politician in his right mind would throw away this opportunity to grow China's global power base and ask for asylum instead?

This was one big hoax. A loser in China's political pecking order desperate to escape?

Probably.

Could she afford to be wrong?

Better sleep on it. She always made better decisions in the morning.

Shaking her head, she dropped the entire report on the floor and slid her fingertips across the computer's screen, seeking distraction in her pet cause—putting a stop to human trafficking on the West Coast. Concerned constituents submitted a report describing a thriving underground network of cargo ships and border crossings. She added notes in the margin, questions to ask, witnesses to subpoena. Did the Immigration and Customs Enforcement Agency need additional funding?

A soft buzz rumbled from the depths of her purse. Her heart stuttered.

Her fingers found the smooth surface of her vibrating phone. She tapped the screen on the way to her ear, closing her eyes and praying that it wasn't another heart attack.

"Dad?" She held her breath, hoping he was still coherent.

"Uh, Ms. DuMont, this is Don Salazar, a friend of your Dad's. Is he all right?"

"I'm so sorry." Janelle heaved a sigh of relief. "I panic whenever the phone rings at this hour. Dad's fine. Thanks for asking."

"Any apology is mine, Ms. DuMont. I assumed I'd hit your voice mail, so it didn't matter the time difference. If you wish, I can call back tomorrow."

"No, I was working late anyway. What can I do for you, Mr. Salazar?"

"Call me Don. I'm following up on an email I sent regarding an American citizen jailed in Inner Mongolia. Did you determine whether valid charges are filed against her yet?"

That's how she remembered his name. Sara had vetted the email yesterday before passing it on to Janelle, confirming Don Salazar had indeed worked with Dad during his DARPA days.

Janelle grabbed the top-most page out of her URGENT folder, marked with a bright yellow paperclip just that morning. "I accessed the official prisoner database and couldn't find her name. Kay Chiang, right?" Her mind raced back to the other email from China. Maybe it wasn't a hoax.

"Correct. We last heard from her directly in early February. Current bootleg video images confirm she's a prisoner, all right."

Janelle tensed. Was she following someone else's playbook? Apparently, one Chinese official held the power to eliminate Kay Chiang's name to prove a point. And perhaps keep American outrage at bay.

"Are you positive it's her?"

"Absolutely. And if the pictures are correct, she's dealing with physical and possibly sexual abuse."

She cringed. "I didn't realize technology could give us such a clear picture yet."

"Silicon Valley has a lot of whiz-bang tools, including new ones perfect for the DOD if they ever get their priorities straight."

"Now you sound like Dad." She quirked her lips into a fond smile. "In any case, I believe you, no matter what official records show. Let me consult with my fellow committee members—"

"Not enough time," he interrupted. "In a couple of weeks, a joint trade mission visits Beijing, arranged by the Commerce Department for high-powered Silicon Valley political donors. Can you shake up the State Department and demand Ms. Chiang's return home with that delegation?"

"Hmm, good idea." If that email wasn't a fraud, she might need all the rare-earths-related attention moved away from her committee and onto the Executive Branch. "What do you think the official negotiating pressure should be to free her?"

"Why her name isn't on the supposedly official and complete database?"

"Unfortunately, both sides will deny it." Janelle squirmed at her unfamiliar duplicity. Kay Chiang must be someone special to warrant all this attention.

"Let me put it this way," Don said. "Either our diplomats or theirs will have some 'splaining to do if our bootleg imagery lands in the media's hands."

"Always the threat of media exposure."

"What can I say? It works."

"With American politicians. China still prevents most Western news from ever reaching their populace," Janelle said.

"Their Great Internet Firewall has chinks in it now, what with bloggers and YouTube posting in the cloud. However, you're correct. Our side responds to media pressure more than theirs."

Tapping her phone, she consulted her calendar. "I have a block of free time tomorrow afternoon. I'll camp on Secretary Akhras' doorstep to get an audience. I'll make it happen."

"Not to sound condescending, but you're a chip off the old block, aren't you?"

"Only sometimes." She laughed. "Other times we're in severe disagreement. However, I'm always glad to help one of Dad's warriors."

"Give him my regards next time you see him, please. And thank you, Ms. DuMont. You have no idea how much this means to a certain other warrior of your father's."

"Call me Janelle. And be forewarned, I intend to find out the details of this interesting prisoner soon. From you and Dad's other warrior." And whoever else came forward, even an anonymous Chinese official.

"His name is Paul Freeman, and he's quite private, Janelle. Maybe ask your Dad."

"Understood. And goodnight, Don."

"Goodnight."

Janelle dropped the phone into her lap, her mind whirling. That email was no joke. Kay Chiang's clandestine imprisonment must be linked to all this rare earths brinkmanship. Could she risk trusting a complete stranger to protect American interests? She'll be out on a limb, and in possible conflict with her party's backers and key endorsements for the next election cycle. Was it worth it?

Damn straight, girl. Whatever it takes to make it right. You swore a sacred oath.

"Thanks, Dad!" She took a deep breath and hit reply to the strange missive. Whatever it takes.

Chapter 26

COLEMAN RESIDENCE

San Jose, California
Early Afternoon, May 3, 19 Days Later

Paul pointed his finger right at Don's face, his cheeks on fire. "So now you're telling me I'm not even qualified to join a mission?" Thank goodness Lynn was off visiting her folks in Boulder, baby in tow. With an empty house, Eric invited the core group to his home for an in-depth discussion of the upcoming trade mission.

"You misunderstood." Lounging back on the sofa, Don ruffled Fred's long ears, shooting a considering glance Paul's way. "I said maybe, just maybe, all of our defense backgrounds might be a detriment to getting Kay out. Let the State Department do their jobs for once. They can do it."

"Yeah, right. They have such a sterling record." Paul wasn't about to apologize for his sarcastic cynicism. Not in this case. His last pang of loyalty to his former employer imploded. Damned if he worried about their hides—they wouldn't lift a finger for Kay's life. Was there pressure from inside the Beltway protecting the Pentagon cover-up?

"Janelle inherited her old man's uncanny ability of twisting arms and inflicting the most pain with a smile on her face." Don's expression reflected only admiration. "She's confident she'll pull Kay's butt out of the wringer this time."

"I don't trust bureaucrats," Paul muttered, slumping down next to Don. But at least Janelle inherited her Dad's brains, and included DuMont's Silicon Valley contacts as part of the larger effort to get a handle on China's motivations, ad-hoc though it was.

"Smart man," Eric said. "But we should have a member of our team join them just in case. They wouldn't suspect a civilian."

"Like who?" Paul asked. Eric had his fingers in all sorts of interesting pies these days, including shaking Silicon Valley's rare metals user community by its throat. Yesterday he'd even shouted down Victor Turtino at Snazzed Up! To date, no CEO dared risk tanking their stock's share price by quantifying the full impact of China's stranglehold on crucial raw materials. Eric claimed he backed off pressing Turtino for public disclosure—this time. Paul wondered how long until Eric pushed again.

"How about sending an up-and-coming entrepreneur with no official ties to any of this?" Eric nodded at Alex coming through the kitchen doorway balancing a jug of lemonade.

"Me?" Alex squeaked. Lemonade splashed over the edge of the frosted jug.

"Why not?" Don linked his fingers and flexed them until they cracked. "You stand in the background, observe and listen. And make sure they pull Kay Chiang out of there. You understand Chinese, right?"

Alex placed the jug on the table and dropped onto a chair, gripping his knees. "Yeah, my parents insisted I learn it so I couldn't be fooled by translators. But . . ." Unease settled on his young face.

"Spit it out, Alex." Paul leaned forward on his elbows, recognizing the dread Alex was trying to hide. He glimpsed it on his own face in the mirror too many times to count. "If there's a good reason you shouldn't join the team, tell us now."

The image of Ernie's pleading face insisting he creep down to the docks instead of Paul danced in front of his eyes. One instant of panic, then Ernie's callow features aged with grim determination. Paul thought he committed to memory only Ernie's grit, not the fear. Apparently, he'd failed even at that.

Alex drummed his fingers on the table. "Eric . . . um . . . do you think the other VCs funding my company are okay with this? I mean, they expect me to keep my nose clean so I can sell the technology to any government, including China. Could they pull my funding?"

"They'll probably plant a rumor you're already in negotiations with China and on a fast-track to international success." Eric grinned. "There's no risk of fallout if this comes up at the next board meeting."

Paul jumped to his feet and paced. How could he let another young kid go in his stead again? Alex's career and dreams could die because Paul couldn't work through the DIA to get Kay out. It wasn't fair—or right.

"It's really too bad Fred's final test for search-and-rescue K-9 certification conflicts," Don said. "Otherwise I'd go. But . . . life sometimes hands us lemons. Lemonade anyone?" He grabbed the jug and a glass and held them aloft, meeting each man's gaze with a determined glint in his eye.

Swallowing hard, Paul nodded and returned to his seat. Alex firmed his jaw and reached out a shaky hand.

"Janelle emailed this morning." Don handed out three glasses before taking a long sip of his own. "She searched the prisoner database again last night. Kay's listed now as a prisoner in Beijing, yet the formal charges are mysteriously blank—and her nationality changed to Taiwanese. She's bringing Kay's birth certificate with her, though who knows if the Chinese will accept that."

"It's a sign China responded to political pressure and settled into a negotiating posture." A satisfied smile wreathed Eric's face. "Otherwise they'd deny she was in their control."

"What are they negotiating?" Alex pivoted his head in a half-circle, looking confused.

"Refining rare earths again, what else? And Kay's life may be the price we pay." Paul grabbed hold of his wayward temper. "Eric, have the VCs freed any additional dollars for investment in either R&D or mining?"

Eric retrieved his cell phone and tapped the screen. He pointed his thumb up in victory. "Yes! New Age Capital committed five million dollars to Precious Metal Corp. Now they'll have cash to produce the prototype solution for gear using only a tenth as much rare metal, which gives us breathing room. We can buy what we need, have the Chinese think they're still starving us for key components, and have the ability to publicly announce the new funding in the future."

"Why wouldn't they announce it now?" Alex frowned.

"You've got a lot to learn, son." Don shook his head, chuckling. "Better study poker. The tricky part is appreciating when to bluff, and when to lay your cards on the table. Right now, China's moves are predictable. It's when we have to shake them loose and show our strength that we'll come out guns blazing. In the meantime, discretion is best."

Alex opened his mouth and snapped it shut. He opened it again. "I hacked around a bit and confirmed the little girl lives at Li's Beijing home address. I'm guessing she's his daughter or sister. And a female journalist is under house arrest there for treason. Who's she—her mother? Sister? Aunt? How did Kay tie into Li's family?"

"You probably don't want to know." Paul rubbed the back of his neck. "Kay always uses unorthodox tactics. I'm confident she was jailed up north in Inner Mongolia because of her connection to Li. Or at least to whatever intelligence she gathered on rare earths. All the politicians overseeing its supply and distribution live in that region. Someone figured out Kay's link and stuck her nearby."

"I got a buddy to translate a Chinese blog mentioning Li," Don said. "Li's a legend in metallurgical circles, both brilliant and eloquent, introducing radically new purification methodologies at mining conferences. He refused a government oversight post, preferring to work in the research labs and mines."

"Had to make enemies, snubbing a plum, official position." Eric tilted his glass in a half-salute.

"China's no different than the U.S." Paul jeered, thinking about DuMont's forced retirement.

"Yeah, well the journalist who wrote this particular blog mysteriously disappeared." Don pounded his fist into his palm. "For all their griping about bad press, our politicians still support freedom of speech."

"Unless it's not politically correct," Paul muttered. Or blows the whistle on the powerful. He blinked twice, regaining focus. "Let's assume Janelle gets Kay out of China."

"She's coming home, Paul." Eric's steady gaze met Paul's across the room. Paul grabbed it like a lifeline and held tight. He took a deep breath.

"We should shelter her from the media, the DIA, and any other outside interests," Paul continued. "Give her space."

"At least for a few days." Don nodded. "What do you suggest?"

"She'll stay with me." Paul made his voice firm, decisive. "I understand the shock and trauma of stress better than any of you. She'll be fighting mental demons. No debriefing until she's ready."

Don and Eric shared weighted glances. Losing the silent argument, Eric spoke first.

"Uh, Paul, the State Department is spearheading this rescue effort. Their friends at DIA will demand their piece of flesh for getting her out."

"Tough." Paul had it up to his eyebrows with the Feds. Hank Shaughnessy's utter disregard for Kay's safety and her critical intelligence tore him to pieces.

"Maybe Janelle can smooth the way," Alex said. "If she's Kay's official escort out, her decision should have the most clout, right?"

"You learn fast, kid." Don's voice was approving.

"And once we spirit her away to Paul's house, no one will find her," Eric said. "You might as well be a ghost, Paul, with no official address.

The redwoods should provide peace and tranquility. She deserves a chance to recuperate and feel safe again. Lord knows we don't have a sense of what she's handling."

"I do," Paul whispered. "Hell."

"I'll have Janelle remind anyone who gives her flack that Kay might have a type of PTSD." Don twisted his lips. "Swarms of reporters or intelligence agents could only worsen it—for everyone involved." He bowed his head toward Paul.

Paul squeezed Don's shoulder. "Thanks . . ." he choked out. "I owe you one."

"Don't thank me. You spilled your guts out for this country already. It's an honor to join your team this time."

"Same goes for me." Rising halfway, Eric stuck his hand out, giving Paul's a hearty shake.

"And me." Alex pulled his shoulders erect. "I'll do my best to keep Kay safe."

Paul's throat closed tight, blocking any attempts of verbal gratitude. He couldn't shake the fears still keeping him on edge. Distrusting everyone, including his team.

Except Kay's life and sanity were on the line.

Maybe sharing her intelligence could wait more than a few days. Let others step up and work on a resolution to the rare earths crisis. This female warrior deserved safety. And maybe, just maybe, they could re-acquaint themselves as a man and a woman, not simply teammates.

Chapter 27

WENG-HAN RESIDENCE

Inner Mongolia, China
Early Morning, May 17, 14 Days Later

Mai glared at her husband as he nonchalantly sipped tea and examined the vivid flowers gracing her favorite heirloom vase. He acted as if this was any routine morning. How could he be so stupid? Didn't he understand the Party just stripped away their power? She reined in her temper as her distinguished father taught. Descending from a family of mere miners, Yu earned his stature solely on the back of his engineering know-how as China raced into the fast-paced 21st century global economy. He still had much to learn of power's subtleties.

"My dear husband Yu, I am certain this niece of the traitor Chiang Kai-shek spied for the U.S. government." Taking a deep drag on her day's fourth cigarette, she clicked her fingernails on the tabletop. "We must inform our Party leaders someone erred in freeing her from prison."

"Do you think they'll admit any mistake?" Yu guffawed. "A person much higher in the Party than you made the decision, wife."

"Still under the oh-so Honorable Wei Jintao's thumb, no doubt." She blew out a plume of smoke. It rankled her that Wei quit his plum government post with the precise amount of pride and regret, earning him positive accolades and well wishes instead of recriminations for his accepting that American tramp into his bed and leaking state secrets. His hints at failing health must be a sham, but the gossip mill spun his version, not hers.

Yu settled his delicate teacup with great care onto the antique table and shook his head.

"Let it go." He sighed. "Your public reprimand allows our higher-ups to save face. Accept it with dignity, write your formal apology letter, and your record will soon be expunged."

"Wei's last official act protected Chiang Kay." Mai tamped out the cigarette with angry jabs. "Why am I the one punished with less power while he smiles and enjoys his plush apartment in Beijing?" She scowled. "Women deserve equal treatment in this country!"

"Don't do anything else you'll regret," he said. "See what happened when you tattled on Wei? You didn't follow the new procedures for whistleblowers—you spoke your mind to a low-level bureaucrat instead. Your disclosures benefitted him, not you. You merely handed him more power."

"At least I had the courage to speak out!" She winced at how shrewish she sounded. No wonder Yu either scolded or ignored her. But she was right about Chiang Kay, and must do her duty to protect the Party.

"They believed my report on the rebel journalist," she muttered, juggling alternative arguments one after the other as she dug for a new cigarette.

"Yes, you acted honorably. I commend you for providing information confirming the formal charges. Soon, she will join the other jailed writers spreading lies about our government's leaders." Yu stood, stretching his arms, and motioned to the maid for more tea.

Waiting for her to leave the room, Mai clicked her lighter shut and dropped the unlit cigarette. Yu preferred she not smoke. On this she could give if it meant winning him over.

"Husband Yu," she crooned, rising and stepping to his side. She brushed his back with the lightest touch. "Don't you agree Chiang Kay may still threaten our long-term strategy for control of the precious metals ripped from our soils by our hard-working miners?"

Yu flinched away and jammed his hands in his pockets. A frown crossed his placid features. "Yes, it's possible she learned of Li's novel approach for purifying the metals. Your plan to put them both in the same jail held promise when I believed we could extract the new purification process he's refused to share with us. What a fiasco instead!"

"I think . . ." she began with slow, deliberate enunciation, ". . . we must protect China's future economic and military might. We can bring the rest of the world to respect China again by controlling the output and price of all refined rare metals." She rapped her knuckles on the table. "The West relies on it for their high-tech products, energy generation and military gear. It keeps their economies booming. They think if consumers spend all their money on gadgets, their culture stays strong."

Mai smiled. "But you and I know better, don't we, old man? You and I comprehend exactly how valuable rare earths are, and how to control our output into the global marketplace . . ." She took a tiny step closer, leaning against his side to whisper in his ear, ". . . and how much Li can destroy China's negotiating power if anything topples the precarious balance we've achieved in the last two decades."

"What do you have in mind?" Yu stroked his chin, eyes focused on the Impressionist painting hanging between the far windows.

She allowed a brief moment of gloating. Since his recent promotion, he considered her a mere wife. He was no longer dependent on her family name and fortune to catapult him to the higher echelons of the political class. But she could resurrect her reputation before it was too late. Before her years caught up with her and she was forced to retire as gracefully as Wei Jintao.

Right now, as a powerful couple, they influenced all of Inner Mongolia—its resources, people and politicians.

"Let's use their values against them," she smiled with glee. "The Party has funded political campaigns in America for decades. This Congresswoman who demanded Chiang Kay's release—Janelle DuMont—let's exert pressure on her in exactly the right way to make her suspend America's new interest in investigating other supply options for rare earths."

"How will this secure our position?"

"If we can confirm we were right—that Li withholds vital secrets and Chiang Kay spied on us—we can deliver to our Party leaders critical leverage to bend America to our demands that they stop supplying arms to Taiwan. What better way to confirm a U.S. subversive policy supporting Taiwan's independence than by proving they used a Taiwanese agent within our borders?" She crowed the last with relief, the plan blooming in her mind. "The Party will thank us and re-assign us to Beijing."

"Wife, you dream of having all your errors in judgment revoked." He wagged his finger in her face. "Be realistic. The Party never admits mistakes."

"Hmph." She jerked back.

Yu's hands weren't pure, either. He should have broken Li's silence while overseeing his imprisonment. Yet Yu blamed all his failures on her. She heard rumors all older female political appointees would be replaced with the younger generation graduating from Peking University. The Party sought higher education and sophistication than what the children of Mao's revolutionaries had to offer. Did Yu also support this grand plan, even to his wife's detriment?

She grabbed her lighter off the table with nervous hands. Raising a fresh cigarette to her lips, she inhaled a long, deep drag. The nicotine delivered its usual calm.

Mai hated swallowing bitter pills. Action always worked best, no matter the consequences. *It is impossible to wrap fire with paper.* Right now, she was fire, and Yu . . . only inconsequential paper.

"I will take matters into my own hands—again—for our Motherland." She crossed one arm across her chest. "I will contact the right people in California, as well as apply new pressures on Li, demanding his cooperation."

"What pressures?" Yu shot her a suspicious glance.

"If jailing his wife's sister wasn't enough to shake him, perhaps taking his daughter from her safe home will."

"It is not honorable to harm family members." Yu twisted his chin upwards. "Only to force their public disownment of the traitor. She is still a little girl!"

Mai blew a smoke ring right in his face. She hated such cowardice.

"One child versus our country's future?" She curled her lip. "Thinking of your bastards, Yu? Hoping they would protect their father? They won't, you know."

Meeting her gaze with troubled eyes, he stared for long moments. His lips pressed together, and his cheeks faded to a pasty white. Shoulders slumping, he nodded his head.

"All right, old woman. We will follow your plan."

Chapter 28

SAN FRANCISCO AIRPORT

San Francisco, California
Evening, May 18, Next Day

The private jet glided through dense evening fog toward the metallic gleam of San Francisco Bay. Kay worried the dangerously close, choppy waves would lick the wheels clean before they hit the runway.

Where the heck was the blacktop? Any lower and they'll swim for shore. But at least it was American water, not cursed Chinese.

Ten feet over the edge and BAM. The jet rocked and rolled with its own roaring rhythm, brake thrusters on high.

"Glad to be home?" Janelle leaned over the wide armrest, her warm smile reassuring.

Home. Did Kay consider San Francisco her home? Or just her past? She didn't anticipate a paternal welcoming hug. Maybe her mother would squeeze her tight in private. She doubted her brothers cared at all, or frankly even knew of her imprisonment. Her mission had been hush-hush. And from what she gleaned, her rescue had been, too.

No, this was not home. Home should mean love and comfort and rest. At best, she earned a chance at the rest part.

Kay curled her lip. A rest home might be where she belonged. A virtual prison no different from the jail in China. What else to do with a diseased, washed-up whore than treat her as a leper? Kay blinked away sudden moisture and faced Janelle.

"Not really," Kay said. "Failed missions don't exactly earn a ticker-tape parade." She bit back the automatic apology for her unbridled comment. In America, she could speak the truth. Maybe Janelle appreciated honesty.

"You did not fail!" Janelle reared upright, sounding like a soccer mom scolding her kid. "You probably gathered priceless intelligence on rare earths." She drew a deep breath, darting a glance down the aisle at the half-dozen businessmen gathering their jackets and briefcases. "I shouldn't be telling you this, but you've earned the unvarnished truth," she said in hushed tones. "Japan is exploring ways to bolster their military preparedness because of China's posturing. They don't trust the U.S. to cover their asses anymore."

"I guess I missed some news cycles." Kay raised her brows. "Have we changed our official policy toward China as a result?" Maybe that would explain her unexpected rescue, and the tight-lipped silence of her fellow travelers.

Chagrin flashed across Janelle's features. "Too many Chinese tentacles attach to our economy . . . and politics . . . for such a big move." She stared out the window, giving the small terminal her undivided attention.

What wasn't Janelle saying? Dare she trust Janelle with all her secrets? She seemed compassionate enough.

Kay opened her mouth, readying herself for full disclosure.

"Excuse me, Ms. Chiang?" Alex's warbling voice brought a smile to her lips. Scrawny and nearly bald, she now resembled a waif swimming in Janelle's oversized clothing. Kay couldn't imagine how Alex could still be smitten. His sex goddess no longer existed.

However, she owed him for his help in rescuing her, despite her numbed state.

"Yes, Alex?" Kay twisted in her seat to face him.

"Will you need help with the stairs? They're a little steep and I noticed you didn't walk much during the flight." He cleared his reddening throat. "I'll lend you my arm if you want."

Her smile grew, the first genuine one in months.

"Thank you, Alex. I'll manage. And please, call me Kay." She hoped her despondency didn't taint him. She adored his Boy Scout manners and naïve outlook on life, proof good guys still existed.

He nodded and proceeded down the aisle. The business executives dipped their heads to her and Janelle in passing. She glimpsed the pilot and co-pilot busy in the cockpit. Kay had no idea how Janelle included her on this private jaunt but she was grateful.

She moved to unbuckle her seat belt. Janelle's hand restrained her.

"Kay, a word in private." The last passenger ducked through the exit and out of earshot.

"It occurred to me you may wish to see an American gynecologist soon." Janelle dug through an oversized shoulder bag, producing a business card and pen. "Better safe than sorry. My doctor understands better than most the cost of hard decisions for those in the public eye." She scribbled on the card and tucked it into Kay's pocket. "I'll ask her to see you at your convenience."

Kay relaxed a smidgen. She had dreaded arranging a confidential examination. Janelle's unsolicited offer confirmed the politician's sincerity and intuition. Maybe Janelle kept her own secrets too, yet overcame them. Kay never met a single woman so self-assured. Could a life not embroiled in men and sex provide such confidence?

She hoped she could achieve a similar state of contentment soon. Right now, a gaping hole substituted for emotion. As if she would never thaw from behind her icy façade. As if she would always be alone . . .

"Kay? Are you all right?" Janelle's concerned tones penetrated her worries. Shaking her head, she became aware of Janelle standing in the aisle, scarf wrapped snug around her neck and bag slung over one shoulder.

"I'm fine." Kay undid her seat belt and jumped to her feet. "When does our connecting flight to D.C. leave?" Maybe Paul would be glad to see her after he reamed her for breaking protocol. And before she quit her job—if she still had one. She hadn't talked to anyone in DIA since last November. Who knew what changes they might have made?

"Oh, gosh, I'm sorry." Janelle halted at the top of the stairs. "I totally forgot to tell you!"

Yep, here comes the bad news. Apologies galore and face the reality. No job, kicked out to the curb ASAP, no debriefing by Paul.

She ignored the surprising pang of regret. Why would Paul want anything to do with her?

"No problem, Janelle. I'll catch a cab to my parents' house." Assuming they'd allow her across the threshold.

"No, no." Janelle pointed at two distant figures hovering in the terminal doorway. "Paul Freeman has a great secluded home in the Saratoga hills. We've arranged for you to rest there before you're debriefed." She stopped halfway down the steps and turned back. "I should have asked you first. Is that all right?"

Kay's heart lightened. Staying with Paul? No groveling on her knees to her father? Perfect didn't begin to describe the arrangements.

"It's fine, Janelle." She clutched the handrail and descended the slick steps.

A brilliant smile lit Janelle's face, a beacon of hope in the miasma. Too bad Janelle still had idealistic stars in her eyes. Toughness and clear-sightedness would benefit the world more. Kay hoped once she started over they could become friends without compromising Janelle's career.

"I think Paul has family obligations, though." Janelle's grin widened, taking in the obvious argument between Paul and a teenage girl. His daughter? Kay ran the math. Yes, she's a teenager now. "Maybe you can advise him," Janelle chuckled

Peering through the mist, Kay watched Paul throw up his hands and stalk across the tarmac in their direction. The young girl slouched against the building, wriggling a gadget out of her pocket and staring at her palm. Did it hold solutions to her teenage woes? Maybe in a country guaranteeing freedom and a safe future. Where ugliness couldn't taint her. Unlike Frannie.

Paul stopped at the stair bottom and caught Kay's arm, steadying her.

"Hello, you must be Paul Freeman." Janelle's voice held a thread of amusement. "Are you sure you're ready for this extra responsibility?" She nodded toward the teenager. "Looks like you have your hands full."

"Nice to meet you and thank you for your concern, Congresswoman. I can handle it." His sharp voice contrasted with his anxious expression. He took in Kay's appearance, halting at her scarred head, suppressing any obvious shock. "How are you holding up, Kay?"

"How do you expect?" Kay injected all the disdain she could muster. Her bubble of happiness popped, as flat as days-old champagne. No way would she subject another pure young girl to her internal demons. Golden hair fell all the way to his daughter's waist, reminding her of a Barbie doll. And her promise to Frannie.

Kay couldn't handle watching another child's innocence stolen.

Paul's brows lifted to his matching blond curls, his cherubic features flustered.

"I . . . uh . . . I don't expect anything, Kay, to tell you the truth," he said. "Simply ascertaining what you might need before taking you home."

"I'm free to go where I want. This is my life, not yours. I've had enough of jailers for a while, thank you very much." She tore her arm loose.

"Let me try this in a language you understand, Ms. Chiang." Paul slammed his hands on his hips, his eyes narrowed to mere slits. "You don't have a choice. The U.S. State Department negotiated your release with the strict condition you stay in my custody until your debriefing. Only afterwards are you just another American citizen with the freedom to choose her life." He jutted his jaw. "Until then, you're mine."

His! Kay's temper spiked.

"I won't be any man's possession—including Uncle Sam's!" She fisted her hands on her hips in mocking imitation of Paul's belligerent stance.

"Kay?" Janelle took a step closer and dropped her mouth next to Kay's ear. "Remember our conversation on the plane? Any intelligence may prove valuable. However, we'll give you a chance to recover from your ordeal in private." She waved her hand at the deserted tarmac. "See? No media, no fuss. Please cooperate with us."

If anyone except Janelle asked, Kay would have replied with a snide remark. But the congresswoman made a good point. Janelle could have arrived at the airport a conquering hero, prisoner in tow, taking all the credit and glory in political brownie points on the way to a re-election bid.

No camera flashes blinded her. No throngs hounded her. Only the pilots hovered on the last step, waiting their turn to go home.

Home. Would she prefer to go to the loveless house in San Francisco, dumped off and forgotten? Or go with Paul where she might earn respect again? It seemed she deserved a rest home after all.

She took a deep breath of frosty air. "I'm all yours, Paul."

Chapter 29

FREEMAN RESIDENCE

Saratoga, California
Late Morning, May 25, 7 Days Later

Kay dug her fingers in the soft dirt, dropped the delicate roots deep into the soil, and patted the last transplant in place. Sinking back on her heels, she surveyed the short row of baby herbs. Would they survive or thrive in their strange new environment?

Would she?

Cocking her head to the side, she allowed the memories of the last time she gardened wash over her. Six weeks later, and still shuddering. Better to keep them buried. No matter how good it felt connecting with the earth again.

She sighed. Paul's protective cocoon would stunt her growth as surely as keeping a plant in too small a pot. She needed to put out new roots and establish her own home.

"Daddy, stop telling me what to wear! You're just like Mom." Tina's commanding whine carried through the open patio doors. Kay wondered what awful outfit she flaunted today. Worse than yesterday's horizontal-striped tights with tiny short-shorts?

A door slammed, muting the childish yells and Paul's frustrated baritone. Tina seesawed daily between adult wisdom and daring childish antics. Paul tried so hard to give Tina a reasonable amount of freedom, yet Tina still rebelled, always pushing for more. Reminding Kay of her teenage years.

Lord, she prayed Tina wouldn't make the same mistakes. Maybe she should pull her aside and give her a little woman-to-woman guidance.

Kay grabbed the watering can, welcoming the seedlings to their new home with a refreshing drink. She'd done little more than sleep and eat for the last week, finally releasing the festering anger and resentment. Paul didn't pressure her for information, even after her visit to Janelle's doctor.

Good thing. She needed more facts before she dared bring that topic up with him.

Setting the watering can onto the bench, she sensed eyes on her. She squinted against the morning glare and stared through the kitchen window. Sure enough, Paul stood at the sink, a somber expression on his face.

Too bad he looked worried instead of turned on. With rest, her hormones had revved back into high gear. Or was it because she hadn't been near him for so long?

Paul usually offered the equivalent of tough love. This week he acted uncertain instead. Maybe he regretted exposing her to his private life and difficult daughter. Well, too bad. He invited her here—she didn't ask. And she loved every minute.

She felt at home.

Disconcerted by the sudden revelation, she waved, forcing a carefree smile on her face. A flock of seagulls flapped overhead in mocking salute, breaking the serene silence with raucous cries to get on with her life.

"Is there a fresh pot of coffee?" she called, crossing the small plot of grass to the patio. Why bother asking? Paul was addicted to the stuff, even the leftover sludge. He always had some brewing.

He tipped the carafe high and poured her a large mugful, adding the cream she preferred. Expression intent, he carried it to the open door.

"What, no smile with the service?" She imitated Tina's grumpy smarminess.

Embarrassment flashed on his face.

"You heard, huh?" He passed the cup into her hands.

"Hard to miss," she admitted.

"She's growing up so fast." He pocketed his thumbs and leaned against the wall in a vertical patch of sunshine. "Too fast."

"At least you can watch it happen and steer her around life's potholes." She blew on the hot liquid and took a tentative sip.

"Speaking of potholes, do you know what she did this morning?"

"Hard telling. She keeps me guessing every day," Kay smiled.

"Ain't that the truth!" He heaved a dejected sigh. She had a fleeting urge to give him a hug.

Down girl! She ignored the familiar cascade of warmth. Would he feel the same rightness if she provided comfort instead of always taking it?

"So what'd she do this time?"

"I realize I shouldn't care, but . . . Jesus, Kay, she carries her passions too far."

"Which passion this time?"

"She slapped a Save the Ta-Ta's bumper sticker on my car!"

"Horrors." She took a long swallow, savoring the rich, bitter taste, and eyed his pained expression.

"Thanks for your support."

"Are you worried about your paint job or what Silicon Valley geeks might think of your Southern roots?"

"Neither. Both. No . . . I don't understand her! Why this? Why not something, well, normal?"

"Supporting breast cancer research is quite personal to her." She paused, tilting her head. "You're aware her friend Naomi's mother has breast cancer, aren't you?"

"Yeah, I listen to her. Now she daydreams about training for a fundraiser marathon in Atlanta, and she's hounding me to ask all my contacts for donations. When will it end?"

"With life . . . or death. As always."

Paul shot her an assessing look, opened his mouth, then snapped it shut. Three seconds passed. Her heart beat faster. She gripped the mug, dreading his inevitable grilling.

"Can you talk about it yet?" His gentle tone surprised her as much as the innocuous question.

What bug was up the DIA's ass to debrief her? Didn't she deserve some vacation time? Any critical information died with Charlie. She only chatted with Li once. The U.S. would have to figure out a new way to get their precious rare metals.

"No, I can't." Draining her coffee cup, she handed it back to him with a firm shake of her head.

"You know, if you want to quit the DIA, all you have to do is say so." Paul jostled the mug in his hands.

A surprising wave of relief weakened her knees, along with a twinge of guilt. If she quit, she couldn't help free Li and return him to Fran. But maybe China would release him soon anyway. She hesitated, chewing her bottom lip.

This was her chance to change her life—right now.

"Then I'm quitting. Today. I need out, to forget the whole experience." She exhaled from deep in her lungs. Tension drained out. Closing her eyes, she breathed in the fresh morning air, smelling the fragrant pines, the pungent bays, the subtle tang of ocean vapor.

A soft touch on her shoulder brought her back to reality.

"You still require debriefing," Paul said.

She nodded, willing her shoulder muscles to stay loose and relaxed, opening her eyes and staring at the sky.

"I've already told you what I know for certain. All else is pure speculation." She met his compassionate gaze and held it, hoping he would cancel this futile conference.

"Your guesses may be better than our facts." A cynical smile twisted his mouth.

"A sad commentary on U.S. intelligence."

"Ain't that the truth." Bitterness permeated every word.

Chapter 30

The telephone's shrill yanked Paul's attention back to the present. Kay waved him away and plopped back on the grass, tending the little seedlings like tiny moppets charged to her care.

He stared after her. What happened to the sophisticated, urbane Kay who didn't take shit from anyone? This back-to-nature hippie reveling in the sun and dirt, appreciating his simple life, was a complete stranger.

Yet compelling. And incredibly sexy.

And still too damned reluctant to talk.

He strode into the kitchen and grabbed the phone on the fourth ring. "Freeman."

"Salazar here. We have news from Beijing."

"Tell me." Paul's gut clenched at Don's grim voice.

"Li's daughter disappeared. Local agents confirmed it with her aunt, the journalist under house arrest. She's frantic. The daughter never came home after school last Wednesday."

"Can we verify who grabbed her and why?" His mind raced through the possibilities.

"We're trying. Our informant network tracked her to a brothel in the eastern outskirts of Beijing."

"She's a little girl!"

"Yeah, well, some people enjoy that." Don paused, giving Paul time to gather his thoughts and shove his emotions deep again. "Do you think Kay could shed light on this new situation?"

"She's not ready yet. Besides, isn't it obvious the little girl is being used to gain Li's cooperation?" Paul clenched his fist. How much would he disclose to keep his precious Tina safe?

The image of Chiang in San Francisco, dismissively waving his hand at the news of Kay's danger, flashed through his mind. Maybe not all fathers cared. Would Li?

Would it undermine America's best interests if Li didn't?

Paul grimaced at the implication.

"Good guess," Don said. "Looks like the brothel owner's in deep with a yuppity-yup high in the Communist Party's food chain, living off too many bribes to track."

"Maybe we'll be lucky and he'll become the next target of these new corruption busts."

"Or maybe a politically-linked little girl is the new currency. We can't push too hard for information—not and keep her safe."

"Safe so we can use her to gain Li's cooperation ourselves?"

"If that's what it takes." Don's pragmatic message rang loud and clear. "If Li is the key to breaking China's total monopoly on purified metals, they've upped the ante in this little game. And if Li spills all his secrets to the Chinese to protect his daughter, his life won't be worth squat."

"He won't worry about his own fate," Paul blurted. "He's her father!"

"Have you met the man?" Don's skeptical tones shot right to his heart. "Kay has. She's the only one who can guess which direction he'll jump." He paused. "We need him on America's team, not China's."

Paul watched Kay through the kitchen window, her beautiful long hair gone. She was still mostly skin and bones. Her constant trembling disappeared two days ago, replaced by this cowed docility. Or had she drifted into an emotionless void?

"She's not ready," he repeated, rubbing his jaw.

Don's heavy sigh filled his ear. "Your call, only remember—Kay befriended this girl. Don't you think she's earned full disclosure of the current situation?"

"Maybe. I'll risk it." He hesitated. Don deserved a tidbit to keep juggling the balls. "One more week. Then I'll bring her up to speed and we'll debrief her fully. Okay?"

"I don't have much choice, do I? Here's hoping the girl stays put." The connection went dead.

Paul kept his grip on the phone, so hard his fingers turned white. Was he screwing up again? Requiring more information ahead of taking decisive action? Delaying when the fates of so many were on the line? Keeping too big a secret from a key person with the right to know?

That's why Ernie died. Paul insisted on one last recon before he sent in his whole team. Ernie faced down a small army on his own, no one watching his back. All because Paul wouldn't risk the team's hideout to send a short message warning Ernie of the impending attack.

Should he consider Li a member of their team? Paul grasped exactly what it would take to earn that respect.

Li must love his daughter more than himself.

Yet just less than he loved doing what's right.

Paul pounded the counter tile in frustration. Dropping the phone with a clatter, he grabbed a dishtowel and hurled it at the refrigerator, wishing he had the nerve to throw the owner's classy china instead.

"Daddy?"

He whipped around. A flush of shame for losing his temper replaced his angry heat.

"I'm sorry, honey. Bad news day." He took a calming breath, retrieved the towel and re-folded it. "What do you need?"

"I want to show you something on the Internet. Do you have a sec?" Tina's subdued voice matched her widened eyes.

Scared eyes.

"Honey, give your old man a hug." He spread his arms wide.

Stepping into his embrace, she held tight to his waist. "Whatever it is, Daddy, it'll be okay." She rubbed her crown along his sternum. Long tresses cascaded over her back in a fall of golden sunshine.

With a shaking hand, he stroked the curls, twisting them around his fingers. Clenching them in his fist as he remembered Kay's missing hair.

And Li's missing daughter.

Lucky him—his daughter was snuggled right here in his arms.

"What did you find, honey?"

"It's better if I show you." She pulled away and tugged his hand, leading him to his office. She pointed to the computer screen. "Look."

Paul sat down and scanned the headlines decrying the growth of the Asia-based sex-slave trade. "Honey, I'm sorry. If I thought you were old enough, I would have told you."

"Get real, Daddy." She snorted and tossed her hair, arms folded across her chest. "Of course I know it's happening. Who doesn't? But why aren't you stopping it?"

"Uh . . . this isn't my job—"

"So what?" Her blue eyes flashed at him, both challenging and idealistic. "These children need help!"

Damn, his little girl was right. When had he stuck his head so deep in the sand he couldn't tell right from wrong?

When Ernie ended up dead. A lesson hard to forget for any leader.

But not impossible. That's why DuMont had asked if Paul had the backbone to stand up against the Pentagon's head-in-the-sand routine. Courage was all too rare among those who'd made fatal mistakes.

But isn't that what he would soon ask of Kay? To forget the horrors of her mission and contribute to the country's success? To pursue the principles of freedom for all?

Especially children caught in adult games.

"You're right, baby, this is too important to ignore." He tugged Tina onto his lap and hugged her tight. "I'll do what I can to help." He swallowed his anxiety. Was he ready to lead again and challenge the status quo? To confront wrongs and still protect his family?

Funny, he included Kay in his family now. Whatever his feelings, they were definitely beyond professionalism, and way beyond friendship. It felt right to see her under his roof, joining him for meals, digging her hands in the dirt and tending his plants.

It took people with special insight and skills to wrest earth's power from its bowels. Like Li. One more hero he could help.

And maybe, just maybe, protect Li's daughter, too—with Tina's blessings adding lift to his refurbished wings.

Chapter 31

VALLEY VISTA MALL

Santa Clara, California
Early Afternoon, June 2, 7 Days Later

Kay studied the chain drugstore's chrome anonymity, tapping her foot. How long did it take to fill a prescription for birth control pills anyway? She recalled the tiny, musty shop in China, where she bought Jintao his virility potions. One to prevent a child, the other to create one. She shook her head. The energy and money spent fighting nature was absurd.

At least she escaped having a child with Warden Deng, despite repeated episodes staking his claim. For power, or a warped sense of protectiveness? She sensed something similar in Paul. He hovered and watched every expression, anticipated every need. Sweet, if a little overwhelming. The jailer, on the other hand—nope, sweet didn't fit.

Tina stepped closer to the extensive condom display, her eyes huge. She darted a quick look at Kay. Her innocent cheeks stained pink and she spun away.

"Tina." Kay pitched her voice low and firm. Paul would have her hide but if Tina was already curious, she'd better have protection.

"What?" Tina kept her back turned.

"Do you have any cash on you I can borrow? I didn't plan on using your father's credit card for all this stuff." Kay grabbed two small boxes of condoms, and slapped them on the counter. The pharmacist delivered her prescription in a plain white bag.

"Sure." Tina stepped to Kay's side, wallet in hand. "Omigod, are you and Daddy hooking up?" She dropped two bills on the counter and pointed to the condoms.

"One of these is for you." Kay smirked, accepting the change and shoving the small box into Tina's purse.

"Me? No way!" she squeaked, blushing a deep red.

"Every self-respecting woman takes responsibility for her own protection." Kay grabbed her shoulder and marched Tina down the aisle. "And I doubt your mother has taught you everything." She pushed open the exit door with her hip. "Does Naomi share all the details of her dates?"

Tina stomped to the car and yanked the door open, dropping her purse at her feet as if it contained cooties. "I'm not stupid," she muttered. "I can read."

"Of course you can." Kay settled in the driver's seat. "However, if you want me to treat you like an adult, you'll have to accept the responsibilities of adulthood, which means you prepare ahead of time."

Tina stared out the side window in silence.

"All those hormones shooting through your body can overwhelm common sense," Kay continued, pulling into traffic. "This way you can minimize any bad consequences of your choices." Or non-choices—when it came down to submission . . . or death. Then, living with whatever the future brought you.

"Umm, you know, these aren't one hundred percent effective." Tina chewed on her nail, darting nervous glances her way.

"Nothing in life is, sweetie," Kay said. "At least they'll block nasty germs and viruses. You'll have to ask your parents for more in terms of birth control. This is as far as I'll go."

"I didn't mean pregnancy. I was referring to STDs."

"So was I." Kay coughed back the tightness in her throat. She had very recent and quite intimate experience with nasty viruses. She braked at the yellow light and grabbed pieces of her tattered composure. The last thing she needed was a car accident.

"We learned all about it in health class." Tina sounded nervous.

"Hasn't your father ever talked to you about any of this? You should ask."

"You're kidding me!" Tina rolled her eyes. "Have you ever asked Daddy to do something he's uncomfortable with?"

The light turned green. Kay turned into the driveway of the trendy shopping mall and pulled into a parking stall.

"I have first-hand experience with your father's stubbornness." Kay curled her lip, removing the key and opening her door. "I'll pass on this one." It'll be hard enough telling him her own situation.

Tina stepped from the car and gasped. "Are we shopping at Nordstrom?"

"Would you prefer a different store?" Kay kept her tone neutral and crossed her fingers. Nordstrom was her go-to destination for a classy, pick-me-up outfit. Paul offered to pay for Tina's new wardrobe. Where better?

"No, Nordstrom is great. Mom won't ever take me. Says the clothes would be wasted on me."

"Come on." Kay bit back nasty words springing to her lips about Daisy's opinion. "We have serious buying to do."

Standing in the dressing room an hour later, outfits dangling off hooks and Kay's favorite dress adorning Tina's slender frame, Kay marveled at Tina's priceless expression of wonder.

"Wow! This makes me look gorgeous." Uncertainty crossed her expression. "Don't you think?"

"I think you're already gorgeous. Your old clothes weren't letting the real you shine." Kay tucked the price tag out of sight with a silent chuckle. It was worth every precious penny in her mind, but Paul might have a coronary.

"I'll wear it home." Tina balled up her old clothes. She grabbed a trendy jacket with coordinating pants and shoved them at Kay. "And you should wear this. Let's blow Daddy away when we walk in the door."

Kay studied her ratty old sneakers. "These pants deserve better shoes." Listen to her, worrying about her appearance. The last time seemed like decades ago. Running her fingers through her hacked-off stubs, she jammed on the cute hat Tina recommended earlier. She'd better get to a hairstylist too.

Her heart lightened. Maybe she turned the corner and her life was back on track.

"Change your clothes, girlfriend." Tina dropped onto the small bench, crossed her arms and legs, and tapped her foot. "We can shop for shoes online at home. Daddy's probably freaking out we're so late."

"He'll live. Let's stop by the toy store before we leave."

"Toys?" Tina laughed. "I've never heard of toys being the way to a man's heart. But it might work with Daddy."

"It's not for your father."

"Ah, you don't deny you hope for a way into Daddy's heart! Cool." Tina sounded a tad too smug, yet Kay wouldn't lie to herself. She wanted to look good for Paul. A different image. A new woman. Refined, gracious, done with adventures and ready to re-engineer her life.

"There's a little girl in China who loves Barbie dolls. I want to get her the newest one with a couple of American-style outfits."

Tina skipped down the narrow hallway. "And a Dreamhouse? Or a convertible? Those are pretty all-American."

"She'd love those." Kay followed Tina to the counter. "Did you play with Barbie when you were little?"

"I preferred my warrior princess doll." Tina handed the cashier Paul's credit card. "Who is this girl?"

"The daughter of an important man in China."

"Politics." Tina sneered. "Of course. Ass-kissing is universal." She jammed the credit card into her wallet and grabbed the bag.

"I'm not ass-kissing." Kay swatted Tina's butt, nudging her toward the mall. "Her father probably won't ever find out, and I'll never see her again."

"Then why? What is she to you?"

Fran's joyful giggle echoed in Kay's ear. She recalled her final memory of Fran's tear-washed cheeks and woebegone expression.

"I made several promises to her." Sadness and guilt blurred Kay's vision. "I should keep at least one."

The toy's triviality bothered her, though. What else could she do in America? Li was alive, Frannie was safe, and Yannan would watch over them—if Yannan kept her opinions to herself for a little while. Surely, she would to protect such a precious angel.

Tina's head bobbed. "If you gave your word, you better keep it. That's what Daddy always preaches."

"Your father's a wise man."

And a very surprised one, Kay reflected once they finally sauntered through the front door. She mentally patted herself on the back at Paul's stunned expression. Didn't he believe she could convert his daughter into a young lady? Or did her own makeover shock him more?

"We're not done spending your money yet, Daddy." Tina tugged Kay toward his office. "We need shoes—lots of shoes."

Worry toyed with relief on Paul's face. Kay grinned, tossing a broad wink in his direction, leaving him to his silent battle. He asked for Tina's makeover. Well, the right shoes made the outfit. And the woman. What a difference boots versus heels versus flats made to a skirt. Or pants.

Maybe they should get all three. In different colors, too.

"You choose for me. I trust your taste." Tina pointed to the desk chair.

"You'll have to develop your own sense of style. I won't be here much longer."

"Why do you have to remind me?" Tina slouched in the armchair across the desk, destroying her classy new image. Sullenness swept her face.

"Because it's the truth."

"I thought you liked Daddy." Tina ruined her adult look with a childish pout.

Kay clicked on her favorite home page. "I do, honey, it's complica—" She gasped, scanning the blaring headlines. "Paul!" Her fingers flew, seeking new details to the story.

"What?" He rushed through the doorframe to her side.

Kay motioned to the screen.

"China cuts exports of refined rare metals," he read aloud. "Holy shit!"

She scrolled down to the story. China reduced its output to only twenty-eight percent of average, declaring its intent to stockpile the rest for its own uses. In the last hour, commodity prices of rare earth elements skyrocketed. The stock value of technology and defense companies were tanking.

China just cornered the market on rare metals. And put America's economy and military at peril.

Chapter 32

SNAZZED UP!

San Jose, California
Late Afternoon, June 2, Same Day

Victor Turtino's hand shook as he reached for an old cigarette crumpled in the back of his desk drawer. Late afternoon rays shot through the top-floor window, reflecting an eerie amber glow off the sleek modern furnishings.

"Guys, I hope you don't mind but I crave this." Victor scratched a match and filled his lungs with the familiar nicotine. Instantly, memories flooded his mind of earlier years when he controlled the fate of his company. He reveled in the immediate relief from today's stress, when China made perfectly clear who really was in control: them.

"Got another?" Nikolai Herzog rubbed his bald pate and extended his hand. "Screw the no smoking law. Politicians have better things to focus on now than worrying about its citizens' lungs."

"Mind if I open this door before you two set off the alarm?" Eddie Morrison coughed, heading to the private balcony. "Reminds me of shore leave after a long sub deployment. More smoke than a forest fire."

Victor waved approval and the cloud circling his face dissipated. "Sounds appropriate. We're smack dab in the middle of a roaring inferno. I thought you of all people would stockpile ample rare metal components, Eddie. What happened?"

"It's simple. There are no more available. So many industries incorporate high-tech gadgets in their design these days, we've created a huge uptick in demand. Prices would've skyrocketed even with a reliable supply. But now?" Eddie shook his head, dropping onto the buff-colored leather chair. "We're out of options. China's played a powerful military and economic chess move. First time since I founded the company I can't deliver. What's the Pentagon going to do now?"

"Whatever they do, it'll be behind closed doors." Victor frowned, loathing his lack of power and influence over Washington politicians on an issue this big. "I doubt they can afford to let the public understand the scope of China's move."

Nikolai stalked around the credenza in ever-widening circles. "Can't you two work together and substitute slightly inferior materials for a few product cycles?" He thumped the far wall. Framed prints of Victor's original design schematics quivered behind protective glass. "Do your products really demand such highly purified elements?"

"I think the DOD might complain if their precision-guided missiles are off by .0001%." Eddie glared at Nikolai over the top of his glasses. "They're aiming for the chest of a single terrorist in the middle of a village via remote-control drone. I'd say they require that kind of accuracy. Inferior weapons are no substitute if they put American lives at greater risk."

"We need radically new ideas." Victor slammed the birch wood desktop. "DOD Tech hasn't come up with anything new in the last few months. So I hired a top-notch chemical engineer to study alternatives for all our products. We've always re-invented the base concepts, right? Basic research in chemistry and physics. Silicon chips morphed into gallium nitride, fiber optics replaced copper-based networks—we can do this with enough time."

"How's he doing?" Nikolai stopped his pacing mid-stride, his expression hopeful.

"He's a she, and no progress yet." Victor raised his hand, waving off Nikolai's predictable sexism. "She's top of her field, named India's best up-and-coming engineer. We recruited her based on a promise of more stock options than my CFO. Believe me, she'll find an easy solution quick . . . and a permanent solution eventually."

"We can't build 'quick' and 'eventually' into fighter jets or lasers. We'll lose our defense contract if we don't deliver on time." Eddie cradled his head in his palms. Victor swore he saw more gray in Eddie's hair than he had a month ago. "Not to mention China's next move may be to stop ordering all new military gear from us. If we don't get those sales, we'll be driven right out of business. We built our next decade's business model on global revenue, not just Pentagon contracts."

"Stop worrying about contracts, Eddie." Nikolai said with an impatient shake of his head. "No one else can deliver without purified metals, either. You've got enough accounts receivables on the books from past deliveries, so you can weather a few more quarters."

Nikolai turned to Victor. "You, however, will lose the entire Christmas season. This is more than a profit miss. This is a major revenue hit. Freeze hiring and plan layoffs immediately, plus identify which offices and plants you can close."

"We can't keep this secret . . . even if the Pentagon can." Victor choked down the guaranteed hit to his stock price—and bank account.

"No kidding. The press will have a field day over this." Eddie moaned. "Wait a sec! Is there any way we can lay the blame on Washington politicians not doing their jobs negotiating better treaties with China?"

"Might work for you as a defense contractor, Eddie, but as CEO of a consumer products company, I have a responsibility to my shareholders to make sure we have second-source suppliers." Victor squeezed the bridge of his nose, pushing against a throbbing headache. "I never thought China would dare push America this far."

"You know . . . if the Pentagon never questioned us about having redundant supplies . . . and our entire military relies on China—" Eddie halted, his eyes widening. "Holy fuck! Then America can't defend itself against any war that China doesn't approve! We just made ourselves beholden to a foreign power for our security . . . and our freedom."

"Both of you better call emergency board meetings. I refuse to be the only member with this knowledge." Nikolai slumped against the desk, grabbing another cigarette. "Maybe someone else will see a way out of this shit pile. I sure as hell don't."

Victor caught Eddie's eye and shook his head. Who would have supposed it would come to this?

Chapter 33

CHESAPEAKE CORNERS CONDOMINIUMS

Washington, D.C.
Evening, June 2, Same Day

Janelle held her phone inches away from her ear. Her father's roar carried over the soft swish of tires on wet pavement outside her townhouse.

"I spent years funding those high-tech companies so America would never be in this pickle! And now stupid bureaucrats who wouldn't recognize a threat unless their crooked noses were bitten off are debating instead of acting? What are you going to do, girl?"

The question of the hour. Some editorials advised welcoming China's overt power grab and putting a halt to all defense spending; others recommended the U.S. nuke the hell out of Beijing and prepare for the next world war. The consensus: it was one big bluff.

She took a deep breath and stared at her ceiling. What if China wasn't bluffing? Snippets of TV interviews showed her normally rational, patriotic colleagues pretending China was a child who needed a gentle scolding for taking thoughtless action.

Thoughtless? Just the contrary. Janelle sniffed years of strategic positioning. He who controlled a key commodity controlled its price—and the world's economies.

Unless a very shrewd player undermined China's stranglehold on rare metals. Like her asylum-seeking Chinese friend. Too bad she didn't have that promised disk with the supposed breakthrough idea in her hands yet. After the way stock prices tanked today, would anyone ever forgive her deliberate caution and prudent delaying tactics in these behind-the-scenes negotiations?

"Well?" Patience wasn't Dad's strength. When all else failed, he reverted to his military bark. "I didn't call in favors so you could sit on the sidelines, Representative DuMont. Are you going to let the Chinese dictate to us?"

"Dad, you always praised American innovation, especially during crises." Janelle chose her words with care. "While I appreciate your efforts to give DARPA a boost, it's an investment in the distant future at best—and a further waste of taxpayers' dollars at worst. I'd rather trust the private sector's decisions."

"Those are fine words, darlin', but that's all they are—words. Where's the good-ol' tech muscle?"

One. Two. Three. He's an old, frustrated man. Cut him slack.

"I've pushed Silicon Valley CEOs hard for weeks, Dad. Not many focused on this issue prior to December. It takes time, not only money, to invent new solutions." Besides, she had more faith in a Silicon Valley solution to the purification quandary. There, each success contributed to a thriving, vibrant marketplace based on the freedom to innovate and experiment. What a random disk from China might contain was anyone's guess.

"How about all those high fallutin' colleges you have? Aren't there brains left in Berkeley and Stanford? Or anyone with patriotism?"

She gritted her teeth. "I've pushed them, too. I've pushed think tanks and venture capitalists. I've pushed our foreign allies—anyone I could think of after China's threats in December. They're making good on those threats, and we're just not ready, despite your warnings."

"Well, hell, Janelle. Your only job is to defend United States citizens. Don't you remember your oath of office?"

"Yeah, I do. I'm not the one losing my memory!" She winced, regretting her quick temper and waspish tones. "I'm sorry, Dad. How could you think I would do anything less?"

He cleared his throat. "I'm sorry, too." His voice dropped a few decibels and most of its anger. "I lost my head. I trust you'll do what you can, and I'll stop butting in where I shouldn't. Good night, darlin'."

Great. More fences to mend. His early onset of dementia didn't mean she could slap him upside the head with a big dose of disrespect. When this was all over, she'll be lucky if he doesn't disown her for a lapse of ethics. She crossed her fingers the end would justify the means.

China could trumpet its stranglehold in terms of economic success all it wanted. In Dad's day, they called it Communism. And what was wrong with that? After all, the Chinese lauded their Communist Party, the decisions made by that six percent of their population, and the results of a command-and-control economy.

The fact they hid their warts by throttling journalistic opinions or demanding unquestioning obedience to their policies would eventually harm their progress. Proof? A damned clandestine offer to swap the keys to the rare metals kingdom for American freedom.

She powered on her laptop and scanned her emails. No reply yet from her Chinese go-between to this evening's urgent request to expedite proceedings—after almost two months of secret negotiations. And after she'd stuck herself out on a limb, going against every ethical lesson Dad pounded into her.

Was her asylum-seeker surprised by the sudden embargo? Or caught, and the offer gone up in smoke? Or . . . was he bluffing, too?

What marvelous answer could really be on that disk?

She scanned a deluge of nasty-grams, telling her to butt out of China's business and do her job. Interesting. She hadn't publicly engaged yet on rare metals, just on her on Human Rights Committee work. So who was choreographing all this posturing? Her anonymous official? The go-between? Maybe the Chinese government had her in their official crosshairs now. Or members of her own party had finally had enough of her ethics.

Wonderful.

Janelle tugged at her hair, making her scalp ache. She was still up shit creek without a paddle, chasing this fantasy solution-on-a-disk. Kay muttered something about a mining engineer in her sleep on the flight home. Maybe she recalled more than she let on.

Time for Kay's debriefing. Janelle should cushion the email with good news about more funding. That might mollify Paul, but not Kay.

Tough.

Janelle shot off an email demanding the meeting tomorrow afternoon. She could grab four hours of sleep on the red-eye flight home, and re-familiarize herself with the details of Kay's case.

The blinking icon alerted her to another incoming email. Clicking it open, she skimmed the contents. Her skin crawled.

Her first death threat. She poised her finger to delete the hateful message but paused. What if it were real?

Squirming, she saved the missive and slammed the lid shut. Good thing she was leaving D.C. tonight. Her presence was no longer valued.

Or was it her life?

Chapter 34

DUMONT CONGRESSIONAL OFFICE

San Mateo, California
Noon, June 3, Next Day

Kay rubbed sweaty palms against her slacks as she examined her inquisitors' faces, ringing the round conference table. The redwood's enduring strength seemed a fitting anchor to the vista soaring westward toward the new-growth forest dotted with fragrant eucalyptus trees. The open window still carried a hint of morning's cooling fog and a taste of simmering mid-summer heat.

She would answer their questions. That's all. This was a simple debriefing about her past career. Time to move on.

She hadn't expected to see Eric Coleman and Don Salazar. She'd broken all of Paul's rules during her stint at SDS Technologies, hoping fantastic results would rescue her from her chosen, damning role.

Didn't happen. In fact, it only forced her into a worse situation—in China.

"Kay?" Eric leaned across the table, hand extended. "Sorry to hear about Wilkins . . . and everything else you endured."

Kay blinked in disbelief at Eric's graciousness in spite of her unprofessional behavior at his last company. She accepted his hand, giving it a brief waggle. "Thanks," she muttered.

Standing next to Eric, Don nodded in her direction but his hands remained in his pants pockets. She returned the acknowledgment before tucking her head against her chest, hoping fresh tears wouldn't get noticed. One person's forgiveness would do for now.

Paul dropped into the chair next to her. Maybe he forgave her antics too. She enjoyed his eyes on her this morning as he took in her new outfit. Hoping was a fool's dream—but she loved his touch at her waist, and playing the lady to his chivalrous escort.

Janelle, seated at the head of the table, cleared her throat. She looked exhausted, as if she spent all night preparing for this meeting. No surprise. Her father's reputation for kicking ass and taking names must be a tough act to follow.

Kay only hoped hers wasn't the one on Janelle's short list.

"You appear much better, Kay," Janelle began with a compassionate smile. "I trust you're well enough to answer our questions. China's control of rare earth metals has become a national concern. We're hoping you can shed light on the issue, based on your recent mission."

"I'm afraid I don't know much." Kay leaned forward, catching each participant's eye in turn. "Charlie Wilkins made the contacts. After he was killed, I dropped all inquiries." She shoved back the image of his dead body from her mind. Not now.

"Why don't you tell us what you do know?" Paul squinted his eyes, tapping his finger in slow, steady rhythm on the table.

Kay took a deep breath. "I didn't find out much about rare earths before Charlie happened upon a game company with leading-edge designs. If those engineers told him their secret, he didn't share any details. He asked me to keep an eye out for other companies potentially using purified metals, which I did within my mission's charter to uncover technology theft."

"Did you find any?" Don linked his fingers on the table in front of him.

"I found a few interesting leads and passed them on to Charlie." She shrugged. "Occasionally, I went with him to translate. Most times I didn't."

"Did you have any reason to suspect he'd blown your identity?" Trust Paul to cover all the bases. She turned to face Eric, hoping he would understand her role at SDS.

"Charlie was a pathological liar who got off on keeping secrets, so nothing was guaranteed," she admitted. "Since they murdered him, not me, it would indicate they considered me a mere translator—and a lowly female to boot."

"Shows how stupid Chinese men are." Janelle sniffed.

"Or not." Eric raised one finger. "Wilkins got so focused he forgot to cover all his bases. Maybe they wanted Kay kept alive for a reason."

"As a warning to our intelligence community?" Don's question carried ominous undertones. "Maybe they didn't take too kindly to us poking through their secrets."

"Perhaps." Janelle tilted her head. "I guess it depends on who 'they' are. Kay, do you believe this recent posturing might be linked to the intelligence you uncovered?"

"I didn't uncover anything." Kay raised her voice, shaking her head. "Charlie did. After he died, I avoided all his contacts. I have no idea who killed him. I'm just putting two and two together. When I sent the email about rare earths from his account . . . he was killed."

Eric and Paul exchanged glances. Paul frowned, turning to face her.

"According to security surveillance video, you met a little girl and a young woman at Tiananmen Square multiple times," Paul said. "Who are they?"

"You saw me?" Kay's mind raced. "Wow, super-advanced technology. How does it work?"

"Never mind." Paul glowered. "Answer the question."

Kay reached for the water glass, willing her fingers not to tremble. She took a long, slow sip. How much should she share? Setting the glass down, she maintained her grip on its wet surface and focused her eyes on the drop sliding down the inside curve.

"I contacted a fellow Berkeley alum for help getting out of China," Kay began. "Tan Yannan is a journalist and I was hoping she might have different sources. She happened to bring her niece with her." She shrugged, keeping her expression impassive. No way would she drag Frannie into this mess. School and her Barbie dolls should be her only concern.

Don's grayed mustache twisted in a scowl as he crossed his arms. A not-so-discreet sigh emanated from Eric's chest. Janelle kept her expression hidden, flipping through a stack of notes in front of her. Paul slapped the table and glared.

They didn't believe her! Tension shot across Kay's shoulders. Why not?

Oh God, did they discover her prison abuse? She yearned to pretend it never happened—if only her body would cooperate . . .

Janelle's hand reached across the table for Kay's. She squeezed once, hard, and kept her grip firm.

"Kay, we know this girl is the daughter of a Chinese engineer with expertise in purifying rare metals," Janelle said. "We can offer him political asylum in return for helping his daughter. Do you think he'll cooperate on the basis of her safety?"

"Fran's safe enough with her aunt." Kay cocked her head. A horrible idea flashed through her mind. "Unless you put her in harm's way in return for his defection." She frowned at Janelle, yanking her hand free. "Are we exploiting children to leverage our political agenda? That's stooping pretty low, even for Washington politicians!"

"Not in my lifetime." Don snapped. "And your information is a little out of date, Ms. Chiang."

Kay whipped her head in Don's direction. "What don't I know?"

Don opened his mouth. Paul slashed the air with his hand.

"Better I tell her," Paul said in a low voice.

"What don't I know?" Kay repeated. Dread crept through her. Had she tainted Fran in her desperation to get out of China? She pushed her chair back far enough to encompass all their expressions. "Tell me!"

"The little girl—Fran—is Li Ying's daughter. Is his name familiar?" Paul watched her with a steady gaze.

"I heard his name once or twice connected to rare earths." Kay locked her eyes on his face.

Paul took a long breath. "She's no longer living with her aunt."

"Where is she?"

"We're not sure."

"Guess."

"Under the control of the Chinese government so they can gain Li's cooperation."

A lump formed in Kay's throat. "Is Fran safe?" she whispered.

"Again, we're not sure."

"What's your best guess?" Kay pounded the table. "Come on, Paul, the DIA has to have some idea!"

"In a brothel." Paul swiped his hand over his jaw, his expression anguished.

"No!" No. No. No. Not little Frannie. Not an innocent girl. Tears flooded her eyes. She was a modern-day Typhoid Mary, ruining everything good she touched.

"We have proof, Kay," Eric said in a somber voice. "Chinese informants tracked her to a notorious house of prostitution."

"Why aren't you rescuing her?" She didn't recognize her own voice, timid with fear for Fran's safety. And sanity, if Fran suffered any of the sexual torment Kay experienced.

"How do you propose we do that? With a magic carpet?" Don somehow mixed compassion with sarcasm. When Kay glanced at him, she recognized her helplessness mirrored in his eyes.

"No, I'm being foolish. Of course you can't." Kay sniffed and wiped her nose. She faced Eric. "Are you sure the government is behind this? If not, there might be politicians willing to earn brownie points for protecting their children . . . even the girls."

Her heart twisted. Chinese still preferred sons, not daughters—to the point of claiming a young daughter drowned to justify having another child, hopefully a son. No body found, no proof of death. Many parents, too many, believed selling their little girl was more humane than killing her. And they got cash on delivery.

Kay wasn't sure which fate was worse.

"The brothel has significant government ties, according to our informants. So, if it's not purposeful, it's a whopping coincidence—and I believe in Santa Claus again," Eric said.

"Paul?" Her voice wavered. "What's the plan? I'll help any way I can."

Pain crossed his face, followed by uncertainty, then resolve.

"There are more moving parts than my unofficial assignment calls for." Paul swept his arm in a broad gesture, encompassing the group. "Let's pool our intelligence and contacts, and figure out the best solution."

"For the intelligence community or the affected individuals?" Kay narrowed her eyes.

"Both, if possible." Don paused. "That's always the goal, Ms. Chiang." Kay met and held his understanding regard. "Sometimes individuals sacrifice for a greater good. Li Ying did by deciding to buck his government. He put his daughter's life in danger. Not you."

"Don's right." Eric nodded. "Fran and her father are in danger because of Li's resolve to use his genius for the good of his fellow citizens, not the politicians. They jailed him for refusing to acknowledge his brain was China's to command and control."

"Given these new disclosures, do you have any additional, relevant details to share?" Paul zeroed in on her, his green eyes ablaze.

Kay recognized the ring of steel that colored Paul's tones many missions ago. Exactly when he lost it, she couldn't say. Maybe after his family deserted him.

"If you connected the dots between me, Li and Frannie, I suppose others could, too." Kay wrung her hands. "And . . . I may have made one nasty enemy in all this. She's spiteful enough to exploit a little girl as payback."

"What's her name and what did you do to piss her off?" Don's focus turned to her.

Kay's cheeks warmed. Maybe they were right to suspect her of being a bull in a china shop when it came to other women. She was never able to make female friends.

Except Tina. Despite their age difference, she sensed a kindred spirit in Paul's daughter. What did that say about her immaturity—or was it Tina's maturity?

"Her name is Han Mai, an ambitious political appointee who's threatened by change, including her own aging." Kay kept her eyes on her hands, clasped tightly in her lap. "She went out of her way to spite me and her boss, Wei Jintao. I think she was jealous of all the attention he paid me. And jealousy can be a powerful motivator."

Silence met her confession. She glanced up, expecting to find derision and disgust. Instead, she found patience and understanding. She drew a relieved breath and straightened her back.

"Her name sounds familiar." Don focused on the screen in front of him, tapping his tablet. "Janelle, do you recognize it?"

"No." She shook her head. "Should I?"

"She has lots of ties with your party's Political Action Committees and their favorite charitable organizations. Quite generous with her father's wealth in our country," he added.

"Whoa!" Janelle shoved back her chair, her arms falling to the sides. "Now it's making sense."

"It?" Eric cocked his head. "What aren't you telling us?"

"This is for your ears only, agreed?" Janelle's teeth bit into her lower lip. "No telling my father. He doesn't need more worries."

"Agreed. I'll worry for him." Don's eyes sparkled with pride.

Kay hadn't met DuMont but the loyalty he inspired was downright awesome.

"I've gotten a number of threatening emails, and they escalated after my China trip," Janelle said. "I wonder if they're linked to this Han woman's personal vendetta because of my association with Kay."

"Describe the threats." Don jotted notes.

Scrolling through her emails, Janelle read aloud the hateful expletives and explicit dangers, keeping her voice calm and light, enunciating the words like a storyteller. As if they were unreal.

Kay squirmed. She knew better. Her all too recent experience proved how quickly intimidation could become a reality.

"For God's sake, Janelle, why didn't you tell us sooner?" Eric implored.

"I'm not in a position to disclose confidential information." Janelle sounded just a tad defensive. "My committee work requires I keep my mouth shut. How could I assume this was linked to Kay's situation?"

"Because you're too damned familiar with how D.C. works!" Paul jumped to his feet and paced the room's perimeter. "Are your colleagues pressuring you to play ball according to any new rules recently?"

"Okay, I'll share a little bit." Janelle fidgeted. "However, this is really, really classified. Get it? Maybe bigger than the rare metals issue."

Digging into her briefcase, Janelle pulled out a sheaf of paper-clipped pages and slapped them onto the table.

"This comprises the list of House representatives under investigation by the Ethics Committee for accepting bribes." She flipped to a middle page and spun it to face them. "These link to Chinese money specifically. I'm working with the Senate Ethics Committee to identify similar problems."

Kay craned her neck, searching for familiar names. Too many politicians to count.

So much for reaching the safe haven of American shores. China bought influence here decades ago. If Janelle were on their shit list because of her, wouldn't that make Kay a more important target?

"Okay, here's where we start." Don cracked his knuckles and caught each person's eye. "I'll see what I can uncover from my contacts in the Justice Department—"

"Discreetly, I hope?" Janelle interrupted.

"Of course," Don said. "I expect limited success if political pressure has already been exerted due to the Ethics investigation."

"We're forgetting about Li." Eric's somber voice broke in. "If money-backed politics has entered the picture, whether political asylum will work is just a WAG."

"WAG?" Janelle and Kay echoed in unison.

"*Wild-Ass Guess* in Southern-speak," Paul said with a quick grin. "A shot in the dark."

"We've got to get Li's rare earths refinement know-how." Eric thumped a clenched fist on his armrest. "He's too important a player to leave hanging in the wind."

"Now you remind me of Dad." Janelle twisted her lips into a wry expression.

"Time is running out," Eric continued. "Either we go in and exploit the situation with his daughter, or this Han woman will—with or without the blessing of the CCP." He shot Kay an apologetic look. "Sorry, Kay. Those are the facts."

She nodded, grappling with their implications in the sudden silence.

Bad things happened to everyone around her, and not just in China.

"I have to find a new place to stay—alone." Kay grabbed her purse and started to rise. "You've got my debriefing, so we're finished, right?"

"Like hell!" Paul stomped to her side and thrust his face into hers, forcing her back into the chair. "Who will keep you safe? Huh?" He wiggled her skinny arms. "No muscles to fight back, and I sure as shit won't let you borrow my sidearm for protection. You're exhibiting signs of outright insanity!"

"My presence in your house puts Tina at risk," she cried. "And you, too."

"I'll determine that," Paul said, scowling. "We have a team of people backing us up. Right?"

"Sure enough." Eric nodded.

"Damn straight." Don rapped the table.

"These threats aren't simply against me," Janelle said. She slid her hand, palm up, in Kay's direction. "They're for anyone on my side. And you're on my team now, Kay, like it or not. Wherever you live."

"I can't help Li." The last time Kay saw him flashed unbidden through her brain. No! She left jail behind! "I won't help you," she quavered, a tear slipping free.

"Even to help Fran?" Paul's tender touch wiped her cheek dry.

"Oh God, Paul . . . don't ask more than I can give!" Kay buried her head in her hands, fighting back the memories of defeat. Of terror.

"Ms. Chiang, you're a key team member, and we will protect you." Don offered his assurance in sonorous tones. Her fear subsided a tiny bit. "If you're watchful and cooperate with our security plans, you'll be safe. I guarantee it."

Kay lifted her eyes, battling the cynicism that stained her soul.

"Thank you, Don. But I don't think life comes with any guarantees. Especially mine."

Chapter 35

FREEMAN RESIDENCE

Saratoga, California
Evening, June 3, Same Day

"Stop telling me what to do!" Kay stormed toward the living room, aiming a wet dishtowel at Paul but missing–par for the course.

"Only after this is all over and you're safe." He followed right on her heels, brandishing the towel like a lame whip. "Until then, I'm responsible for you."

Tina rolled her eyes and turned to the wall, adjusting her ear buds. Kay ignored her and spun on her toes.

"Like hell you are." She glared at Paul.

"Dammit Kay, follow orders for once in your life!"

"Even nonsensical ones? Ones that put others' lives in danger instead of our own?"

Ghosts flickered in Paul's eyes, pain whispered across his face. He sank to the sofa, shoulders hunched.

"Stop shouting." Tina yanked her ear buds out and glowered, her set jaw identical to her father's. "I can't hear my music."

"Learn to share, young lady, or go to your room." Paul scowled at Tina.

"My room is too small. I get claustrophobic." Tina's childish whine topped her exaggerated pout.

Kay whirled on her. "Do you have any idea how other children live?"

"I don't like being told what to do any more than you do. And you're not my mother!"

Kay narrowed her eyes and opened her mouth. Tina stuck out her tongue.

"Paul, would you tell your baby to grow up—fast? She's no longer the center of the universe."

"Kay's right. Until you act as an adult, you'll be punished as a child." Paul pointed to the hall. "Go."

"Just because you two are fighting doesn't mean you have to take it out on me." Tina uncurled her legs and rose. "Get real. You still have to work together." With a resigned expression, she turned the corner and disappeared.

Kay crossed her arms against her chest. "She's right. There's no point in fighting. I'm going to bed." Spinning on her heel, she marched down the hall and slammed the door shut behind her.

Hours later, Kay still hadn't slept a wink. She'd huffed and pounded her pillow into a shapeless mass, dampened by a seemingly endless stream of tears. She checked the clock—after midnight already.

What was that? A muffled sound. A thump. Footsteps? No, not regular enough. Was she glad or relieved Paul wasn't on his way to comfort her? Unless he was right, and they weren't safe. She shivered in the cold air.

An owl hooted once. Twice.

Hugging her waist, she hoisted upright and shoved a pillow behind her back. She held her breath, listening.

And hiccupped. Loudly.

Great. She lost all her talent for covert ops. More tears rolled down her cheeks. She sniffled and reached for a tissue.

"Kay?" Tina's troubled voice drifted through the door. "Can I help?"

"I doubt it," she managed, surprised by Tina's offer.

In a nanosecond, Tina slipped inside the room. "Try me. I'm mature for my age."

"Oh, honey, trust me, you don't want to know about this."

"About what?" Tina patted the wall, bumped against the nightstand, and climbed under the comforter, seeking warmth.

"My life as a woman." Kay sniffled.

"I assumed women had it great these days. You know, we can have it all . . ."

"Yeah, right. Only if we're willing to pay for it all."

"What awful price have you paid?" Tina stuck a pillow under her head.

"Self-respect."

"So pay yourself back."

"Easier said than done." Kay tossed the sodden tissue in the general direction of the wastebasket.

"Because?"

"Because . . . basically . . . I whored myself out on my missions!" Tears burst from a black hole deep inside. She buried her head in the covers.

"So . . . you did what you had to . . . for your country. You're a patriot, not a whore." Tina patted Kay's shoulder reassuringly.

"What guy cares . . . or wants anything to do with a bald woman?" Fresh sobs shook her.

Tina edged Kay's head onto her shoulder, running her hand over the stubble. "You know, Naomi's mom felt the same way after her cancer treatment and mastectomy. Hair grows back." She paused. "Her breasts won't."

"I'm sorry." Kay's breath hitched. "I'm too self-centered. I get that. But . . ."

Seconds passed. "But . . . what?" Tina prodded.

"There are other consequences of my choices. Ones not so trivial." She hesitated. "Ones that will keep anyone from loving me, or having sex with me." A wry laugh escaped. "Maybe I've enjoyed all the sex I deserve already. Lord knows, it's more than most women my age."

Tina stroked Kay's back in long, repeated sweeps. Kay relaxed with every breath, following her instinct to trust another woman, even one so young. Somehow, Tina knew how to comfort her.

"Did your gynecologist have bad news for you?" Tina whispered.

"How did you guess?"

"Woman's intuition?" Tina squeezed her hand. "What did the doctor say?"

"I'll need re-testing, but I've been diagnosed with AIDS." Kay shuddered and blotted her eyes.

"It's not a death sentence. Not these days. Especially if they treat it early."

"Maybe not, although I may as well be a leper. No one comes close to an AIDS victim for fear of catching it."

Tina pulled her closer, dropping her cheek on top of Kay's head. "I'm close. And I don't worry."

"Maybe your father doesn't feel the same way." Her heart smarted.

Tina shrugged, jostling Kay's head. "He should. It's not your fault you caught AIDS." She hesitated. "Is it? I mean, did you use condoms?"

"I couldn't all the time." Kay lifted and braced herself on one arm, missing Tina's warmth right away. "One situation controlled me. I traded off my life for my health."

"The same as the young girls forced into the sex trade." Tina nodded. "They don't have a choice, either. It's just not right to turn our backs on them when they finally have a chance for a normal life."

"Like Fran." Kay shivered. "God, I hope she stays safe."

"Why wouldn't she?" Tina's tones carried hints of confusion.

"Because she's apparently been kidnapped and is being held in a brothel, God knows where!"

"In China?"

"Yes. What does it matter?"

"Some cultures mutilate female genitals. I don't think the Chinese do, though–right?"

"God, Tina, don't tell me they teach that in school!" Kay winced and clamped her legs together.

"No, but they should. I read it on a blog." Tina sat up, hugging the pillow to her chest. "Breast cancer research doesn't really need more walkers, do they? I want to help those girls. Who else is going to help this cause?" She heaved a heavy sigh. "Daddy will probably freak out and say no. Can you talk to him?"

"Really?" Puzzled, Kay scratched her head. "Why?"

"Because my life in America is so easy compared to theirs." She gave a self-deprecating chuckle. "I know . . . I fussed like crazy tonight. I was just joining in with you and Daddy."

"So glad we could entertain you." Kay tilted her head in feigned admonition.

"Seriously, can't I help Fran? You know, find a family to adopt her?" Tina sounded so sincere. "Too bad Mom would go nuts. I'm sure someone would be willing to give her a home."

"Me." A slow ember ignited in Kay's chest.

"Help you?"

"No. Me." The warmth grew, expanding into Kay's heart. "I'm willing to adopt Fran."

"Cool." Silence. "Umm, what do you think Daddy will say?"

"Paul will probably growl and grumble, but he's a real softie." Kay laughed, joyous at the notion of adopting Frannie. "Especially with women–have you noticed?"

"Yeah. Like the song says, it's a Southern state of mind."

"Fran will need a new family, one who loves her and accepts her, no matter the trauma she's going through." Kay clenched her fist against her chest. "We're going through," she whispered.

"Everyone deserves forgiveness and a fresh start once in his or her life, don't you think?"

"I do."

"Let make sure Daddy believes it, too."

"Deal." They bumped fists in the dark.

Done.

Chapter 36

FREEMAN RESIDENCE

Saratoga, California
Late Morning, June 4, Next Day

Paul tugged his backpack from the pile of crap cluttering the hall closet and peered into the main compartment. His smaller daypack lay right on top. Thank goodness.

Yanking it free, he eyed the remaining gear nestled in the larger pack. He'd assess Tina's and Kay's strength and hiking ability today, and sort out the rest tomorrow. A camping trip next weekend would be a welcome escape from this isolated pressure-cooker.

Did Kay guess how strong his attraction had become? Her life was so promiscuous . . . while he practiced monogamy all the way. How could they mesh? She stood for everything he always condemned. What was he thinking?

No doubt his little head was thinking for him.

The sounds of slamming drawers reached his ears. He shuddered in anticipation of the clothes Tina would surprise him with today. Maybe Kay's influence from their shopping expedition would stick. He stuffed the daypack with first-aid kit, water bottles and energy bars, and hefted it onto his back, the familiar weight at once reassuring and disconcerting.

"Will I be warm enough in this?" Kay stepped out of the hall shadows, opening wide his loaned windbreaker and exposing a form-fitting tank top with mid-thigh gym shorts.

Paul nodded, lost for words. Guess his home cooking helped. She had curves in all the right places again. Better yet, she sounded relaxed.

"Fog's burning off now," he recovered. "And we'll be in sunshine soon, according to my neighbor. This is his favorite hiking trail."

"Have you heard more about Fran?" Kay whispered, glancing over her shoulder.

"No. I trust Don and Janelle are doing their best." Paul hated to see worry pucker her face again. He brushed her forehead with his thumb, smoothing the lines, anticipating her pulling away. Instead, she smiled and followed his motion with her head.

He stared into her eyes, hunting for her real feelings. After their arguments yesterday, did she finally trust him to keep her safe? She couldn't live inside her mellow cocoon forever. With her by his side, he sensed an elemental rhythm of home life pulsing with promise. Filling his empty voids. He hoped his tender caring soothed her, yet he couldn't resist pushing her at every zesty sign of life. He wouldn't stop searching for his lost woman, or praying for her scars to heal.

Her soft breath warmed his palm. He spotted signs of confusion and remnants of fear in her expression, accompanied by unanswered questions. Warring in the liquid depths of her brown eyes.

Who was Kay's role model? An uncaring father? Obedient mother? Tormenting brothers? What if she'd sought his guidance years ago? He'd ignored her and his basic, unexpected attraction, opting for the head-in-the-sand routine instead of the honesty she deserved. Leaving her all alone.

Sure, he'd been married and determined to create the right environment for Tina, even with the turmoil of heart-wrenching separation and ultimate divorce. But was he emotionally equipped for a new family now? Kay and Tina found an endearing camaraderie he hadn't expected. Maybe he could do it right this time.

Tina's footsteps pattered down the hall. With regret, he slid his fingers in a lingering caress along Kay's cheekbone and dropped his hand.

"Ready, Tina?"

"Ready, Daddy." Tina's curls bounced through the back of a white baseball cap festooned with pink ribbons.

Fighting the temptation to tug her ponytail, he shook his head. His little idealist. Like father, like daughter. He enlisted in the Army the day after high school graduation.

"Let's go." Herding them to the Jeep, he tossed in his pack and drove south on Skyline Boulevard to the trailhead. He snagged a map to show them their anticipated route and key landmarks.

"Will we be in danger?" Tina patted his arm, pointing to a sketch of a mountain lion dominating the display board.

"I doubt it." He squinted against the noonday sun beating down on the parked cars in shimmery waves. Kay tied the sleeves of her jacket around her shoulders. Her shirt clung to her small breasts; his palms inadvertently curled into the exact shape. "Most wild animals stay hidden during the day, so the chances of a mountain lion attack are lower than a double lightning strike. Snakes though—"

"Ew! Snakes?" Tina shuffled her feet.

"Your dad's teasing. Snakes enjoy sun, not this damp trail." Kay tugged her down the path. Another hiker turned the corner and passed with a friendly wave.

Paul let his favorite girls stay a few feet ahead, watching their antics in the mottled sunlight. And enjoying the soft sway of Kay's hips rolling with every dip and step. Approaching a junction a mile in, two mountain bikers zoomed past from behind. Paul jumped aside, cursing.

"Wow! Did anyone see them coming?" Tina whipped her head and watched them reach the distant corner.

"They're supposed to yield the right of way," Paul muttered.

"Good luck with that." Kay snickered. "They're bigger and faster."

He scanned the map. "We'll be okay on these wide fire roads. If we meet a bike on a narrow track, yield by stepping toward the hillside, not to the outside edge. If anyone takes a tumble for going too fast, it'll be the biker, not you. Got it?"

Tina and Kay nodded, resuming their animated conversation and heading uphill. Glancing back, Paul noticed the bikers stopped near the junction. One scrutinized a piece of paper in his hand and peered back at them.

Paul hesitated. Were those men lost? He shrugged, following the girls. If they were newbie bikers, the park was easy enough to navigate. Ascend whatever trail you could find, and you hit the main road again. Down carried you into a steep canyon beyond civilization, where the silent embrace of hard redwoods and oaks smoothed away technology's rough edges.

He dug a water bottle from the pack and sipped. The stillness invited him to replay yesterday's meeting. If Kay didn't have any more intelligence to share, why toss her in a Chinese jail? Had someone else jumped to the wrong conclusions—or was Kay holding something back? He remembered her guarded belligerence at the beginning of the meeting. What did she still have to hide? What other choices had she made during her seven-month absence that she didn't dare share with the group? Or was she afraid of sharing them with him?

Tina's sweet laughter drifted into his reverie. Would he forgive her bad choices, aside from clothes? Or disown her like Kay's father? Praying he'd never face that decision, he hustled, joining them near the next trail junction.

"Which way, Daddy?"

Tina's endearing tones softened his troubled conscience. He wormed the map out of his cargo pocket.

"Hmm, let's take the left fork. It'll bring us back toward the parking lot and we can decide then how much longer we'll hike." He offered them each a bottle of water. "Drink up. You've probably sweated out more than this already."

"Exercising again feels great." Kay wiped her face with the bottom of her shirt, affording him a glimpse of slender waist and sturdy exercise bra. A bead of sweat worked its way to her navel. He followed every centimeter of its progress.

"You and Kay should walk together." Tina kicked his ankle and winked. "I haven't had alone time in for-ev-er." She loped down the soft dirt trail, scattering leaves in her wake. She put about fifty yards between them before she slowed, descending deep into a sheer canyon. Her golden curls lit the way forward in the dim forest light.

Kay's uncertain expression tugged his heartstrings. He extended his hand. Staring into his eyes with an uneasy smile, she gripped his fingers. He led her onto the trail, contentment settling through him. Fragrant laurel bay trees whispered and waved in the faint breeze amid the solid redwoods soaring above, welcoming them to their safe, quiet haven.

"Paul, what do you think of my chances of legally adopting Fran once we rescue her?"

Paul dropped his jaw and stared at her. "Are you serious?" He tripped over a tree root.

"Totally. She needs a loving, safe home. Why not mine?"

"Um, because you don't have one?"

"I searched the local listings and found a number of condos for rent in good school districts," she said.

"How will you support her? Didn't you just quit the DIA?" Or did only men worry about how to support a family?

Kay notched her fragile jaw higher. "In the middle of all my intelligence work, I racked up an impressive resume." Doubt crossed her features again. "If you and Eric serve as references."

Paul swallowed the lump in his throat. What a fool he was, living one day at a time, assuming she'd stay with him indeterminately, dependent on him for food and shelter while he saved the world. Once again, Kay got the jump on him.

"I can't speak for Eric, but you can count on me." He squeezed her hand. Letting go, he preceded her down the narrow, twisting path. He couldn't see Tina ahead, only heard the sound of an occasional twig snap. "You've always believed that, haven't you?" His voice dropped to a mere whisper.

"Of course." She tugged him around, meeting his gaze. "Don't you realize I relied on you to find those messages and not abandon me? To cover my ass every time I went rogue?" She bit her bottom lip. "It wasn't only professional support, was it?"

He shook his head, searching for the right words. His true feelings. Their current reality, especially with her recent bombshell. How could they develop a lasting relationship? She aspired to create a home for a Chinese girl, and he had no idea how long his Silicon Valley job would last.

A blur of motion ten yards behind Kay's shoulder caught his eye.

"Watch out!" He yanked Kay sideways, pushing her halfway up the hillside into an exposed root ball. He twisted, pressing his back against the damp earth, and held his breath.

Two bikes barreled toward them, chrome handlebars glinting in the filtered sun. Dust filled his nostrils. A blaze of shiny helmets and colorful lycra blurred past them.

The same two bikers they saw earlier. And Tina was somewhere ahead.

"Be careful—there's another hiker!" The lead biker waved him off, rounding the hairpin turn with an ominous rattle of loose stones and muttered curses. The other followed with the same disregard for his safety, skidding on the damp leaves and pedaling on.

"Tina! Watch out!" he bellowed, grabbing Kay's hand and pulling her off the hillside.

She stumbled, clutched onto his arm and regained her balance.

"Go!" She pushed him forward. He charged up the trail.

A soft slither of sound. The suspicious rustle alerted him two seconds faster this time. The same bikers returned around the bend, heads up. Aiming straight for them.

"What the—" Paul swallowed his curse. "Kay—jump!"

Praying she remembered to leap up the hill, he stretched his arms and legs wide. He dug his boots into the duff. The front rider's wheel skittered.

With a reckless twist, the biker aimed for the trail's edge. Soft dirt crumbled off the cliff. The front tire wobbled, slowed, and slid a foot down the steep ravine.

Paul grabbed at the handlebars but the forward momentum pushed them out of reach. He caught onto the biker's fanny pack instead and braced to counterbalance their weight. The biker kicked his legs free, arms waving in the air.

Snap!

The belt fastener gave way to inertia. Paul fell back against the hillside in a thud. His breath knocked loose. The biker's body was airborne, fingers flailing in horrific slow motion. A crash, a broken-off yelp, the uneven thuds of a body plummeting downhill. Then . . . silence.

Still clutching the pack, Paul looked to his right, struggling to regain his footing. Kay clung to a manzanita bush, her face pressed to the damp earth.

Whoosh!

The second biker whipped by, avoiding the gouge in the trail.

"Hey!" Paul waved at him. "Your buddy's hurt!"

The biker pedaled furiously, eyes on the trail. He disappeared around the far bend.

Kay turned her head. Her worried gaze met his.

"Tina!" she screamed.

Tina! The first echo bounced back. He scanned the direction the bikers had come, torn. Maybe Tina had gotten far enough ahead they never saw her.

Tina! The second echo . . . an eerie mockery of his daughter's name. Crawling to the edge, he spotted a colorful patch nestled in the broad arms of a madrone tree. The biker's twisted body matched the graceful spirals of the golden-hued trunk.

"Tina!" His stomach heaved at this brush with death. All because he insisted on exercise.

"Daddy! Kay!" Tina ran around the curve, hurtling toward them. "Are you all right? What happened?"

Paul scrambled to her, yanking Tina away from loose dirt on the edge of the trail. He hugged his daughter tight.

One of Kay's arms gripped his waist, the other held Tina's shoulders. Kay's tear-filled eyes searched his. He raised his eyebrows in silent query.

"I'm okay," she mouthed.

"A biker went over the edge, honey." He released a shaky breath. "We need to get help."

Tina wriggled away and extricated her phone.

"I'll call 911." She tapped the phone, stared, and frowned. "No signal? Where are we, Mongolia?"

"Actually, Mongolia has pretty good cell coverage these days." Kay's chuckle carried an ironic tone. "It's harder to conquer Mother Nature."

"What? The redwoods? Because they're so tall?" Tina twisted her head upward.

"And we're deep in a canyon, under the signal's spread." Paul walked to the edge and shook his head. "I don't dare a rescue without rope."

Kay grabbed his arm, pulling him back. "You don't dare rescue him alone. They were maniacs!"

"They charged us like angry bulls." Paul stroked his chin, recalling those adrenaline-filled moments. And not liking the suspicions pounding for attention.

"What do we do now, Daddy?" Under normal circumstances, he'd laugh at Tina's bewilderment of technology's limitations.

"We hike out of this ravine and get back to the car, fast. We should get a signal there. If not, we drive until we do." Paul grabbed the ripped fanny pack lying in the leaves. "Let's hustle, ladies." They darted forward.

Keeping one eye on the trail, he followed at a slower pace and unzipped the pack, searching for the biker's identity. A crumpled sheet of paper was crammed into the front pocket. He unfolded it and stopped dead in his tracks.

Two smiling faces stared up at him—photos of Kay and Janelle. Cryptic Chinese characters leapt off the page. What the . . .

He stuffed the paper back inside the pack. Too bad he hadn't learned to read Chinese so he could avoid asking Kay to translate. No doubt they spelled trouble in any language.

Jogging, he caught up with Kay and Tina. They hiked silently up the hill, huffing all the way, and finally reached the parking lot.

"Tina, would you walk a little farther and see if you can get a signal?" Paul pointed to the road. "If you can, give a yell and I'll place the call. You weren't a witness to the accident." Besides which, he'll call Don, not the police. Phone in hand, Tina headed out.

He crooked his finger in Kay's direction, pulling out the paper and smoothing it onto the hood of his car. "What does this say?"

Kay flinched and paled. She grabbed his wrist. "Targets," she whispered.

"Targets? Are you sure?"

"Oh, I suppose there might be subtleties or nuance to the words, but essentially that's what it means." She shuddered. "This was no accident."

"No, it wasn't." His anger built with fortifying strength.

"Daddy! Here." Tina waved from the lot's far corner.

"Don't say anything to Tina," she hissed.

"Of course not." He strode off toward Tina and pulled his phone free. "Honey, go sit with Kay. She's a little shaken by the close call." He tapped Don's number.

"No problem." Tina hurried to Kay's side.

"Salazar." Don's sturdy voice afforded Paul a small measure of relief. Finally, someone to share his burden and take his suspicions seriously.

"Don, Paul here. Listen up." He detailed the afternoon's events.

"Any other cars in the parking lot?"

"Nope. They must have come together and the other guy took off."

"Is the biker still alive?" Don had a way of getting to the heart of the matter.

Paul squinted at the bright sun, considering. "If he is, he has serious injuries." He refused to let his conscience bother him for leaving the biker.

"I'll call the ranger and let him arrange a search and rescue," Don said. "Do you have the GPS coordinates where he went over?"

"No. It was approximately half-a-mile south from the junction of the Manzanita and Sunset trails."

"Got it." Don exhaled. "Kay has dangerous enemies."

And secrets. All the afternoon's good feelings evaporated. He fingered the paper in his pocket with the astonishing photos.

"What about Janelle?" Paul hoped Don might shed some light on this current mystery. Don hadn't commented on the photographs, but that didn't mean he didn't have a theory—or two. "Maybe they're her enemies and Kay got caught up in the net." Desperate men grasped at any possibility. He learned fast.

"After I call the ranger, I'll head to Janelle's townhouse and bring her up to speed. She needs extra protection, and I can help out there. Kay's your responsibility. Keep her safe."

"I intend to. Both she and my daughter could have been hurt."

Don grunted. "Fate has a nice way with payback. Talk to you later."

Paul's brain flooded with questions. Did China's ambitions really reach this far?

Opening the driver's door, he slid in. He met Tina's worried eyes in the rearview mirror and handed his phone to Kay.

"The ranger is handling this," he said. "They have my contact information. In the meantime, why don't you do a little searching on the Internet for who might know this guy."

"How about local bike clubs? I can help." Tina's eyes reflected genuine concern. Where'd she learn so much compassion? Not from him. His mother? Probably.

"Good idea. Thanks, honey. Kay will try a different search." He shot Kay a glance, and she nodded, looking strained and anxious. He threw the Jeep into gear and floored the accelerator. Between the isolation and locked doors—and his choice of weapons—he could protect them at the house.

A soft gasp escaped Kay's lips. He glanced over. Her anguished expression made him lift his foot off the gas. She shook her head, pointing to the road home. Her hand trembled mid-air.

Now what? He pushed faster, taking the turns at high speed, whizzing past cyclists. Kay leaned her head against the headrest and closed her eyes. A tear escaped and trickled down her cheek.

He braked hard in the driveway. They all jerked forward. He tossed his key chain to Tina.

"Honey, would you mind running in to see if the ranger called and left a message already? Kay and I will bring in the gear."

Tina nodded and scampered up the walk.

"What happened?" Paul cupped Kay's jaw.

"There was an explosion at Janelle's and they can't find her." She swiped the cascade of fresh tears. "They think she's dead."

Chapter 37

WENG-HAN RESIDENCE

Inner Mongolia, China
Late Evening, June 4, Same Day

"Wife, we must talk."

Mai loathed the disapproval tinging his innocuous words. Yu walked home straight from the club, where political gossip and favors floated in the air like ash. A member must have tattled on her.

With deliberate calm, she arranged a pot of tea and two cups on a tray, adding delicate cookies. She preceded him to their living area and glanced out the window overlooking the vast barren desert to the north. Still silent, she offered him his tea, poured hers, and relaxed into a chair.

"Well? What is so important you don't greet me first?" Maybe her querulous tone would put him on the defensive so he would listen and support last week's unauthorized order.

Yu slurped a few sips. "We were sent here to ensure the great success of mining rare earth elements. Why do you pursue an unattractive vendetta? Heh? Is this American girl worth tarnishing our reputation?"

"It's not Chiang Kay I'm worried about, you fool," she said. Her husband didn't deserve the whole truth. If the girl died in California, who could ever tie it to her? She bit a tiny cookie. "It is protecting our information. Comrade Wei Jintao may have stupidly compromised our security when begging for what nestles between her legs."

"What does Wei have to do with our mining efforts?"

"That whore Chiang was observed gathering Li's secrets at the prison, yet a Party official let her leave the country, nonetheless. I reasoned it prudent to move Li farther away, in case another spy tries to contact him."

"You moved him so far even I can't contact him!"

Mai's eyes widened. Her husband never yelled. Maybe she pushed him a little too far this time.

"He may as well be in another country," he said with a grumpy glare.

Well, of course. The remote prison isolated Li from his family and colleagues. No one could get to his secrets now . . . especially, nosy American journalists. With one masterful stroke, Mai controlled all information. What more could one person do?

"Old man, you must face the truth. The Party assigned us to Mongolia as punishment, not reward. It will take extraordinary efforts to earn our rightful place back in Beijing."

"You are being punished, not me." Her husband stood, and stomped about the room. "This is an opportunity to help my country. I require Li's brains by my side to do so."

Lighting a cigarette, Mai conceded his point. She preferred unorthodox methods, such as planting seeds years ago in the American political party. As more Chinese emigrated worldwide, her influence followed. Whenever she needed to exert pressure on foreign soil, she identified which favor to call in, which political lever to pull.

Dragging on her cigarette, she rose. "I must check my email for an important communiqué." Walking to her desk, she opened the laptop, already powered on and ready to report on her far-flung minions.

Her San Francisco contact sent photo confirmation of the fire raging in the DuMont woman's home. She smiled in satisfaction. Clicking to an American news outlet, she scanned the headlines, searching for details. The DuMont woman escaped with only minor burns! Scowling, she swatted the desktop. What kind of idiot was hired? And no update yet on Chiang Kay's disposition.

"What is wrong?" Yu called across the room.

Should she tell him? Oh, why not? They were in this together, according to him.

"I sent a message to the U.S. Congress to mind their own business." She shrugged. "While the envelope arrived . . . sadly, it was empty."

"You fool! Why do you complicate matters?" Her husband stepped over and stuck his face into hers.

"I suppose you think we should kowtow to the Americans—yet we have the biggest economy now!"

"Soon enough, the world will kowtow to us. We both manufacture and buy their products. They rely on us for their refined metals, which drives all their high-tech devices. Without our labor and our consumers, the world would experience a deep depression." He threw up his hands. "China doesn't seek control over U.S. citizens or its politics, only the economy. Soon, we will be the most powerful country in the world. The military is irrelevant. Don't you understand yet?"

"Enough! You sound like the Party leaders at a convention." But she lowered her head in a conciliatory gesture. "You may be right." Better to pretend giving in than to battle him. She might need his influence in the future.

"One by one, countries are buckling under our sphere of influence. Can't you just wait a little longer?" He sighed, dropping into a chair.

No! She bit back the cry. Didn't he see she was becoming a useless old woman, good only as a nursemaid for her aged mother-in-law? She only had one year left before her forced retirement. If it took strong tactics to make her mark, so be it.

"What would you have me do, then, husband?"

"Believe in me. I already arranged a reduction in the charges against Li's sister-in-law to disclosing state secrets, instead of treason."

"What?" She flung her teacup against the wall.

Yu's face remained calm and composed. Shaking his head, he held her gaze. "It is a negotiation tactic, woman, and one the Party leaders approve of. If Li sees I helped his family, maybe he will cooperate."

"And his daughter?" Mai forced breaths in and out of her lungs. "Have you freed her already?"

"No. I hope never to use her." A pained expression crossed his face.

"You will if you must? We can't afford to fail, you and I."

"Ah, so now we are a team again, wife?" Yu's laugh was laden with irony. "Why is that?"

"Because we do not have the freedom to be otherwise."

For a brief moment, Mai allowed herself to imagine another culture. One allowing freedom, where she could tell her husband and her colleagues to take their antiquated ideas of revering elders and go hire themselves a caregiver.

Taking a deep breath, she calmed herself. This was China, her homeland. Her life.

Chapter 38

COLEMAN RESIDENCE

San Jose, California
Late Afternoon, June 4, Same Day

Paul pulled into Eric's driveway with a sigh of relief, overriding Tina's objections. She's safer here with a guard dog than in the isolated redwood forest as Don's crisis team was assembled.

Lynn opened the front door with a wave and Fred scooted out, barreling down the steps. His friendly woof and wriggling body undermined his reputation, but Don swore his hearing and guard-dog demeanor were excellent.

"I don't wanna be here," Tina whined for the umpteenth time.

Kay shifted in her seat. "What, a stay-cation, complete with a swimming pool and a chance to earn money for more clothes doesn't interest you? I'd trade places in a heartbeat if I could."

Tina twisted her mouth, grabbed her bag, and shoved open the door. Leaving the engine running, Paul jumped out and introduced her to Lynn. He kissed Tina goodbye with promises to call tomorrow and ran back to the car.

"At least she cooperated with minimal fuss." He slapped the car in gear, gunned the accelerator, and tore out of the driveway onto the wide-open back road, his mind racing just as fast.

He finally mixed his professional and personal lives—and look what happened. His little girl almost lost her life today. Those bikers didn't care who they took out, as long as Kay was injured—or killed.

"I think she understands the stakes are pretty high." Kay touched his hand resting on the gearshift.

"I hope so. Has Don sent an update on Janelle?"

"Yes. Second-degree burns on her shoulders and face only. The hospital will release her soon."

"She was damned lucky." Kay had found an online news story describing Janelle's mad dash to safety. One whole corner of her townhouse was gone due to the inferno. She was in the bathroom when the explosion occurred, not cooking dinner. Sheer coincidence—or poor timing, depending on your perspective.

"Where to now, boss?" Kay tossed him a smug look. "Right? We're not taking these attacks sitting down, are we?"

"DOD Tech. It should be deserted enough." And hopefully not linked to Kay's whereabouts for anyone to guess she might be there. Those bikers spooked him with their kamikaze attitude—and photographs of Kay and Janelle.

"Enough for what?" Her eyes searched his for clues.

"You'll see." He needed a safe place to grill her in private, and it was the first location that came to mind. It should work.

Kay scowled and stared out the window.

He thrummed his fingers on the steering wheel, pointing the car into the stark afternoon sun. What had he missed? He kept Kay's whereabouts a secret, yet someone still found her and linked her to Janelle. Was there a leak in his multi-faceted team? He hoped not. Although the women were alive, it came too damned close.

Unless Kay's reticence to disclose all the details of her missing months and imprisonment undermined their mission. And put Tina's life at risk, too. How could he ascertain the complete truth? For all he knew, Kay withheld the solution to the country's entire rare metals dilemma, inadvertently or not. They couldn't wait any longer.

Considering options, he swerved into the lot at DOD Tech, noting one other parked car. He got out to escort her across the deserted space, one hand resting at her waist. She trembled. In fear of him? Or of what was to come?

He unlocked the outer door and pointed right. "My office is at the far end."

Peering in the opposite direction, he spotted light shining through Gideon's ajar door. Good. Maybe all this pressure would motivate the engineer to find a solution.

Kay sauntered ahead, her snug jeans calling attention to every sway. She seemed ready to face danger again. Maybe he'd overdone his protectiveness. Maybe he should have tossed her back into the deep end sooner so she'd remember how to swim the swampy marsh of espionage and intelligence work.

Careful to lock the office door after him, he sat in his desk chair and steepled his fingers, uncertain how to start. She watched him patiently from the adjacent guest chair.

"Kay . . . um, Don thinks there's something pertinent to your time in China that you haven't yet disclosed." He frowned. How lame was it to pin this on Don? He took a deep breath. "And I agree."

"Are you calling me a liar?" The tiniest bit of remorse flickered through her eyes, undermining her angry tone.

"No, but you see the danger we're all in. Have you been afraid to tell me something?"

Bingo! He recognized that look. Surprise mixed with embarrassment. Her defensive posture would come next . . . wait for it . . . here it comes.

She crossed her arms and legs and set one foot swinging in a slow, deliberate rhythm. Yes!

"Why should I be afraid of you?" Her mockery didn't quite ring true. And she avoided answering his question. Again.

"Stop playing games. You've never been a team player, so why should we think otherwise?"

"Yeah, well at least I haven't conned myself that I'm a good team leader."

He gritted his teeth. Just like Daisy—change the subject and go on the offensive. "Are you referring to me?"

"Who else?" She smirked.

"It's hard to lead a team when the team is comprised of two people— that would be you and me, sweetheart—and one of them—again, you— doesn't tell the other what the hell is happening."

"Oh come on, just because you didn't receive daily updates from China didn't mean the end of the world. I'm good at what I do." She studied her nails, avoiding his glare.

"Maybe not the end of the world—but definitely the end of my job!"

"What did you say?" Kay sounded startled.

It was about damn time.

"I lost my job because I lost you! What do you think my job entailed, anyway? Being your personal cheerleader? My sole responsibility was to keep track of your mission and use your intelligence. You disappeared right when this rare metals situation blew up. It reflected poorly on my ability to manage you." He shook his head. "I got fired...and you got forgotten."

"By you?"

"You have to ask?" He slammed his fist on the desk. "I called in every single favor owed me to find your stupid ass. And then I tapped your former contacts at SDS—the ones you pissed off, by the way—to help me help you. So who the hell is more of a team player? Me? Or you?"

"You, okay? You're the best, and I trusted you would find me. Don't you remember all those cryptic emails you figured out?"

"Damn straight." He folded his arms. "So start talking. You screwed your professional reputation with everyone else. I should probably have my head examined for still listening to you . . . I. Don't. Care. What. You. Did . . . So tell me everything."

Kay slouched, tucking one leg beneath the other, and stared out the shaded window. "After Charlie died, I tried to leave China. My visa got yanked and the government blocked me every time. I tried leveraging my family name, but no go. So . . . I . . . um . . . I . . . became a mistress to Wei Jintao."

"The guy who invented the Great Chinese Fire Wall?" He fought to steady his tone. This was always Kay's MO. Why should he be surprised?

"He's high up in the political food chain. I hoped he might help me arrange a new visa."

"And how did that work out for you?"

"Isn't it obvious?" She scowled. "Not wonderfully. But . . . he leveraged his influence and protected me in jail."

"You thought they treated you well?" He grimaced, instantly regretting his harsh mockery.

"Relatively." Her subdued voice spoke volumes.

Paul scooted his chair next to hers. He laid his arm on the desk, palm up, hoping she'd remember their trail confessions. "You always told me everything. What's different this time?"

"I felt helpless. Oh, God . . . Paul! It was so much worse . . ." Her face crumpled. She clutched his hand. He covered her cold fingers with his.

"Tell me," he whispered.

"I never heard Li's name until Tan Yannan told me he was a member of their family." She took a deep breath, shudders marring her effort. "I assumed it was coincidence, you know? There aren't a lot of subversives working together in Beijing." She smiled wryly. "Then, I promised Fran I would get her father back. Once I got stateside . . . I didn't see how I could." The tears came.

"Well, you were probably right. None of us have figured out how yet." A pang of guilt flashed through Paul. Had he let Kay's recovery and obfuscations undermine his promise to Colonel DuMont?

"I haven't even tried to help Li!" Kay hiccupped. "And now Fran's in danger, too."

"I don't think one is related to the other, sweetie."

"Everything is related." She sniffed and wiped her nose with the back of her hand. "Including Tina's safety. If she'd been hiking at my side instead of you, one or both of us would have gone over the edge instead of that crazy biker. Even if we find Fran, she wouldn't be any safer in America . . . obviously. Why bother?"

"Because you care for Fran. And you'll make a good mother if you decide to adopt her."

"Yeah, right. I'm the best role model on earth for a little girl." Her tone dripped with sarcasm.

"Courage is an admirable trait. And communication." He tapped the tip of her nose. "Work on your honesty a little more and you'll have the basis for a committed relationship."

"I'm no better than a whore."

Her whispered confession shocked him.

"You survived," he said, lecturing himself as much as her. "Most assault victims face the same dilemma, and choose life over death."

"You know?" Tears filled her eyes again.

"We watched . . . snippets." Vivid snippets that still ripped his guts in two. "I can't begin to imagine what it was like for you." He forced down the lump in his throat.

"You're disgusted with me." She covered her face with her hands.

"No! No, it wasn't your fault!" He inched closer and touched her knee.

"Wasn't it? Shouldn't I have stayed in touch with you? Obeyed your orders?" She peeked through her fingers, eyes glistening. "Listened to my father in the first place and never gone to China?"

"Really? You think this is all about a bad career choice?"

"At least I still might have the respect of my family." She bit her lip. "Or a family of my own. And friends who admire me and enjoy my company, not run away because I'm bad news."

"Who's running? From where I sit, the only one running from your past is you."

Silence.

He let her stew on his accusation a good long while. It was about time she faced herself.

"Grow up, Kay. Stop making excuses for your choices. Make new ones and stop cowering in the shadows. Live, goddammit! Live!"

"Do you believe I can be different?" Her reedy voice trembled.

Dumbfounded, he stared into her tentative brown eyes.

"You have to ask?" Damn, this woman managed to yank his chain. Didn't she see he was risking Tina's life to be with her?

She leaned forward, cupped his face, and kissed him full on the mouth.

What the . . . Hell, his mama didn't raise a stupid man. He lifted his hands to her cheeks and held her in place.

Slowly . . . he tasted her lips, inhaled her scent. He increased the pressure as her mouth softened, parting her lips with his tongue. Waiting for her. Uncertain if she meant the kiss as an introduction to a future or a salute to their past friendship.

She slid her mouth away. "You're buzzing."

"Huh?"

"Your phone." Smiling, she slid her hand along his thigh to the cargo pocket.

"Oh." He dug into the pocket with more difficulty than usual. "Freeman here."

"Alex thinks he found Li." Don's curt voice carried loud enough for Kay to hear. She gasped and wrung her hands.

"Alive?" Paul stilled her fingers with a firm grip.

"For now. Janelle and I are heading to Alex's office."

"Kay and I will see you there." He ended the call, meeting her uncertain gaze. "Are you ready for this? It might bring back bad memories for you."

"Too bad. If it stops these attacks, I'll do whatever it takes."

"That's my girl!" He smacked her on the lips and rose, pulling her to her feet.

Kay got her gumption back. It was a start.

Chapter 39

PANVISION TECHNOLOGIES

Cupertino, California
Evening, June 4, Same Day

Alex confirmed his earlier search results just as Paul and Kay rushed through the entranceway. He'd managed to track down more drone video footage floating through the ether by hacking into rebel circles. Their cryptic messages battered the world's technology cloud, seeking justice.

Shaking his head, he considered the five ad-hoc team members crowded into his tiny office. He'd have to arrange for larger quarters if this would become a typical use of his technology. He thought all his office needed was whiz-bang computing systems, a desk, a table, and a few chairs. He'll confer with Eric and Lynn soon on that issue. They always gave him great advice.

Janelle dropped into the plastic guest chair looking haggard from her ordeal, repeating her arguments to Don about not cowering in a safe hotel. Don played her temporary bodyguard but based on his numerous phone calls, sought a more permanent solution.

Tapping the zoom button on his outsized screen, Alex enlarged the bootleg image. Kay crowded close; he leaned back into her soft warmth. With her new weight gain, she embodied his teenage fantasy once more, not an emotionally drained waif.

"Kay, you're the only one who met Li. Is this him?" Alex glanced over his shoulder.

"Any way to improve the resolution?" Kay peered at the screen, tilting her head left and right.

"WYSIWYG." Don called out from across the room.

"Pardon me?" Kay's face twisted in confusion.

"*What You See Is What You Get*—and be damned grateful Alex is so smart," Don said.

"I am, for my sake and for Li's," she murmured in Alex's ear, patting his shoulder. Straightening, she nodded. "He looks like Li and walks like Li. If he quacks at me, I'd say he's a duck."

"Most engineers quack at a pretty woman." Paul chuckled. "Right, Alex?"

Warmth climbed the back of Alex's neck. He unrolled his tongue and re-focused on the conversation at hand, not his body's reaction to Kay's soft breath and sweet smell.

"This guy's prisoner number matches the classified Chinese transfer orders Janelle provided," Alex said.

"How did you manage that tidbit, Janelle?" Paul leaned against the doorjamb, arms folded across his chest.

Janelle toyed with the end of her scarf. A guilty expression crossed her bandaged face. "Um, let's just say hackers work for all kinds of companies, organizations . . . and governments." She grimaced. "Sorry for being obtuse, but I really can't say more."

"Where is the prison?" Kay leaned close again. "That background has high mountains, not the high deserts of Mongolia, where I saw him."

"Bingo," Don said. "Our young genius, Alex, just put the puzzle pieces together. How does 'near Tibet' strike you?" Don pulled a chair away from the table and dropped into it, sipping coffee from a dinged, metallic travel mug.

"Tibet? Oh, no! Did I cause that poor monk trouble because he carried my message?" Kay's worried glance bounced from Paul to Janelle.

"We don't think so." Janelle shook her head.

Alex twisted around to face Kay, catching her flash of uncertainty. "I researched this jail. It's the favorite holding site for unusual political prisoners, probably due to its obscurity. Out of sight, out of mind."

"You can't get more out of sight than the outskirts of Tibet," Don said. "That's why the rebels there love these new camera-equipped drones–keeps them in the public eye."

"And you have Alex's invention to help." Kay topped her praise with a gracious smile.

"I enjoy searching for beautiful women." Alex dared a wink.

Kay threw back her head and laughed. "I'll tell Li. He may be surprised how much his prison stint has changed him."

"So we've found Li. Now what?" Paul's no-nonsense question wiped the smile off Kay's face, much to Alex's regret. She stepped away and crossed her arms, matching Paul's attitude.

"I'll keep tracking him, of course." Alex waved at the array of monitors.

"You may need to do more, son," Don said. "Each member of this tiny team must do his–or her–best." He nodded toward Kay and Janelle.

"Absolutely." Paul turned to Janelle. "Does your influence in Congress extend to Tibet?"

"That's a real stretch." Janelle wrinkled her nose and shrugged.

"So stretch a little," Paul prodded. "This rare earths crisis gives you an excuse to push. Work those diplomatic muscles. Don?"

"Yo." Don waved a half-salute.

"Can you find a good reason to get someone over there to check out the prison personally?"

"Just 'good,' or one that gets results?" Don's dry question made Alex smile.

"Results are all that matter." Paul pounded his fist into his palm. "Bottom line, we have a rescue operation on our hands. Now that Alex found Li, we've got to get him out of China, and do everything we can to ensure his safety."

Alex gulped. Was this his turn to step up? After fleeing Vietnam's oppressive regime, his parents felt they owed America a debt of gratitude for their sea rescue and political asylum. How often had Mom and Dad pushed Alex to excel in order to repay that debt? Maybe he needed to do more than just show off his software skills.

"Janelle, I have an unusual idea about how I can help." Kay's voice wavered, but she lifted her chin high. Such courage! She coped with so much already.

"Why am I not surprised?" Paul muttered.

"I wouldn't want to ruin my rogue reputation." Kay jammed one hand on her angled hip and glared. "Stop coddling me and let me stretch a little too."

"Go for it." Paul threw his hands in the air and perched on the desk corner.

Alex detected a tiny bit of relief—or was it pride—in Paul's expression. Had he finagled their discussion to provoke Kay's active involvement again? If so, kudos to Paul's leadership style.

Kay blew out her breath. "If I publicly testify in Congress about my first-hand experience in a Chinese jail where political prisoners like Li are kept, and link it to China's motivation to control rare metals, wouldn't we have a negotiation advantage to free both Li and his immediate family?" She turned a worried face toward Paul. "Fran's included in this rescue, right? I mean, we're not abandoning Li's daughter in the middle of all this. They might use her against him—and us—and we'll be right back where we started."

"You'll appear for us?" Janelle jerked upright in her chair. "Wonderful! It will solidify our committee's credibility."

"I'm only doing this to help Fran and Li, not because I've developed a patriotic conscience." Kay wagged a finger in Janelle's direction.

"It's the right thing to do and you know it, Kay." Paul jumped up. "It should have been part of your debriefing. You've gotten off easy."

"Easy?" Alex leapt to his feet, too. "You sweated and cursed with the rest of us watching Kay's prison video. You punched that hole in the wall, remember?" He pointed to the dent.

Kay paled. Her gaze locked on Paul's tortured features. "Thanks, Alex."

Alex beckoned him, "Can I speak with you in private?"

Paul resigned a nod and turned toward the door. They stepped into the empty hallway. Alex shut the office door on the other three and walked to the nearby window, hoping Paul would follow that extra distance to insure confidentiality from the others. Turning, he met the older man's troubled eyes.

"Sorry, Alex. I was out of line. Lord knows what she's gone through." Paul inclined against the wall, arms crossed, head bent. "Thanks for pointing it out."

"You're welcome," Alex said. "However, I didn't ask for privacy to yell at you."

"Then what?" Paul's eyebrows lifted.

"I'm not sure I'm the best person for this team." Alex shuffled his feet, keeping his gaze lowered.

"Why not? You've been a great asset so far."

"Because I considered this one big chance to show off my technology's capabilities, not take a political stand. In fact . . ." Alex hesitated, not sure how to phrase what was gnawing at his conscience.

"Spit it out. We don't have time to waste."

"Don't you find it all hypocritical? America criticizes China's horrible environmental policies, yet is furious when China dares to halt this mining which contaminates its land and water." Alex scratched his head and met Paul's eyes. "If we need refined rare metals so badly and the output is so critical, why aren't we mining it ourselves? We shouldn't bash China for filling our technology orders. Basic supply and demand, right?"

"Out of the mouths of babes." Paul rubbed his forehead.

"I'm not a babe!" Fists clenched at his sides, Alex glared at Paul.

"No . . . you're not . . . but this isn't a simple case of competitive disadvantage. It's touch football versus the NFL."

Mollified, Alex waved his hand, wanting to hear more.

"Look, China's political gambits and power plays put the U.S. on edge," Paul said. "The NRC came up with unnecessary rules that broke the U.S. rare earths value chain. That's how we lost control of our fate. Bottom line, we simply can't match the scale of China's enormous program. This is really about state-sponsored industries and government-sanctioned monopolies used for geo-political warfare against America."

"Yeah, well, I'm concerned any more involvement on my part will tank my future." Alex admitted. "China's a big market to ruin when I don't have a stake in this outcome."

"You don't? Don't you aspire to land defense contracts eventually? Doesn't that fancy computer on your desk use some of these refined metals?"

Alex could almost hear his father lecturing him in one ear about his patriotic duty, his mother nagging in the other about his moral obligation to help.

"Okay, okay." Alex sighed. "I guess I can justify helping to rescue a political prisoner and an innocent child. But I have to keep my company's success in mind. I'm accountable to my investors. They expect me to keep my nose clean."

"What makes you think you won't?"

Alex pointed his finger. "Because I think Don and Janelle may be considering using the girl as a negotiating tool, no different than the Chinese government. And that isn't right."

"Besides which, it would destroy Kay." Paul's voice lowered.

"How do you figure?" Alex's brain raced, re-playing earlier conversations . . . his video hunt . . . his scanning of hacker message boards. Had he missed something important?

Paul stared at the fluorescent light fixture, its incessant hum reminding Alex of a relentless insect, irritating and ubiquitous, especially in the wee hours of the night.

"Kay cares an awful lot for Fran," Paul said. "I should have gone over all those images with you and figured out Fran's connection to Li sooner. Maybe then, we could have protected Fran. And Kay wouldn't be hurt again."

Alex cracked his knuckles one by one, considering. "You worked non-stop pulling this informal team together to rescue Kay. Wasn't that your first priority, keeping a team member safe?"

"Well, sure—"

"And once Kay was home, wasn't your next highest priority to get her healthy again?" Alex searched Paul's face. "So she could help us, not be a burden?'

"Yes, especially once we realized how drained she was." Paul clunked his head against the wall, closing his eyes. "But—"

"But nothing. If anyone failed Kay, I did. I could have asked more questions or gotten involved earlier." Alex took a deep breath. "I didn't think an engineer should."

"You think you're a simple engineer in all this?" Paul opened one eye with a squint.

"Well, yes. I had expertise and technology, and you used them. Case closed."

"Case re-opened. You're an honorable young man who's working hard to support his investors, his family's integrity, and his colleagues' requests. Expertise and technology mean nothing without values."

Alex linked his fingers together and stared down at his clasped hands. Paul's assessment shook him to the core. He grew up in Silicon Valley's pressure-cooker schools, where technology was God and failure to achieve top grades provoked more senseless suicides among his fellow students than he'd care to admit.

"Is that what guides you in critical decisions?" Alex winced at the tremor in his voice and cleared his throat. "Your values?"

"That's what life is all about." Paul took a few steps down the short hallway before turning back to face him. "Lacking values to guide you, you might as well be a soulless mercenary."

"Then . . . I'm proud to serve on any team you lead. Starting now." Alex stood firm, ignoring the caution swirling in his brain.

"Thinking of saving the world, kid?"

"No, just making it a better place, one tiny step at a time." Alex lifted his head and forced a confident smile.

"You're on." Paul slapped his shoulder and reached for the office door handle. "Now let's go plan a rescue. For Li, his daughter, Silicon Valley . . . and the rest of America."

Chapter 40

FREEMAN RESIDENCE

Saratoga, California
Night, June 4, Same Day

"Wine or coffee?" Paul poked his head out of the kitchen and tossed his sweatshirt onto the vestibule's coat stand. Kay burrowed against the sofa arm, tucking the afghan around her shapely legs. With the fog rolling in, his high-up rental home had the feel of a romantic bed-and-breakfast get-away along California's famous coastline.

"If you brew decaf-Irish, I'll take the hot stuff," she called. "I forgot how cold and damp it can get in the summer."

"Imagine the shock to a Southern boy like me." He dumped decaf grounds into the coffeemaker and splashed a healthy jigger of whiskey into each mug. "At home, I strip to my boxers until summer's sweet dawn."

"Now that's worth paying to see."

He smiled, relishing her teasing lilt. Advancing into new-relationship territory was just fine with him. As long as she wasn't scared off again. "Yeah, well, you'll have to fight off the Georgia skeeters for the best seats in the house."

"Ah, and here I thought you already sported the best seat . . . well, tush . . . in this house."

"Depends on your perspective." Pulling the carafe free, he filled the mugs half full. "Last I looked, your tush beat mine, hands down."

"Wouldn't that be 'pants' down? Anyway, how long ago did you look? Two years ago? Three?"

He halted in the doorway. The back of his neck prickled. Whenever the old Kay sought compliments, she had an agenda.

Handing her a mug, he settled on the sheepskin rug. He stretched out his legs onto its plush warmth, remembering their interrupted kiss hours ago.

"I looked every time." He searched her eyes for her reaction to that confession.

"I'm shocked." Winking, she took a quick sip of coffee and gazed out the window toward the glistening silver of shrouded moonlight. "And glad, too," she murmured. "I hoped you'd notice."

"What red-blooded man wouldn't?"

"I wanted you to notice. I didn't care about the others." She met his gaze full on.

"I noticed more than a married man should." He grappled with a flood of memories. "It tore me apart."

She slid her foot out from beneath the afghan and nudged his knee. "I never meant to break up your marriage."

"You didn't, not really. It's just . . ." He sipped his coffee, welcoming the liquor's punch. ". . . I tried every which way to ignore you, but I couldn't." Boy, what an understatement. His body still reached for her whenever she came within fifty feet. "To keep my commitment to Daisy, I became a professional hard-ass instead of dealing with my feelings out in the open."

"Did Daisy find out?"

He shrugged. "Daisy grabbed the chance to marry me and leave her small town behind. When she felt secure enough, she started her own life—which didn't include me. I don't think she cared one way or the other, as long as I provided for her and Tina." His gut twisted. "Having a family anchors me."

"And you anchored me."

"Then why?" Years of tormented imaginings roughened his voice. "Why did you purposely put yourself in roles to be used by so many men? You could have asked me for help. I would have moved heaven and earth for you."

"Don't you get it?" She tilted her head, eyes welling with emotion. "I didn't find my true self until that damned prison. I couldn't risk losing my only support when I was out on all those limbs."

"You put yourself there!"

"What choice did I have? You were married, and I didn't want to harm you. I figured if I was the least of your burdens, I could stay on your team."

"You cared that much?"

She darted a glance at him and compressed her lips. "The first time I saw you I actually tingled. Those tingles turned to heat . . . then fire. I craved an intimacy I couldn't have. Oh, I tried to act all cool and professional, tried to treat you like one of the guys . . . but I couldn't." She drained her coffee and slapped the mug on the coffee table. "Can you blame me for seeking a poor substitute?"

"Damn straight! Even after my divorce, you kept your distance, waltzing into D.C. for only a few hours." Hours planning her next seduction, how she would use targeted pillow talk for needed intelligence. He'd twisted in knots between jealousy and worry, anger and desire, and an overwhelming shame that he'd handed her the ultimate power with barely a whimper. "Why did you avoid me?"

"I was afraid you'd abandon me, too." She took a shuddering breath.

"Ah, honey." He pulled her down to his lap, rocking back and forth. "Daisy filed for divorce, not me." Resting his cheek on the top of her head, he sighed. "As much as I wished I could be with you, I never would have left my family."

"Really?" Her muscles relaxed.

Memories resurfaced of his struggles to pay monthly alimony and child support. He kept crazy schedules to free up time whenever Tina visited. How could he ever doubt he was a good father and protector?

Because my shame as a man ate away my confidence as a husband.

"Really," he whispered in her hair. "And you're feeling guilty you've abandoned Fran. Am I right?"

"How did you know?" Kay stirred, searching his eyes.

"Because I've never seen you so passionate. It's obvious you care for her." He toyed with her fingers.

"She's special, Paul. Full of life. Similar to Tina, only deprived of freedom—and the security of a family."

"Why would you take on such a responsibility for a virtual stranger?"

"To prove I've changed . . . That sounds kind of selfish, I guess. But this is a chance to be the person I choose to be, not the person I imagined I had to be." She met his gaze. "To show I can love someone more than myself. And to create a family, not ruin yours."

"You didn't wreck my family, honey. I allowed it to disintegrate, right in front of my eyes . . ."

"Paul?" Kay's tender touch pulled him back to the present. "The future is what matters. If you're by my side, pushing away obstacles with me, I'll get better." Her eyes searched his. "Can you . . . will you . . . be there for me?"

"I always have, Kay. And I always will." He framed her jaw with his hand, tilting her face up toward his kiss. She met him halfway, twining both arms around his neck, pulling him close. Her lips parted, warm whiskey breath tempted him to lower his guard, to relax in her embrace. To trust.

Pressing his mouth to hers, finally tasting her, he half-throttled the groan rising in his throat and slid his fingers through her short hair. She tensed. Waiting for his repulsion?

"Relax," he murmured, exploring the bumps and tiny ridges of her skull, enjoying the unexpected intimacy. "Trust me."

She melted against his chest, easing into his hardening lap with abandon. He slid his hands along her neck, swept the afghan off her shoulders, and wrapped her in his arms. Long hair or not, this was the Kay of his dreams. His long-time friend. His teammate. His partner.

His lover.

Kay's tongue dueled with his. Her fingers clutched the fabric against his shoulders. Tiny, hard nubs pressed against his chest, tempting him. He unbuttoned her vest and pushed it down her arms, delving beneath the soft vee of her shirt and cupping one breast.

She jerked and tore her lips free. "What's that?"

"This?" He pinched her nipple. "Or this?" He thrust his hip upward, pressing against her butt cheek.

"No . . . listen . . ." she whispered.

She straightened. He held his breath and cocked his ear.

Silence. Too silent. Even the birds and the insects seemed to wait and watch.

Disentangling from their embrace, he nudged her to the soft rug and rolled to his knees, peering over the top of the sofa. Ominous darkness filled the exposed window.

Pop.

A silent bullet tore through the back cushion and pierced the wall.

Holy shit! He ducked. A second bullet missed him by inches, smacking into the wall behind him. He looked over his shoulder. Kay was coiled into a crouch, wide-eyed.

"Stay down!" Paul hissed, his brain racing, ears straining.

The front door eased open. Damn! His firearm was buried in the hall closet, too far away to do any good. He should have been better prepared. Now he only had the element of surprise on his side.

A shadow slipped through. A floorboard in the front hallway squeaked.

He motioned Kay to cover her eyes.

Squinting in the door's direction, Paul clapped his hands.

The torchiere blazed to life with the strength of sudden summer lightning. Dressed all in black, the assassin's wide face contorted. His hand shot up to shield his eyes before he dove back outside.

This afternoon's biker!

Scrambling to his feet, Paul tore across the wooden floor. He grabbed the doorframe to stop his forward momentum and provide cover. He stuck his head out in time to glance at the dark form retreating down the driveway.

He dashed onto the porch and jumped over the steps, peering into the gloomy woods. A shadowed movement faded rapidly into the blackness.

Should he give chase? He shot toward the Jeep's driver-side door and skidded to a halt. A loud hiss from the front tire took that option off the list. If it still had air in it . . . when did that goon have time to slash it?

Maybe there was a third assassin.

His blood surged. He spun and raced back to the house. Kay stood in the doorway.

"Did you recognize him?" Kay asked, white-faced and trembling.

He nodded, pressing a finger to her lips and grasping her cold fingers. He closed the front door and secured the safety bolt. Better late than never. Pulling her after him, he tiptoed into the kitchen, relieved to see the sturdy chain still in place. He hustled down the hall to his bedroom and bath, checking every possible hiding place.

Nothing.

Retracing their steps, he released Kay's hand and pointed her toward Tina's bedroom. He searched hers and the bath. No sign of forced entry.

He let out his breath. There was at least one gunman, possibly prowling the driveway. Did the intruder count on an instinctive flight along winding roads to get back to civilization? There was only one road out of the house. The gunman could take potshots along the way.

Or did the invader hope for a fight: seeking vengeance, calling for back up, re-grouping, and succeeding this time? The memory of Ernie's futile, fatal stand raced through his mind. His attackers had outnumbered and outgunned a trained soldier armed to the hilt in only minutes. What were the odds he could protect Kay with just a handgun against a swarm?

Paul considered his team. Eric already guarded Tina, and Don belatedly had Janelle's back. Alex was just a kid. It would take almost an hour for local law enforcement to navigate the windy roads to his remote home. Too damned long if these assasins were deadly serious and ready to attack. Besides, calling for help might put more people in danger because he hadn't prepared.

Third option . . . evade.

Chapter 41

Still in shock, Kay stared at Paul, a blur of motion as he snatched the huge backpack off the floor, sticking water bottles in its side pockets.

"Grab jackets and shoes." He yanked the ties of the pack tight. He looked up and his expression softened. "Kay, move it. We gotta go."

She blinked, the last few minutes smacking her upside her head. Someone tried to kill her—again.

Why?

Rushing to her room for her warmest hoody, she jammed bare feet into old canvas shoes. She bolted to the hall, pulled his sweatshirt off the coat rack, and dashed back to the kitchen. Paul squatted, fastening his bootlaces with swift, sure motions.

Kay tossed him the sweatshirt and pulled hers on, tying the strings tight below her chin.

"Ready." It was a miracle she managed to steady her voice. Tremors floated along her spine in mocking imitation of Paul's fingers only minutes ago. Passion or fear? Disappointment or adrenaline crash?

Paul almost died, all because of her.

He hoisted the pack onto his back, cinching the straps against his broad chest and narrow waist, wearing the burden with ease. Sliding the chain sideways, he twisted the deadbolt on the back door and opened it six inches. The fog reflected back glimmering moonlight, brightening the dark. Pushing it wide open, he examined every direction, his blond curls a soft beacon.

Kay grabbed a ball cap from the rack.

"Here," she whispered, stuffing it on his head. Following him outside, she closed the door behind her with a tiny click.

He threw her a grateful smile and wrapped his hand around hers, going along a gloomy path to the edge of his property. A horse whinnied in the neighbor's corral. Paul stopped.

"Can you ride a horse?"

"A city girl like me? Get real!"

"Just a suggestion." His grin gleamed in the darkness. He peered to the left, the hillside falling away from the crest. The road—and the assassin—led up to their right. "This way." He tugged her hand and she fell into step next to him, heading down.

A tiny, winding trail met them on the other side of his fence, the redwoods rising like spooky sentinels in the foggy mist off the ocean. Acorns crunched underfoot. The crackle and pop reminded her of the firecrackers at Wei Jintao's Chinese New Year celebration. How long ago that seemed! A different time, a different place.

A different Kay.

Paul gestured to match his rapid steps and traverse single file. He stayed in the deepest shade, anticipating dangers ahead. The leaf-strewn path dipped and dropped, paralleling Skyline Boulevard, she guessed. Climbing a steep section, Kay stumbled. She caught herself on her hands. Paul pivoted and grabbed her elbow, hauling her up and forward, toward the exposed road.

Headlights pierced the darkness. Twin beams swept the forest in an eerie imitation of a Hollywood premiere. Paul dropped to his knees, avoiding their indiscriminate glare. The tall, straight redwoods offered surprisingly little cover, their branches soaring upward to drink ready moisture settling on top of the little mountain.

Kay fought for breath. Too bad she hadn't spent more time getting back in shape.

"Come on, we can take a break after we go over this crest." Paul's repeated urging made her smile. Apparently, he already forgot how he powered up the last incline without pausing once. She pushed herself hard, digging for the inner strength she used to rely on as a matter of course. She'd gotten too soft living as a fledgling in Paul's comforting nest.

The fog thickened into cold, heavy clouds. Hoody soaked, shoes squishing with every step, she clenched her hands in the jacket's pockets. She willed the shivers to a low shudder, reluctant to succumb to simple physical discomfort. She so missed her heavy head of hair. How did bald men ever stay warm?

Paul halted at the top, gazing down the steep canyon. Pulling his phone free, he aimed it in every direction.

"No signal." He didn't sound the least bit surprised—or alarmed. "Let's hike this section off-trail. There's shelter ahead. Maybe we can beat the worst of the rain if we hurry."

Jamming his phone back inside his pocket, he clasped her hand and pulled her up a steep slope, hopping from one slick rock to the next with the ease of a mountain goat. Kay didn't dare let go. He pulled, steadied, and pulled again, bending into the sudden, pelting downpour.

She distracted herself by remembering the details of one childhood summer in San Francisco when it poured like this. They'd been at the coast, and the June rain surprised picnickers and ruined outdoor weddings. It was the very last time her parents took her to Ocean Beach.

A brown sign smeared with dirty raindrops announced their entrance to Castle Rock State Park. They entered a crisscrossed intersection of wide fire roads and tendrilled trails. He cocked his head and raised one finger. She held her breath.

Bike tires splashed and swished below them—heading their way.

His jaw clenched.

"I was hoping we could avoid this." Paul adjusted his straps and bootlaces. "Can you handle heights?"

"Is there a trail?" She gulped.

"Sort of." He headed out, his stride determined and swift, winding through an abandoned campground of lonely fire circles. Kay dreamed of a bonfire thawing her frozen toes. Why hadn't she put on sturdier shoes?

Because she hadn't anticipated this assassin would still be on their tail. Who was he?

Head down, Kay followed Paul's footsteps right to the brink of a canyon. A gray curtain hid what was probably a stunning ocean view on a clear day. The sheer drop of a five hundred foot fall terrorized her.

Better than the Golden Gate Bridge for suicide. One misstep and you're a goner.

Paul halted and held out his hand. "Hang on. This is slippery."

Kay took a deep breath, gripped his fingers tight and followed him along the edge. One gingerly stride at a time, they traversed the goat path. Up, down, scrambling over huge rocks, clinging to a safety wire. Kay kept her eyes on her feet. Otherwise, she'd surely freeze in her steps from fear. And freeze to death in the cold rain.

"The good news is no biker in his right mind would follow us." She forced a smile at the lame joke and gripped the soaring rock face.

"Assuming he's in his right mind." Paul jumped off the boulder and held his arms out toward her.

"What a positive attitude." She collided with his body and reveled in the brief moment of warmth.

"Only speaking the truth, honey." Paul trudged forward. "His partner's crazy trail maneuver may have killed him. We have no idea why they're after you."

"Meaning they'll die trying, rather than face failure alive?" Kay shuddered.

"Meaning we convince whoever's behind it to stop, or make sure they're next."

The trail widened and flattened until the next downward bend. Kay drew in a breath, relieved for the break. This obviously linked to her last mission and rare earths somehow. But she didn't know anything! Even if she possessed any critical information, she wasn't in a position to do much with it. Anyone with a brain would guess she disclosed all her secrets during a debriefing.

Well, except the personal ones.

Paul skidded the length of the trail, halting his slide at a wooden bridge crossing a rushing creek.

"Finally! I don't think I'll attempt that again," he said.

"Maybe on a bright sunny day to appreciate our accomplishment." Kay dared a look behind and cringed. She picked her way along the stable, inner edge. Reaching his side, she hugged him. "Thanks for your help."

He rocked her for long seconds. "I didn't want to lose you again," he murmured in her ear. "And if I don't get you warm soon, I might."

"What, you can conjure up a warm, cozy hotel with room service? Did we hike all the way to Yosemite's Ahwahnee Hotel?"

"I have something nearly as dry in mind. Come on."

Curious, Kay ignored the slap-slap of her soggy soles and the constant drip of her drenched sleeves onto frozen fingers. Negotiating a series of rises toward the peak, she shoved back her hood and peered at the massive rock formation towering above her.

"Let me guess—Castle Rock."

"Better. A cave serving as a castle for your rest, milady." Paul bowed with a flourish of arms and pointed ahead.

"Rest? I'll take it." Lord, she was tired, too tired to fuss about Paul's unorthodox shelter. He'd kept her safe so far.

Hang on! Did they both experience brain freeze?

"Paul, what about that biker?"

He hauled her up one final step. She faced a limestone cave, tall enough to stand upright and large enough for ten. Urging her to the rear, he dropped his pack with a heavy sigh.

"If we stay out of sight, I doubt he'll find us," he said. "He'll expect us to head down the hill for help, so we'll do the unexpected. Let him wear himself out in this rainy forest. I'm bushed."

Kay sank to her knees on the smooth, rock surface. Paul burrowed through the pack and pulled out a dark tarp. The next item, thin and silvery, gleamed in the cavern's darkness. Reaching in one more time, he dug out and tossed her a water bottle.

"Drink up, then we rest." He flapped the tarp and laid it into the back notch. Shaking open the silver blanket, he grabbed a bottle and drank half of it. He fiddled with his tangled laces and toed off his boots. "Take off your clothes."

"My, my, what wonderful foreplay." Kay quivered with nerves. She never expected the night to end like this.

"Cut it out, Kay. The survival blanket only works if we radiate body heat back at ourselves. Clothes will waste it, not use it." He struggled with his wet sweatshirt, and pulled it and his T-shirt over his head with one jerk. A handgun protruded from his waistband, gleaming metallic against his pale, bare skin. He pulled it out and set it on top of the pack. Unbuckling his belt, he shoved his jeans to his ankles and stepped out, shivering. "Do you need help?"

She shook her head, staring at his taut body. He never lost the broad shoulders and muscled chest from his football years to flab. His hard thighs glistened in the dim light. He squatted and lifted the narrow blanket high enough to crawl under, taking the entire space.

Anxious about the forced intimacy, she slipped shoes off icy toes, slid out of ruined pants, and peeled off her tops. Following his example, she left her panties on and darted beneath the blanket, landing right on top of him.

Delicious heat radiated below her. She moaned and grabbed the last ounce of pragmatism remaining in her mushy brain. "If you scoot over, I'll stretch out in front or back—your preference."

His chuckle jiggled her. She tried to slither sideways but he gripped her waist and positioned her squarely on top of him, her legs between his, her crotch nestling his unmistakable bulge.

"This blanket isn't made for two, honey," Paul said. "This is the only way it will work."

"I beg to differ." Kay dropped her head on his chest, too weary to argue. "The Kama Sutra suggests many more positions for the adventurous."

His laughter filled the cave, echoing back an invitation to relax, to enjoy. To forget all the dangers and revel in their closeness.

Tears moistened her eyes. She didn't deserve him.

"Soon, honey." He kissed the top of her head and squeezed her tight. "I've had all the adventures I can handle for one night."

Now or never.

Sliding her fingertips through the wiry hairs on his chest, she took a deep breath.

"There's something you should be aware of before we . . . um . . . ever do anything," Kay said.

His arms jerked.

Heart in her throat, she waited for them to drop away, to put her at a distance.

Instead, his arms snuggled her closer, one hand drifting down and resting on her butt cheek, as if he found it a more comfortable spot.

"What is it, honey? We had this conversation already. You know, the one where you can tell me anything."

"I don't think you meant this." She dropped a quick kiss on his exposed throat. Would it be her last?

"Try me."

"There's a good likelihood I have AIDS." She squeezed her eyes closed, preparing for his rejection.

He didn't breathe. Tension filled his muscles, from his thighs and abdomen to his neck. Head pressed against his heart, she felt his pulse stutter and break into an uneven rhythm. Glancing up, she watched his eyes open, blink, and stare at the rocky ceiling.

"Paul?" She couldn't stop the uncertainty coloring her voice. Dammit, his opinion mattered. She couldn't rope him off now. He made a promise of sorts, right?

But he made no commitments. She wouldn't lie to herself. Maybe he was simply horny and hoping to fulfill some fantasy before turning his back and walking away.

"It wasn't my fault," she added in a small voice.

"I'm so sorry, honey." He inhaled, his chest lifting her inches higher. His long exhalation dropped her down again.

"Sorry for me? For us? Which is it?" A sudden urge to force his fears to the surface and join hers took over. Poking at him probably wouldn't help, but it sure relieved her building apprehension.

"Kay, I understand. You were in no position to defend yourself. Your . . . condition is an unfortunate circumstance. It's not your fault." He paused. "If it's anyone's, it's mine."

"How do you figure?" She lifted her head a few inches and stared at Paul.

"I failed again on my mission." Shame colored his low tones.

"Again? When did you fail me before?"

"Not you. Ernie." He cleared his throat.

Ernie's name hung in a ghostly echo.

"Go on," she whispered, gripping his shoulders and squeezing. She'd wondered often enough what knocked the stuffing out of him. *I guess I'm about to find out.*

"I convinced my CO to act on an unexpected tip about a major drug trafficking ring coming into the States," Paul said. "He ordered me to plan and lead a mission to stop the drug shipments by blowing up their processing and storage facility."

His muscles turned to stone underneath her again. His breath came in short, shallow spurts, as if memories had turned to nightmares.

"And?"

"My plan had a major flaw, one we didn't discover until we were hours away from blowing the place. I couldn't come up with a new one. Ernie did."

"Who's Ernie?"

"A guy who died because I'm a bad leader!" He slid out from under the blanket onto the tarp, flinging the cover over her.

She shivered, missing his extra warmth. "Did you order him to die?"

"No, he volunteered for recon. And then . . ."

"Yes?" Kay reached out and touched his face with her fingers, aching with sympathy.

"Neither of us grasped the full danger until his ass waved in the wind. And I had a choice to either risk the whole squad to rescue him, or leave him to fend for himself until more backup came . . . I took the coward's way out."

"How do you figure?"

"Because our job was to watch his six." He pressed the back of his hand across his eyes.

"Don't you think he recognized the risks? Do you think he wanted more lives put in danger to save his?" She laid her hand on his chest. "How would he have felt if you saved him and another teammate died?"

"You can't understand. You weren't there!"

"I was in China." She kept her voice soft and gentle. "Same mission, same rogue team member planning on the spot, same risk-taker willing to let her ass wave in the wind."

"You made it home." He rolled out from under, placing his back to her.

"Due to your efforts." She itched to stroke the expanse of bare skin and soothe away his deep, scarring hurt.

"Ernie didn't!" His low voice was tortured and insistent.

She grappled with his twisted logic. "So, you think you're a bad leader because in an effort to help your country, you took on a dangerous mission that went awry."

"Yeah," he shrugged.

"The fact a teammate died doesn't reflect on your ability to lead. To the contrary, it shows you're one of the good guys."

He rolled over and faced her, sneaking under the blanket again.

"I'm afraid I'll fuck up."

"So am I," she whispered. "Please help me. And I'll help you."

"Deal." He pulled her close, burying his face in the curve of her shoulder.

She breathed in a potent mix of sweat and fresh rain. Cradling his head in her hands, she held him tight, hoping he could feel the power of redemption. Of self-forgiveness. Of hope.

He raised his head and dropped a light kiss on the tip of her nose.

"Thank you. I never shared Ernie's story with anyone."

"I guess I'm flattered." She sniffed, pretending to pout. "You could have chosen a better place."

"To a Southern Boy, this seems pretty classy—and it has all the privacy we could hope for." He maneuvered her spine against his chest, her butt cuddled into his groin.

"Too bad we're too tired to care." She yawned, all energy drained.

"Next time." He ran his hand the length of her torso. "I promise."

"I'll hold you to it." She closed her eyes and fell fast asleep.

Chapter 42

"I don't think you're supposed to be in there." The high-pitched voice reverberated in the silence. "Mr. Ranger told us we couldn't climb inside."

Paul blinked awake. A small figure shaded the cave's opening. Brown cap, brown shirt, neckerchief tied neatly—Boy Scout, through and through. Even his brown eyes and skin matched.

"Hey buddy, how ya doing?" He coughed, raising himself on one elbow. The blanket shifted, exposing Kay's bare shoulder to a sliver of sunlight.

"Daddy! A man and woman are in the cave. And they got to sleep there!" The youth turned wide eyes back in Paul's direction. "Can I climb up?"

Kay elbowed his stomach.

"Uh, no, you shouldn't. We, uh, we got special permission from Mr. Ranger." Seeing the skepticism on the boy's face, he searched for a better explanation. "We're conducting research."

"Cool! We do research in science class."

The eager expression painting the boy's features sent Paul's optimism plummeting. How could he get them out of this mess with integrity—and composure—intact?

"So what are you researching?" The youth rested his elbows on the opening.

Kay snickered. "And when you answer that, big boy, explain why we're half-naked." Her quiet amusement made him bite his cheek.

"Forrest—get back here with the troop!" The boy pouted, throwing them an apologetic look. His head and shoulders disappeared.

"I can't believe we dodged assassins, but a Boy Scout snuck up on us." Paul let loose his stifled chuckles.

"His Mom must have been a hard-core Den Mother." Kay poked him, a huge grin splitting her face. "By naming him Forrest, he was destined to become a pain-in-the-ass Boy Scout."

Paul fumbled for his cell phone, powered it on, and checked the time.

"Geez, how did we sleep so late? It's after nine."

Kay stretched under the blanket, fumbling for her stack of clothes.

"Sheer exhaustion." She wrinkled her tiny nose. "Ugh. I hate wriggling into cold, wet jeans."

Yet she did it with such elegance and grace. Paul shot his legs in the air and just yanked the heavy fabric up his legs, watching as she slid hers along slender limbs, one at a time.

"If you prefer, feel free to hike out wearing lacy panties for the Boy Scouts to ogle." He winked.

She tossed his damp sweatshirt, effectively cutting off his view. Chuckling, he pulled it on, followed by wet socks and boots. He gathered the tarp and blanket, stuffed them into the pack alongside his handgun, and jumped out of the cave.

"Hey, wait for me!" Kay scrambled to the edge, feet dangling over the side. "Whoa, I don't remember this being so high."

Paul braced himself and opened his arms wide. She pushed off into his waiting embrace.

"Good morning," she sing-songed, giving him a quick kiss.

"Top of the day to you, too, madam. I trust your accommodations were satisfactory." He linked arms with her and headed up the path leading to the road.

"Perfect. I especially enjoyed the custom bed warmer."

He loved it too, so enthralled he forgot their danger. Or was it the sheer relief of sharing his nightmares with someone who cared? Usually, Ernie's face appeared as a demonic ghost, taunting him, reminding of his failure. Not last night. No. Last night he slept soundly for the first time in years, despite Kay's awful news.

AIDS. Paul shook his head, climbing the fire road with ease, even with the extra weight of Kay dragging at his arm. If he became more involved with Kay, he had to deal with the disease and all its permutations. Forever. Unavoidable. Could he handle it? Better yet, did he want to?

His body screamed *Yes*. His feelings went beyond physical attraction, though Lord knows that placed high on his list.

Her strength, her willingness to accept responsibility for the consequences of her life-altering decisions, her commitment to do an about-face after the dire results of previous choices—these drew him like a storm-tossed boat to the gleam of a lighthouse.

Could he do the same?

Damn it all. Enough of this BS. If Kay could leave the past behind, so could he.

"How much farther?" Kay huffed, trying to keep pace.

"Almost there." He stopped dead, pointing to the tree line at the top of the short incline "Once we reach the top, I should get a cell signal, and we can finally call in the cavalry."

"And here I considered the Boy Scouts our rescue team." She poked him in the ribs.

"Very funny." His conscience pricked him again. Too close a call.

Time to stop playing defense and plan an offense. Reaching the crest, he called Eric.

"Is Tina safe?" he blurted out, too worried to say hello. At Eric's puzzled reassurances, he summarized last night's dangerous flight. "We've got to go balls-out on solutions to our rare metals supply. No one's life should be in danger because of this—especially civilians!"

"I just talked to the CEO of a mining operation in Missouri. They can modify production to get us the minimum minerals in two years or less. That might work." For once, Eric's pragmatism didn't calm him. It drove him nuts.

"Not good enough. We need to get Li on our soil and find out what breakthrough would cause China to spirit him away to the far boonies. Why Tibet of all places? And why hasn't Janelle found a way to offer him political asylum yet?"

"Hey, cut her some slack," Eric said. "She's been a little busy saving her own life and keeping the media at bay."

Janelle wasn't the only one in danger. His eyes drifted toward Kay, perched on a redwood log, head buried in her crossed arms. "I'm only trying to figure out who's friend or foe."

"Yeah, but in the meantime if the press gets wind of this, tech stocks will sink to the bottom faster than a waterlogged submarine," Eric said. "And our economy right behind it."

"So we find natural allies—ex-military guys in the tech fields, smaller VCs with links to colleges." Paul's brain kicked into high gear. "If we can identify a viable solution, Janelle can release that to the press. Then China might re-consider."

"Great strategy." Eric's approving voice boosted Paul's confidence. "I'll check back with university kids, see what's percolating underneath the surface with these next-gen geniuses."

"That's how the Web exploded, right? A college kid figured out a way to add a user-friendly interface to the standard Internet protocol."

"Now that kid's a prominent VC, wealthy as Midas."

"And a poster child for game-changing success. He'll understand our dilemma if anyone could." Out of the corner of his eye, Paul watched

Kay raise her head. Weariness and uncertainty blanketed her features. Impatience gnawed at him. "We need to take a lesson from the '90s."

"Lynn's well acquainted with him and others. With Tina babysitting, she has free time to help us. I'll get her started . . ."

Satisfied that Eric understood his urgency, Paul shoved his phone in his pocket and waved to Kay. "Let's walk the road. It'll be easier."

"Another workout–great!" A valiant smile wreathed her face. "I'm still a little out of shape. I wouldn't mind hitching a ride for part of the way, if it's safe."

Watching Kay drag her foot with every step, Paul stuck out his thumb. As luck would have it, a pickup truck with an empty flatbed slowed to a crawl next to him.

"Where to?" A bearded face appeared in the open window, weathered wrinkles sharpened by the driver's inquiring eyes.

"Up Skyline to the Palo Alto border," Paul said. "Okay if we crawl in back?"

"Suit yourselves."

Paul assisted Kay onto the metal bed, flipped his backpack in and hoisted himself up, waving a hand to the driver. With a cough of smelly exhaust fumes, the truck traversed the few miles, depositing them at the end of his long driveway.

Pistol at the ready, keeping a sharp eye on the woods lining the way to the house, Paul hustled Kay inside.

"Take a shower. I have a call to make." He steered her toward the bathroom.

"No argument here."

Paul headed to the kitchen, filling the coffeemaker to the brim and flipping the switch. Pops and sizzles accompanied his fruitless search for a clean coffee mug. He called Don and filled him in on the intruder.

"I'll arrange for a sketch artist later this afternoon." Don said. "If we're lucky, maybe one of Janelle's neighbors can identify him at her place before the arson." His contacts and competence had no bounds.

"How's she holding up?" Paul gulped his first jolt of caffeine.

"Still shaken and sore, but safe. I've stashed her in a motel with a private security guard. Do you need one, too?"

Paul dropped into a chair, considering this. "Not a bad idea. At least to watch the perimeter. I could use someone watching my six while I change a slashed tire."

"Done. And I'll fill Janelle in on the increased threats. She seems to think she's invincible. Maybe when she hears they took potshots at you—"

"At Kay. She made some bad enemies."

"And you're her friend in the line of fire, too. Don't underestimate these guys."

Thanking Don for his advice, Paul ended the call and took another bracing swallow. How far would they go? Torching Janelle seemed extreme for a casual acquaintance of Kay. Of course, her local address was a matter of public record. It was easy enough to track down for a very serious warning message.

Should he bring Tina home again, or would it be in his daughter's best interest to distance her from Kay?

And how would Kay interpret that? As a reaction to her disease or to human enemies?

Dropping his phone, he buried his face in his hands. What kind of protector was he? He fought back waves of anger and guilt that he ever let Kay get into this situation.

Kay's arms circled him. Her head rested on his back.

"It'll all work out," she murmured. Soft, comforting kisses penetrated his damp sweatshirt, pulling him out of his self-recrimination. Reminding him of lives yet to defend, yet to be shielded from a potentially more hostile enemy.

He pulled her onto his lap and held tight. She made no protest about his dirty, wet clothes against her freshly washed skin. Unlike Daisy, who'd fussed and held him at bay when he rushed home straight off a mission. Grateful for the difference, disconcerted anew by where his instincts led, he concentrated on the immediate dangers.

"I don't know how to keep Tina safe," he said, toying with her sleeve.

"She's fine where she is, and can probably handle anything." Kay tilted back, resting her hands on his shoulders. A frown crossed her face. "Haven't you figured out by now she's pretty grown up?'

"No father ever looks forward to facing that." A crooked smile escaped. "We relate to horny teenage boys all too well."

Flashing a conspiratorial grin, she winked. "Teenage girls quickly learn how to handle male teenage horniness. Especially if they ask sage old ladies for advice."

"Who's old?" He pinched her butt.

"Hey, stop that! I give!" She patted his chest and rose. "I'll prepare lunch while you shower, okay?"

"Sounds like a plan." He hopped to his feet.

The ring of his phone startled them. He grabbed it to his ear.

"Freeman here."

"Paul, this is Alex. I have good news—well, sort of." His dubious voice set Paul on high alert.

"Spill it, Alex." He sat back down and motioned for Kay to resume her spot on his lap. He positioned the phone so they could both hear. "Kay's listening, too."

"Well, I kept working on what I know best, like you said. And, well, I found out Fran was moved," Alex said.

Kay's hand flew to her lips, pressing back a tiny gasp. Hope crept into her eyes. Paul slid his arm around her back.

"To where?" Paul anchored Kay in place.

"The coast near Tianjin."

"Interesting," Paul commented. "I wonder why."

Silence.

She scowled. "Alex, what else did you find out?'

"Kay . . . um . . . maybe you should, I don't know, go watch TV?" Alex's stammering put Paul on even higher alert. "Paul can fill you in on the details later."

Her eyes narrowed. She tilted the phone sideways. "Listen young man, I can handle bad news. Contrary to popular belief, I'm fully recovered— even got a training exercise in last night." Her chin jutted higher, daring Paul to contradict her. He squeezed her and nodded instead.

"I think they stuck Fran in another brothel." Alex paused. "Only this one is full of kids her age."

Kay looked at Paul, her expression pained. He tapped his finger on the table, thinking hard.

Shit.

"Alex, can you tell how far away she is from the wharf?" Paul grabbed Kay's hand and held on tight.

Keyboard taps filled his ear. "A hundred yards or so. You think sailors on shore leave visit them? Ugh! We've got to get her out of there—fast!"

Paul would take Alex up on his offer soon enough.

"Track all the activity coming and going—especially trucks leaving the brothel." Paul dared not look at Kay. "That could be the perfect locale to aggregate girls until they have a full boatload."

Kay pulled against his grasp, shaking her head. Denying his words and their stark reality.

Fran was a sex slave, bound for ports unknown.

Chapter 43

SAN FRANCISCO AIRPORT HOTEL

*San Francisco, California
Early Afternoon, June 5, Same Day*

Janelle loosened her scarf. The acrid odor of singed hair lingered in her nostrils. Aspirin turned her burn pains to bearable stings, thank goodness. She needed all her wits to handle this meeting and catch her D.C. flight.

Her sturdy bodyguard shut the door of the rented, sparsely furnished meeting room with a resounding click. He nodded in her direction. Hair pulled into a haphazard ponytail, Alfonso Delrio's ill-fitting blazer revealed the lethal handgun nestled beneath his armpit. Having constant protection wasn't in her official job description. But she'd accepted it as a consequence of her rogue actions, despite the hit to her meager savings account.

She sipped lukewarm coffee, provided by the hotel at an exorbitant price, and studied Paul Freeman's motley crew. They gathered elbow-to-elbow around the conference table. Despite the odds, this civilian team was shouldering the responsibility to protect a free market and keep the U.S. strong. Would her fellow politicos face this dilemma with the same ready zeal as these fervent citizens, or continue burying the truth with a careless shrug?

"Okay, folks, let's begin." Janelle rapped her knuckles on the table. "We only have an hour to deal with new developments."

All heads turned in her direction, anxious eyes intent.

Flipping open her manila file, she took a deep breath.

"The State Department refused my request to be a delegate on any near-term trips to China." Janelle toyed with the page corners. "There will be no sanctioned negotiation for Li." Making that damned disk more critical to America than Middle Eastern oil. Whatever scientific breakthrough Li had uncovered, it was a whopper.

Silence met her statement but their expressions spoke volumes. Bitterness on Paul's, determination on Eric and Kay's, cynicism on Don's. Alex's youthful features twisted first in relief then confusion, his eyes darting to each face. And for some reason, Delrio smirked.

"I've done what I can through official channels." Janelle shoved aside any guilt for not disclosing her unofficial ones. "Diplomats are already scrambling so China doesn't retaliate for interference in their domestic affairs by releasing Kay."

Janelle kept to herself the harsh criticisms from leaders of her own party. Human Rights Committee colleagues turned their backs on her. Despite their pretty speeches in the well of Congress, too many relied on the fountain of Chinese money and favors for their ongoing campaigns. Compromising ethics apparently took precedence over surrendering political careers.

Would she be next?

"What about DIA?" Paul leaned forward, green eyes boring into hers. "Have you contacted them?"

"Yes, this morning," Janelle said. "Hank Shaughnessy offered help only if I agreed the mission secures Fran and holds her as a bargaining chip for her father's cooperation, pending his release."

"Asshole," Paul muttered.

"And you answered?" Don's controlled voice matched his steady gaze.

"I told him I'd get back to him this evening." Janelle shrugged. "I want all options open." Including one so farfetched, she didn't dare bring it up . . . yet.

"That borders on exploitation!" Kay slammed her hand on the table. "Using a little girl that way is something terrorists do."

"We're running out of time." Janelle met her eyes, wishing she could communicate sympathy for Kay's feelings. "Li has been sentenced to death for subversive activities while in prison."

"Because of me!" Kay paled. She sank back in her chair, extending a trembling hand to Paul. He caught it mid-air, held it fast, lifted it to his lips. Janelle felt one level of guilt drop away. Kay's sojourn with Paul seemed to have its rewards, despite Janelle's underhanded interference.

"China could be bluffing," Eric said in dubious tones.

"We can't take that risk." Paul fingered back his hair. "How long do we have?"

Janelle consulted her notes. "According to their official records, it's scheduled in twenty-nine days."

"FYI, China expedites executions when convenient," Don said.

"We have to move fast!" Kay leapt to her feet, stalking a wide circle around the conference room. "What are we missing? What else can you do, Janelle?"

"To be honest with you, I've already called in all my favors." Janelle spread her hands wide. "If I get re-elected, it will be a miracle."

"Thank you for your sacrifice, Janelle." Eric's voice rang with confidence. "We recognize there are and should be limitations on what our government can do. Otherwise, we're no better than China. It's time for the private sector to do its part."

Paul swiveled to face Eric. "What do you have in mind?"

"Our direct approach is meeting resistance," Eric admitted. "Maybe it's time to leverage ancient grudges."

"Cut the cryptics, Eric." Don said with impatience. "Spit it out."

"A lot of rich Americans openly support the Dalai Lama and the Tibetan resistance against China." Eric tilted his chair back and meshed his fingers below his chin. "We could cobble together a delegation to meet with provincial leaders under the guise of addressing the displaced herders' complaints. Once we're in Tibet," he shrugged, ". . . officials can be bribed . . . maybe we can smuggle Li out."

"My monk!" Kay exclaimed. "We can ask for help in return for helping his cause. It's the exact story Tan Yannan wrote that put her under house arrest. Maybe her fellow journalists could use that angle to give us media cover, too."

Janelle squirmed, fingering what remained of her wild and wooly mop. Perhaps she was more her father's daughter than she appreciated. She hated using sneaky tactics to win, and never considered having to condone actions so blatantly illegal. But rescuing Li from prison, however accomplished, may be the only option left. Her clandestine, negotiated asylum efforts had stalled out. She hadn't heard from her Chinese go-between in too long.

"I can email that monk again, plus search blog posts for allies in Tibet and surrounding areas." Alex looked nervous but game. "And I'll retrieve more recent images."

"Thanks for the help." Paul shot him a gratified smile.

"It's a long shot, Eric," Don grunted, "mostly because it'll take a heck of a lot of time to coordinate that many interests and pull it off. We need other possibilities. Let's get creative, people."

Tense moments dragged on. Delrio tapped his watch. Janelle scowled at her new leash. Li wasn't dead yet. This team might still be able to secure his secrets. But how?

Kay stopped behind Paul and gripped his shoulders, pressing down so hard his chair back tilted.

"Janelle, can you find out the status of Wei Jintao?" Kay's voice quavered but her face looked damned determined. "Maybe he'll help."

Janelle's brain raced ahead, sorting out possibilities.

Paul snapped his head around. "Kay, what the—"

"It's the only way." Kay's fingers dug into his jacket.

"Why the hell would he get involved?" Paul yanked free and turned his chair to glare at her in full.

"He already was. And because I would ask him to," came Kay's quiet answer.

"In return for what?" Don's curiosity was laced with skepticism.

"For me." Kay sat back down, keeping her eyes lowered. "I'm willing to become his mistress again in return for freeing Li and Fran."

Janelle pressed her lips together, considering the idea's implication on her carefully laid plans. They might not have any better choice. She turned to Eric. "What do you think?"

"I think the idea has merit." Eric's compassionate eyes flashed to Kay's downturned head and back to hers.

"Over my dead body!" Paul roared.

"It's not your decision." Kay's head jerked up, her dark eyes blazing. "I'm willing to do my part. Teamwork, remember?"

"Last I checked, I led this team." Paul's face flushed a deep red. "It's in our national interest to rescue Li, not his daughter. They're thousands of miles apart, and this issue doesn't fall into Wei's jurisdiction."

"The Chinese Communist Party really doesn't define jurisdictions for their highest-level officials." Don's dry observation floated unchallenged for long moments.

Kay placed her hand on Paul's forearm. "We need Li on our side," she said. "He'll owe us loyalty galore if we protect his daughter for him. Besides, I promised Fran . . . and she's only a little girl!"

"Millions of little Chinese girls are in trouble. We can't help them all." Paul slapped the table.

"I know." Kay's voice was subdued. "But Fran believes in the United States, and what it stands for. If our country can instill hope in their youth—especially one we know, who's in real danger—isn't that worth defending . . . and cultivating . . . no matter the cost?"

"You've already paid enough." Paul shook off Kay's hand. "The answer is no."

"Kay, I applaud your willingness to return to China, especially given your recent trauma," Janelle said. "No one expects this of you, especially me. Don's right, all these options are long shots." No kidding. But could she really guarantee that Kay's offer wouldn't be necessary?

"I expect it of myself." Kay scowled. "This completes my mission."

"Your mission ended weeks ago. You're a private citizen now." Paul looked first at Eric, and then Don, as if pleading for corroboration.

"So are you! Besides, I can't live with myself if I turn away and let others try. What if they fail?" Kay shook her head and straightened her shoulders, determination etching every line of her proud posture.

"What if we succeed?" Eric's confidence caught Janelle's attention. He passed a note to Don.

Janelle watched and waited with the others, wondering if she should allow optimism to take root. She prayed Eric's solution would protect Kay better than she could.

"Listen up, people, Eric's right. We can do this." Don leaned his forearms on the table and met all their gazes. "It'll just take two rescue efforts, launched simultaneously."

"Just?" Paul shook his head. "We'll split what few resources we have."

Janelle noticed Delrio appeared skeptical. Was this getting more hare-brained by the moment? How hard could it be to process rare earths to the right purification levels, anyway? Didn't Silicon Valley have enough smart engineers without having to rely on Chinese technologists?

She smiled to herself. Now she sounded like Dad. *At least he'll be proud of me for that.*

"So we double the resources." Eric directed his comment to Paul. "Unless you're surrendering. I've spent the last few days making clear to Silicon Valley bigwigs the implications of China's monopoly power on their businesses. They'll fund whatever we need if it secures their future. They're on board. Are you?"

"Hell, yes."

"Eric," Kay's voice strained, "um . . . once you rescue Li, tell him his daughter will be safe, all right?" There was no doubt she understood the exact implications of her words. "He loves Fran. He'll cooperate with us."

Surprise flashed across Paul's features. "You're no better than Shaughnessy . . . or the Chinese!"

"It really may be necessary." A stricken expression settled across her face.

"Sometimes the only moral choices left are unorthodox," Don added.

"Amen to that," Delrio chimed in.

Janelle started at the unexpected comment, yet agreed completely with his sentiment. Especially given the long-term implications of her questionable tactics to date.

"Congresswoman DuMont, it's past time for us to go." Delrio swept his arm wide. "After you."

"Well, I really shouldn't know any more details of Li's possible rescue once you work them out." Janelle gathered the papers and stuffed them into her satchel. "Plausible deniability and all that. But I trust you'll find a solution and alert me if and when I can shove away any bureaucratic hurdles. Especially to help free that little girl." She hesitated, ignoring Delrio's impatient glare. "I'm sorry our government won't do more."

"You've done plenty." Kay rose to her feet and hastened a hug. "It's our turn now."

"Just . . ." Janelle met their eyes in turn, dreading having her lies and Li's death on her conscience for the rest of her life. "Please hurry."

Chapter 44

SNAZZED UP!

San Jose, California
Morning, June 6, Next Day

Nikolai Herzog tapped his gold pen on the polished granite conference table, its metallic echo underscoring this meeting's agenda. "Eddie, are you telling me that DOD Tech still hasn't come up with an alternative for refined rare metals? What's wrong with our technologists these days?"

"Our lousy schools?" Victor Turtino took another drag from a half-smoked cigarette. Nikolai rarely saw him without one nowadays. "Instead of teaching science and math, we're teaching kids how to create pretty presentations, or use social media to stop bullying. Software apps and service companies replaced Silicon Valley's core strength in engineering hardware solutions years ago."

"Yeah, you're right about that," Nikolai said. "Every country in the world does a better job educating their kids than we do."

"At this point, placing blame doesn't get us anywhere." Eddie Morrison waved a dismissive hand. "I pushed DOD Tech's engineers to the wall, Nikolai. No go. I actually considered buying them out if they'd come up with any inkling of how to fix this. I could get them for a song, but if all I'd get for my money is excuses . . ."

"We can't rely on young Turks to save our ass." Victor jabbed the cigarette into an ashtray.

"I emailed my contact at the Pentagon with the same bad news yesterday," Eddie continued. "Needless to say, they're sweating over this issue, big time."

"What about the new government research dollars?" Nikolai sought one last viable idea before he accepted Eric Coleman's unusual proposition. "Have we gotten our hands on any?"

"Yes, but we can't invent more time." Eddie threw up his arms. "Look, even with the whole country working on Apollo in the '60s, it took years for each iteration to be conceived, developed, tested, and implemented—and we still had mishaps on the launch pad."

Nikolai rose to his feet and clasped his hands behind his back, choosing his words with care. "You know, that decade showed how this country could pull together against an emerging threat without actually going to war, didn't it?" He paced the perimeter of the conference room, keeping an eagle eye on the other two men.

"Yes . . . but what does that have to do with China?" Eddie tilted back to lift one foot across the other knee and shot Nikolai a measuring look. "We're not in a Cold War stare-down with them—at least not yet."

"It has to do with investing for the long-term success of large industries, and setting the stage for developing truly breakthrough technologies for both defense and commercial applications," Nikolai said.

"I hope we can do better than Tang this time." Victor laughed, lifting a bottle of flavored water to his lips in a half-hearted toast.

"You're missing the point." Nikolai scowled. "Why do you think China has its teeth in rare earths? Because it likes polluting its natural resources?"

"Military prowess." Eddie clenched his fist.

"Economic and political influence on the world stage." Victor stroked his trimmed beard. "After all, they have to make up for Mao's incredible fiasco and the waste of decades of productivity while the rest of the developed world took off."

"How about simple ROI?" Nikolai stopped and tapped the whiteboard filled with numbers. "With a four-billion-dollar investment, they turned the by-product of mining simple iron ore—rare earth elements—into valuable and purified oxides. Now China controls seven trillion dollars in finished goods. Whether they turn that investment into political goodwill or new manufacturing jobs for their populace or negotiating power for Eddie's newest military gear . . . they're in command." Nikolai sat back down. "Too bad we didn't think of it."

"You forgot to mention a simply great financial return on their investment." Eddie pointed to the whiteboard.

Nikolai smothered a smile. Better for these two CEOs to reach their own conclusions about how best to proceed than for him to present an idea as a *fait accompli*. Nothing had ever stopped these two from accomplishing their goals. Why would this time be any different?

"You know, every time we set-up a new production line in China, the terms of the contract include sharing every little detail, down to the blueprints of the building," Eddie said with a rueful twist of his mouth. "That means, under the guise of simply being a manufacturer, China has acquired all the intellectual property behind our proprietary technology, too."

"So you funded your own competitor without any protections? That was stupid," Victor said. "You should have killed any threat before it had a chance to begin."

"What makes you think your products are handled any differently?" Eddie sneered.

"I made sure our brand is what makes the difference, not just the technology." Victor pointed to a framed picture of their latest product launch's vibrant color offerings. "Nothing compares to the panache of a Snazzed Up! device, whether it's a simple computer pad, a smart phone, or our newest line of wearable devices. I spend as much money on marketing and advertising as I do on the product itself. And my brand is what people buy—not the technology."

"Well that's great, Victor, only my customers actually require a product that works, not one that just comes in snazzy colors!" Eddie jumped to his feet. "And the most important customer is the Pentagon. Unless you plan to run off to another country once you've made your billions, you better start worrying about whether our nation will even exist in another year."

Victor scowled at Eddie, but didn't refute the assessment. And Nikolai knew why. Victor had just informed the board of his intent to sell the bulk of his founder's stock over the next thirty days, offering his early resignation as CEO as part of the package. What better time to retire than when he could make the most money and leave untenable problems for his successor? Victor's term wouldn't end for many months, though. And his ego would be wrapped up in the long-term success of his company for years to come.

"Well, gentlemen, do you think your supply requirements overlap sufficiently to consider a higher level of cooperation than you're used to?" Nikolai glanced between the two men.

Eddie leaned back in his chair, twiddling the pen between his fingers. "I would be willing to kick in some significant dollars to co-fund a domestic mining concern equivalent to China's if—and this is a big if—American companies are guaranteed first dibs on its output. How about the few million I would have put in to buy DOD Tech?"

Victor grimaced. "I don't have the kind of profit margins you do, Eddie, to warrant investment dollars on a dream. I need the low cost option every time."

"Even if that short-term focus leads to your company's demise in the long-term?" Eddie pointed his pen at Victor's face. "C'mon, Victor, think beyond what Wall Street thinks of next quarter's deliverables."

Nikolai turned to Eddie. "There might be legal obstacles on this kind of co-op. As a defense contractor, are you under any special restrictions?"

"The WTO places strict parameters around government subsidies on specific industries, but since we carry a line of products for both military and commercial customers, I don't think that's an issue." Eddie shrugged. "I'd have to double-check with my corporate counsel, though, to be sure."

"Victor?" Nikolai faced the other man. "Are you really against investment that would protect your company's future? As a board member representing your other shareholders' interests, I've got to say that I would rather you invest some dollars now for a second-source supplier, rather than rolling the dice on China's willingness to keep supplying what you need at the price you can pay."

"Won't China simply respond by lowering their prices to beat ours?" Victor countered. "It's hard enough keeping our retail prices low and protecting our profit margins. We always negotiate for the lowest cost supplier, regardless of who or where they are."

"You know, Victor, the coffee industry had a similar situation years ago dealing with the influence of drug cartels on small coffee plantations." Nikolai rose and stepped to the window, staring out at the bustling Valley below. "They came up with the Fair Trade moniker, and convinced consumers their decisions were worth the extra price."

Eddie nodded. "If you're so good at branding, Victor, we could probably use your guidance in this."

Somehow, Eddie sounded gracious, not needling. Good, Nikolai thought. Maybe these two CEOs could start the core group and pull in others to form an effective cooperative. They could even use the shell of an existing tech company so investors would be able to buy proportionate shares, rather than start up something brand new.

And give the U.S. another option than simply rolling over and playing dead.

Chapter 45

FREEMAN RESIDENCE

Saratoga, California
Evening, June 6, Same Day

Tina helped herself to a forkful of string beans. "Aren't you gonna fill me in? You shouldn't keep secrets from your family, you know."

Paul rubbed his forehead, looking pained. "Who's your expert this time? Oprah or Dr. Phil?"

"Pul-eeze," Tina said. "You're so last century. It's all over YouTube now—tell the truth or else."

"Could you pass the salad, Tina?" Kay portioned a small amount and squeezed lemon juice over the greens. "And I'm curious—do you tell your family all your secrets?"

"Important ones." Tina's cheeks flushed.

"So, Paul, do you agree secrets are safe with family?" Kay stifled her grin.

"Personal ones affecting family members, sure. Professional ones? Not on your life." Throwing aside his napkin, Paul stepped to the coffeemaker and poured a cup.

"That's just it." Tina sounded calm and reasonable–grown-up. "I'm part of this already. I was with you when those bikers tried to knock you down. So your professional secrets already affect my personal life. Therefore, you should tell me what happened."

"She's got you there." Kay chuckled and waved a lettuce-tipped fork.

"She's still a schoolgirl." He scowled. "And you're always preaching how we should watch out for them, right? So put your money where your mouth is and support me in my own home, please."

Well, that put her in her place! Kay dropped her fork and shoved the plate away. "You're correct. She'll mature soon enough. I'm sorry."

"Damn straight." He stomped out, spilling droplets of coffee on the linoleum.

"I'm not as young as the girl in China–Fran–right?" Tina chased after Paul to the living room, Kay following. "Who's watching out for her?"

"We both are." Paul cradled the coffee cup. "She's not in a real nice place, honey."

"I know." Tina rolled her eyes. "Way to reassure Kay, though."

"Do I require reassurance?" Kay twisted her lips and dropped to the sofa.

"Yes!" Tina matched Paul's tone and volume exactly. They grinned at each other.

Tina plopped next to her and patted her arm. "The stuff I showed you on the Internet, well . . . um . . . it's the worst. You know, sensationalistic. They probably treat the majority of girls well. I mean, they have to stay healthy enough to, you know, work. Right, Daddy?" She threw him a pleading glance.

"True, baby. A lot of girls in the world have it worse." Paul settled into the armchair.

"And none have Woman Warrior Kay protecting them, either."

"Woman Warrior, huh?" Paul smiled. "Great nickname."

Kay stuck out her tongue. "Girls need strong role models, too."

"Maybe we can get a Laura Croft outfit for the Barbie doll you bought Fran." Tina puffed out her cheek. "Or Kung Fu fighter, or Mulan. See Daddy, lots of women can handle the dark side."

"We're not the Jedi force honey, only a bunch of human warriors with a humdinger of a fight on our hands." He slurped his coffee.

"I think most Jedi knights would turn their noses up at the password Fran and I concocted, anyway." Kay wrinkled her nose.

"Password?" Wide-eyed, Tina looked at Kay. "Way cool. What is it?"

"We were really clever—'California Barbie'."

"Did you play spy games with her or something?" Tina leaned forward on her hands.

"Or something." Kay's sadness was tinged with guilt. "I wanted her to trust that if I sent help, she would accept it. It seems silly now, considering her situation."

Tina nudged her shoulder. "Barbie is a heroine to a lot of little girls in the world. It's not shameful to be feminine or attractive."

"Thanks. I counted on that every day." Kay searched Paul's stony features. He clenched his jaw tight.

"C'mon, Daddy. Kay fought for the good side, not evil. Is it her fault men have this stupid weakness for pretty women?"

"I don't see how holding sexual power over anyone can be good, honey." Paul placed his cup on the side table with deliberate precision.

"Mom said it's the only power women have." Tina crossed her arms.

"Not true." Kay straightened, her eyes latched onto his. "Not in a loving family . . . But that's my own experience." She grasped Tina's fingers and squeezed. "Your parents love you."

"Tina realizes that, don't you pumpkin?" At her emphatic nod, Paul leaned on his forearms and dropped his eyes to the floor. "Your Mom and I loved each other once. It's just . . . love isn't always strong enough for what life throws at you. A family should pull together as a team and solve problems in harmony, not acrimony. We never developed that skill."

"I finally figured out a family can be a strong, stable structure to build on, not just a cage." Kay tugged the afghan around her shoulders. "My parents stifled me with their strictness."

"So that's good, right?" Tina beamed. "You feel like being part of a team again?"

"Don't jump to conclusions, cookie." Paul tossed a half smile in Kay's direction.

"Get real." Tina hopped to her feet. "I'll leave you two alone. G'night."

"Good night, Tina," Kay said to her receding back.

"Night, baby," Paul called out.

Shadows lengthened in the comfortable silence.

"Your daughter is remarkable." Kay scooted into the sofa corner and patted the cushion. "You've taught her well."

Paul eased his body onto the opposite end. "I can't take all the credit. Daisy certainly influenced her. And she's as fearless as her grandmother. But in this situation . . ." Worry lines aged his face.

"Is there something new we should fear?" She'd shoved all thoughts of assassins aside for the last few hours. Facing the possibility of returning to China's spider web took all of her excess energy and nerve.

"Not anymore, thank goodness. Don texted me a minute ago. His rent-a-cop friends caught a trespasser hiding in the bushes at the far end of our driveway late this afternoon." He finished his coffee, letting his words sink in. "It will take a couple days to slow-roll all the paperwork, so we have breathing room—and a new lead."

Kay's muscle tension eased a tiny bit. "Protecting us isn't all that concerns you, is it?"

"Protecting our country's future, its economic assets, my family, and the lives of my team—that's my mission now. The trick is prioritizing which comes first."

"And this differs from your previous missions how?"

"After Ernie died, I couldn't care about my teammates anymore. It hurt too much. This time, it matters."

"Because Tina's in danger? I think she's safe now, with Don's extra guards on duty." Her nerves jangled tight, anticipating a looming battle of wills.

"Tina matters, sure." Paul's gaze latched onto hers. "Look, you're barely recovered. And I'm not willing to trade Li's life for yours, even if America needs a wholesale solution to this rare earths debacle."

"Would you trade your life for Tina's if she were stuck in the hell-hole Fran's in?" Kay narrowed her eyes at his challenge and searched for remnants of familiar confidence.

"Every father would!"

"And mother—and hopefully any adult who loved her." She thrust out her chin. "Fran's precious to me." How did that little girl get under her skin so deep? Their shared love of all things Barbie? Her infectious giggle? Being a real-life heroine to a desperate child?

"Please admit rescuing her is a long shot." Paul scrubbed his face with his hands. "And in your condition . . ."

"My condition?" She uncoiled her legs and rose to her toes. She took on the balanced stance of a fully trained operative. If she convinced Paul she was ready, maybe she'd convince herself.

He gave her a deliberate once-over. "You're still mostly skin and bones." He dropped his forehead onto his fingers. "You don't look as good as you used to," he muttered with a strangled voice.

Kay fought back stinging embarrassment.

"Meaning?" She put all the disdain she could muster into her question and flexed her newly developed bicep muscles. They rippled the tiniest amount.

"Meaning while I still find you sexy as hell, Wei Jintao might not." Paul's throat pulsed in erratic rhythm. "You've always relied on your beauty to enthrall men. If the mission depends on that single fact, it may fail."

A warm glow started as a tiny ember beneath her sternum and spread all the way to her toes. "Sexy?" She fingered her crown of layered wisps.

"You have to ask?" Incredulity colored his tone.

"I wanted to ask." *And loved his answer.* Kay swallowed the emotion rising in her throat.

He extended his arm, inviting her into his warm embrace. "This mission is too critical to take unwarranted risks, sweetie. We need different tactics."

Nestling her cheek into the hollow of his shoulder, she regretted her single-mindedness. Could she help Paul get his job and self-respect back, plus avenge Charlie's death and free both Fran and Li with one masterful swoop? Talk about ambitious!

But . . . America's current negotiating posture wouldn't be possible if not for her sacrifice and imprisonment. Her fleeting sense of pride grew bigger. She created this opportunity– along with Paul, who never stopped believing in her.

Payback time.

"So let's get creative," she said.

"Regarding Wei Jintao . . ."

Kay tensed, marshaling her arguments, and took a deep breath.

". . . I didn't give you a chance to explain your plan," Paul said.

The surprise in her eyes was undeniable. He kissed the top of her head. "As team leader, my responsibility is to consider all options, and only then choose the best one. Otherwise, it's a team of one. And Lord only knows my track record isn't sterling." His fingers gripped her waist. "What do you have in mind?"

"Jintao has contacts up the ying yang. He never hid anything. In fact, he only refused helping me leave China. If I arrive on his doorstep–"

"And in his bed?"

Kay gathered her courage. "Perhaps. Does it bother you?"

"Hell, yes!" He shifted out from under her and bolted upright, putting inches between them.

"I promise I'll extract all the favors I can before having sex with Jintao. Feel better?"

"Hell, no!"

"Why on earth not?"

"Because that's what you always do!" He jumped up and paced the living room's length.

"Oh."

"Oh? Great answer! Fantastic! So concise!"

Kay glanced at the hall doorway. "Keep your voice down. Tina might hear you."

"Good! She should learn the right way to attract a man."

"And you're saying I use the wrong way?"

"Don't you?"

"I did, Paul. In the past. Not anymore." How could he not see her transformation? She blinked back hot tears. It was all too easy to return to the old Kay. "Why won't you believe me?"

"I want to." Paul stepped in front of her. His angry expression turned uncertain.

"Then sit down and listen up, team leader. You need other options, and promised to be open-minded. Don't rip me apart because you can't keep your own professional and personal opinions separate."

He sank to the sofa, one hand over his closed eyes, the other hand clenching the afghan's folds. "Okay, I'm listening."

"Old Wei Jintao relies on a little purple pill to get it up. He enjoys the promise of a sexual interaction more than the act itself." She touched his white knuckles. "I'll be acting a part, nothing more."

"Unless he asks for more."

"At one point I was willing to submit to gang rape by a bunch of filthy jailers to stay safe. It's not a stretch to endure a much more pleasant experience to keep Fran safe. Don't you get it?"

"Maybe," he muttered. His hand dropped, exposing an agonized expression.

"If I knew Fran was captured, I never would have left China. I would have gone straight to Jintao and bargained anything for her release. This time, if I have you as backup, I'll be in a much better position of power. I know you'll get me out of there if things fall apart. Don't you agree?"

A strange expression settled on his face amid the stark silence.

She shook her head. "Thank you for hearing me out. Ultimately, it's your call."

Nothing.

"Paul?" She brushed his thigh, uncertain how to proceed. Or if she should proceed.

"Promise me one thing."

Kay recoiled from his iciness. "Anything."

"Use a condom." Paul's hand snatched hers. He stared down at their enjoined hands for long seconds. She watched a muscle twitch in his cheek, then his chin rise up, eyes flashing. Focused. Tortured.

Committed.

"I don't know what might happen." He ran kisses across her knuckles. "Since I obviously can't be at your side every minute, please protect yourself. Don't risk another disease or a pregnancy on top of all this." A flush of red stained his cheeks. "I realize a condom may be old fashioned. But last I heard it's still pretty damned effective."

"A repeat of the lecture I gave Tina last week." Kay curved her lips into a crooked smile.

Paul groaned, his eyes searching hers. "Thanks?"

"Tina has a better head on her shoulders than I did at her age." Her heart clenched with poignant regret at her own father's distance. "Trust her to make the right decisions and tell her she can come to you if she fails."

"You need that from me, too, don't you?" His fingers stroked her cheek and lingered.

She nodded, rubbing her face against his palm.

"You got it. Let's keep you safe and healthy so when this mission is complete . . ." He brushed her lips with his.

She placed her fingers over his, staring into his green eyes. His breath quickened.

"I'm not healthy now, remember? I have . . ." Kay choked on the word.

"Another reason to get accustomed to condoms, don't you think?"

"What do you want?" she whispered. Tears filled her eyes.

"Hmm, what a loaded question." He nibbled her ear as one cold hand wormed under her shirt and inched its way along her ribcage. "I'm not sure about the future, but I sure as hell intend to grab whatever time we can before our mission takes precedence—again."

"Country before family, right?"

"Eventually." He breathed in her ear, his tongue swirling the lobe.

Warmth flooded her. She pushed against his chest and eased on top of him, returning kiss for kiss, touch for touch. Fire for fire.

His muscles hardened as he slid his hands along her spine, rocking her in place. Slipping her hands beneath his sweater, she ran her fingernails across his wide chest, reveling in his shivering response.

This intimacy is what was missing with all her previous lovers.

No lies this time. No seduction. No calculations of power.

Only this special feeling of true caring. Proven repeatedly—as colleagues and friends under fire. Now as lovers.

She craved it.

Did she love him? Did he love her?

Did it matter? They might be risking their lives again soon. She scooted up his chest and met his voracious kisses with her own, lost in the fiery sensations.

"Daddy! Kay! You should see what China's announcing now." Tina's distant voice broke over them with the impact of a barrel of cold water.

"Shit!" Paul jerked upright, jolted out of his trance. "Coming, honey." He rose, pulling his shirt over his waistband and glancing at his tented pants. "Do you think this little girl of mine can handle seeing her daddy with a boner?"

Kay giggled, tugging her disheveled clothes back into place. "Stand behind me and we won't have to find out."

"Is this country before family or family before country?" Grabbing her hand, he marched her down the hall. "I get it mixed up at times."

"We all do. Because when all is said and done, they're one and the same."

Chapter 46

CHESAPEAKE CORNERS CONDOMINIUMS

Washington, D.C.
Early Morning, June 7, Next Day

"Congresswoman DuMont? Come see this." Delrio's polite tones didn't mask the urgency.

Grabbing a modest robe from deep inside her closet, Janelle tugged it on and opened her bedroom door. Being a prisoner in her own home sucked to high heaven.

Muffled sounds confirmed Delrio on the job, alert, suspicious, and being a pain-in-the-neck. All under the guise of protecting her. She followed the television's blare to her living room. CNN's familiar logo graced the screen, its grim-faced business reporter facing the camera.

"Last night China made good on its threat to halt all exports of rare earth elements in any form," a reporter droned, "including valuable highly refined metals from those elements. Our technology industry is tossed into a tailspin."

Janelle sagged against the wall, dazed by the implications. She clutched her robe's lapels and stared at the TV. A red arrow flashed in the bottom corner, confirming in real-time the economic impact of China's power.

"World stock markets plummet as China's embargo impacts all future shipments and sales of leading-edge technology products, automobile control systems, and military equipment," the reporter continued. "In addition, the energy sector is under pressure as analysts calculate the widespread effect of delayed installations of wind turbines. Stay tuned for updates when the U.S. markets open."

The familiar news anchor looked up from her notes. "Thank you, Brandon. Now, let's switch to our Washington bureau reporter, Camilla Pertowski." The background changed to the emerald White House lawn. "Camilla, is there an official response?"

"Not yet. Sources tell me the American public is demanding action now. Congress is inundated with emails urging retaliation on Chinese imports." Camilla tucked her hair behind her ear, her face set in serious lines. "Back to you."

Delrio muted the volume and faced Janelle.

"So what are you going to do, Congresswoman?" He smirked. "Wait for political consensus? Watch our economy tank because we're held hostage by a country we never should have relied on in the first place?" He pointed to her laptop charging on the corner table. "Maybe one of your constituents has the balls to tell you what to do. Sure as shootin', your colleagues don't."

Janelle's temper snapped. Between Delrio's bossiness, Dad's hourly check-ins, and having to constantly monitor her private email account for details on that damned disk's contents before she officially requested asylum on behalf of some still-unknown Chinese official, her patience finally failed her.

"Look, Delrio, your business is to protect me, not tell me how to do my job. So butt out!" She didn't dare share her strategy—with anyone—and keenly missed Dad's advice.

"Don said your job got you into this pickle." His eyes narrowed. "So I have to butt in—whether you like it or not."

Fuming, she marched toward the kitchen and poured a cup of coffee with shaking hands. *Get a grip, girl.* Delrio had a point. The same one Dad made every time he could. It was downright dangerous to be a politician, especially since she bucked her party at every turn and shed a light on questionable alliances and unethical practices. Alliances compromising America's strength.

Really, who was she to harp about unorthodox behavior? Hers was one big humdinger, and no longer a sure bet.

She sipped the hot coffee, considering Eric Coleman's declaration at their last meeting that their government had run out of options and private citizens needed to step forward. What other choice did they have except planning Li's rescue, with or without official sanction? Instead of an implausible backup plan, it may be their salvation.

Her own party would buck regulatory reforms necessary to bring rare earth resources back to the States, even if it created a new taxable value chain and put the Pentagon and its defense contractors on a strong footing. Unless she could find a radical, metallurgical solution, it was only a half measure, and she could anticipate an attack from all sides. Worse yet, the public would never understand any of it.

The caffeine calmed her rattled nerves. She toasted a bakery-fresh bagel—hurrah for Delrio's few redeeming qualities—and smeared it with cream cheese. Taking a big bite, she carried her breakfast to the living room, settled into her armchair, and pulled up the avalanche of emails. She prayed they didn't give her any more indigestion than she could handle.

"OK if I raise the volume a little?" Delrio waved the remote in her line of vision.

Nodding, she scanned for replies to her formal requests for help to rescue Li, sent out yesterday. Two emails carried the prized reply format. Only two of dozens. She frowned. Not an enthusiastic show of support.

Opening the first, her heart sank. The Defense Department could transport her to their base in Okinawa, no further. And no assurances they could ever get her into China proper. *Not their purview, sorry Ma'am.*

The second email promised help with correct, flowery words—in three months. The United Nations welcomed her on a scheduled inspection of Chinese prisons, except it was highly inappropriate to earmark a specific locale to visit. Sorry, effective diplomacy took precedence.

Resting her head on the chair back, her unfocused eyes jumped from knickknacks to draperies to Delrio sprawled on her sofa to the flickering television. What would Dad say if she cried *uncle?* Better yet, what would he do to win this fight? She imagined his boot in her ass, his blistering words burning her ears.

A familiar tone alerted her to incoming email. She tapped the screen. A wave of relief washed through her at the Chinese email return address. Finally!

Opening the missive, she cocked her head at its brevity.

Ready.

Janelle took a deep breath. She didn't have any more time to negotiate details. She had to act now, and test her months-long plan. She'd laid the secret groundwork with the utmost care, battling her conscience every step of the way, waiting for this final go-ahead sign.

Her gaze fell on the television. A different kind of image flashed on the screen. Shaky cameras, people tottering against store shelves and out unstable doorways.

"Earthquake! Where? San Francisco? My district? Turn it up." She shot upright.

"Don't worry. California's not shaking. China's at it again, only this time in a remote area near Tibet. This happened hours ago." Delrio shrugged. "Who cares? Their government sure won't. We'll be the ones sending in rescue teams." He flicked the remote control, surfing the channels.

Sanctioned rescue teams into China near Tibet? Hmm. Janelle thrummed her fingers on the armrest. Did her idea have merit, or was she just desperate? She paged through her emails, fumbling with her phone and searching for the right number. She crossed her fingers the UN phone lines wouldn't be swamped.

Introducing herself, she got through to the person in charge of emergency relief efforts, explained her idea, and got verbal permission to assist putting together their official rescue team. Promising to provide names later, she contacted the State Department and obtained approval for expedited emergency visas.

Taking a deep breath, she made her last call, wincing at the early hour in California. If her idea worked, it would be worth losing sleep.

"Don? It's Janelle DuMont. I need your help."

"Uh, sure, Janelle." Don cleared his throat. "What can I do for you?"

"A massive earthquake hit the Xinjiang province of China, bordering Tibet. American rescue teams are joining others under the United Nations banner." She hesitated. How crazy was she to suggest this? "Do you have any contacts who might be willing to go there, and afterwards help us free Li?"

"Great idea, Janelle. K-9 rescue teams allowed? Dogs can sniff out buried survivors."

"Actually, they're preferred."

"I'll go. I've got a fully-trained buddy who's eager for the job."

"A dog or friend?" Janelle wrinkled her nose.

"Both." Don chuckled. "Fred's a dog and my friend."

"Relief workers will be flown into Xinjiang province from Kyrgyzstan via helicopter." She checked the time. "The plane departs SFO in four hours. Can you make it?"

"No problem, but we should get one more person on my team. In the meantime, someone had better figure out fast exactly how to rescue

Li. It's a big country with potentially damaged roads. I'll have my hands full with the earthquake for a few days, maybe a week."

"I'll call Paul. He's the most logical person."

"Roger that. I'll call you prior to takeoff and confirm any last minute details." He clicked off.

There! She could help in Li's rescue after all. At least Don didn't think she was crazy.

"Creative solution—congrats." Delrio crossed his ankles, pausing on the news channel and staring at the stark images. "Any chance we'll be travelling to China? I've never been."

"No, I can run interference with the different agencies if I stay stateside." No telling what communiqués the CCP might intercept if they feel threatened. She couldn't risk her political refugee or his disk.

"Don will get the job done. He's a miracle worker."

"Has he worked miracles for you?" Janelle squinted, her curiosity roused.

"More than I'll ever tell, Congresswoman." He twisted his head, pointing to her phone. "But even miracle workers need angels on their side. Don't you have more phone calls to make so his ass isn't left wagging in the wind working alone on Li's rescue effort?"

She stifled the impulse to make a face at him. Delrio wormed into her skin like a tenacious tick. She wished she never promised Don and Dad to keep him for protection. However, he had a good point.

First, though, she had to start the ball rolling to get that disk safely into her hands. And that meant getting Kay back in front of Wei Jintao with a believable story. Janelle's part in the plan: publicly distracting the Chinese powers-that-be with a bigger international issue to worry about than a defection.

She tapped the Assistant Attorney General's private phone entry, mentally constructing her arguments. "Letitia? It's Janelle DuMont. I need your help." She briefed her on the Human Rights Committee's most recent findings on the booming slave trade coming out of Asian ports, and ended with her unorthodox request. No surprise—the AAG squawked.

"Letitia, let me put it this way. Aren't you ashamed human trafficking isn't being stopped on your watch? Slave girls are sailing in right below the Golden Gate Bridge and docking in my district, for God's sake! I won't tolerate it."

The tiniest bit of doubt shadowed the AAG's clarifying questions. Shoving back her shaggy hair, Janelle caught Delrio watching her beneath lowered lids, the expression on his face approving. Well, what do you know—he has a conscience despite all his toughness. Would he be so supportive if he knew the whole truth behind her unofficial negotiations?

"If we form a UN human rights inspection team to break up a slave trafficking ring, it should give us diplomatic cover. What self-respecting leader would complain?" She grinned at Letitia's answer. "Let's focus. My confidential witnesses repeatedly name Tianjin as the last port in Asia for boats headed to American shores."

She counted the seconds, fingering some singed strands of hair. "Great, Letitia. Yes, as fast as we can pull it together. No longer than seven days." She grabbed her calendar and jotted notes. "No, I don't think I should join this contingent. Let's keep it under UN auspices. However, I do have people I highly recommend. I'll confirm with them and get back to you."

Grinning, she raised her phone in the air, pumping her arm in celebration.

"Way to go, Congresswoman." Delrio uncoiled from his lounging pose and stretched. Scrubbing his bristles, he yawned. "What can I do to help?"

"Book us on the next flight to San Francisco." She pulled up Kay's number. "And shave, would you? You're no one's idea of a professional bodyguard."

"Appearances can be deceiving, can't they, Congresswoman?" His mocking tones echoed down the hall.

Janelle shrugged, focusing on managing Kay instead.

Kay's enthusiastic response surprised her. "If we can rescue Fran, I'll claim her as my daughter or sister to get her out of China. Wei Jintao will help."

"He may not have much influence anymore, Kay. He retired due to health reasons." She paused, tiptoeing through the conversation's minefield. "After all, did he ever admit he might give you AIDS? I'm sure his priority is to get good care. Why would Wei help us?"

"He would want to keep his political reputation intact even more so. I'm sure he'll help me. Besides, if he publicly decries the horror of child slavery, and explains why he acts precipitously, who will chastise him?"

Janelle cocked her head with a smug smile. Kay's face-saving story was right on the mark. "How will you arrange a private conversation with him? I can manage an emergency visa, but you're still persona non grata."

"He has a room at a private club. I'll bribe the concierge to slip him a note, and wait." Quivers shook Kay's deep breath. "I'll dig up a sexy dress, but there's not a whole lot I can do about my hair. Tina tried trimming it even, but I still look like a boy!"

"Don't worry. Hair doesn't define a woman—style does."

"So Paul keeps telling me."

"Speaking of Paul—can I talk to him?"

"Sure."

Paul's baritone soon filled Janelle's ear with a greeting.

"Paul, Don is heading to northwest China as part of an earthquake rescue mission. Would you join him? While you're travelling there, we can figure out how to get to Li and convince him to seek asylum with us."

"No fucking way. If Kay's in Beijing calling in favors from Wei Jintao, I'm with her."

Surprised by his vehemence, Janelle softened her plea. "Don needs backup."

"Call on Alex. His Chinese would help more in a remote area."

Paul was right. "Do you think he'll agree? He seems awfully concerned his business will suffer from all our unorthodox activities."

"I'll convince him. Give me an hour."

"In the meantime, I'm pushing for a UN-sanctioned search of all vessels leaving Tianjin. I don't know if that will help little Fran Li in time. Hopefully, we'll eventually find all the slave ships and free anyone caught up in this terrible trade."

"That's great, Janelle. I'll tell Kay. A UN search will give her an excuse to see Wei Jintao without disclosing the direct connection to Li."

"I hadn't thought of that angle, but yes, that might work." Janelle winced at her outright lie. "This is an awful lot for your small team to take on, Paul. Are you guys ready for this?"

"As much as we can be. Have you arranged whatever official papers we'll need?"

"I'll hand deliver them myself. I'm flying into San Francisco shortly."

"Roger that. And Janelle?"

"Yes?"

"Thanks. You've become as great a hero to me as your Dad . . ."

Janelle dropped the phone on her lap, drained and exhilarated. At least she tried something different. Something she could be proud of. But nothing heroic.

Because, sure as hell, she tossed a clear conscience and untarnished reputation out the door with this rare metals gamble. Even if her plan succeeded, she lost.

She prayed it was worth the cost.

Chapter 47

DOD TECHNOLOGIES, INC.

Sunnyvale, California
Noon, June 7, Same Day

Gideon slapped the arm of his wheelchair. "So that's it? We give up?" He rolled the six feet across their shared office. Years of work tossed in boxes decorated the cramped corners.

"Do you see something I don't?" Adam threw his hands in the air, all energy wrung out of him. "A way to wave a magic wand and force China to export again? A method to purify rare earths in enough quantities to meet our customers' demands? Ain't happening! Don't you understand? Everyone just got snookered by China."

"What . . . what happens to our company?"

Adam closed his eyes. Another fiasco. This time he'd even vetted the concept with potential customers and engineering experts, years in advance. Squeezing in conferences, networking with venture capitalists, he'd identified which firms he would solicit for another round of funding to leverage him right to the top.

Now this disaster. He might as well superglue FAILURE to his fading entrepreneurial resume.

"Adam?" No longer belligerent, Gideon's voice carried doubt. And shame.

He took a deep breath, forcing the supportive demeanor of CEO one more time. "Gideon, we have no supplier, no product, no money, and two employees—you and me. No one's interested in funding nothingness. What would they invest in? Our patents require refined metals, which we can't get. Why risk money in a guaranteed loser? The VCs have moved on to market-moving, creative-destruction opportunities."

"So we just . . . shut the doors . . . and say goodbye?"

Staring at the best technologist he'd ever worked with, Adam's conscience nagged. This was Gideon's first loss, and not really his fault. He'd worked magic within the context of existing market conditions. No one could force creativity and innovation out of anyone's mind. Was Gideon shouldering the entire failure of Silicon Valley to come up with an alternative solution?

"Yes . . . and no," Adam said. "We shut the company down, sell whatever assets we can, and hope we end up with a couple of dollars in our pockets. If you choose to work with me again—"

"Yes!" Gideon's face lightened with hope.

"OK, get cracking on new ideas, because I'll be grabbing whatever job I can to stay afloat." Adam recalled the all-too-familiar mental checklist. "We'll have to work on weekends to get a new business off the ground—assuming we can identify a growing market niche to match our talents."

"I may have one already." Gideon rolled to one corner and snagged a drive out of a cardboard box. "Let me finish the final pieces and show it to you in a couple of weeks, okay?"

Adam nodded in resigned commitment. *I'm nuts to start all over again.*

Chapter 48

COLEMAN RESIDENCE

San Jose, California
Late Afternoon, June 10, 3 Days Later

Paul arrived at Eric's house in a blaze of heat. Switching off the engine, he glanced in the rearview mirror. "Just in time for a quick swim before supper, Tina. Lucky you."

"Aren't you coming in?" She gathered her duffel bag and nudged open the door, pointing ahead. Eric paced the front porch, phone pressed to his ear. His fingers morphed from a friendly wave to a clenched fist.

Paul looked over at Kay. "Okay if we check in with Eric?" They could spare thirty minutes.

"Sounds good." Kay hopped out the opposite side and they jogged up the broad steps. Eric ended his phone call with a few terse words.

"Hi. Glad to have you with us again, Tina." Eric gave her a hug. "Lynn's poolside. Why don't you change into your swimsuit and join her?"

"In other words, get lost." Tina planted one hand on her hip.

"Honey . . ." Paul hesitated. But she was right. "Listen sweetie, this is classified government information. Notice Lynn isn't part of our discussion, either."

"Yeah, well I bet she gets the rundown tonight, while I have to wait for-ev-er."

"I'll call before we leave." He swept her into a bear hug. "I'm proud of you, young lady." He kissed the top of her head, mussing her curls.

Her return hug surprised him with its fierce strength. Grabbing her duffel, she headed inside.

"Good news." Eric led them to the living room, motioned them to sit, and settled in the recliner. "We're finally getting results from the VCs."

"Thought an A-bomb going off might get them moving." Paul perched on the sofa.

Eric smiled. "With all the tech stocks tanking in value, they understand their private little gold mines are threatened in a powerful way—and by a formidable competitor."

"Remember, China's favorite symbol is a dragon," Kay offered. "Bold, ambitious, and intelligent. All of Silicon Valley's characteristics."

"Any progress in the universities, Eric?" Paul couldn't stop the hope coursing through his veins.

"Their competitive juices are flowing, too. Hopefully some genius will discover a solution shortly, and we won't face total ruin." Eric's expression turned proud. "Brainpower will solve this problem, not our military, not long-term government sanctions. Our tech companies can't afford to miss a single day of production."

"I bet the student who solves it will earn millions. Right?" Kay mused. "He—or she—will be in an incredibly strong negotiating position to extract a huge price for a breakthrough idea. Companies will clamor to buy the solution or license the intellectual property, no matter the price."

"What are you suggesting, Kay?" Eric's brow wrinkled.

"If we can convince Li to work in the U.S., we need more than just a visa or research grant to dangle in front of him. We need to make him rich. China's nose would be well and truly snubbed, their efforts to blockade our products will fade away to pathetic posturing, and Silicon Valley will bounce back, as usual."

"As good a summation as any." Paul grinned.

Kay met his gaze, her expression serious. "With China's complete embargo, his rescue just became more critical than Fran's. Your presence is required elsewhere, team leader, not babysitting me." She turned her head. "Don't you agree, Eric?"

Lips clamped tight, Eric's head swiveled between the two. "I'll do my part arranging a well-paying post for Li to settle in, and stay out of everything else. However . . ." he held up one finger, ". . . I do agree with you on one point, Kay. As our team leader, what Paul says, goes."

Paul released his held breath and glanced at Kay. A disappointed pout flashed across her face, followed quickly by one of determination. His gut twisted. He anticipated another argument on this point. And soon.

"Thanks." Paul rose and thrust his hand out to Eric. "Keep us posted on your progress, and we'll keep in touch to the best of our ability. If Kay's experience is anything to go on, it might be days before you hear from us again."

"Good luck, and watch your backs." Eric shook their hands. "With such high stakes, there's no telling what side-deals might be cut."

Resting his fingers on Kay's waist, Paul escorted her to the car and shot Eric a final wave. They sped back down the country road toward civilization, his brain on overdrive, too.

"We're meeting Janelle at Alex's office," he said, entering the packed freeway. "She'll drive us to Moffett Field to catch the military transport to Okinawa." He maneuvered through the heavy traffic with ease, taking advantage of carpool lanes, zooming past stuttering lines of cars.

Kay's silence unnerved him. Her head leaned against the headrest, eyes half-closed. She twisted her knuckles in her lap, hinting of a volcano, ready to erupt.

At him.

"Kay, I'm not letting you handle Wei Jintao and Fran's rescue on your own." He set his jaw. "Two teams of two is safest—one for Li, one for Fran. And that's final."

"Oh, really?" Her eyes opened wide. "No discussion? No input? The great Oz has spoken?"

Slamming his hand on the steering wheel, he accelerated into the open fifty yards in front of him, releasing only a tiny bit of frustration.

"You're too emotionally involved," he said through gritted teeth. He glanced in the mirror and slapped on his turn signal. "Either act as a full-fledged member of this team, or you can goddamn stay home for all I care."

"Yeah, well, being an emotional icicle doesn't suit me."

"You think I don't care?" He darted through an opening and caught the exit ramp. Tires squealing, he negotiated the tight turn and slammed the brakes. "I'm so knotted up I resemble my Mom's goddamn needlepoint!"

"What's the difference if I go alone or not?"

"You need a partner. I can keep my perspective about Fran. You can't."

"So what's knotting you up?"

"You! You and this Wei guy. I can't do much to help out with him, but don't tell me to stay away while you're in the clutches of a Chinese official again."

"Oh."

Paul shook his head in disbelief. He steered into the lot behind PanVision's office and parked. Staring through the windshield at the oak-shaded boundary, he opened his mouth, ready to pepper her with more arguments.

Her silence floored him.

She stopped fighting.

Twisting in his seat, he nudged her chin to face him. "Are we agreed?"

"Yes, Paul." She pulled his hand to her lips and dropped a soft kiss in his palm. "I think I may enjoy being on your team." She offered a tremulous smile.

"Damn straight." He pulled the keys out of the ignition, opened the door and stepped to the rear, hefting their duffel bags over his shoulder.

Chapter 49

PANVISION TECHNOLOGIES

Cupertino, California
Early Evening, June 10, Same Day

Paul escorted Kay into Alex's claustrophobic office. Equipment blinked with intermittent flashes mirrored in the blackened monitors. Alex's precious software ran in his absence for their convenience. What a huge concession from a budding entrepreneur. What about this mission inspired Alex so?

"We've got almost an hour until Janelle arrives. Let's see what's new." Paul slid onto the chair and fished in his wallet for the password Alex entrusted to him.

Kay lifted a sticky yellow note off the flat screen and scanned it. "Here are the file names containing all his stashed video images. Alex says Fran was stable and safe when he left."

She read a string of characters and he typed them into a preset form. With a hand on his shoulder, Kay leaned forward. "Do you see what I see?"

"A line-up?" He zoomed in on the image, fumbling for his glasses. The fuzzy figures grew distinct.

"They're counting heads. See?" She pointed to a lone figure who tapped each smaller figure before waving them away.

"This can't be good," he muttered. "How many guards?"

"Hmm, I count seven—no, eight. How many earlier?"

"Four, according to Alex. Why would they double the number?"

"Because they have more arrivals to deal with?"

"Great." He pulled off his glasses and thrummed the desktop, letting his vision relax and take in the whole, blurry picture, not the details. "That's an awful lot of movement for a routine head count."

"They're getting ready to ship them out." Kay sank to her knees. "We're too late."

"Didn't you contact a Taiwanese rebel network in Tianjin?" Pity tore at his heart. "Maybe we can call them and ask for help stalling this shipment of girls."

"Can't. They only work face to face. No way they'll get involved on their own." Her eyes welled with tears. "What's in it for them to help a bunch of worthless females?"

Paul's mind raced. Any remote attempt would be fruitless. They would have to pray for luck on their side—for once.

Unless . . .

He fought the ugly memories and wrestled inner demons back into the murky corners of his mind, praying this time they'd nest there for eternity.

It was Fran's only hope.

Taking a deep breath, he crouched next to Kay and eased her into his arms, rocking her back and forth, reveling in her sweet, soft warmth. How he wished this moment would never end.

"New plan," he whispered in her ear, combing her short hair with his fingertips. "You go to Beijing on your own and see if Wei can help. I'll go to Fran ASAP, using any and all of Janelle's connections I can wangle. I promise I'll free her."

"What happened to teamwork?" She lifted her head, wide-eyed, hopeful.

"The best teams meet changing conditions head on." He shrugged with a nonchalance he didn't feel. "Fran's safety takes a higher priority than whether Wei paws you."

"I can handle Wei." Her smile was tentative. But, hey, it was still a smile. "It's you who's been a challenge all these years."

"Past tense, I hope?"

"Past tense." She nodded, her gaze clinging to his. "Do you remember my password?"

"Password?" He blinked, searching his memory. "Are you hacking his computer?"

"No, silly." She shifted in his arms and tilted her face up to his. "For Fran. Remember? I told her if I ever sent help, she'd know it was safe if the person said 'California Barbie'."

"Oh, yeah, right." He chuckled. "Whose idea was a silly password again?"

"Mine. It carries great meaning to a lonely, brokenhearted, twelve-year-old girl."

"How sweet," he admitted. "And far-sighted of you." He kissed her upturned lips.

"I'll sacrifice anything to free Fran—even my freedom." Her gaze slid away to the far window.

Fear snaked along his neck and tightened his throat. "Why would they care about little old you after all this time?"

"I'll make sure they care." Her fiery eyes met his, full of grit and resolve. "I can pretend to have Li's precious information on rare earths, so Wei and his assistant Mai save face. They can swap me for an ignorant little girl. I'll stall until you get Fran safely out of the country."

Staggered, his thoughts flew back to Ernie's voice, crackling and faint, assuring him he would be fine on his own. Paul's duty lay with the team. In this case, one for all.

Did he have what it took to put himself out there? Since Ernie's death, he avoided any situation requiring commitment. Including his marriage.

But Tina . . . for his little girl, he would gladly give his life. The ultimate declaration of love. He stared into Kay's misty brown eyes, drowning in their complex depths—and craving more.

How could he let her face her foes alone?

Realization slammed him. If he loved her, he couldn't just protect her. He had to put her happiness above his own. Even if it compromised her safety.

Because he had no doubt, after all.

Tugging her close, he kissed her, all his emotions rising to the surface. Pleasure hummed under her breath, a tiny vibration across her tongue, on her lips, and in her throat's deep recesses.

He stretched out on his side next to her and delved to taste every part of her. Sliding one hand to her jaw, he held her fast and slipped the other beneath her top. She moaned and returned the favor, tugging his shirt free of his pants, scratching his back with kittenish innocence—piercingly sweet, agonizingly provocative.

A potent mix of lust, love, and frantic recklessness grabbed him and held tight. If only he could freeze time and mark this moment as theirs, not their country's. Rising to his knees, he grabbed the zipper of her jeans and tore it down, hastily pulling the stiff material from her hips. His fingers caught in the lace of her panties. He ripped them away and shoved her back on the linoleum floor, straddling her hips, lowering his shoulders over her.

Kay's hand flew to her mouth, muffling a fearful cry.

He froze. *I'm an idiot!*

He pulled her off the cold floor and onto his thighs, squeezing her tight.

"I got so carried away I forgot." He kissed the top of her head, praying she would forgive him, hoping she could get beyond the bad memories and create new ones with him.

Damned if he would let her take precious years to forget. He faced his last mission's horror all alone. Daisy's token comfort had been worthless. He would offer so much more to Kay.

"I'm all right." Her long inhaled breath quivered, contradicting her. "It's just . . . the hard floor reminded me of the last time . . ." She dug her face into the hollow of his shoulder.

"I'm so sorry . . . I wanted to show you how much I love you . . . and, well . . ." He followed the arch of her brow with his lips, stroking her back with a long caress.

Kay's body tensed. "You love me?" Raising her head, she met his eyes.

"Yeah, I do." He gave her a crooked smile. "Took me too long to realize it, though."

"Me too." Biting on her lip, her breath hitched.

"Me too, what?" How pathetic was that? But this time, he wouldn't shortchange himself—or their future. He needed the words, goddammit.

A brilliant smile lit her face. "I love you, too." She wrapped her arms around his neck and caressed his earlobe with the tip of her tongue.

"Are you sure?" He traced her slender curves with a possessive palm.

"Very much so." She leaned back, her expression serious. "I got uptight on the bottom. If you're willing . . ." She gestured at their position with one hand. The fingers of her other unbuttoned his shirt with effortless speed.

"Baby, if you're eager for a wild ride, I'd be pretty stupid to dissuade you." Sliding his thumbs beneath the hem of her top, he hoisted it over her head and tossed it away. She lifted her weight and leaned to the side, reaching for her purse and pulling out a foil packet.

Cursing under his breath, he struggled with his zipper and bunched fabric, halting for a fleeting second to admire her lithe limbs and satiny skin.

"Let me help," she crooned, tugging and pulling the tangled pants off his ankles. He wrestled his arms free of the shirt and reached for her. She clambered on top, sliding the condom on and taking him into her heat in a single motion.

His breath caught. He froze, memorizing her face. Her body swaying in tempting rhythms above him. The sweet sensation of her inner muscles gripping him tight, tighter. Her shivering release.

Blinding heat shot through him, washing away all doubts. All hesitations.

He finally came home from his last mission.

With gasping breath, he sent a prayer heavenward, asking they both come back safe from their next.

They lingered on the cool floorboards in a close embrace. Their murmurs created an odd counterpoint to the incessant hum of Alex's computers. Paul kept one eye fixed on the wall clock. Too few minutes remained before reality—and visitors—invaded.

"Janelle's due soon." He extended his arm and gathered their scattered clothing.

He helped her to her feet and took her head in his hands.

"You know, I'm getting fond of your new look." He caught one small lock between two fingers and tugged. "Messing around won't muss your hair. Could be quite convenient. Might even set a new fashion trend."

"Yeah, that's gonna happen." She snorted, breaking away and stomping into her ankle boots. "Give me a break. No woman would cut her hair this short to look good." She scrubbed her scalp, frowning. "I'm not sure if Jintao will recognize me, let alone accept me again. He has pretty high standards for his mistresses."

"Long hair was in his job description?"

"Actually, I feel sexier with long hair than not. And for a man his age, how I feel sets the stage for a successful interaction."

"Too bad." The words caught in his throat, but her attitude needed fixing for her rendezvous to work. "I think sexy is as sexy does. Based on this last half hour, you're still one damn smokin' hot lady—long hair or not."

She danced across the room toward him, rose on tiptoe and smacked him on the lips.

"You're just stroking my ego, and I love you for saying it. But it's not reality." She shrugged. "It'll grow back, I know. Until then, I'll simply fake it."

"Do that often?" The irony-laced words spilled from his lips. He winced at her hurt expression. "I shouldn't have said that. It was unprofessional and . . ." He trailed off, spotting the hurt in her eyes. Hanging his head, he shook it in shame. "I'm sorry."

"You're forgiven." Her small hand grasped his and squeezed. "We have a field of emotional land mines to cross. If we do it together, we should succeed." She eased his head up. "Teammates, right?"

"Right." He lifted her hand and gave it a swift kiss. A car engine rumbled outside the window. He reached for their bags. "The cavalry has arrived."

Scooping up her purse, she followed him out the door, waiting for him to lock it and pocket the key. A black limousine idled in the parking lot, one back door opened in invitation.

"Janelle has a certain kind of style, doesn't she?" Kay strode over, ducked her head, and climbed in. "Oh my God!"

Paul dashed over. He tossed the bags through the opening with no regard for where they might land. Clambering inside, he peered around the darkened interior for lurking danger.

And met Tina's grin, Janelle's wide smile, and Lynn's piercing blue eyes.

All sporting hairdo's identical to Kay's.

His eyes popped wide at Tina's golden halo. Similar dismay filled Kay's expression. He slammed the door, speechless.

"Hi, Daddy." Tina waved. "What do you think of our matching haircuts? Pretty sexy, huh?" She patted her head and preened, pouting like an innocent porn star. "We couldn't let Kay have all the fun."

"You did this to imitate me?" Kay slumped in the bench seat, her hand at her heart.

"Well, in fairness, the flames singed off a big chunk of my hair." Janelle chuckled. "It was best I cut it all off."

"I've had enough of the baby pulling out my hair by the fistfuls," Lynn smiled.

"I needed an adult hairdo," Tina piped in. "Mom can't style it different. What you see is what you get."

His baby, all grown up. No more curls to play with. His throat locked with emotion.

"I think you're all fantastic," Paul said. "See, Kay, I told you short hair was trending. Glad you ladies proved me right."

"Thank you." He barely heard Kay's whisper above the engine noise, but her new friends apparently understood. They leaned close, patting, hugging, and crooning silly chitchat.

Two minutes later, Kay's full-throated laughter joined the others. Paul relaxed. A mere male could only say so much to reassure a woman about her looks. Some wounds took a female touch to heal.

Including his own.

Chapter 50

EARTHQUAKE ZONE

Xinjiang Province, China
Evening, June 12, 2 Days Later

Alex wretched alongside the dirt road, his empty stomach heaving an eruption of foul-tasting acid. For just this one moment, he focused on his own misery.

Weak cries for help added to the din of barking dogs, squawking chickens, and the ancient, clanking bulldozer clearing rubble off the main thoroughfare. A stench unlike any he'd ever smelled before rose up from the village.

Local officials had declared the area free of all living victims before Don and he arrived the day before last. So far, the bulldozer unearthed an occasional arm or leg—or severed head. With only a few hours remaining, the rubble that was once a village would officially became a mass grave.

He blew dust from his watch and peered at the luminous dial. Eleven o'clock by official Beijing reckoning. Squinting at the setting sun, he wondered how many more hours before Don took pity on Fred's quivering nose and allowed the poor mutt a rest. Fred had already found ten survivors in the crumbled homes, including an unconscious baby trapped beneath his dead mother.

The other five UN-sponsored canine teams headed for high-population areas in the quake-stricken region. Don volunteered them as the rescue team for this remote town for a reason. It was just over eleven miles from Li's prison. Equipped with minimal supplies, their sole link for backup was a satellite phone, pre-programmed to call the official evacuation helicopter for a pick-up when they decided their work was done.

No Chinese national government assistance had yet reached this remote town; only regional volunteers arrived with little more than water and bare hands. Alex overheard the local's angry cries about the lack of responsiveness from Beijing, and the bitter acceptance of their fate. Their poor village didn't contribute to the Party's political power structure—why should any CCP politician care?

Don had already eyed the bulldozer, hoping their unexpected help would grease the skids for its loan. He figured they could drive to the local monastery three miles in the opposite direction from the prison and ask for help freeing Li. Even with their official UN emergency insignias emblazoned on their safety helmets, a few more local faces to confront suspicious guards wouldn't hurt.

"Alex, over here." Don waved him toward a toppled building at the outskirts of town. The leash attached to Fred's collar strained tight, his wagging tail a blur.

Rising, Alex crammed on his helmet and walked on unsteady legs through the center of the hamlet. He averted his eyes from a scrawny teenage girl's body, smashed and tossed aside like garbage, and reached Don's side.

"Not another kid . . ."

A pile of dirt covered Alex's boots. He looked up and caught the eye of an old man. Fresh dust covered a build-up of months-old grime around his wrinkled neck. The unmistakable odor of unwashed flesh turned Alex's stomach again. The old man shifted his attention back to the wreckage. His bony fingers dug toward a saffron-colored scrap of cloth with swift, steady movements.

Shoving back his helmet, Don shook his head and pointed to the distinctive material caught underneath the fallen wall. "This monk will die if we don't unearth him. He's the last sound Fred has heard in hours."

Fred whined and wriggled. His bloody paws burrowed through loose rocks and debris.

"You really think we can do this?" Alex considered the four-foot high mound of rubble.

"Sure. By sunset." Don's confident words didn't quite match the telltale twitch in his cheek. He tossed Alex heavy leather gloves, pulled on a matching pair, and wrestled a large section of roof off the pile.

"Youch!" Don dropped the piece and grabbed his back, wincing. "Goddammit, this is all I need." He dropped to his knees.

Arranging a handkerchief over his nose, Alex positioned himself a few yards from Don and planted his feet. He grabbed a long, worn plank and used it as a makeshift shovel, scooping pulverized rock mixed with broken pieces of primitive pottery. A flattened brass candleholder caught the setting sun's rays and glistened. He set the religious keepsake aside for the monk—if he survived.

Four more hands appeared. Surprised, he glanced up. A young couple joined the old man, heaving and shoveling in a frantic pace.

"He came home to visit his father," the youth explained in Chinese, nodding at the old one. "He is one of ours."

The pile was growing taller behind them and shorter in front. Fred woofed and whined in discordant rhythm as he buried his nose in rubble and licked it clean only to do it again. More villagers joined them, silent of chatter.

Alex raised his plank and scooped a load of stones away. An elbow appeared, worming its way upward.

"Here!" He repeated the word in Chinese, pointing to his feet.

A swarm of bodies joined him. Resembling an underworld god, the trapped monk pushed himself upward, back first. Grainy waterfalls spilled from his bloody shoulders. The saffron robe remained snagged beneath the fallen building's weight, his nakedness revealed in slow motion.

Anchored in dust, his lean, sinewy body straightened like a flower seeking light. His head lifted to the indigo sky, and his hands joined at his chest in a prayerful stance.

"*Ami tou fo*," he chanted weakly. The villagers halted all activity and bowed their heads.

Breathing hard, Alex looked over at Don sitting on the ground with a pained expression, patting Fred's head. Alex swore the dog was grinning with satisfaction.

"I think Fred deserves a reward," Alex said. Grabbing the precious water bottle, he took one sip and stepped toward them.

Don nodded, cupping his hands low. Alex poured a handful and Fred lapped it up.

"Thank you." The soft Chinese words, heavy with an accent Alex barely understood, drifted over their heads. Shifting to his knees, Don motioned Alex to lend him his arm. With a grunt, Don rose and straightened, facing the naked monk. Blood trickled down the monk's forehead and across his nose, a macabre mask that contrasted starkly to his serene expression.

"Translate for me," Don said. "Tell him we were happy to help."

Fumbling for the right words, Alex stuttered Don's reply and listened to the answer.

"He says he owes you his life, and his elderly father owes you the life of his only son. Whatever you need that they can provide, they will." Alex paused.

"Now we're getting somewhere." Don stared into the monk's eye. "Tell him we hope he and his village can help us."

Alex complied and listened to the answer.

"He asks what he can do to repay our kindness so he can begin working on it immediately," Alex paraphrased.

"Tell him we'll require an escort to Li's prison tomorrow to check on the damage there." Don scratched his chin. "If he's smart, he'll figure out what our true purpose is soon enough."

Alex rattled off the translation, watching the monk's face for signs of comprehension. A slight widening of his dust-crusted eyes betrayed reaction to the favor's scope. To his credit, the monk nodded in simple, silent agreement.

"We'll meet at sunrise," the monk murmured. "I will bring others to assist. Too many of our order are also imprisoned because of their religious beliefs. We will bring spiritual counsel to our brethren."

Turning his back, he re-joined the villagers and picked up his tattered robe. The monk wiped his face with one corner and swiped the blood from his shoulders. He wrapped it around his torso with practiced gestures, his melodic voice reassuring the villagers that Buddha will surely answer every prayer. Yet perhaps not with the answer they sought.

Chapter 51

Dawn spread delicate hues across the vast sky, dusting the mountaintops with amethyst shadows. Alex stretched awake from a tiny knoll above the flattened village and examined his blistered hands. Should he feel grateful he got a break from digging today, or guilty there were no more lives to save? What a stark contrast between the villagers' minimal resources for survival and the excesses of Silicon Valley.

Really, what was the point of accumulating so much personal wealth? To drive a fast car? Glancing toward the village, Alex sobered, his vision filled with life's true challenge—stark rows of roughly shrouded bodies.

A melodic chanting filled the quiet.

"*Ami tou fo.*" Five monks filed with processional dignity along what remained of the village lane. Villagers stepped from their meager night's shelter and bowed deep as they passed.

"Don." Alex tossed a stone on the lumpy sleeping bag nearby, interrupting another snore. Fred appeared above the bag, rising with a yawn-stretched jaw.

"Huh? What?" Don shoved back his covering and propped up on one elbow with a muffled groan. His eyes darted in every direction. They stopped at the human chain heading their way.

"What do you want me to tell them?" The reality of their true mission hit Alex. His empty stomach knotted.

Don unzipped and eased to a sitting position, patting Fred's head. "Ask if we can borrow the bulldozer so we can help at the prison. The front shovel might come in handy smuggling Li out."

Alex blinked grit from his eyes and scrambled to his feet. He approached the familiar young man leading their escort. Gesturing to the machine and pointing at the distant hills, he communicated their goal. No questions, no comments. No resistance.

Don limped over, Fred pattering behind, and nodded to each monk in turn. They acknowledged in kind. The leader gestured to follow him to the village center. Alex stayed back, calculating Don's elder status should enhance the unorthodox request.

One man stepped from the circle of villagers, bowing to Don and the monk. Alex studied the body language of the village elder. His reluctance and hesitation was as clear as his respect and deference to the holy man. So much for China's effort to wipe religion out of the minds of its people. Out here in the boonies, it was probably their citizens' only hope.

Long minutes later, Don climbed behind the wheel, wincing. He started the engine and bounced across the rubble to their makeshift camp.

"Help Fred up to me," he called. "You can walk and chat with the monks. Make new friends."

Alex conceded Fred's paws deserved more of a break than his boot-encased feet. Lifting him to Don's side, he tossed their belongings into the well and joined the line of monks heading northeast.

"*Ami tou fo.*" The haunting chant lifted over the bulldozer's coughing motor.

Alex shrugged and joined in the chant. Dust spitting from its wheels, Don thankfully brought up the rear in this procession.

They crested a high hill just as the sun passed its zenith. Don coaxed the old engine up the incline. Walking to Alex's side, the leader pointed to a building a quarter mile away. Alex discerned three crumbled outer walls and people milling in a large bunch, surrounded by what appeared to be guards.

Don cut the engine and rummaged in his pack, pulling out a wad of cash. "Tell that young monk we have plenty of money to bribe whomever we need. We gotta find out which one is Li under the guise of searching for buried bodies. Can they do that?"

Alex translated. Disappointment crossed the leader's face, replaced by his usual resignation and serenity. Too late, Alex remembered the monks took vows to renounce all earthly goods beyond essentials. Having to participate in Don's mercenary tactics must roil their consciences.

Nodding agreement, the monk gathered the others, speaking in soft tones and controlled gestures.

"You think there's enough money for Li to walk out of prison? No questions asked?" Alex muttered under his breath.

"Shit, no, son." Don yanked out the packs and helmets and handed Alex his. "Give me more credit. Listen up." Shrugging on his gear, Alex paid attention to the plan, marveling at Don's cunning.

Alex joined the lead monk, making their way down the hill, side by side with Don following in the bulldozer. Early afternoon sun highlighted a layer of dust suspended above a long line of motionless bodies. At fifty yards, the stench of decay began to fill Alex's nostrils. He tugged a handkerchief over his nose to stem another tide of nausea. Fred jumped down from the cab, running to the front of their odd procession and back to Don, woofing as if asking for permission to search for survivors.

A disheveled guard limped toward them. Don cut the motor and slumped in the seat rubbing his back, more haggard and drawn than Alex had ever seen him. Alex stepped forward and held up his hand to help him down, but Don shook him off. Instead, Don wiped his brow and slapped on his UN helmet in an exaggerated motion.

The lead monk spoke in a respectful voice, asking if one of their order survived and requesting the body be returned home if not. He waved behind his back. Alex took this cue to grab some cash and shove it into the monk's fingers. With a graceful bow, the monk slipped the bills into the guard's pocket and clasped his hands to his chest, shaved head bowed.

"*Ami tou fo.*" The other monks joined in the chant. "*Ami tou fo. Ami tou fo.*"

Fingering the money, the guard's expression lightened. He gestured them ahead, scrutinizing each face. His brows rose at Don's western features but motioned him forward, too.

They scattered throughout the prison. Don powered on the engine and poked the bulldozer's prongs through the rubble in random thrusts. Alex positioned himself in the center courtyard, praying Li wasn't one of the poor victims rotting in the sun.

A ring of prisoners surrounded him, muttering and suspicious. Outside the circle, a few others loitered with speculative hope on their expressions. More emaciated than Kay had ever been, their clothes hung in tatters. Political prisoners or murderers? Religious dissidents or thieves? Alex wished he could help the innocent escape. But how could he tell which was which? Perhaps there would be some money left over, and the monks could come back.

"*Pssst.*"

Spinning on his toes, he peered through a darkened doorway. Two wraiths lurked, one in a robe, the other listing to the right. Alex peeked back at the guards. They seemed fascinated by the bulldozer's mechanisms. Darting inside, Alex met the stranger's skeptical eyes.

"I'm Li Ying. This monk tells me you look for me. Who are you and why are you here?"

Triumph washed through Alex, mingled with relief. He introduced himself and summarized Don's plan in hushed tones. "We can get you to America where you'll be safe," he concluded.

"Do you think I would leave my daughter and future wife in China while I am safe?" Li scowled.

Wife? They missed something pretty important in all their grandiose plans.

"You're not helping them much shut up in this prison, are you?" Alex gestured at the stone wall, surprised at Li's pig-headedness. Had he any idea what the team had gone through just to have this conversation with him?

Of course not. Alex hadn't shared the details. But he would give Li an earful once they were airborne.

"Look, someone else is freeing your daughter right now." Alex crossed his fingers that his statement wasn't a lie. "Once you're safe, we'll work on the other."

"Freeing?" Li's face darkened.

"Shh!" Alex ducked and pulled him farther into the gloom. "We think she's being detained as a bargaining chip to use against you for your know-how about refining rare earths. If we can get you to America, her continued detention would be meaningless."

"Or more important! You don't understand Chinese politicians. A defector is a terrible loss of face. And Yannan? We must free her, too."

Of course! Alex should have anticipated this possibility. Kay was so adamant Fran had no one else, and Li would happily come to America with his daughter. Now what? He peered at the monk tucked in a meditative squat. Maybe he would offer sage advice.

"*Ami tou fo.*" The monk's lips moved in silent rhythm.

Nope, he was on his own. Alex sighed. "Staying here isn't getting you, Fran, or Yannan any closer to freedom, right?"

"No, I want out of prison." Li peered outside. "I just do not wish to worsen the situation."

"Then follow our plan."

"Do you understand if I am caught, I will be executed on the spot?"

"Do you understand you're scheduled for execution any day now?" Frustrated, Alex shook Li's shoulder, ignoring the wince crossing the man's face. "Why not try?"

Li nodded. "Tell me what to do."

"Hold your breath." Alex extricated the tarp from his pack. "I'm wrapping you with the largest body we can find. Then, we'll haul you to the bulldozer and smuggle you out. Can you handle it?"

"Our old, revered profession of corpse walker carried a dead body on his back, at times for weeks on end, to bring the deceased home." Li's chin rose with pride. "I can handle a few hours."

Alex peeked out the doorway and jerked his head back. Three guards strode by, wooden bats in their hands, gesturing and ordering the circle of prisoners to quiet down.

"Wait . . . get ready . . . now!" Alex scrambled out the door behind the guards' backs, Li and the monk on his heels. Eying the bodies, he squatted next to the widest corpse, who fortunately had all his limbs attached underneath filthy garb. Along with a crushed face. Maybe a guard wouldn't demand a close inspection underneath this gruesome sight. Or would he?

Li dropped to the outspread tarp. Alex and the monk hefted the dead man on top. Cramming cash into the ripped neck of the corpse's tunic, Alex took one last look at Li's resigned face, and rolled the two bodies together as one.

"We can't lift this ourselves," Alex hissed at the monk.

Nodding, he straightened and with controlled, graceful gestures beckoned the rest of his entourage to gather close. With ceremonial dignity, the monks lifted the burden and carried it to the bulldozer, Alex supporting the two heads. Don dropped the shovel to the ground and slid down from the cab, standing next to the solitary guard.

The lead monk motioned the guard close.

"We have found our relative." The monk flipped the tarp's corner aside and hefted the load near the guard's face. The guard reared back with a disgusted expression—and filched the fat wad of notes. Pompous satisfaction replaced revulsion.

A commotion broke out in the courtyard. Two prisoners ran toward them, pleading for assistance in loud shouts. Four guards tackled them to the ground. They beat the prisoners' heads and shoulders, screaming obscenities all the while.

Alex flinched at the violence. He glanced around, wondering if anyone would halt it. In the distance, he spotted a uniformed man step into the doorway of the corner building still anchoring the courtyard. The officer pointed and gestured at their small grouping.

Their guard paled. "Go! No visitors permitted." Stretching his arm wide, he swung his baton hard across Don's back.

Don fell to his knees. Pain contorted his face.

"Your machine is not needed." The guard smacked Don's back again.

The lead monk stepped forward, putting himself in the path of the upraised baton. The guard hesitated.

"We will leave now." The monk motioned to the others. They maneuvered their burden into the shovel. It tumbled down the scoop's side, the tarp unrolling halfway.

Alex held his breath. An exposed foot jerked out of sight. Alex shot a glance at the guard, praying he hadn't noticed.

"Fred! Come boy!" Don whistled from his hands and knees. Fred scurried around the corner. Alex lifted Fred and tossed him on top of the tarp.

"Bluff. Show him Fred's bloody paws," Don muttered.

Alex gestured to the panting dog, explaining how hard he worked on behalf of Chinese victims in the remote village. He re-positioned the tarp, patting Fred and recounting how Fred's keen nose saved a tiny boy. The guard squinted at the dog, curled a disdainful lip and waved them off.

Squatting at Don's side, Alex helped him rise.

"Are you hurt?" Alex kept one eye peeled on the guard shouting orders on his way to the prison's courtyard.

"What do you think?" Don grunted and limped to the bulldozer. He eyed the high step up. "My back was already killing me from yesterday, and bouncing over here didn't help. You'll have to drive this thing back to the village." He threw Alex an assessing glance. "You can use a stick shift, right?"

"No, I can't." Dismayed, Alex stared at the long rod poking through the rusty floorboard, at the intimidating array of pedals and knobs, chokes and clutches. Fitting names for how he felt.

"No time like the present to learn, then." Don grasped the metal frame and rose to his toes. "Boost me up, kid. There's no way I can walk."

Grunting with effort, Alex got Don settled on the edge of the cab and jumped into the driver's seat. He followed Don's commands to start the engine, and stared at the line of monks already climbing the first hill. He took a deep breath.

"Now what do I do?"

"Now we see if you have coordination to go with your genius brain." Don explained the essence of the controls, and closed his eyes. "Practice makes perfect. Just try to reach perfection before you stall out on that hill. You'll have one helluva time clutching otherwise. And I don't think Li's stomach would appreciate that one bit."

Alex gulped thinking of Li, wrapped up with a decaying corpse surrounding him. He focused on getting his feet and hands in the necessary rhythm. The bulldozer lurched forward and died.

"Try again," Don said. "You almost had it."

Why hadn't he listened to his father and learned on his little pickup when he had a chance? No, Alex assumed no one in his generation would ever need to learn manual gearshifts. Maybe just for fun, certainly not for necessity. Who knew an emergency would put him in this situation with other people's lives at risk?

He gripped the wheel, positioned his feet, and worked the choke, clutch, and accelerator. The engine coughed and caught. He got it moving forward in an unsteady line. But moving forward.

"Good job." Don rested his head against the back of the cab. "You can take it from here. Mission accomplished. Getting out of here will be a cinch."

Chapter 52

Alex crested the first hill and glanced over his shoulder at the prison a safe distance away. He squinted at the sun and estimated their journey would take a few more hours. Pitying Li suffering in the building afternoon heat, he pressed on the accelerator, coaxing the bulldozer and building up speed on the downhill slope.

He took his first relaxed breath in hours and tapped Don's shoulder.

"We have a glitch in our plan," Alex said.

"Who says?" Don shifted, pain evident on his face.

"Li. He's not feeling real cooperative until he's sure we'll free both his daughter *and* his sister-in-law . . . who apparently is his next wife." Alex shifted into lower gear at the bottom of the hill, the loud scrape filling the pastoral valley with incongruous echoes.

"Great. Just great." Don peered ahead. "At least we can get him to Okinawa, and out of China's clutches."

"Yeah, I think he'll be okay with freedom."

Long shadows marked their path back to the village. Finally accustomed to the bulldozer's fits and starts, Alex let his mind wander to the other rescue attempt. Were Paul and Kay successful in getting Fran out of the clutches of the slavers? And how would Kay take Li's insistence on freeing that journalist, too? That might throw cold water on her determination to settle Fran and Li in America, if she'd imagined herself a surrogate mother. Alex shook his head, nibbling his energy bar. He sure hoped Kay's unlucky streak ended soon.

Spotting familiar boulder formations bordering the monks' processional path, Alex nudged Don's upraised knee. "Shouldn't we call for the UN helicopter?"

"Yeah, good idea." Don dug out the satellite phone. "We're close enough now to our original GPS coordinates." He pointed ahead. "That crest should work as a pick-up location." The engine whined and screeched, starting its ascent up the last hill.

Alex leaned forward as far as he could to tap the shovel three quick times, hoping Li would interpret it as a message of reassurance, not danger. Don punched in the pre-programmed number for UN rescue teams, arranging a rendezvous for three.

Reaching the top, the monks stopped dead. They dropped to a crouch in unison. The leader crab-walked down the incline to the bulldozer and waved. Concern lined his face. Swearing under his breath, Alex braked and turned off the coughing engine. Battling that clutch again to re-start the uphill climb would be a bitch.

"The national government has finally sent help to my village." The monk's sedate voice belied caution. "They will ask many questions."

Alex translated for Don. Fred took advantage of the break to jump out, sniffing and peeing on the low shrubs along the dusty roadside.

"What does he suggest?" Don straightened upright and dangled one leg out the cab.

Alex asked. Dread crept up his spine at the monk's blunt answer, in direct contrast to his calm demeanor. He turned to Don and translated.

"He says he has paid for his life, and has no other advice to give. They will return to the monastery where they belong." The monk bowed, turned away, and re-climbed the hill. At the peak, his followers fell in line.

"*Ami tou fo.*" The chant drifted away.

"Let's pray the new government officials don't come exploring this racket too soon." Don sank to the hard earth and whistled. Fred ran over, panting, and dropped his jowls on Don's thigh. Don stared at the bulldozer for long minutes, scratching behind Fred's ears.

Alex crept to the summit and peeked over. Floodlights lit the village. Six uniformed guards circled the outskirts, rifles slung across their backs. The villagers squatted in a circle, their hands moving from their laps to their mouths with provisions apparently provided by the government. One guard stopped the monks at the base of the hill, gesturing upwards.

Busted!

Alex slid backwards on his stomach. Sharp rocks poked his ribs. Digging his toes in to stop his descent, he jumped to his feet and ran back to the bulldozer.

"They're coming our way!" Alex gasped for breath. His heart was pounding.

"Get Li out of there and behind that boulder. Then stall them." Don struggled to his feet, grabbing onto the cab for support. "The chopper should arrive within an hour." He crawled into the seat, tossed Alex his helmet, and cranked the engine.

Clambering into the shovel, Alex unearthed Li and re-rolled the faceless corpse back in the tarp. He told Li about the coming helicopter and the unexpected army presence. Li paled but kept silent. With a nod, Li darted behind a large boulder ten yards away.

Alex scanned the effectiveness of Li's hideout. Satisfied their prize was secure, he glanced up, jamming on his helmet with the UN logo.

A lone, gun-wielding figure silhouetted at the hilltop pointed his weapon, waving them forward. With a loud cough and masterful manipulation of gears, Don inched the bulldozer up the hill.

Alex grabbed Fred's collar and strode ahead, pondering which part of their day's journey to embellish, which details to censor. His stomach knotted tight. Would their official story pass muster to one pissed-off Army dude?

One hour. One hour until the roar of spinning blades would fill the night skies. The rare metal needs of America rested on Alex's shoulders. And ironically, his people skills mattered most, not military prowess or technology gadgets.

He never would have guessed it would come down to this.

The anger on the soldier's face glowered vivid red by the sun's setting rays. He brandished his rifle at Alex and pointed in the direction of the monks' path.

"What are you doing with these terrorists?" the soldier hollered.

Puzzled, Alex took his time climbing the few yards to the soldier's elevation. Did the Chinese government judge Tibet such a threat they broadened the definition of terrorism? Considering the monks' tranquil behavior, he prayed not.

"We are Americans, here to help the villagers after the earthquake." Alex raised his hands to shoulder level with a smile meant to reassure and pointed one finger to his helmet. The soldier squinted at its emblem in the dim light.

"China does not need your help." The soldier took a menacing step forward. He looked down the hill at the bulldozer. "If you are here to help this village, why did you leave it, heh?"

Fred wagged his tail and sniffed the soldier's shoes. So much for a dog sensing who was friend or foe.

"To retrieve the body of one of the villager's family, who died at the nearby prison." Alex held his trembling breath.

"Show me."

Waving Don to the top, he waited until the engine stopped. The soldier nudged him forward by the rifle tip. Alex approached the wheezing vehicle.

"Don, this soldier wishes to see the monk's body." The possibility that the soldier understood English stayed foremost in Alex's brain. As much as he would like on-the-spot strategizing with Don, he didn't dare. He prayed his formality would relay this to Don. "He thinks we are helping terrorists, instead."

Eyes narrowed and assessing, Don grabbed his helmet and plopped it on his head. He stepped with deliberate motion from the bulldozer's cab. With gritted teeth, he walked to the shovel, leaned over the edge at an awkward angle, and eased the heavy body to the front tips. Now wincing with silent pain, he flipped the tarp away from the mangled head.

"Ugh!" The soldier grimaced. "Who can identify this man as a monk if he has no face?"

Alex's brain went blank. He shot a quick glance at Don and translated.

"The monk's father, of course." Don's bland expression complemented his deferential nod. Switching to a low murmur just for Alex's ears, he muttered, "Get ready to run to the village and do some quick talking to our favorite monk's old man. He owes us a favor for digging out his only son."

Alex faced the soldier. With elaborate gestures, he invented rescuing a monk from the collapsed prison wall. He struggled to keep his voice steady even as his heart raced with the deception. "His father awaits his body to burn incense in special brass holders I pulled from his home's rubble. He was a very special son."

"Special? He was in prison!" Skepticism swept over the soldier's face. "This shamed his father."

There was that. Alex scrambled for an explanation.

"As a monk, he investigated alternative religions, always seeking the truth. His father says he fell in with bad people, the Uyghur Muslims, and lost his way." Alex bowed. "We did not understand this when we agreed to help a poor Chinese father bring his only son home for burial."

"Did I just hear you say Muslim, son?" Don nudged Alex's toe. "No wonder he thinks we're helping terrorists."

"The Uyghurs are not terrorists," Alex said in English, aiming a gracious smile at the soldier. "But the wise government officials consider any religion against the best interests of the Chinese people."

"Introduce me to the father." The soldier pointed downhill. "I will determine if you speak the truth."

"I'm guessing he wants to check out your story, Alex. Tell him I'll drive to the village and bring this boy home to his father." Don opened his arms wide and gestured at the bulldozer. "He can ride with me as an escort, and a sign of faith you aren't fleeing."

Alex complied, pointing and smiling.

The soldier strutted to the far edge and pissed over the hillside.

"You get your butt down there and give the father the rest of that cash," Don whispered rapidly. "Make sure he verifies our story. Otherwise, that copter will take off with only Li." He limped forward. "Boost me up first."

Alex assisted Don into the cab then walked to the soldier's side. He started his five-minute sales pitch on why he needed to get to the village first. Good thing he'd practiced with the VCs. This one counted for more than money. This was his life.

Chapter 53

Alex ran down the hill. The old man sat with the other villagers, looking weary and defeated. No wonder. His only son returned to the monastery, leaving his homeless father to fend for himself. Fighting back a pang of guilt he was about to do the same, Alex placed his hand on the man's bony shoulder and asked to speak with him in private.

Glancing at the soldiers grouped nearby, the old man shook his head, shrugging off Alex's hand.

"You owe us," Alex hissed.

"My son already paid you back. Do you require a second life to save?" He tilted his jaw at the soldiers. "I'm sure they would provide you one, starting with yours."

"I will pay you for this help." Alex slid half of his cash under the man's hip.

The father dropped his hand and fingered the width of the stack. "Not enough."

"For this, you will do everything I ask." Alex shoved the remainder into his claw-like hands and bent at the waist. Gagging at the overpowering stench of days-old sweat, he whispered his requirements into a withered ear.

A satisfied smile settled onto the old man's face. He nodded, and rose with an alacrity defying his years. With an exaggerated tug, he re-settled his tunic about his waist. The money disappeared into his worn belt.

"I must greet my son's return to his rightful home." His announcement caught the attention of his neighbors, who watched with a mixture of curiosity and wariness. "Please join me after you have finished your meal."

Alex grabbed the tip of the old man's elbow and nudged him toward the bulldozer descending the last twenty-five yards of the hill.

"You will cry and scream and wail your grief loud enough to make these soldiers believe the man we have brought here is your son," Alex said. "Then, you will convince your neighbors his face is not to be looked upon ever again, in a sign of respect to the Chinese government who has come to help your village."

"What help?" The old man protested. "You and your friend saved more lives than our government."

"Remember that, and remind your friends, too." Facing the oncoming vehicle, Alex raised a hand.

Don braked and stopped the motor. The soldier jumped out and scrutinized the old man. Don followed, limping, Fred at his heels.

"Is this the father?" The soldier squeezed his nostrils shut with one hand. A look of disgust crossed his face.

"Is that my son?" The old man could have been a Hollywood veteran. Tears spilled from his eyes and his face crumpled in feigned grief. He stumbled to the edge of the shovel and struggled with the tarp. Horror filled his face as he pulled open the corner and gasped.

"Well? Is that your son?"

"Yes . . . yes!" Wailing, the old man climbed in and threw himself down on the body, hugging it to his chest.

"Enough!" the soldier roared. "Get down from there—and bring your son's body, too."

The father raised his head, pretend-dismay covering up the flash of cunning.

"Do you expect an old man to carry such a fine son?" He pointed to the group of soldiers. "You promised assistance to our village. You were too late to save lives. Here is your chance to help."

"That is not our job." The soldier sneered.

The father rose and clambered to the top of the cab.

"Neighbors," he bellowed. "Do you not think all of us here tonight should honor my son and carry him home?"

As one, the villagers scrambled to their feet and hurried up the incline. The half-dozen soldiers had no choice but to follow, disgruntled expressions on their faces.

Alex stood by Don's side, Fred at their feet, and watched the father tossing orders with the confidence of a five-star general. He commanded soldiers to harness their rifles and hoist the body out to the upstretched hands of the villagers. He jumped down and positioned himself at the front of the mourners. The other soldiers flanked the procession and started toward the old man's crushed hovel.

Whop-whop-whop.

The distinctive sound of the incoming helicopter filled the night air. Alex peered over his shoulder, spotting the top of Li's head at the crest. Li waved at the copter and they both dropped out of sight.

The last soldier in line stopped and turned with a suspicious scowl on his face.

"Our transport home." Alex gave the soldier a respectful bow and took a side step up the hill.

"Halt!" He flipped his rifle into his hands. The villagers milled along the hillside, some pointing to the sky, others with wary eyes on the remaining soldiers.

Rifle tucked into his armpit, the soldier stepped to Don's side and grabbed his shoulder. Don dug his heels into the dirt, not giving an inch.

"I think we will need to question you and your pilot before we grant permission to leave," the soldier said.

Don glanced between the helicopter rising twenty feet above the crest, and the distance to the crowd. The look he gave Alex was unmistakable.

Of course. Don needed extra minutes to scramble up that hill. *Create a distraction and fast!*

"Old man," Alex called, shoving back his fear. "Is this the thanks we get for saving your village people?"

"Friends!" The father responded on cue, waving his hands. "The UN sent these fine men to help us days before our own government could. We should let them leave and go home to their families, don't you agree?"

The crowd roared their approval and surrounded the soldiers. They pressed close, closer, pinning the rifles and arms of the soldiers in a downward position. Turning like a giant swarm of bees, they headed downhill as a mob, taking the helpless soldiers with them.

Damned effective pacifist technique, Alex thought. Wonder where they learned it?

Better yet, would it work long enough to let them escape?

"The United Nations sent us in peace. You must let us go now." Alex tore the soldier's hand off Don and glared at the soldier, daring him to object.

The soldier stared back. "You obey my orders!" He raised his rifle to his shoulder.

Alex shook his head, pointing Don up the hill. Giving him a shove, Alex twisted around to face the soldier, standing toe to toe.

The soldier aimed his rifle at Alex's chest.

"Fred—attack!" Don's yell washed over Alex from behind.

A snarl, a scurry of paws on the dirt, and Fred flung himself at the soldier.

The soldier yelped, surprised, and fell to his knees, dropping his rifle. Fred persisted, his open jaws aimed at the man's throat.

Alex grabbed Fred's collar, praying they could get out of here with no bloodshed. The dog snapped his teeth at the air, growling and tugging with fearsome strength. Alex stepped back, dragging the dog with him.

"You are safe." Alex huffed, wrestling with Fred. "Let us go in peace."

With a glower wreathing his sweaty forehead, the soldier tucked his feet under him and rose to one knee. His eyes locked on Fred. His hand groped for the rifle a yard away.

Alex bent to the side and pushed at Fred's hindquarters. If he could get the dog to sit, perhaps the soldier would see they were cooperating and let them go. Fred resisted. Threatening rumbles rattled from his throat. Alex pushed harder, turning his back on the soldier and holding his breath. The quivering dog sat. Releasing his collar, Alex rested his hands on his thighs and released a shuddering sigh.

The rifle butt whizzed past his face. It smashed onto the top of Fred's head. The mutt yelped and fell limp next to him.

"No!" Don pushed past Alex and dropped to his knees next to the prone dog. He lifted Fred's head; blood poured out of the long ear onto the dirt. No muscle twitch came from the poor animal. No breath lifted his chest. Alex dropped his head, ashamed he couldn't protect this helpless creature.

The soldier knocked Don aside.

"You Americans are so stupid. Dogs are worthless." He pummeled Fred again with his rifle, a sick grin contorting his face.

The helicopter blades appeared in front of them. Wind gusts almost knocked them flat. It hovered at an angle above the descending road.

Li crouched in the open doorway and jumped out. He streaked toward the soldier. Catching the downward path of the rifle aimed at Fred's limp body, he tore it out of the soldier's hands.

"Go! You are a little man trying to prove his greatness by killing a helpless dog." Li flung the rifle far out of reach and spat in the soldier's face. "All you proved is how worthless you are." He cocked his chin high and raised his fists halfway.

Alex stepped to Li's side and assumed the same posture.

"Bah!" The soldier curled his lip and kicked Fred one last time. With a curse, he turned to retrieve his rifle, yelling curses and flailing his arms.

Alex glanced down at the bloody carcass. His heart wrenched. Sliding his helmet off, he placed it over the heroic dog's head and snapped off a small salute.

"Come on." He tugged Don to his feet and linked arms. Don's chest rose and fell in great heaving gasps. Whether from back pain or grief, Alex couldn't be sure. Either way, the old warrior struggled taking that first step.

Li joined them, linking Don's other arm and bending against the blast from the hovering helicopter.

Dust coated Alex's mouth, hot and bitter. Tension gripped his muscles. Relying on Li to keep Don upright and moving forward, he dropped behind. He expected a shot in the back at any moment, but they had to keep Li alive any way they could.

The three men clambered into the open doorway of the copter and fell inside. Li slammed the door and they lifted up, flying away from China's death grip.

Chapter 54

PORT OF TIANJIN

Tianjin, China
Morning, June 15, 2 Days Later

The ferry's lonely wail announced their impending arrival into port. From Okinawa, Kay and Paul flew to Seoul, meeting Janelle's arranged transport to the Tianjin Straits. Constantly moving became second nature to Kay after the first twenty-four hours. And sneaking in along the coast on this commuter special was one of the dozen ways Janelle had contributed to their back-door entry into China.

Unfortunately, this was the end of the road for their plan. The rest was all up to her and Paul.

Kay shivered and rubbed her arms. The land coalesced in bits and pieces through heavy humidity, with dozens of ships anchored wharf-side. Was it the chill in the air or sheer weariness that sapped her energy?

Or simply fear of returning to Beijing without her constant protector? Funny how much she now relied on Paul's reassuring presence.

Paul climbed the ladder and crossed to her side at the bow. "Janelle just texted. Apparently, your Taiwanese connections made good on their promise."

"That's a surprise." Kay turned and leaned her elbows on the railing. "I forgot all about Yannan's leads. What's up?"

"They identified the name of a cargo ship carrying questionable containers. *Happy Landings* is the rough translation, if you can believe it. It's in port right now, preparing for departure." He pulled her close. "Janelle alerted the Attorney General and is contacting the United Nations too, just in case."

"In case we fail or in case we succeed?" Kay twisted her lips. "To politicians, failure may be the best outcome. They'll negotiate an acceptable solution behind the scenes, short of admitting guilt or placing blame. Saving face, in other words—on all sides."

"Janelle isn't a typical politician. We can trust her."

"I truly hope so." She nestled her head on his chest. "Make us proud, team leader."

"Easy for you to say. If Wei Jintao doesn't come through with some official orders on our side, I'll have to create a diversion to separate Fran and hustle her off the ship."

She bit back her offer to stay at his side. As angry as she was with Jintao for infecting her with AIDS, he was too powerful an ally to dismiss. Janelle said he retired due to health reasons and was now the target of an informal investigation by the CCP. Kay wanted far, far away from Chinese politics. But if Wei could use whatever clout he had left to help free Fran, she'd take it.

"Look!" Kay pointed to the massive container ship entering her view. "That one." Its towering black hull gleamed in the morning light, throwing an ominous shade over the ferry. The long arm of a crane wavered above its deck, a single strand of cable swinging a container in the cool breeze. What were the conditions inside for the living? No light, little water or food, crammed side by side with other trapped souls.

Kay shuddered. "Has anyone ID'd their first port of call?"

"According to Janelle, San Francisco, which justifies her official involvement and why she was able to obtain high-level attention for this particular shipment."

"So even if I can't get Wei Jintao to open some doors locally, we can help Fran in San Francisco."

"Still not a comforting prospect, hon." He hugged her tight. "We won't fail. Trust me."

"I do." Otherwise, she'd drive herself nuts worrying.

Hours later, staring out the window on the train whisking her to Beijing and Wei Jintao's side, she started worrying anyway. Her own assignment was no cakewalk. It would take every bit of acting in her repertoire—and then some. Even though Jintao's invitation to come by any time sounded sincere.

Could she pull this off? Last time she failed, she landed in jail.

Exiting the taxi at Jintao's private club, Kay's steps faltered crossing the foyer. Instead of heading straight to the elevator, she veered left and into the ladies' room. Mirrors from every angle greeted her. They reflected multiple images in descending sizes, each depiction more distorted than the last, and every one different from what she remembered.

Skinny, not sexy. Nervous, not confident. Determined, not flippant.

Sinking onto a small stool, she stared into her own eyes. Searching for the necessary courage.

She took a deep breath, fingering wisps of hair with one hand. She fished out her phone and laid it on the counter, pulling up the group photo snapped outside the limousine. Zooming in, she stared at Tina, so precious with her new halo of curls. And who would have guessed without wild, wooly hair Janelle's long neck would show off a shapely head? Lynn's white streak was quite striking.

Kay studied her own picture. Not horrible. If she didn't remember her hip-length hair, she would think she appeared cherubic. Gamine, with a touch of vulnerability and innocence. Younger.

Paul seemed to think she was sexy. In fact, he proved it to her quite well. Glancing in the mirror, she caught a glimpse of satisfied humor twitching at her lips. Very sexy.

Good to go.

The elevator delivered her in quiet splendor to the top. Beijing's skyline fell farther away with every rising second. Exiting the glass-walled cage, she pressed a button adorned by intricate carvings of a tiny dragon, and ignored her pounding heartbeat.

Footsteps approached from inside. Swinging wide, the door framed an older-looking Jintao. A welcoming smile erased his weariness. He straightened slumping shoulders. His gaze fell on her head and his eyes popped wide.

"Kay?" Confusion crossed his gaunt features.

"Of course it's me, Jintao." She sauntered through the door, willing her ankles to remain steady in stiletto heels.

She spun and flipped open her suit jacket, displaying a lacy camisole. She prayed his tastes hadn't changed.

"Don't you recognize your number one mistress?" She tsked while circling and studying his figure with deliberate blatancy. "You look well," she purred. "Life must agree with you."

"Let's not lie to each other more than we have to, child." He stepped in front of her, gently lifting her chin and shaking his head. "We appreciated that in each other many months ago." He released her and turned toward a silk-upholstered armchair facing a stunning view above the city. He sunk into it and motioned her to sit across from him.

"I retired recently due to health reasons. I am no longer a vital man." A pang of sympathy tore at her heart. "Maybe because you left me. When I am with you all my youth comes rushing back with the force of a swollen creek in the spring, or darts forward with no concept for the future, only to experience life to the fullest."

"I am sorry, Jintao." She lowered her head, confused. Surely he knew of her arrest. The warden mentioned receiving his instructions! Or had the warden lied? She glanced up, searching Jintao's face for proof of his integrity.

"That is the past." He waved a dismissive hand. "However, I kept something of yours you left behind." Reaching into his breast pocket, he pulled out a tiny photo disk.

Yannan's! Kay's hand flew to her lips. Her mind raced. She would bet good money the disk contained subversive material. Had he agreed to this visit just to blackmail her and keep her in China on his terms?

"Thank you Jintao. I . . . I don't know what you thought of it—"

"I never looked at it, my dear." He slid it across the small tea table. "Nor did I allow anyone else access." His kind gaze met hers, full of understanding—and acceptance. "After all, if you chose to memorialize our playtime, it is only our business what pictures you keep. No one else's."

She blinked in disbelief. Was this a bluff? Or was this a good man after all?

"Thank you, Jintao. How generous of you to believe in me after all this time." She bowed her head and tucked the disk into her pocket.

"You were my lover. And my—what do the Americans call it—ah, yes, soul mate." A nostalgic smile wreathed his face, taking ten years off. "With you, there were no power games except for sexual play. Simply pleasure in each other's company. From each other's bodies." He sighed. "How sex is meant to be, and so rarely is."

Maybe he didn't realize he'd given her AIDS. Or even that he had it now. Kay's conscience battled with guilt. He'd tried to protect her in prison. Her ploy might ruin this poor man's favorite memories.

Squirming, she fiddled with her hair, not quite meeting his gaze. His eyes followed her movements. A sad expression settled on his face.

"Tell me, dear," he said in a soft voice. "Why did you cut your hair?"

Startled, she crossed her legs and re-crossed them. "I had to."

"Tell me, Kay. Tell me everything."

Unprepared for the flood of painful memories, she jumped to her feet and stared out the window, forcing back tears. She didn't dare share her burdens with Jintao!

Slow footsteps approached. His gaze met hers in the window's reflection, full of compassion, wisdom, and a tinge of sadness. Hers was a mix of anxiety and relief, framed with hope. With a regretful smile, he turned her to face him, wrapped her in his arms, and rocked her.

"Ah, child, I never meant to cause you harm. I have many enemies. Tell me what happened."

Kay burst into tears, sobbing out pieces of her imprisonment. Her total abandonment in the complex bowels of Chinese justice. The guards' harassment. The ugly way the warden hacked off her hair.

Her rape.

"This should not happen in our country." He cradled her head against his tear-sodden shirt. "This is my fault."

Kay forced her brain to re-engage, to remember her mission. Was it right to transfer the guilt to his shoulders? Well, he had given her a fatal disease. She drew a shuddering breath, too weary to sort it all out.

Jintao led her to a loveseat tucked away in the corner. She opened her mouth to speak but he pressed two fingers to her lips, shaking his head. Digging into his pocket, he pulled out a round coin with a missing center.

"I carry this old Chinese coin to remind me that modern China lacks a soul." He worked it between his fingers with practiced ease. "I realized something was missing in my life. I filled the void with a unique sensuality—my individualistic stamp on a life forbidden by so many edicts."

"Did it work?"

"To a point." He shrugged. "I enjoyed women who made a conscious decision to explore their sexuality with me. In my position it was one luxury I made sure I could afford." He reached out and brushed her short hair. "Apparently I didn't always understand the consequences of our passions."

"Because I was jailed? Jintao, I don't think you can take on all the blame yourself."

"You were simply the message." He fell back against the cushions looking years older again. "Many of my colleagues considered me a hypocrite enforcing such strict standards blocking pornography over the Internet, and yet still enjoying my little amusements. They didn't understand the moral compass I used for my policies."

"And what was your compass?"

"Little girls are precious," he whispered. "While our stated policies ensure equality for our women, they don't protect them. For generations, my family understood a Chinese girl's life is at risk from conception to adulthood. I believed . . ." He stopped with a choking sound, his eyes closing.

"Go ahead." Kay detected moisture at the corner of his eyes. She moved close to him, placed a hand on his knee and squeezed. "Please. I understand."

"Of course you do, dear. . .In my official position, I felt honor-bound to prevent all sexually exploitative images of little girls from entering our country's borders. This is why I insisted on the Great Internet Firewall."

He held up the coin, twisting it so it caught a glimmering sunbeam. Its shadow fell on the opposite wall, the inner hole massive.

"To fill our country's soul with values beyond making money. To care for our entire populace, not only a handpicked few. To fulfill a promise I made to my father, and he to his father before him. Generations of commitment.

"My enemies turned my love for women against me." He threw the coin at the ominous image. It clinked and fell soundlessly on the carpet. "Against you. And sadly, against China. Because I don't yet see a change in our actions. Official words, yes. Policies, sometimes. Culture?" He sighed. "Perhaps. I will not see it happen in my lifetime."

"Oh, Jintao." She grabbed his hand. "You will live many years still."

"There is much you do not comprehend about my health, although my colleagues relish the gossip." He trapped her palm between his two hands. "I would be happy if you could stay with me. Would you?"

Kay hesitated. Raw pleading softened his voice and painted his usually proud face.

"I . . . I can't, Jintao." Pity engulfed her, pulling at her heart.

"I will always desire you, Kay." He kissed her knuckles. "A desire no pill can ever impart. To the point of obsession, it seems." He glanced up. His eyes searched hers. For what? Agreement? Sympathy?

Love?

It struck her. They had been soul mates in loneliness, tackling the world's problems, sensing in each other the sheer courage it took to wake every morning and go to battle again. With no one at their sides.

Except she had Paul on her team now. Loving her. Supporting her.

"Jintao, I can't stay. It is too dangerous." She lifted their joined hands to her cheek, her eyes damp.

"Simply an old man's dream, my dear." He sighed, nodding.

"But–" She paused, hating herself for what she was supposed to ask. But she must. For her team. For Paul.

For Fran. Yes, he would understand Fran.

"I could use your help, Jintao."

"Of course, child." He brushed her short hair. "Tell me what I can do to atone for your pain and suffering. I desire to put a smile on my soul mate's face . . . rather than remembering the troubles I caused."

Kay recounted Fran's situation in as much detail as she dared, omitting her link to Li, simply admitting she met the little girl in Tiananmen Square and was struck by her vivacious personality.

"We must find a way for the government to save face in all this. Otherwise they will not let the little girl leave the country." Jintao rose and paced the room, hands clasped behind his back."

"I couldn't figure out a solution. How can anyone put a good face on such a horrid practice?"

"Isn't that what you are doing, dear Kay? Helping one little girl at a time?"

"I wish I could do more." She wrung her hands. "I feel guilty helping only my friend. All of those other children are friendless, too."

"It is not your responsibility." He wagged a finger in her face. "It is our government's. I will shame them into admitting it—while still letting the politicians save face."

"How?"

"There is only one crisis that motivates politicians to act more quickly than they intend."

"Shame?" Kay ventured.

"Uncontrolled plague. If the population falls ill and starts dying with no end in sight, they will eventually turn on their politicians. A simple matter of survival, dear."

"I still don't understand."

"Leave it to me." He patted her hand.

Crossing to the corner where a small desk sported a stunning view, he sat and picked up his phone.

"You will do as I order, Physician Fang," Jintao commanded. "Disassociate with me, and you will re-gain the Party's respect for your expertise in communicable diseases. I no longer need your help. This little girl does." He paused. "You owe me a large favor, remember? Or do I have to remind you of those circumstances?"

Kay followed the continued arguments and counter-arguments, grinning at Jintao's creative plan. This should work. She paced the length of the room, staring eastward. She would see Paul again soon. And Frannie too. She hugged her arms and fought back tears of relief.

Jintao ended his call and walked to her side. Leaning forward, he kissed her cheeks and placed his hands on her shoulders. He ran his gaze over her entire length.

"Go, child." His voice quivered, but he stood straight and tall again. In charge, confident of his direction. Proud of his actions. "I will always remember you fondly."

"I will remember you that way, too, Jintao." She kissed the back of his hand. "And thank you."

He nodded and stepped away, turning his back to her in dismissal. He stared out the window as if searching for a China he once loved. With one final glance, Kay retreated, and closed the door behind her.

A soldier, left to die all alone. With a magnanimous gesture as his parting shot.

Yes, she would remember him. Forever.

Chapter 55

PORT OF TIANJIN

Tianjin, China
Evening, June 15, Same Day

Paul turned off his phone's ringer and approached the sole figure standing beneath a dim streetlight. Kay had called him earlier from the train heading back to Tianjin and given him the doctor's name. She seemed confident Wei had come through for her.

Paul couldn't imagine how Wei would manage such a miracle—a cooperative doctor this late at night, and English-speaking no less. He would follow Wei's plan. Lord knows he couldn't come up with a better one of his own. The only lucky break he'd had so far was managing to buy a pistol on the black market, courtesy of the ferry captain's questionable family ties.

"Dr. Fang?" Suspicious eyes turned to him. The doctor bobbed his head. "I understand you can help identify a potential illness. It could spread to the citizens of China if not stopped right here, right now. Correct?" Paul recited the expected justification Kay gave him in precise, slow language.

"I am asked to examine one little girl on a boat. Which one?" Fang clutched a wooden box to his chest.

"There." Paul pointed to the hulking cargo ship anchored at the last piling.

The doctor flinched. Fang must have presumed it would be a routine examination on a passenger ocean liner. Whether he understood the grisly underbelly of human trafficking was another story.

Paul headed down the wharf, listening to the matching echoes of Fang's footsteps. The last time he walked a commercial dock, he was on a mission, too. Stalking a different kind of cargo. One to destroy, not save.

One leading to Ernie's destruction . . .

Paul shoved his negative memories aside. This time he would succeed. He had to. They all had to. He pictured Colonel DuMont's fist shaking in his face, demanding their absolute best—and then some. This time, more than Ernie depended on him. His country's future did.

"Halt!" The call rang out from above them. A menacing line of sailors stared over the ship's railing.

Fang stopped, nodding his head. His shoulders folded around the little wooden chest he clutched like a life vest.

"Minister Wei Jintao did not tell me this is what he required." Fang's voice trembled. "I do not owe him a favor this large." He stumbled taking a tiny step backwards. "They will take away my license if I help you."

"A very sick girl is on board. If we don't identify her and keep her from spreading the disease, many people will die. Are you a doctor or not?" Paul failed to keep the impatience out of his tone.

"We have already handled the AIDS disease and SARS successfully. If it is so bad, our government will send resources to contain the illness." Hands shaking, Fang unclasped the chest and fumbled with a pad of paper. He scribbled a few characters, tore off the page, and shoved it in Paul's hand. "My official diagnosis. It is all you require to declare her ill."

"Thanks, but I need you to get on board." Paul jammed the paper into his pocket.

"No. I will not do this." Fang took a step back toward the road.

"Yes, you will." Paul jumped in front of him and whipped the gun from his waistband. "Do you understand there may be one hundred children onboard? This is a slave ship! The United Nations approves the search of this particular boat. You should be willing to save them all." He pressed the gun barrel to the doctor's head, hating himself for doing so. "If you don't care for your own life, imagine the shame your actions will bring to your wife and your family."

Confusion replaced the doctor's fearful expression.

"I'll ask Wei Jintao to tell everyone you visited this wharf to rape a young girl." Wincing at his own crudity, Paul pressed on. "You'll be remembered as caring for your own selfish pleasure, not your family." He recalled an essential custom in Chinese culture. "No one will tend your grave if you're killed here in such a shameful manner."

Fang's posture crumpled. His bowed head dipped in agreement. Paul tucked the gun under his shirt and pushed the doctor forward. Reaching the well-lit gangplank, Paul nodded at the two large guards at its top.

The doctor waved his hand, gestured to his medical chest, and yelled in a commanding voice. One guard turned away. The other one grinned and shouted back. At Fang's reply, he blanched and signaled them aboard, cowering.

"What did you tell him?" Paul whispered.

"The family of one girl all died horribly, their flesh eaten away."

Topside, Paul pushed Fang to repeat the conversation. A worker directed them to a cargo container with an open top panel. Paul clambered up the side and assisted the doctor to join him. Catching his breath, he caught the distinctive odor of human waste and steeled himself. He took a deep breath and jammed his head inside the hole.

Dozens of faces turned upwards. Outstretched arms faded into the huge container's dark corners. Tearful pleas reached a crescendo and diminished, repeating in rising waves of desperate panic and confusion. Paul searched the almost identical young features. The digital imagery never delivered a clear enough picture of Fran to differentiate her in this dim light.

"California Barbie!" His shout reverberated within the container, overwhelming their cries. A brief second of silence. Their wails came again, louder. More frantic.

Fang poked his head through the opening and he gasped.

"No, no. This is terrible. This isn't right!" He glanced at Paul. "Contagious disease or not, many children will die if their journey is a long one."

"Destination, San Francisco." Paul scanned the faces below. "California Barbie!"

What else could he do except holler? If he dropped into the hole, there was no way to climb back out. Not with this crew. If they bought their cover story, soon they'd seal this container tight and avoid it and the children altogether.

"Here!" A thin arm waved from the side. "I'm here!" A taller girl shoved and pushed her way forward. She peered up. "Who are you?"

Paul opened his mouth to answer truthfully, and thought better of it.

"We think you and your family may be sick."

"Auntie Yannan? Daddy?" Even in the gloom, Paul could discern Fran narrow her eyes and tilt her head to one side. Her thumb and one finger created a surreptitious O. He breathed a sigh of relief. Kay was right—this little girl understood how to play the game.

Dr. Fang cleared his throat and barked a long sentence in Chinese.

It was as if he were a modern day Moses. The mob split away, leaving a gap below the opening. Paul levered himself halfway and anchored an elbow around a large, metal handle on the container.

"Jump." Staring at Fran below him, he swung one leg.

She leapt high and grabbed on to the bottom of his pants. They slid to his hips and dug into his bones. Fran latched onto the other leg. Paul prayed the fabric wouldn't rip.

Hoisting herself higher, Fran stepped on one foot. He braced himself. She held fast to his belt and inched herself upright. Her head cleared the opening.

The doctor released his wooden chest, stuck his hands under her armpits and tugged. With one heave, Paul swung his legs above the opening and collapsed with relief.

Pandemonium erupted from the abandoned children. How could he leave them behind? Too many individual faces suddenly stamped themselves onto his brain, no longer a crowd, each a young child confronting a horrendous fate.

"We must go!" Fang picked up his wooden box and hurried to the container's ladder. Fran stumbled after him, her face mirroring Paul's guilty anguish. Could they save another? And another? At what point did their mission turn impossible?

With a heavy heart, Paul uncoiled his arm and lurched away from the edge of hell. Somehow, he would help these children. After he completed this operation and got Fran to safety.

Joining the other two, Paul peered over the side. Hulking sailors milled about the deck, gesturing upward. He pulled Fran to the edge, and motioned Fang to explain.

Damn it, Fang's voice was warbling. No one would believe him. Paul kicked his shin to shake him up. Fang coughed loudly and pointed to three sailors, motioning them forward.

They scattered like frightened chickens.

"The crew won't stop us," Fang muttered. He stuck his foot onto the top ladder rung. Securing a foothold, he inched his way down. "I told them she carries a deadly virus and must be quarantined. If she just breathes in their direction, they'll probably jump ship."

Or toss them all overboard instead.

Following the doctor, they joined him crouching in the gloom. Paul peeked back at the small figure.

"How are you, Fran? Strong enough to run?"

She hesitated. "How . . . how do you know my name?"

"Your Auntie Kay told me." His glance lingered in her direction. "You were very smart to pre-arrange a password."

"I help Auntie Yannan all the time." A broad grin slashed her face, and then faded. "Is she sick, truly? And Daddy?"

"No more than you are, honey. We needed a way to get you out."

"Those other children . . . can you help them, too?" Fran touched the container's wall.

Dr. Fang waved an urgent hand at the gangplank.

"First, we must get off this ship. Kay is waiting nearby." Paul stood, scanned all three directions, and grabbed her hand. "Let's go!"

They dashed out into the open, work lights creating harsh shadows of their fleeing figures.

"Stop!"

Paul recognized the Chinese command and veered right, away from a uniformed man charging down the wheelhouse stairs. Fran stumbled against Paul, her full weight tangling his feet. He skidded on one knee and leapt up again with her in his arms—all in one smooth motion, eyes focused on the ship's railing. Fang's footsteps fell farther behind.

So close.

He jumped down to the gangplank, letting Fran slide down his body. Inky seawater slapped the hull, reeking of diesel fuel. For a brief instant, he considered their chances of diving overboard. Not as good as running.

Clasping Fran to his side, he pulled out his pistol and aimed it at the ship's edge.

"Come on, Fang, come on," he muttered.

The doctor leapt onto the gangplank. Without a glance, he pounded past them and down the deserted wharf. Paul aimed at the sky and pulled the trigger.

Nothing. Damned black-market piece-of-shit. Can't even deliver a warning shot.

He spun around and pushed Fran in front, following Fang. A bullet would do less harm to his large bulk than her skinny frame.

Of course, it might kick off World War Three, but that issue was way beyond his pay grade. He prayed Janelle had all her ducks in a row with the State Department and the United Nations. After what he witnessed in the ship's hold, he hoped she came out with both barrels blazing.

Tina was right. This slave practice must stop. Right here. Right now.

Reaching the wharf, he guided Fran to the dim cover of barrels and waiting pallets. Shouts filled the air, but he couldn't hear any footsteps.

Mission accomplished. Almost.

He gestured to the next cover. Fran nodded and darted ahead. Her lithe figure slipped between containers with barely a sound. She paused for him and they repeated the steps. Just two wharves over, Kay waited on their transport back to Seoul, worrying about Fran's safety.

And hopefully his safety, too.

Where did that new doubt come from? Because she visited Wei and hadn't told him any details yet? Because he felt dwarfed and inadequate next to the man's obvious influence in such a large country?

He shoved his foolish insecurities aside and caught up with Fran. Sliding an arm around her shoulders, he slowed their pace. "Only a couple more minutes, honey, and you can see Kay."

"And Auntie Yannan?" She skipped, matching his longer strides. "And Daddy?" Her high-pitched voice rose with hope.

Paul's thoughts flew to his other teammates, whose mission had to have been twice as grueling, risky, and uncertain. Had they rescued Li? He sure hoped so, otherwise this was all for nothing. Fran didn't hold the secrets. Her father did. She could still be used as a pawn if his teammates had failed to get Li to safety.

Or Fran might be one disappointed little orphan.

Then again, maybe he could handle another little girl in his life. Or two.

Chapter 56

WENG-HAN RESIDENCE

Inner Mongolia, China
Afternoon, June 16, Next Day

"You are announcing our esteemed engineer died in the earthquake?" Mai dragged in a quick breath, stabbing her cigarette toward Yu. "To our leaders? Where is the proof? Where is his body?"

"According to his jailer's official report, a collapsed prison wall killed him. They threw his remains into a group burial pit."

"No!" She dropped her forehead onto her palm. "We need his know-how to control the next generation of American technology."

"Give it up, wife." Yu sank into the adjacent chair. "Your plan failed. We must resign."

"Resign?" Her piercing gaze was incredulous. "Never!"

"We don't have a choice. You ruined your reputation within the Party." He sighed and shrugged. "They seek any reason to push elders out, and replace us with the younger generation."

"Bah! So many of those children have no connections, no maturity."

"Perhaps. But they do have education and familiarity with other countries. Most have studied in the United States and return full of remarkable insights of triumphant strategies."

"Would they have contemplated handling Li with such finesse, such subtle pressure on our American allies in this way?" She waved her cigarette, fuming.

"Would they have bungled the sensitive Tibetan question by moving Li to a region outside your assigned influence?" He countered, shaking his head. "You went one step too far, a step off the safe bridge. You never should have mixed the mining business with politics. It is China's official position that the two are not intertwined."

"I won't resign!"

"No, I will, due to a bad heart. And you, dutiful wife, will regretfully leave your esteemed position to care for me in the warmer climates near the South China Sea."

"No! Humidity will kill me. No, husband, we can fight this!"

"You will be lucky not to be charged with treason and betraying state secrets." He snatched her cigarette away and stomped on it. "Have you not learned from Wei Jintao's plight?"

"He will lose his life to the AIDS disease anyway." She sniffed. "No Chinese doctor will treat him now. They do not want news of his condition to create a stampede of fear about another outbreak. If it can infect Party members, too, the poor are doomed." She tapped another cigarette out of the pack and lit it. "However, perhaps Wei Jintao's fate will remind young Party members their private and public lives are one."

"Don't you understand yet? You were just as bad following your own personal vendetta." He rapped his fingers on the table. "Call off your dogs, Mai. Don't let any more unsanctioned actions get traced back to you—including the ones you began in America with that Congresswoman."

"But—"

"No!" The thunder lacing his voice shattered any remaining objections. "Li is dead! You have no more to gain with this childish grab for power. You lost. Our world is changing. The next generation is taking over."

"Your children, you mean. From your other wives." She crossed one arm over her chest and inhaled from her cigarette.

"Accept it, wife." He met her gaze with polite calm. "There is nothing else you can do and survive."

Outflanked, outranked, and outmaneuvered. So much for being a role model for future female politicians.

Red embers disintegrated the cigarette paper in tiny increments. Maybe they were right. You can't wrap fire with paper. A woman cannot follow the edicts of the Chinese Communist Party and survive.

At least . . . not yet.

Chapter 57

UNITED STATES MARINE CORPS BASE

Okinawa, Japan
Afternoon, June 19, 3 Days Later

Kay glanced at the clock in the Captain's office. Its snug quarters offered blessed peace and quiet. In only two days, Fran bored of her new Barbie doll and began pestering her with questions. Even Paul's patience with her enthusiastic dreams about living in Hollywood finally petered out this morning.

How could Kay soothe the child's anxiety? They had no clue whether Li was even alive. The last message from the earthquake rescue team simply requested transport out. The route to Okinawa from the Air Force Base in Kyrgyzstan was long, circuitous, and covert. Until they landed, they had no idea how many passengers made it on board.

She pulled out Yannan's photo disk from her pocket and wriggled it into the slot of the borrowed computer, smiling at Jintao's unexpected loyalty. Protecting her at every junction, wherever he could. She owed him her life.

Tapping the icon, she pulled up the first photo.

A blurry image of two lovers filled the screen. She recognized the black sheets and red roses scattered on Jintao's bed. The faces were obscured but the bodies way too familiar.

What the hell?

She clicked again, faster and faster. Dozens of photographs taken over many days, erotic and compelling. And completely anonymous—except to her.

Jintao played her for a fool! He still possessed Yannan's disk. Contents unknown.

Scratch that. Whatever it contained must be important otherwise he would have returned it. Unless he was simply a dirty old man, titillated by sharing pornographic images with his lover.

She shook her head, disconcerted. Jintao had more class. More pride in his sexuality. He wouldn't cheapen himself this way.

Then why? And what had Yannan smuggled out to her so many months ago?

A loud roar penetrated her confusion. Glancing out the tiny window, she caught a glimpse of a small jet taxiing down the runway.

The door burst open. Paul's head appeared. "They've arrived."

"Any word on who made it out?" Yanking the disk free, Kay jumped to her feet.

"Nope." He dashed toward the hangar.

"I'll get Frannie," she called to his back. She ran out the door, her emotions in turmoil. If Li were alive, he and Fran would go wherever he found a position, maybe even at a National Laboratory. If he were dead, it would devastate Fran, but Kay would give her the closest she could afford to a California-Barbie-style life. No more worries, no treachery.

No father. Unless Paul . . .

"Is that Daddy's plane?" Fran ran to her side from the protection of the barracks.

"I hope so, honey." She spoke with stark certainty. This excited little girl deserved happiness. Kay grabbed her hand and forced them to a slow jog.

Paul turned the corner, a limping figure at his side.

"Daddy!" Yanking her hand free, Fran lunged forward. "Daddy! Daddy!"

Li swept his daughter up in his arms. Love, relief, and sorrow all melded into a beautiful family portrait.

Paul passed the entwined figures and joined Kay.

"Don and Alex are safe, too." He pointed to two weary figures crossing the tarmac. "Apparently they encountered one major scare with the national army and lost Eric's dog to a rabid Chinese soldier. They managed to smuggle Li out with a couple of well-placed bribes and a replacement corpse."

"Won't officials come looking for him?" Kay remembered all too well China's tenacious, awesome bureaucracy.

"I doubt it. I asked Janelle to check. Officially, he was killed in the earthquake." Paul shrugged. "So he'll have to change his name in America. That shouldn't be too hard to arrange."

"America?" Li stepped to Paul's side. Fran clung to his leg and stared up at her father. Adoration brightened her face. "I am not going to America." His English was perfect.

"You want to stay in China?" Paul's face contorted with confusion.

Li pressed his hand to Fran's head, his expression combative.

"My family is here and my battle is here. So, my life is also here." He nodded to Kay. "Hello, Chiang Kay."

"Greetings, Li Ying." She pointed at Fran. "We would arrange for both of you to go to America, just as I promised Fran months ago. Right honey? You want to go to California, don't you?"

"I'll live with Auntie Yannan and Daddy." Fran pressed her face against Li's dusty trousers.

"But—"

Don's hand landed on her arm and hauled her backwards. "Li's apparently ready to give Fran a new mother in the form of her favorite auntie," he whispered in her ear. "Surprise!"

"Yannan is under house arrest." Kay stepped right up to Li's face. "You can't go back to the mainland and join her. Especially if you're officially dead."

"Paul, maybe you can talk some sense into our young engineer. I sure couldn't." Don rubbed his back and winced. His face fell into gaunt lines. Swollen eyelids drooped over bloodshot eyes. Even his beard stubble looked grayer than a few weeks ago.

"Uh, Li, America put out substantial resources to rescue you and your daughter. We'd like to offer you asylum to work on better use of rare earth elements." Paul cleared his throat. "We understand you're the leading expert on its mining and purification. Many private organizations, including prominent universities, stand willing to offer you the highest position on their staff in return for sharing your knowledge."

"Oh, really? Name one."

Kay sympathized with Li's skeptical retort. After his ordeal, she imagined he didn't feel very accommodating. He craved freedom—of choice, of locale. Of values.

"Berkeley. Stanford." Alex's grimy face joined the circle. "Lots of Silicon Valley companies need good solutions for purified rare metals. Any of them would jump to bring you on board."

Tentative gratitude replaced Li's determined expression.

"I am honored by your generosity to a total stranger." He met each team member's gaze in turn. "Also grateful for your dedication to save my life and my child's. However, China is my home."

"Li Ying, I understand exactly what you've experienced." Kay leaned forward and patted Fran's shoulder. "Your life and your daughter's will be in danger if you go back. Is this what you wish?"

"I'll make Taiwan my new home." He sighed and rubbed the back of his neck. "There, I can help move my country forward in a new direction and away from totalitarian rule. Freedom is coming to China. Eventually."

"You owe us your help." Don's abrupt tones cut through Li's idealism. "America can't be held hostage to China's dirty politicians."

"Didn't Yannan get you all my files?" Li turned to Kay, his brows wrinkling. "In her last email to me she swore she met with an American woman she could trust. I have no other record of my life's work. The police destroyed it all during my arrest."

Her stomach clenched. Yannan relied on her to get Li's know-how to America, and twice she left it in Jintao's hands. No wonder he passed her a bogus disk. With Li imprisoned—or dead—he held the power of China's economic negotiations in the palm of his hand.

"Yes . . . she did. However . . . they confiscated all my belongings." Enough said for now. "Please, Li Ying, give America a chance—for at least a few years. We can keep you safe and you can pay your debt to our government by sharing your ideas."

"Not to mention getting a bundle of money in the process for your innovations," Don said.

"When will we see Auntie Yannan, Daddy?" Fran's high-pitched voice tugged at Kay's heart. "She must be so worried."

"I don't know what to do." Li hauled Fran up to his hip, his face tormented.

"Paul?" Kay placed her hand on his arm and squeezed. "How can we solve this?" She owed him a full debriefing, including her stupidity with Jintao. They must somehow satisfy Li and gain his cooperation; otherwise, this entire rescue mission was one huge, expensive fiasco. And she might have to return to Beijing and confront Jintao again. Or worse.

"SNAFU says it all." Paul scratched his head and paced in a wide circle, muttering curses.

Kay faced Li, tossing pride to the wind. Time to beg.

"Are you sure, Li Ying? America can offer you and your family safety. Fran would surely thrive."

"I want to stay with Daddy, Auntie Kay." Fran laid her head on Li's shoulder and threw her an angelic smile. "Thank you for the Barbie doll. And remembering our password. You and Uncle Paul."

"Yes, thank you." Li bowed to them all. "I will always remember your help, and aid you if I can. My first priority, however, is to free Yannan."

Scowling, Paul re-joined the circle. "American policy doesn't include kidnapping or imprisonment of ordinary refugees—"

"Hardly ordinary," Don grumped.

"It's not a crime to be brilliant." Alex elbowed Don. "His ideas are his own, not ours."

"Hopefully we can work out a common sense solution for all of us," Paul continued. "In the meantime, I'll ask our congresswoman to arrange for asylum in Taiwan for you and your family." He held up his palm. "It's now your responsibility to assist Yannan. We can't get any more involved."

"Thank you. You are more than fair." Li stuck out his hand. "There are many rumors of America's generosity. I now believe it."

"Fran, why don't we let your Daddy and the others bathe and eat?" Kay hoisted the girl from Li's arms to her own, hugging her close for a long, last poignant moment. "The men still have work to do."

Blinking back tears, she marched toward the barracks. What a mess! No Li, no disk, no solution in sight. Damn the whole CCP and Wei Jintao for their manipulative games! Vengeance welled hot and fierce. She would get back at them all—when they least expected it.

Chapter 58

COFFEE FOR TWO
SAN MATEO, CALIFORNIA

Morning, June 20, Next Day

Janelle studied the suave Chinese man across the table at her favorite coffee shop. His tailored jacket hung a little loose but the smile seemed genuine in his gaunt face.

"All right, Mr. Wei," Janelle said. "I've done what you asked. Where is that disk?"

"I believe this will give your negotiators the tool to lift China's silly embargo of all those minerals." Wei Jintao presented her a photo disk with a flourish. Only a slight accent colored his words.

She held the tiny piece in her hand. Did his cynical view of the issue have merit? How many ethics had she compromised arranging asylum for this man, including under false pretenses?

"I reserved a room at the best AIDS hospital in the world, San Francisco Medical Center. How long do you plan to continue this charade?" She dropped the disk into her purse and took a sip of steaming coffee.

"As long as it takes me to re-gain my weight." He chuckled and patted his stomach. "It is harder than you think to fake this disease's symptoms. Besides, won't my complete cure reflect well on the American health care system?"

"You're apt to create enemies in San Francisco by making light of the illness. Your asylum is based on keeping this a complete secret," Janelle warned.

"Yes, it is always best to let your negotiating partner save face. In this, the CCP is better off believing I came for treatment and chose to stay, rather than admitting your government arranged my freedom." He tilted a teacup to his lips.

"We arranged it? You plotted it all out before you contacted me."

"Everyone played a part, true. My colleagues would never believe I am so stupid as to contract this AIDS disease."

"Including Kay Chiang?"

"She is far from stupid. Your doctor's false diagnosis proved necessary." Sorrow settled on his attractive features. "Han Mai's informants carried back the confirmation she sought. Trust me, the CCP rumor mill is a very efficient communication network."

"You exploited Kay more than necessary. How will you apologize to her?"

His eyes narrowed. "You played a willing partner in the deception, Congresswoman."

Squirming, she dropped her gaze. She hated every moment of this game, yet continued playing it. And good thing. Although Li's miraculous rescue had come off, his stubborn refusal to come to America even for a short stint threw the rest of their plans out the window. This smuggled disk hopefully carried all the country needed to bring China to heel.

"All right, once we deliver the good news to Kay she doesn't have AIDS, what then? Kay deserves our support to get back on her feet."

Wei Jintao tapped his cheekbone for long seconds, staring out the gingham-curtained window.

"Last time I talked with her, she seemed quite passionate about rescuing one little girl from those horrendous sex slave traffickers," he said. "Is more than her heart involved in the cause?"

"What do you have in mind?"

"Bribes I received as a CCP official are now stashed in American banks." He leaned forward, crossing his arms on the table. "I choose to fund an organization dedicated to ending such dreadful practices. She can put my money to excellent use and rescue more children."

"Bribes? You expect her to touch your dirty money?" Janelle folded her arms across her chest and glared at him.

"Not only her, my dear, but you too. Do you really believe you can keep your position after word of my defection reaches your party's leaders?" His hearty laugh drifted through the coffee shop. "In many respects, America is no different than China. Corruption is a human, not a cultural, condition."

Prepare for unintended consequences. How often had Dad drummed the concept into her? As often as she disbelieved him, always the idealist. Or was it naiveté tripping her up this time?

"Why would you choose this cause? Why not a politically based one, or funding technology education as befitting your reputation?" She leaned back in her chair, considering the odd character.

"With each generation my family corrects a wrong of an ancestor." A crooked smile graced his face. "My quest commenced in 1869, when a San Francisco slave trader snatched a beautiful daughter from our home just as she reached marriageable age. Since that tragedy, our family revered daughters equal to our sons. Frankly, I'm curious if I can trace her life here." He fiddled with his shirt cuff. "These days, technology is used for everything. If exploring a database nets results, isn't that most appropriate in this land of free speech and open access?"

Janelle started at his subtle message. Others knew of the database hacking and therefore must know of her involvement smuggling him to the United States. How many more political enemies did she have? Better yet, how many more days could she effectively represent her district with a compromised reputation?

Very few.

She folded her paper napkin in half, and again, creasing the folds. Maybe she could atone for her unsanctioned actions by giving herself to a cause that, by definition, never glimpsed the light of day.

Maybe then, Dad might forgive her serious breach of ethics. Or would he conclude, as she did, that America's future was worth any risk?

"All right, Mr. Wei, let's make another deal. Assuming this disk has the information you promise . . ." She broke off and frowned, daring him to dispute its value. ". . . I will assist you and establish a non-profit organization for the purpose of supporting local victims of modern day slave trafficking. If Kay aspires to join it, so be it. If not, I'm sure I can find other people who will."

"Agreed." He thrust his hand over the tabletop. "I hope Kay will follow her passion. However, the Silicon Valley winners in this modern-day Gold Rush might find it hard to face these ugly truths."

"Perhaps. But if so, I will enjoy my new mission issuing the clarion call." A hint of pride colored her voice, and finally crept back into her soul.

Chapter 59

CHINATOWN

San Francisco, California
Afternoon, June 24, 4 Days Later

Paul helped Kay into the passenger seat of his Jeep and tossed the long box in the back seat. He ignored her father's grim face peering through the apartment's draperies. Rounding the hood, he climbed in and twisted the ignition key. "Have everything?"

Kay nodded. Her father's message saying he had a gift for her had brought Kay scurrying to San Francisco, clutching the framed photo of Fran and Li, taken as they waved goodbye in Okinawa. Kay hoped Li's poignant story might remind her father how to treat a daughter.

But she'd been disappointed—again.

He glanced in the mirror and gunned the motor. Traffic blocked them for a few seconds more. He checked out Kay under lowered eyelids. He wasn't sure he could handle more tears. She shed so many at their farewells to the Li family. More than he expected. Yet apparently not all.

Sniffing, she wiped a tear with the back of her hand. "Did you hear back from Eric yet?"

"Yeah, he was able to fast-track DOD Tech as the leading defense sub-contractor to study the information on the disk Janelle passed on. Apparently, with Li's improved purification techniques using some form of molten salts, their engineers confirm it's possible to cheaply refine a more concentrated, malleable form of rare metals without the use of powerful acids and other toxic by-products."

"So Li's discovery reduces cost and environmental waste?" She whistled. "No wonder China controlled him."

"With his knowledge, any country with even a moderate concentration of rare earths could refine it, and then sell their purified metals in the global marketplace." He flipped on his turn signal. "America's military and technology companies will have their choice of supplier. Janelle even convinced her committee to force regulatory changes related to Thorium's categorization, which will soon impact our next-gen energy needs, too. Best yet, China can't manipulate the market with this key commodity again." And the Pentagon would be able to cover up their glaring misstep and crow about their fail-safe procurement process.

Paul wasn't sure how he felt about that. On one hand, hearing Colonel DuMont's congratulations on a successful mission had been the final, healing touch. On the other, they both rankled that DOD policies and career bureaucrats had even allowed this crisis to develop in the first place. With Janelle's formal resignation from her congressional seat, they had even fewer allies with a backbone willing to speak up about this systemic breakdown. He took a deep breath, letting the politics go. The ball was in their court. He hoped they'd follow through.

"So I was right," Kay said. "Li's intellectual property will be licensed to DOD Tech and others?"

"Yep. Eric has already arranged new VC funding for DOD Tech to do so." He darted into a brief gap in the traffic. "In turn, both a defense contractor and Snazzed Up! committed to buy their products using the purified elements once they ramp up manufacturing again."

"Won't it still take years to develop?"

"Yes, but now China recognizes they have a viable American competitor. They'll probably flood the market with cheap, refined rare metals very soon. Silicon Valley is back in business." He twisted his lips in a wry smile. "And China will find new ways to negotiate their economic and political agenda."

"Mission finally accomplished." Kay took a deep breath, staring at the fog bank forming ahead.

It still irked Paul that Janelle refused to disclose how the disk landed in her possession. Had someone besides Wei Jintao snagged it months ago after Kay's arrest? Corruption permeated the police force in China, too. Maybe Wei truly was a poor, sick man sharing erotic memories.

"So, what's in the box? Your Dad's welcome home present?" He tossed Kay a sympathetic glance. Her father issues would haunt her for years to come, he was certain.

"No. It arrived at their house yesterday." Twisting in her seat, she reached behind and tore open the end. "From the Feds, no doubt, clearing out my desk. It's still my official address."

Guarding the gearshift while she maneuvered the package, Paul downshifted to climb the steep hill.

"Ugh. It's heavy." She grunted. "Here's a note." She ripped the square envelope open, dropped it in her lap, and extricated the letter. And gasped. "It's from Wei Jintao!"

"You're kidding me." Braking hard, he avoided a car turning into his lane by mere inches. He swore under his breath and steered toward a freight-parking zone, steeling himself for more bad news. "What does he want now?"

Kay's lips trembled but she made no sound. He switched off the engine and held his breath.

Her eyes widened, glimmering with new tears.

"I . . . don't . . . have . . . AIDS!" Shoulders heaving, she clutched the note to her breasts and sobbed.

He pulled her against his chest. "How could Wei know?" Relief battled with skepticism.

"He . . . he made it all up so he could defect." Her breath came in jerks. "He brought Yannan's disk to Janelle while on a sanctioned trip to America. He used the excuse of needing AIDS treatment as his cover."

She sat up straight. Smoothing out the creases, she continued reading the letter.

"He demanded Janelle's doctor lie to me," she whispered.

"Sneaky devil." Paul stared out the windshield, searching for answers. "So Janelle wasn't much of a loyal team member after all."

Kay fumbled with the envelope and withdrew a photo disk. "Jintao says this disk contains all the information China collected relating to slave trading in the region. He's funding an organization to fight the practice and wants me and Janelle to run it."

"So he can dictate to you again? I don't trust the bastard." Paul slapped his palm against the steering wheel. "And I'm not a huge fan of Janelle right now, either. So what's in the box?"

Kay reached inside to pull out its contents. Soft fur brushed Paul's arm.

"My sable coat." Her brow wrinkled. "What's he trying to do? Make nice? Apologize?"

"Buy you with gifts?" Paul wrestled back jealousy and guilt. Would he ever be able to provide Kay with luxury goods on a whim?

"Well, it's not working!" She shoved the box aside. The expensive coat spilled onto the dirty floorboard. "If he thinks he can just pick up where we left off . . . That was my job. This is my life." Kay grabbed his hand and lifted it to her cheek. "You are my life. Do you believe me?"

Paul's heart skipped a beat. He nodded.

"Actually, Wei's bigger gift is this." He touched the disk clenched in her fist.

"I'd love to help more children, not just commiserate over their plight." Compassion settled on her face. "Jintao understands me well, tempting me with a way to stop this horrible practice." She met his gaze, looking both confused and hopeful.

Paul re-started the engine and darted between delivery trucks. He headed west to the coastal highway.

"I bet it's just as irresistible to Janelle, and that's why she resigned," he said. Or maybe her resignation was another big cover-up of her underhanded tactics.

"Tina could work with us this summer setting it up," Kay mused. "Maybe find families eager to open their homes to these poor children. Create an adoption network. Leverage my family name and gain more support." She sighed. "Even if my father doesn't agree."

"Kay . . . I'm so sorry." He placed his hand on her thigh. "His loss. He won't ever appreciate what a fantastic daughter he raised."

"I used to think I would never meet a good father." Kay squeezed his fingers. "You and Li are great dads. I'm proud to know you both."

"How proud?" Time to announce his news.

"What, do you need a number?" She held up her thumb. "You've earned one hundred likes."

"Probably biased, but I'll take it." He threw her a quick smile. "Hank Shaughnessy offered me a promotion to team leader—if I return to Washington."

"And . . ."

"And the only team I'm leading is a home-grown one—starting with you. Eric's offered me a permanent position in his company."

"Really?" She beamed. "Do you think we can do all this?"

"Do all what?" He laughed. "Live wherever we like? Work where we choose? Sweetie, we can do all of those things . . . especially if we watch each other's six." He turned on a wide boulevard leading to Golden Gate Park.

"Pull over."

"Huh?"

"Pull. Over." Her stern voice brooked no argument.

Flustered, he checked the cross-town traffic moving on all sides. Spying an empty parking spot, he shot in front of two cars, ignoring their blaring horns, and pulled into the space.

"What's wrong?" He switched off the engine.

"I love to watch your six, especially naked. And I'd love to serve as your home partner, too." She leaned across the center console, intimately close.

"Fantastic!" He lowered his lips to hers, giving her a searing kiss.

"But . . ."

"But?" His spirits tanked.

"If you want to grow our family, I intend on setting an example and adopting."

"You're a great example." He stared deep into her eyes. "I agree—on one condition."

"What?" She bit her lip.

"You have to tell Tina. I don't think I could handle her squeals of joy."

"You think so?" Kay's face brightened with hope, looking more beautiful than ever.

"I know so. It's time you took all the love bottled up inside and put it to good use." He tickled her ribs. "And I'm first."

"Whatever you say, team leader," she beamed. "That's one order I'm happy to follow."

AUTHOR'S NOTE

In 2010, China did indeed threaten Japan with its lock on purified rare metals, in retaliation for a territorial dispute, later resolved. In the meantime, commodity prices for various rare earth elements shot up in the worldwide marketplace. While American politicians discussed the implications on our economy long-term and ordered the Pentagon to come up with solutions, they failed to make any policy changes. And Silicon Valley companies, while concerned, continue their dependence on these purified minerals, with no better alternative.

ALSO BY ANN BRIDGES

Private Offerings *(Balcony 7, 2015)*

Get the backstory for *Rare Mettle* and uncover the human element driving the modern-day Gold Rush, full of deceits, desires . . . and dreams. Top-secret technology, up for sale, coveted by competing interests across the globe. Wall Street financiers clash with government interests—both domestic and Chinese—throwing a monkey wrench onto the path of a Silicon Valley entrepreneur about to cash in on his dream of a lifetime.

A NOTE ABOUT THE AUTHOR

Ann Bridges is a Chicago native who fell in love with Northern California while attending Stanford University. Now a longtime resident of San Jose, Ms. Bridges creatively incorporates the dynamics of her Silicon Valley business experience into new works of fiction. Extensive insider knowledge of operations, finance and marketing in the entertainment, communications and technology industries form an authentic underpinning for her sexy, intelligent style of Silicon Valley novels. Follow her on social media.

Chris Hardy Photography

CPSIA information can be obtained
at www.ICGtesting.com
Printed in the USA
LVOW12*1535120516

487958LV00006B/38/P

9 781939 454645